DON'T LET THE SHADOWS IN.

THE
SCARLET
STAR

JENNIFER KROPF

RIGHTS AND NOTES

Published by Winter Publishing House
Edited by Melissa Cole
Interior Portrait Illustrations by Kyannah Durocher
Cover Character Illustrations and Design by Jennifer Kropf

Isaiah 42:13

ISBN Ebook: 978-1-990555-42-8
ISBN Paperback: 978-1-990555-45-9
ISBN Hardcover: 978-1-990555-46-6

DEDICATION

For my friend Melissa Jensen

and the mighty light within you.

And for the Life Bearer women

I went to South Korea with in December 2023:

Never stop.

IN THE BEGINNING...

"There was a great war in the heavens. The skies bled gold and smoke, the air breathed ice and fire on the great morning the Celestial Divinities became heroes of old, men of renown. The gods of the sun, the moon, the night, and the evening stars overcame the bright, nameless beings of the sky through great talent and cunning. For this, they shall forever be praised by mortals.

After the *Heavenly War*, the Celestial Divinities chose to descend to the world of men and live among the human race to guide them, nurture them, and to be gods among them so that humanity might not lose its way. Such boundless grace was theirs, to humble themselves and walk among the Adams and Eves. Therefore, to the great Divinities of the stars, honour should be given, always."

- Excerpt from the *Four Collections of Divine History*, approved in the courts by the Intelligentsia

*Record Note: In the seventh year of King Draco's reign, this version was contested by High Priestess Geovani, Adriel representative of the one hundred and twenty-seven provinces

1

XERXES

The human mind is the most terrifying thing in existence.

It's a powerful marvel capable of altering the heavens and the earth, yet it believes lies. Therefore, it's easily manipulated and controlled. After hearing just a few words, a single mind can tear apart another, influence a hundred souls, or burn a kingdom to the ground. One mind can be the difference between peace and war, between truth and a whole nation falling at the feet of deception, between a great future and sudden death. Therefore, the state of one's mind is *everything*.

He should never have gone outside.

Xerxes slammed his palms over his ears, hot moisture pooling into his eyes as he stumbled down the hidden staircase to the palace basement. Had anyone seen? Would reports arise of a rampaging beast in the courtyard? He knew better than to walk through the gardens this close to his hour of hunger.

His pulse pounded against his mind, muting out the many voices that told him to do terrible, unthinkable things. Voices he refused to obey, ever since…

Since…

Xerxes swallowed and squeezed his eyes shut. His boots scraped over the basement floor from uneven strides as he rubbed his temples, willing himself to think about *anything* else.

He stopped short at the arched entrance to the oval room. He blinked twice, forgetting where he was for a moment as he beheld movement.

Someone was in there.

Who would *dare* take a step into this place?

Xerxes's hand came against his belt before he realized he hadn't brought his sword. He eyed the middle-aged man in a worn vest examining golden pears dangling from the great, crooked tree in the centre of the room. After a moment, Xerxes shook the clouds from his mind and pulled his eyes shut again. When he opened them, the man was still there.

Xerxes tilted his head. If this man wasn't a figment of his imagination, he'd be the first person in almost ten years to set foot in the oval room apart from Xerxes himself.

"You should kill him," one of the voices said, and Xerxes smacked his temple.

"Quiet!" he whispered, demanded, *begged.*

The middle-aged man in the vest reached for a fat pear hanging from the nearest branch. His fingers curled around it, turning it right and left. He tugged, and Xerxes's stomach dropped. But the man's fingers paused before they could do the unthinkable.

As if sensing he wasn't alone, the man glanced over his shoulder into the shadows circling the room—the space where moonlight from the oval skylight didn't quite reach—and Xerxes ducked behind the arch. The pear held to the tree by a mere thread.

A second passed by. Two. Three.

The man turned back to his task.

Xerxes slipped into the room, his boots a whisper over the floor, his black cloak transforming him into a shadow himself. He came up behind the thieving intruder, and he spoke in a voice low and dreadful, "Entering this room is forbidden."

"Kill the trespasser!" all the voices in his mind pleaded at once.

The man's hand went still on the pear. When he spun around, his wide gaze drew up Xerxes's body, stopping on Xerxes's face several inches above his and mostly obscured by darkness. The man's eyes grew rounder, his thieving hands sliding behind his back.

Crumbs littered the man's chest, making it obvious this thief had helped himself to the baking in the dining room on his way down too. He wasn't dressed as a servant or a guard, or even a noble. In fact, grass stains covered his clothes and the salty scent of his skin indicated he hadn't bathed in a while, which was practically a crime for anyone who belonged in the palace.

"You've entered the palace grounds, you've trespassed into a forbidden room, and you've stolen from the King," Xerxes informed the man. "I'll have you killed."

"Yes, let's kill him!" the voices agreed.

The man dropped to his knees. "Please!" he begged. "I... I came here only because..." He glanced around and scratched his head. "Because I promised my daughter I would find her a midnight rose!" he shouted with a clap. "It's *her* fault, really. If she

3

wasn't so greedy for a flower, I never would have come here!"

Two seconds of strange silence rang through the room.

Xerxes was used to overhearing the murmuring taunts of the palace dwellers: *"crazy, lunatic... evil"* they'd say. But as he looked upon this man, Xerxes recognized a different sort of evil. A duller, less exciting one, maybe. But evil, all the same.

"How old is your daughter?" he asked. The sensation of cold water tickled over his flesh, creeping along his fingers, prickling behind his ears, and threatening to take the rest of him and bring his mind to another state. Xerxes shook it off.

The man looked Xerxes up and down. "She's about your age, I think," he guessed.

"Then what does she want with a midnight rose? Aren't flowers for little girls?" Xerxes didn't know why he was asking. This man should die. Any moment now.

"Well," the man huffed an odd laugh, "it's been a while since I left to find her a rose..." he admitted, and Xerxes raised a brow.

"How long? Hours? Days?" Xerxes folded his arms, imagining a father vanishing for days on end for a silly flower. "Weeks?"

"Years." The man clasped his hands behind his back and dropped his gaze to the floor.

Xerxes blinked.

He blinked again. "Years?!"

"Seven years. My daughter was... uh, let me see..." The man looked off and scratched his head.

"Don't say twelve." Xerxes thought he said it in his mind, but when the man snapped his fingers and pointed at Xerxes, he realized he'd said the strange plea aloud.

"Yes, that's it! She was twelve!" The man made a face after. "How did you know?"

4

Xerxes stared at this man who had a daughter exactly his age. Who left the same year Xerxes's own father had, only this man left his child by choice. Also, he'd clearly made up a cowardly tale for his daughter about going to find her a rose so he could flee from her forever.

No wonder Xerxes sensed this man was evil.

"Never mind. Let's make a deal," Xerxes said. "Give your daughter to me and I'll let you leave this room alive and unscathed. I swear it by the Celestial Divinities."

It was a shallow deal no man would accept, Xerxes knew. Because what sort of father would trade his own daughter for—

"Deal! She's beautiful! And *a noble*—" the man emphasised the word 'noble' too strongly "—and she'd be a great prize for a distinguished palace guard like yourself! You can have her if you'd like!" The man's expression changed, his eyes going wild as he nodded and smiled. "If you let me go free, I will happily give her to you!"

Xerxes's mouth tipped down at the corners. He couldn't remember the last time he felt like the least crazy person in a room. He'd nearly killed men for lesser crimes than this man's impulsive self preservation.

At the thought, his flesh turned cool and moist, and this time, when the voices took over, he found it more difficult to stop them. He perhaps didn't want to.

"Fine. Write her name on this stone." Xerxes tapped a cobblestone with his foot. The man nodded quickly and grabbed a nearby pebble to scrape the information at Xerxes's feet. And as the man handed over his daughter, the thing that should have been his most precious possession, Xerxes began to laugh.

"You fool," he whispered as the man finished, tossed the pebble aside, and glanced up in question. Though Xerxes didn't have his sword, he was sure he wouldn't need it. The man's face fell at Xerxes's expression.

"Don't you know who I am?" Xerxes asked the most foolish father in the kingdom.

The man looked hard at him and squinted. And so, of Xerxes's two identities, he decided to admit the worst one.

"Haven't you heard of the manic beast that's been spotted in the palace gardens?" Though his faulty evenings were rare, Xerxes knew rumours had trickled out of the palace and into the city streets these last years; all of Per-Siana must have heard by now.

Across the room a shattered mirror was pegged to the wall at exactly Xerxes's height, and in it, Xerxes saw his vilest self: his flesh sinking to ashen purple-gray, slick and damp, and dark crescents forming beneath his eyes, stealing away his handsome, youthful face. His muscles grew tighter, his body, colder.

The man took a shaky step backward toward one of the arch exits, his own face paling at the sight of the creature before him. "You said you'd let me leave this room!" he reminded. His throat bobbed. "You made me a deal bound by the Divinities!"

"I did. And now your precious daughter is mine," Xerxes agreed. He inhaled, ignoring the scent of the golden pears just an arm's reach away. "So, go ahead and leave this room untouched. And then start running."

Soil and dust puffed over the feast table where Xerxes dropped the unearthed cobblestone with a loud *thud*. The renowned sages of the Intelligentsia looked up, their long navy hoods casting shadows over their repulsed faces as they eyed the dust breathing over their dinner plates from the dirty stone. Flames spurted to life over charmed candles at Xerxes's end of the table, as though the candles expected he was there to eat, and a cloth lifted from its folded state to polish Xerxes's dinner plate before fluttering through the air and folding itself in its place again.

Xerxes dropped into his chair and slouched back against it. A second later, he kicked his boots high up onto the table and crossed his legs, ensuring even more dirt spoiled the tablecloth. And his freshly cleaned plate.

Two seats down, Belorme, the esteemed Chancellor, slowly set down his cutlery and raised a cloth to dab the remains of dinner from his mouth. It was a drawn-out spectacle, and Xerxes folded his hands on his lap to wait. He licked the taste of pears from his lips to keep busy so he wouldn't speak first.

Finally, Belorme turned in his seat and faced Xerxes. "What is *this*?" He nodded to the cobblestone resting between them all. His voice remained cool and calm, as always.

Xerxes tapped a finger against his chin, thinking about the fool in the vest he'd chased out of the palace. The man had gotten away. Barely. "It's number four," he informed the Intelligentsia.

Belorme's face twitched ever so slightly. "Number four of what?" he asked with his mouth while his eyes made it clear he didn't want to know. Or, perhaps by his divine *insight*, he already knew what Xerxes was up to.

Xerxes pulled his boots off the table and leaned forward to look the sages in the eyes. "I have recently acquired ownership of this

7

young maiden in a deal. Since she's mine, I'd like you to bring her to me."

Belorme pursed his lips, tightening up the soft wrinkles around his mouth. After another long second, he asked, "And?"

Xerxes rarely smiled, but every so often a 'somewhat-smile' threatened his face. This was one of those glorious moments. "And she shall be number four. Four maidens will compete, not three."

Down the table, one of the Intelligentsia coughed. Another glanced at Belorme to see what he would do. Even the charmed serving spoon piling hot rice onto Yelenos's plate stopped moving as though it sensed the tension in the air.

Xerxes and Belorme stared at each other in silence. Of course, this was expected. Xerxes never made demands. He rarely went against the Intelligentsia, against Belorme. He hardly ever even raised his voice, but at Belorme's request, he'd courted six different noblewomen in secret now since *the incident*, and it always ended the same. Xerxes could not stand them, and he couldn't hide what he was from them. It left him miserable and even crueller than before.

At least this time he could perform a noble deed on behalf of a stranger while conveniently undermining the Intelligentsia. Ever since they'd announced to the whole kingdom their intention to audition three of the fairest young maidens in the kingdom to be his next wife, and demanded "he" choose one by the end of three months, he'd been looking for a chance to retaliate.

That announcement was a slap in the face. But no surprise, really, as they must have all been eager to replace the Queen they'd formerly been using as their political puppet. Belorme likely already had Xerxes's next wife picked out, thus why this grim event was announced without Xerxes being notified. But what angered Xerxes the most was that the Intelligentsia sages were using the Queen's open seat as a horrifying display of power against him during a time when Per-Siana was at risk of being crushed by their neighbouring kingdom. The sages should have been strategizing over battle plans, not putting on a ghastly show for the people.

He would not marry any of the women anyway. He would never marry again. He didn't care if the kingdom had no heir.

Belorme turned his attention back to his plate. He picked up his fork and resumed eating. The rest of the Intelligentsia watched in uncomfortable silence as he took a bite, chewed, and swallowed. Only after he made sure the whole table was waiting for him to speak did Belorme say, "You're not exactly in a position to make demands, Your Majesty."

Xerxes's 'somewhat-smile' vanished. He wondered why the Intelligentsia even bothered to call him "Your Majesty" when they made all the rules.

Xerxes reached for the cobblestone.

"What is this maiden's name?" Belorme asked, and Xerxes's hand paused in midair. Rather than take the cobblestone away, he turned it so the sages around the table might see the name messily carved into the stone. Everyone leaned in to read it.

"At least her last name is one from the noble class," Damon murmured from down the table.

Belorme sat back in his chair, his mouth twisting in contemplation. He went back to his plate again. "I suppose including her in the trials is a necessary disturbance to keep you happy, Your Majesty."

Happy?

Xerxes bit down hard on his pursed lips.

"But let me be clear," the Chancellor articulated. "She won't win." Belorme seemed to have forgotten Xerxes was there as he took a bite of spiced meat. As he lightly dabbed the juices from his mouth again with a napkin.

She. Won't. Win.

As in, *"She won't steal the King's heart."*

"Because the King has no heart to steal."

"Because I'll be choosing your wife, Xerxes, not you."

Xerxes stood from his chair and huffed a bitter laugh. "For her sake, I hope she doesn't."

The King left the Intelligentsia to their midnight meal. A meal where they discussed kingdom affairs. A meal he'd stopped attending long ago, ever since the day he lost control of himself.

2
RYN

A *bang* against the front door shook the house, and Ryn's heart nearly leapt from her chest. She dropped her apple; it rolled across the kitchen to where Kai stood from the table, his emerald Priesthood robe swishing behind him as he went to the door.

"What was that? Did a bird fly into the house again?" Ryn knelt and searched beneath the table for her apple, rubbing a hand over her heart. She spotted it under Kai's chair.

She jumped when another *bang* sounded.

Bang! Bang! Bang!

"Divinities," she cursed.

Kai cracked the door open, not far enough for Ryn to see who was outside. A husky voice shouted before Kai could offer a greeting, "We're here for Lady Estheryn Electus!"

Ryn grabbed the apple, stood, and tossed it into the basket with the rest of the unwashed apples. She wiped her hands on the skirt of her gardening dress, listening to the surprise in Kai's voice when he asked, "Estheryn? Why? What business does the Folke have with my cousin?"

Ryn's hands went still against her skirt.

The Folke? The King's *personal* guardsmen?

She peeked through the sheer kitchen curtains, counting six large bodies in navy blue and silver standing outside: the King's colours. One of them had a sword drawn.

The last time she'd seen Folke at her door with their swords drawn...

"If she won't come willingly, then move aside. We'll take her ourselves."

Ryn's hand came over her mouth, and she held her breath, not daring to make a sound. Her heel scraped over the floor when she moved back, and she froze.

A second passed where Kai said nothing. Neither did the Folke.

Ryn inched her gaze toward the rear of the house. The turns of the hall obstructed her view of the hidden cellar door that led to the woods. It was at least seven strides and a long staircase away.

She could only think of one reason the Folke would come for her. One terrible, crippling reason.

Kai slammed the door in the Folke's faces.

Ryn gasped as Kai grabbed her arm and turned her toward the hall. "Hide, Ryn!" he whispered, reaching back into the kitchen and grabbing the parring knife off the counter. The metallic sounds of swords being drawn lifted from outside.

"But—"

"*Hide!*"

Ryn raced for her bedroom. She yanked the door shut behind

her just as a loud crash filled the house, and she dove beneath her bed, dragging herself by her elbows until she was encompassed in shadow.

She went still in the quiet. Her ribs ached from falling against the floor, but she didn't dare move to get comfortable. She didn't even blink, fearing she'd miss something. She thought of the parring knife Kai had grabbed, wondering what, by the Divinities, he would do with that. He couldn't really be planning to *fight* the Folke... Kai would never...

Noise erupted in the hallway, and Ryn's heart doubled over as a muffled shout lifted from Kai, followed by a dense *thud*. She slapped a hand over her mouth so she wouldn't scream, wouldn't charge into the hall with a pathetic fist raised and try to rescue her cousin. Her bedroom door swung open, and the thumps of heavy boots filled her room—at least four pairs. She bit her lips together.

For a moment, all Ryn knew was the light squeaking of the floorboards as the Folke crept around.

One second passed. Two.

Her ankles were grabbed. Ryn released the scream she'd been holding, digging her nails into the grooves of the floor as she was torn from her hiding place and wrestled to her feet.

"Jump out, Ryn!" Kai shouted from the doorway, clutching his ribs and pointing to the open bedroom window. Ryn thrust her elbow into a guard's nose and lunged for the window, but the guard caught her around the waist and dragged her back.

"Don't be so rough with her!" Kai snapped at them.

"I don't know what you've been told," Ryn pleaded with the Folke, "but I'm a Weylin noble and whoever says otherwise is—"

"Silence! You've been summoned by the King," the guard

14

stated. "Refusal to obey is punishable by death."

Ryn glanced at Kai. They had no rehearsed answers for a situation that involved the King.

Kai's brows pulled together, moisture glossing over his eyes as he slid down the doorframe into a heap of swelling and silence on the floor. "I'll find out what's going on. I'll come for you," he rasped as the Folke shoved Ryn out the door and down the hall.

Ryn looked back at her cousin, at the bead of blood running down his chin. It dawned on her this might be the last time she would see him. The moment the last two members of their family would be torn apart, and the Cahana family would officially be dissolved.

"Don't," she called back. "Don't come for me."

She tore her gaze from Kai, her knees going weak as the Folke pushed her ahead. Kai's ribs might have been broken. What if no one came by this house for days? What if he died on the floor outside her bedroom because he wasn't found in time?

Ryn grabbed a basket of medical supplies as they passed the kitchen counter and threw it toward the hall where Kai was. The nearest Folke shoved her shoulder, turning her toward the door as fresh, cool air rolled over her heated body. She was blinded by the sunset burning over the distant mountains when she stepped outside.

A topless glass carriage with large brass wheels awaited, pulled by four black steeds. The luminescent carriage walls glowed against the fiery sun, turning the roadside into a lake of prismed colours. It was the most spectacular sight to ever grace Ryn's street in this part of the Mother City. The city she and Kai had been hiding in for exactly six years, two months, and five days.

A Folke cleared his throat and unrolled a scroll to read. "Estheryn Electus, you have hereby been summoned to be a Heartstealer in the upcoming trial period. Should you succeed in your task, you will inherit the second highest throne in the kingdom of Per-Siana and be glorified over all one hundred and twenty-seven provinces. Should you fail, you will be returned home to this location at the end of the period. Your obedience is required." His gaze flickered up with the last sentence. Then he rolled up the scroll and folded his arms as if he was waiting for something. "Do you agree to come willingly?" he asked. "Or shall I take you by force?"

Ryn couldn't have formed a reply even if she'd wanted to.

A *crash* filled the road, and Ryn noticed a red-cheeked Matthias, one of Kai's closest friends, with a spilled basket of figs at his feet. His shaggy blond hair fell in his eyes as he stared at Ryn and the Folke in horror. He took a step toward them, his hand falling on a dagger in his belt, but Ryn shouted, "Stop!" She pointed toward the house. "Kai's hurt! Please go help him, Matthias! Don't do anything foolish—"

A black bag was pulled over Ryn's head, and the vision of Matthias, along with the burning glass carriage, disappeared. Rope was tied around her wrists, and large hands lifted her into the transport she feared would take her to the palace.

The palace. It was the one place Ryn swore on her life she would *never* go. The place her mother had warned her about, had cautioned her not to wander too close to or look at too hard. The place Ryn promised to avoid like it was the very *cinder plague* that had killed her mother six years, two months, and five days ago.

The kingdom-wide marriage ban had sent waves of astonishment through the cities. Ryn had laughed when she heard the news. She'd gone to the market as usual that day and listened to gossip as Per-Siana citizens speculated why the King would do such a thing as *banning the marriages* of ordinary nobles. Of course, Ryn knew it was because he was crazy. Perhaps everyone knew, and no one would come out and say it.

The rumours grew dark after that. Word leaked into the Mother City that King Xerxes had lost his mind and murdered the first Queen, and now he was looking for another.

But why had the Folke arrived at *Ryn's* door? Most of Per-Siana didn't know she existed; even her neighbours knew little about her or Kai.

The carriage ride was bumpy and awkward without sight. After a while, sounds of chatter flooded in along with the smells of burning firewood and strong perfumes. Ryn was lifted off the carriage and guided into a warm space buzzing with murmured conversations.

Her wrists throbbed by the time the black bag was removed from her head. A strand of dark hair was stuck in her mouth as she looked around with stinging eyes, finding herself on a wide tiled floor before a crowd of nobles who seemed eager to inspect her and three other maidens who stood with her; *pretty* girls with smiling faces, dressed up in their best starlight garments and standing with packed bags at their sides. None of them wore a rope around their wrists like Ryn did.

"You've reached the Folke security building. Maidens, please

17

be patient as we assign each of you to one of the King's royal guards. They will act as your protection from here on in." The husky voice boomed over them at an unnecessary decibel, and Ryn spotted a tall man at the head of the room dressed in blue armour inlaid with silver details. Rich stitching of a long, serpentine white dragon curled down his sleeve. In fact, all the Folke were clad in symbols of the King.

She shrieked when a guard appeared beside her with a blade. He cut the rope off her wrists, and her arms fell to her sides. The Folke walked away without a word.

Nearby noblewomen chuckled as they studied her, and Ryn looked down at her gardening dress, her bare feet, her unwashed hands. Soil was wedged beneath her fingernails from her afternoon of vegetable planting and apple picking too.

A gasp lifted from somewhere across the room, barely noticeable over all the chatter, and Ryn spotted an old white-haired woman by the far wall in a green robe. The robe reminded her of Kai, and a lump sank through her chest. The woman only stared at Ryn—no one else—and Ryn brought a hand up to her cheek, sure there was dirt on her face. Sure that everyone noticing *the girl in the dirt-stained dress* was horrified.

The old woman whispered something to a female Folke guard beside her, but Ryn dropped her gaze to the floor before she might lipread the words.

Only hours ago, she was washing apples for Matthias's birthday pie. She'd made him a promise to bake him one, and then she'd laughed to herself the whole walk home afterward at how red his cheeks had gotten over it. It dawned on her now she wouldn't be keeping that promise.

In fact, she might never bake for Kai or Matthias again.

She took a small step backward, inching into line beside the triad of beautiful, colourful maidens. Folke guards filed in, one standing before each of the first two maidens and whispering a pledge to guard them during the trials, likely also silently pledging to trap them into this event of the King's delusional madness, even if the girls didn't realize it. Ryn swallowed as a sturdy fellow in blue and silver walked in her direction. He was only a step away when another Folke swooped in and cut him off.

Ryn blinked at the female Folke guard standing before her. The girl didn't look to be any older than Ryn. She wore the glassy blue armour of the Folke with silver shoulder plates, the coiling white dragon up her sleeve, and a long sweeping blue guardsman cape covering her back. A nametag was stitched into her protective vest with Weylin letters Ryn struggled to read. She thought the first letter was an 'H'... then an 'E'... She couldn't know for sure, but the nametag might have spelled 'H.E.V.A.'

Ryn eyed the sword strapped to the girl's belt, then brought her gaze back up. The guardswoman, even though Ryn looked her right in the eyes, said nothing.

The Folke who'd been on his way to claim Ryn grunted and stepped to the final maiden instead.

As Folke continued to introduce themselves to their maidens down the line, the guardswoman before Ryn—*Heva*—didn't speak. She just stared. She looked directly into Ryn's face with a hard gaze as if searching for something.

A large set of doors swung open at the front of the room, and the Folke led their maidens out into the darkening sunset. Ryn watched them go—one, two, three—along with the crowd of nobles cheering after them. The security building was nearly empty when her guardswoman finally moved. *"Heva"* spoke for the first time as she turned and headed for the door, revealing silver beads in her slick black ponytail. "Stay close to me, Maiden. Don't wander off, and don't trust anyone. Not even the other Folke." The last part she murmured.

Ryn stole a glance toward the security building halls, imagining a back door somewhere past them. Imagining slipping away before she could make it into the palace. Imagining—

Heva's boots stopped tapping over the floor, stealing Ryn's attention back.

"Don't risk it," the guardswoman advised.

Ryn swallowed. "Why not?" she rasped.

The first flicker of sorrow crossed Heva's face; her brows tugging in, the corners of her mouth tipping down. "They'll kill you," she said. "They won't listen to you explain or beg for mercy. They'll force you to spill the names of your loved ones, and then they'll send an arrow through your back. You'll be nothing more than a spirit in the wind by morning."

Bumps formed over Ryn's arms, and she brushed her fingers along her tight flesh. Yet, still, she said, "I don't fear death."

Heva cracked a dull smile. "If that's true, maybe you'll survive in the palace after all," she said.

This time, when the guardswoman took another step to lead the way out of the security building, Ryn followed.

The evening sky was a crystal blue canvas with one last brush of gold lingering from the setting sun. Ryn watched the serpentine white dragon slither back and forth in the high heavens; a gift from the Celestial Divinities. It was meant to guard Per-Siana and watch all its citizens across the one hundred and twenty-seven provinces so the Divinities would know what judgements to bestow upon each person after their death. Ryn never bothered to acknowledge the great judge of the Divinities before now. She thought the dragon wouldn't spot her among the Per-Siana people. Now, she wondered if all her secrets were written across her face for the great judge to see, and if he would smite her with fire.

She was the last one to board the new silver carriage. She sat in the back row, eyes closed, lips sealed, her heart sinking further and further until it was a weight upon her stomach. Crowds formed at the street sides, cheering and tossing glitter and blossoms that brushed along Ryn's hot cheeks. She peeked an eye open at them.

A Heartstealer.

There were legends of ancient kings who'd invoked the practice of Heartstealers. It was a courtship system that allowed the three fairest maidens in the kingdom to be rewarded with trials to try and "steal the heart" of the King. The maiden who won the King's heart would be wrestled into a silver crown and trapped in the palace forever.

Whispers from other maidens lifted from the front of the carriage. Ryn almost put her hands over her ears to drown them out until one said, "I hear the King is handsome. We'll finally see if the rumours of his striking beauty are true." A series of giggles followed, and Ryn cringed.

"I'm sure we'll learn the real story about all that's happened this year, too. I know he didn't do it. Our sweet King would never do such a horrid thing!" another maiden chimed in. Everyone knew what "horrid thing" she referred to.

Ryn released a tsking sound and shook her head. These girls. These poor, easily fooled girls. If the King was handsome, why did he hide away in the palace? If he was civil, why did he murder the first Queen? What sort of upbringing made these maidens so naïve? How were they foolish enough to get dressed up and enter the trial period by *choice*? Who cared about becoming Queen when they could be murdered in their sleep?

The carriage wheels crunched over the last of the pebbles as they turned onto the smooth Navy Road, and Ryn finally peeled her eyes open. They stung as they adjusted to the brilliant colours of the main street.

The first thing she noticed was all the silver magic in the air—coin-sized balls of light illuminating the path. Her brows furrowed as heaviness settled on her shoulders like something was pushing her down, trying to crush her body.

Magic. Ryn had felt the effects of it before, but not like this.

The magic was so thick this close to the palace, she could taste hints of metal and sweet, buzzing sparks. She blinked away the dizziness that rushed in as the carriage drew closer and enveloped her into an invisible sea of pressure. The maidens ahead were smiling; none of them affected by the magic, or if they were, they didn't care.

The Navy Road was a deep blue stone, scattered with crystals to mimic the night sky and to offer praise to the Celestial Divinities—at least, that's what was preached by the heralds outside the Temple of Nyx by Ryn's home. The road's straight line cut through the centre of the Mother City and pointed to the glittering palace whose spokes pierced the heavens with glass, catching the sunset and making the building glow as if consumed by white fire. The glorious structure rested in the exact middle of the kingdom of Per-Siana. The beautiful slaughterhouse where Ryn would die.

Ryn had never been on the Navy Road. She'd never once attended royal parades, or the Festival of Stars, or Celestial revelries, or night dances. She'd never crossed paths with the King, couldn't possibly have caught his eye. She hadn't even made friends with anyone outside of Matthias and Theo; Kai's closest allies. She lived a quiet life at home washing clothes in the stream behind their house and nurturing apple trees. She imagined the orchard would rot without her, and she doubted there were cool streams inside the palace.

Ryn rubbed her sore wrists as she studied the passing alleys between the tall white buildings. Her sandals and gardening boots were back at the house since the Folke hadn't allowed her to grab them for the journey. But maybe, just *maybe*, even with bare feet, she could make it into an alley, and then she could race to...

To where? Ryn studied the unfamiliar glass roofs, the silver towers, and gold sculptures painted with star runes. She'd never find her way home from here without a map. And if she was caught escaping, she'd be tortured like her guardswoman said, and she might give up Kai's real name.

Ryn swallowed the lump in her throat as the carriage pulled through the great palace gates. They swept by enormous vertical banners with stitched artwork portraying members of the *Intelligentsia*—the wisest and most elite sage magicians in the kingdom. There were at least twelve of them.

Ryn grabbed the rail of the carriage, her lips peeling apart when she spotted three banners of the maidens. The banner trio depicted young women with lovely, smooth faces and long silhouettes in sparkling gowns; the truest beauties in the land—the same girls sitting in the carriage ahead of Ryn.

She slumped back into her seat. The Heartstealer maidens had already been chosen weeks ago. So, why had the Folke arrived at her door and claimed *she* would face the trials?

There was no banner depicting an ordinary, unsuspecting garden girl with a terrible secret. There was no banner of the King either, nothing to confirm or deny the circulating rumours of his beauty. Ryn imagined he was hideous, like his soul.

As the carriage headed across the palace grounds, maidens gasped at glass buildings spearing out from the main palace in the shape of a great star with bridges and balconies ten stories high. Dark silk spilled from the rails, inlaid with starry crystals and flowing in the evening breeze alongside vines of ivy dangling like a vertical garden. There was so much glass, so much marble and silver, and too many depictions of the starry heavens to count. The carriage passed through a small orchard last, and when the fragrance of fruit filled the air, something squeezed in Ryn's chest.

The carriage came to a halt at wide entrance stairs. Folke guards helped their maidens down from the transport one at a time, and the young women tapped their way up the staircase into the tall, gaping mouth of the palace.

Heva stood at the bottom of the carriage with her arms folded. Ryn paused, wondering if she was supposed to wait for her guardswoman to take her hand and guide her down the steps like the other guards had.

Heva shot Ryn a look when she realized. "Do you want to hold hands or something?"

Ryn made a face and climbed from the carriage on her own, jumping off the last step and wobbling when her feet hit the dirt. "Aren't you supposed to protect me?" she mumbled, barely loud enough for her guardswoman to hear.

"Protect you from what? A few scrapes on your way down?" Heva grunted. "You're already covered in those."

Ryn glanced at her arms where tiny cuts speckled her elbows, leftover from being pulled out from beneath her bed. Fresh bruises were blossoming over her wrists from wrestling against the guards too. Even the shoulder of her dress was torn.

She hugged her arms to herself as she followed Heva up the wide stairs and through a tall silver archway. The evening wind picked up, tossing her hair and tugging at her hem, and she shivered. But she paused at the top of the stairs, her toes coming along a blue line of tile where the palace doors might reach once closed.

Ryn thought of her warm kitchen where she'd just been with Kai. She turned and gazed back at the city, her throat thickening as she imagined Kai, Matthias, and Theo gathering without her in the empty house, sitting around the rickety table in the kitchen for Matthias's birthday.

Her gaze fell on a temple with a gold domed roof glittering beneath the last sliver of sun a few blocks from the palace. Something about it made Ryn forget about her guardswoman waiting for her inside. She'd heard of a building with a golden roof before.

Her throat constricted so she wouldn't scream for it—that building just past the wall of the palace grounds. It looked exactly how Kai had described his temple; the building where he worked. The building where he spent his long days studying with the Priesthood, along with the occasional nights he didn't come home.

Ryn traced the road from the temple with her eyes, over the white wall encircling the palace grounds, through a large garden inside, and all the way to a narrow path before the entrance where she stood.

If there was ever a right place to escape to…

Heva's hand found her shoulder. "I said don't risk it."

When Ryn met her guard's eyes this time, there was more than a command there; a sharp warning rang through the silence between them.

Ryn's shoulders relaxed. It wasn't like she could run for the temple right now anyway.

She turned her back to the Mother City, to Kai's temple, and stepped over the blue line of cold tile in her bare feet.

Maidens squealed and pointed at a starry ceiling mosaic sweeping from the entrance across a glass atrium. The ceiling hosted a depiction of a war in the clouds where the seven gods of the Weylin people fought at the beginning of time. It was the biggest mural Ryn had ever seen in her life. Every stone sparkled; every detail was intricate.

Her gaze dropped to a giant fountain piercing the middle of the room surrounded by statues of the seven Celestial Divinities. Ryn couldn't remember the names of the primary Divinities apart from Nyx. Beyond the fountain, two broomsticks floated by, sweeping all on their own. Ryn nearly fell over as she leaned to watch them around the fountain. She'd heard of the magic of the Intelligentsia flowing through the palace, she'd even felt the weight of it on her way in, but she'd *never* imagined that the gossip about the palace cleaning itself was true. Warmth bled into her stomach as she became aware of it—that heavy presence no one else reacted to. She rubbed her temples as the atrium went in and out of focus around her.

Groups rushed for the other maidens. Ryn blinked the fog from her eyes as two maidens were escorted away and disappeared down a hallway. "What's happening?" she whispered to Heva.

Her guardswoman sighed. "The artists are choosing the maiden they wish to beautify. None of them seem interested in you though," she said, then added, "The best artists were paid by rich benefactors or politicians who hope their chosen maiden will inherit the second throne of the kingdom. It's a power struggle." She waved a hand through the air like it wasn't worth explaining to someone like Ryn.

Ryn watched the last maiden receive a group of helpers along with trunks of supplies and a rack of gowns. She, and her crew, disappeared down the same hallway as the first two maidens.

Only Folke guards remained in the atrium, securing the entrance at Ryn's back, and Ryn glanced at Heva. She didn't have a chance to ask another question before the sound of clumsy, clunking boots met her ears, growing louder until finally a young man raced into the atrium with pink cheeks and a large suitcase beneath his arm.

He skidded to a stop, wiping a bead of sweat from his forehead. When he looked around at the empty entrance, his face fell. Then he noticed Ryn.

His face fell again.

He glanced back the way he came as if debating whether he should run away. "This is what I get for arriving late, I suppose," he muttered under his breath—not quietly enough. He sighed as he hauled his suitcase over, looking Ryn up and down with a scowl. "You're the only option left?" he asked.

"She is," Heva answered for her.

The young man nodded. "Come with me, then. I'm *Marcan*." He emphasized his name and waited for a moment, like he expected something. Ryn looked over at Heva, then back at Marcan.

"Divinities, do you really not recognize my name? Did you grow up over the border or something?" Marcan asked, still talking to Ryn. "I'm Marcan. *The* Marcan."

Most Weylins might know who Marcan was, Ryn realized.

"Ah, right," she said, nodding in feigned recognition. *"Marcan."*

Marcan rolled his eyes. He stomped over the tiles to the hallway after the others, waving for Ryn and Heva to follow. He remarked without missing a beat, "You don't look noble."

Ryn clasped her hands and squeezed her palms together. She glanced at a passing servant, then at Heva, then back toward the atrium. "My name is Estheryn Electus." She stated the name she'd learned to say with ease. The name she'd spoken so many times it was starting to feel like her real name.

"Alright, Estheryn Electus, your name passes. But still..." Marcan glanced over at her, at her *dirt*, specifically. "How, by the Divinities, did you manage to get chosen as a Heartstealer?" he asked.

Doors were left open down the hall, giving Ryn glimpses of the other girls trying on silk dresses and glistening gold jewelry in their rooms. They probably really were the fairest young women in all of Per-Siana. Ryn couldn't come up with one reason as to why she dared to walk among them.

"I have no idea," she admitted.

Marcan made a face without questioning her further. "I should warn you; I am *not* this kind of artist. I do stunning mosaics with glass and jewels, rare gem paintings, and coveted wall art," he bragged, but his voice shook when he added, "I've never decorated a woman in my life. I don't even know how to beautify a mess like you, and now my reputation will suffer for it. Don't you know what we're up against? Calliope Ingrid has at least *three* political figures backing her, along with her family's deep pockets!" He took in a deep, shuddering breath and let it out slowly. "I wasn't given a choice about coming here, you know." Marcan swallowed and put the back of his hand against his pink cheek.

It shouldn't have been a relief that someone else did *not* want to be here, and while Ryn would never allow herself to feel kinship with a Weylin, she studied Marcan's back, seeing a soul just as lost and alone in this vast building as she was.

Ryn had no interest in being beautified, and she especially had no interest in standing out. Maybe Marcan would keep her look simple and she could stand at the back until the King chose a wife and the fuss would pass over. It occurred to her that when the Folke had come to her house to collect her, the man reading the scroll had said, *"Should you fail, you will be returned home to this location at the end of the period."*

So, there was hope. If Ryn couldn't find a chance to escape, all she had to do was blend in, stay quiet, and keep out of the King's sight. Maybe—*maybe* no one would ask questions about her, and she could make it through this trial period alive.

"Do a simple mosaic on a dress, then," Ryn said to Marcan with a shrug. "If that's what you're good at." The suggestion was the least she could do for a fellow palace prisoner. Though, thinking about wearing any kind of *'maiden dress'* made her stomach turn.

Marcan scowled like it was the most absurd idea he'd ever heard. But after a moment of walking, he tilted his head and tapped his chin.

They entered the room at the very end of the hall—furthest away from the others. Heva grabbed a torch from the hallway and began lighting candles when she came inside. "Wow," she said as she looked around.

Silk furnishings filled the living area, and a great spoked bed covered in dangling pink-blossom ivies rested at the far side of the room. But while every piece of furniture was meant to catch the eye, all Ryn saw was the wall of windows. She moved for the closest window, and as dusk consumed Per-Siana, she stared out at the city that didn't feel all that far away, at a particular temple just a few blocks from the palace with a domed gold roof, straight in her view.

"Do any of these windows open?" she asked with a dry voice.

Marcan grunted as he clattered around with his suitcase and began setting up a station in the living area. He murmured, "How should I know?"

Ryn looked down the row of sills, her heart fluttering when she spotted a lever. She rushed over and cranked it, gasping when the window opened with a *pop*. She turned until the window was a wide, gaping doorway, inhaling the wind and filling her chambers with the sweet fragrances of fruit and the flower gardens outside. She slapped a hand over her mouth so she wouldn't let a sob escape as her eyes filled with tears, keeping her back to the room where Heva and Marcan were.

A long time ago, Ryn had a mother. She never had a father she cared to speak of, but she did once have a mother who loved her. A mother who used to brush her hair so it never grew tangled the way it was now, who used to wash her dresses so she didn't wear stains like she did now, who used to whisper beautiful, loving words so that Ryn didn't feel alone the way she did now. One thing her mother always said was, "When a door closes and traps you in, the Adriel God will open a window."

Ryn bit her lower lip and held her breath so she wouldn't reveal that her heart was screaming for her mother, for her home, for her people. She didn't believe in the power of an Adriel God, not since her mother died. Nevertheless, the saying proved to be true. Perhaps her mother's spirit was out there, watching over her. Maybe her mother had been checking in on her from time to time and had sensed Ryn's distress.

Ryn laughed, tasting the metallic flavour of blood from biting her lip so hard. She lifted a hand to her punctured lip, not caring if Heva and Marcan were exchanging strange glances behind her, wondering if she was crazy.

The King could have his fun with the three girls who wanted to be here. Ryn would be long gone before he ever learned any of her names—her false one, or her real one. What a fool he was to have tried to take her hostage in the first place when in her very room she had a doorway to freedom.

CHAPTER

3
XERXES

Apart from being disgusted at the sight of how happy everyone was, Xerxes was relieved the palace workers had something else to focus on for a while. He watched from a high balcony above the lobby, blanketed in the darkness he belonged in, as the first two maidens entered the palace and gazed at the great artwork of the atrium. If only these maidens knew how they would be paraded among the citizens, talked about, painted onto tapestries, and worshipped like the Divinities themselves. How unforgiving the people were about their stardoms. He could have warned the maidens if he cared. As it was, he imagined he'd play along for a bit to keep the Intelligentsia pleased and then disappear until the excitement died down. After Belorme chose the woman he foolishly planned to make Xerxes's wife, Xerxes could ignore her the same way he ignored…

The first one.

Xerxes couldn't bring himself to think her name. His first wife, daughter of an esteemed lord of B'rei Mira. The woman was horrid and selfish, openly disobeying Xerxes's orders since day one. It was why Xerxes avoided her and barely spoke three words in her direction since she'd arrived. Perhaps it was childish of him, but he couldn't stand how she did what everyone else did—making every decision about his kingdom for him, whispering in the hallways with the Intelligentsia, plotting their next move.

Yes, Xerxes had brought the threat of war upon his kingdom all on his own. If the B'rei Mira kingdom ever found out that he was the one who had *murdered*—

Xerxes closed his eyes, letting the visions of the new maidens vanish from his sight, from his mind. No, he would never marry again. Belorme would have to tie him down and drag him to the altar.

You wanted to kill her, one of the voices reminded him. *You wanted her gone.*

"I didn't *want* to. It was an accident," Xerxes muttered. "I don't even remember doing it." But he knew it was no use arguing with the voices. If he couldn't even convince the Intelligentsia sages, if he couldn't even convince his kingdom enough to stop the gossip, then how could he convince the voices of his own imagination?

With that in mind, Xerxes left the atrium, not waiting to see the last two maidens who'd rushed from their comfortable homes to see him. To court him. To *marry* him.

He headed down the long hallway, the late evening sun kissing his cheeks as he came beneath a domed glass ceiling. The Celestial Divinities were spying on him tonight, he could feel it. They must have known the maidens were the least of his true concerns. They must have realized that Per-Siana was a mere breath away from the greatest war they'd ever faced. That the second Alecsander of

B'rei Mira learned that a noble of his people had been killed by the King of Per-Siana, the great warlord would sweep into Xerxes's kingdom and destroy everything in sight.

Xerxes had hardly been able to sleep for the past six months—since *the incident*. Even with all their tricks and insight, the Intelligentsia hadn't been able to stop the news from slipping out of the palace and into the Mother City. They'd chalked *the incident* up to silly rumours. They'd claimed through their heralds that the former Queen had died of a highly contagious disease and they were taking measures to ensure the disease didn't break out into the city.

Though Xerxes avoided their meetings, he knew the Intelligentsia would likely create a false disease with their potions, release it into the kingdom's water supply, and call it an "outbreak" to ensure their story was believed. It would ultimately benefit the sages, too, since anyone with a sound mind knew that to control people, all one had to do was create a disease and strike fear into the citizens' hearts about it. Months later, they would conveniently develop a cure, and the citizens of Per-Siana would line up to receive it. The Intelligentsia would look like heroes.

To Xerxes, it looked like diabolical madness. But he knew better than to utter the word "madness" from his own mouth when he was the one hearing voices.

He ventured down a flight of stairs, then another, and finally, two more, until he came deep into the palace basement where his oval room was hidden away. He walked around the hole in the floor where he'd unearthed a cobblestone, and he approached the bright tree of golden pears thriving with lush emerald leaves. The mighty trunk and limbs glowed beneath the evening light piercing downward through the circular skylight that stretched up all the levels of the palace; an opening to the sky cut off from everything. No one in the palace knew why there was a large pillar in the centre of the structure. No one apart from the Intelligentsia and a few select servants who had once come into this room—ten years ago—and had planted this tree and had made the room beautiful. The tree had grown on its own after that by Celestial magic.

The hunger had not begun yet, but Xerxes didn't care to wait until the burning filled his stomach or the icy dampness covered his flesh. He imagined the pulls of it would be magnified this evening after he'd watched the spectacle in the atrium. If he got his mind right, maybe he could sleep through the worst of it. He plucked a pear from his tree.

Most days, one bite of spellbound fruit was enough to quell his starvation and keep him sane and alive. A gift of medicine from the Celestial Divinities and the single reason he was forced to rely on the great stars of the sky and the Intelligentsia. It was the same reason Xerxes could never take control of his own kingdom.

He both needed and cursed this tree.

The light of the moon painted the garden in a milky white. The relaxing aroma of the blossoms turned the air to perfume, instilling a temporary pulse of serenity to the quiet congregation of plants. Xerxes lounged flat on his back over a stone bench, staring up at the sparkling souls of the Divinities in the heavens and the white dragon doing its slow dance across the sky. Back and forth the dragon went. Never growling, never making a sound or moving off course. Just a constant promise in the sky that the Divinities were watching and had infinite knowledge of the kingdom.

Soft buzzing rose from the bushes as the night bugs conversed, and the air turned chilly when the time crossed midnight's threshold and the new, dark day began. It all tickled Xerxes's ears.

He'd just closed his eyes to doze off when *a girl* broke through a cluster of bloom-bushes, nearly startling him right off the bench.

He lifted his head to watch her scurry across the garden, the wind stealing her long dark hair into a dance. She jogged until she reached a tall, square water fountain, and Xerxes raised a brow as she stared at the great weeping pillar like she didn't know what it was. She turned to go right, but she paused. She redirected to go left instead, but she only took one step before hesitating again.

Xerxes couldn't take it anymore. "Are you lost?"

The girl whirled. Her hand went out to grab for something like she wanted to defend herself or some other outrageous thing, but when her gaze found him, she breathed a sigh of relief.

Relief.

Xerxes was sure he'd never seen another person *relieved* at the realization of his presence.

He pulled an arm up behind his head to get comfortable. She'd disturbed his peace long enough; she could flutter off now. He tried to close his eyes and resume his almost-nap, but her breathless panting filled his ears, and he cracked an eye open to find her a few steps closer.

"Excuse me," the girl tried, though—this close she didn't seem like a *girl*. More of a young woman. There was dry mud on her dress, and her hair was a wild lion's mane atop her head. "Might you point me in the direction of the outer wall?" she asked. "This garden is much bigger than I expected."

It occurred to Xerxes only then that this young woman did not realize whom she spoke to. He glanced down at his own garments, noticing his white shirt was covered in soil from when he'd tripped and fallen into the melon patch on his way out of the palace. His hair was tousled too from tossing and turning on the bench. She probably thought he was a gardener, or worse, a *servant*.

It served him right for never wearing his blue robe of nobility unless forced.

"Forget it," she said when he didn't answer. The young woman dipped her head in apology and headed back toward the square fountain. Xerxes watched in disbelief as she paused—again—and turned back to face him.

"Actually, I could use a hand, if you don't mind," she said.

She could be killed for asking the King of Per-Siana for "a hand."

"With what?" Xerxes asked anyway, though he didn't get up. He was ready to announce himself at this rate, just so she'd draw back in fear and be on her way. But he cast her a look when she crept in close like she was going to tell him a secret. She came right over him, blocking out the moonlight, and he flinched when she brought her face within inches of his.

"You're strong," she commented, looking him over in a way that made him wish he was wearing at least seven coats. Then she whispered, "I need you to lift me over the wall."

Xerxes stared at her for several moments. He didn't recognize this young woman, so he couldn't guess why she needed to leave the palace, and *over the wall*, of all things. He studied her build, her height, guessing her age. She was undoubtedly pretty, but her dress made her look like a maid. A poor one, too, incapable of keeping herself tidy even in the presence of nobles.

"Why would I do that?" he asked. "Just walk out the front gate like a normal person."

"I can't," she said. She bit her bottom lip in distress, and Xerxes didn't mean for his gaze to snap to her mouth when she did that, but it happened. "I'm one of the Heartstealers being trapped in the palace—"

"Trapped?" Xerxes couldn't believe his ears.

"—I'm escaping." The way she looked at him so desperately put an odd flinch in his abdomen, a flutter that may have been anger, perhaps, or insult, or... Something else entirely. She reminded him of a rabbit in a snare. Until she added, "You can't really be that blind if you live in this palace. You must see how the King has gathered these maidens, herding them all in like animals being led to their *slaughter*."

For a moment, the whole garden and courtyard swallowed Xerxes whole. He forgot how to blink. And then... the edge of his mouth tugged. He couldn't help it; his misleading clothes, her abruptly honest words... This was possibly the most amusing thing he had ever seen in all his years as King.

He burst out laughing.

The girl's face fell, and she drew back a step as her pretty lips pinched together into a scowl. She looked like she might run away from him now, as she should. She headed back toward the fountain, but Xerxes sat up, his eyes narrowing, his muscles flexing.

He should have her killed.

As the thought went through his mind, he became increasingly aware of the stillness of the garden. Of the quietness of the breeze. He looked around, waiting. He glanced up at the stars with a questioning face.

Where were the voices? Why had they not urged him to destroy this woman like they always did when he had a dark thought?

Either way, he should not let her leave. Something within him told him so, but… But it had been a while since he'd found something so outrageously funny. He'd forgotten the sound of his own laugh. He cleared his throat, finding it strained and strange.

"If you'll excuse me, I have a terrible situation to escape from." The girl bid him farewell as she *finally* chose which direction to go in and began heading that way.

"Wait," he said.

She stopped, turning back to him one last time as he rose from the bench. Xerxes folded his arms and studied her.

Drag her back to the palace to be punished?

Drag her back to the palace to be executed?

Drag her back to the palace and force her to finish the Heartstealer courtship like he was being forced to?

Have the Folke kill her on the spot? It would be nice to be done with it.

There were too many options. And though he was a young man who often craved the power he'd lost forever, there were times such as this he wished someone would just tell him what to do so he didn't have to think so hard.

CHAPTER

4
RYN

The young landscaper's face turned silver in a moonbeam, making his features clear and sharp. Ryn wondered if her own features were so obvious. She'd made the mistake of stepping out of the shadows to ask this lazy servant for help, and now he'd seen her. Her best chance was to run, but with the garden being so tall and the paths so twisted, she was sure she'd get lost and sprint right into a Folke.

She meant to leave this servant behind, but the moment she began heading further down the garden path, he spoke.

"Wait."

It was spoken like a command, and even though a mere landscaper shouldn't have influenced what she did, the tone made Ryn go still.

When she looked back, she found him standing with his arms folded. It was the second time she noticed his broad shoulders and the muscles in his arms. And though he wore no Folke armour, she wondered if maybe he was a Folke guard off duty since he was built like one. A bead of fear dropped through her at the thought, especially when he walked after her—She staggered back. He stopped a few inches away, demonstrating his height and swallowing her in his shadow. He didn't try to grab her. Yet.

"You know that if the King discovers this betrayal, you'll be killed." He said it like a question. There was a slight tug at the corner of his mouth, almost too subtle to see in the night. It made Ryn's insides turn.

Ryn swallowed. "I don't fear death," she said.

The amusement left his expression. "No?"

"Death is a gateway to the ones we lost before us," Ryn told him. "I welcome it."

Several seconds went by of him saying nothing, and Ryn wondered if he wasn't fully right in his mind. She stole a look at his unkempt garments again, at his messy hair. He was too handsome to be a village idiot, but he also seemed to have trouble keeping himself together—

"The wall is right through these trees," he said, nodding toward a cluster of tall, bushy lilacs.

Ryn glanced at the bush, calculating the turns of her new path. "Thank you," she said. She didn't wait to hear what the landscaper might say next; she'd never see him again anyway. She pushed into the lilacs, the branches scraping across her arms and cheeks. A huff of triumph escaped her when she caught a glimpse of the white stone wall on the other side. She was so close; she could nearly taste the freedom of the Mother City. She could already imagine what she'd say to Kai when she surprised him.

She pressed her hands flat against the cold wall in gratitude when she reached it. The white stone was formed into tightly stacked bricks half her height, leaving almost no ledges to climb on. She ran her fingers along the one and only dent in the stone, chewing on her lip. It wouldn't be easy, but she could find a way over if—

She nearly yelped when two hands came around her waist. Ryn was hoisted off her feet, her toes leaving the garden, the top of the wall coming closer. She strained to reach it, her fingers curling over the edge. The hands released her waist and she hung there, looking down to find the landscaper taking hold of her ankles next. With one shove, he pushed her up and she climbed onto the wall, straddling the barrier with one leg on either side, a song of victory rising in her heart. From this height, she could see nearly the whole garden below where the landscaper folded his arms again, watching her curiously. She could also see the Navy Road on the other side—her road to escape.

She meant to thank the landscaper once more, but the thrill of her success took over. She turned back to the palace and blew it a sarcastic kiss goodbye instead. "Goodbye, Maidens!" she said in a loud whisper. "Goodbye, Folke!" And last, but not least, "Good-bye, you ugly, heartless King!"

The landscaper's face changed.

Ryn shot him a smile and waved. She'd never forget his kindness.

With that, she flung her leg out of the garden and toward the Mother City. She would have kicked the dust off her boots on her way out if she was wearing any. She leapt down, landing silently so she wouldn't alert the Folke guards around the wall, and she scampered down the Navy Road.

The Priesthood Temple was vaster than Ryn expected, reaching the clouds in height and wide enough to host a small village inside. She studied the burn marks up the pale walls, wondering who would attack such a beautiful, sacred temple. Other dark stains like filthy water or animal blood were splattered against it too. Ryn's heart sank as she imagined Kai being splashed with filth as he stepped out of this temple. She knew he never wore his priestly robe on his walk home for safety reasons, that he'd been careful to not let their neighbours know his occupation, but she hadn't realized that even the Priesthood Temple of the Adriel God had suffered.

The front entrance was sealed shut, and everything was quiet and dark in the yard. Ryn knocked against the door a few times, eyeing the buildings nearby. No one answered, so she ventured around the cool grass in her bare feet until she spotted a ground-level window. She dropped to a knee and pushed against the glass, but it didn't budge.

A sharp, metallic sound filled her ears, and she flinched as a cold sword touched her throat, the tip hovering just below her jaw. She raised both hands slowly. "P... please... I wasn't trying to trespass," she stammered.

"Stand," a deep voice instructed.

Maybe this wasn't the Priesthood Temple at all. The thought raced through Ryn's mind as she stood and turned, keeping her hands raised and lifting her gaze to a swordsman with a dark hood.

A set of brown eyes looked back at her. They widened, and

Ryn gasped.

"Theo?!" Her voice came out high and loud. "Divinities, Theo, what are you doing with a weapon—?"

Theo sheathed his sword and grasped Ryn, pushing her against the wall with one hand and slapping the other over her mouth. "Shh!" he instructed. "Are you out of your mind, Ryn?" he whispered, looking her up and down. "What are you doing here?"

"What are *you* doing here?!" she wanted to ask, but it was muffled through his fingers.

Theo chewed on the inside of his cheek, then huffed. "Forget it. I'll take you in." He tugged her off the wall and ushered her around the corner to a moss-covered staircase that led to a door she didn't see earlier. Ryn watched his sword sway at his side as he walked. She took in his black hooded cloak, the cuffs of his emerald Priesthood garments peeking slightly from his wrists.

He knocked in a complicated pattern, and the door swung open. The priest inside looked Ryn over but didn't ask questions as Theo pulled her into a hallway filled with the distant murmur of voices. A brighter room lay at the end of the hall, and Ryn marvelled at how she hadn't seen a single drop of light from outside.

"Did you black-out the windows?" she asked Theo.

He didn't answer.

Ryn tried something else. "Where are you taking me?" They reached the end of the hall. "Theo—"

"To Kai," he finally said. "You shouldn't have come here, Ryn. We would have contacted you. Kai sent someone in as soon as you were taken."

"Sent someone in where? What are you talking about…" Ryn's voice trailed off as they entered a large, bright room with dozens of priests in emerald green conversing in heated debates around tables. Most of them appeared to be in their twenties or thirties, and many wore swords like Theo.

One at a time, they hushed as they noticed Theo and Ryn standing there. Theo pulled his hood off.

"Ryn?" Kai's voice filled Ryn's ears as a priest moved from his spot, running around a table. She gasped at Kai's swelling bruises as he grabbed her shoulders, his jaw dropped. "You lunatic!" He slapped a hand over his mouth, his eyes stricken with horror. Then he smiled; it crept past his hand. "You escaped?! You're such a lunatic," he said again.

Ryn grinned. "Now we can run to a remote village and start over!" she told him. "Or we can go hide in the wasteland deserts with the tent people."

Kai's face fell. His eyes lost focus for a moment, and he stared off, dropping his arms to his sides. "I despise myself today, Ryn," he admitted. His throat bobbed when he swallowed. "First for letting the Folke take you, and second for…" He bit his lip.

Ryn became acutely aware of the rest of the Priesthood watching them. They stared at her like they recognized her even though she only knew Theo and Matthias. She didn't see Matthias now. "For what?" she asked.

"Adassah." Someone said her name—her *Adriel* name.

Ryn spun, her body warming. She hadn't been called that name in over six years.

A young man with long blond hair down to his waist and a green robe came to meet her. "I'm the High Priest. My name is Saturn, but that's not important. The only important name right now is *yours*."

"Please, let me be the one to ask her," Kai cut in, and Saturn hesitated. A second later, the High Priest nodded and took a step

45

back, folding his hands neatly in front of him. With his light hair and gentle movements, he looked like a god in a painting. He also looked way too young to be a High Priest.

Kai closed his eyes and inhaled, his chest expanding and deflating.

"Ryn, I despise my Priesthood for even suggesting this," he said. "But we've been talking about it for hours and they're not wrong. I hate that I have to ask such a thing of you, but we've never had an opportunity like this," he said and then swallowed. Ryn scooted back a step as something sunk into the pit of her stomach. Kai never fidgeted, yet he clasped and unclasped his hands now.

"Kai, what's going on with you? And why does Theo have a sword?" Her voice wavered. She looked around the large room, at the big chandelier overhead, at the tall, pointed windows covered in black paint. "And why are you meeting at night in secret?"

When Kai opened his eyes, they were rimmed with red. "We're a private branch of the Priesthood that's *doing something* about the persecution of the Adriels. The rest of the Priesthood either don't know we exist, or they turn a blind eye because they know what we're doing is right," Kai said. "We've been training in combat to defend our people. We've been covertly trying to gain influence across the city, especially in politics, and waiting for a chance to enter the palace." He took hold of Ryn's shoulders again, tighter this time, and Ryn blinked at him. She'd never heard Kai plead, either. "Ryn, I wish it wasn't you. But you're the only Adriel who's ever snuck inside with an influential position."

For several seconds, Ryn thought she was somewhere else. Like the person standing across from her wasn't the same Kai who spent his evenings reading his studies to her. The same calm, soft-spoken priest who tended to the needs of the children on their street with his medical supplies when they scraped their knees, and who delivered spare apples to all the houses down the road. Never would she have dreamed he was a part of something secret, and she couldn't imagine him learning to fight or speaking up against the Weylin ways.

Only now did Ryn notice Kai wore a sword as well.

"Kai," she began in her softest voice, "I'm not sure what you're asking me to do, but if I go back to the palace, it's only a matter of time before someone figures out I'm lying about my name. Adriels are forbidden from entering the palace grounds, and I've already done that. I'll be killed for breaking the law the second my identity comes out."

How could he ask this of her?

Moisture layered Kai's gaze, and he nodded. "I know the risk. I hate this, Ryn. I wish I could take your place. But there's no seat more powerful in the kingdom than the Queen's seat. Ryn, if you could take it, you could *save the Adriel people*—"

"Don't you know the things that go on inside that palace?!" Ryn felt the weight of magic all over again, the same stomach-turning heaviness that had made it difficult to breathe when her carriage first pulled through the gate. "Don't you know what happened to the last Queen?" It came out high-pitched and raw.

Ryn's whole life she'd been told to stay inside, to keep quiet, and to *avoid* the palace at all costs. She rarely even left the street she lived on with Kai so she wouldn't be discovered. She always wore popular Weylin clothing if she needed to leave the house, she made sure to use common Weylin phrases in her conversations with merchants, and she took the time to bow to the goddess statue when she passed the Sixteenth Temple of Nyx on the road. Now

47

Kai wanted her to parade herself in front of all of Per-Siana? Within arm's reach of the very people who'd love to see her dead? She pointed back in the direction of the palace. "There's something evil in there, Kai! I could feel it, and I escaped it! You can't ask me to go back there!"

Kai dropped his head and released her shoulders. He nodded, and a second later, he turned to the rest of the Priesthood. "You heard her," he said quietly. "She said no."

Theo made a deflated sound at her side. Ryn noted the looks around the room—men biting their tongues, frowning. She studied their reactions with a weak stomach, not noticing when Kai turned his attention to someone behind her.

"What do you want, Heva?" he asked.

…Heva?

Ryn glanced toward the hall and faltered at the sight of her guardswoman standing there in her navy and silver Folke armour. Ryn looked between Kai and her guardswoman when neither of them explained how they knew each other.

"I almost didn't come here," Heva admitted to the Priesthood. "I'm not a part of your fight."

"But you did come," Kai replied. "So, you must have a reason to be here, like us."

Heva didn't answer. Her gaze shot to Ryn instead.

"Did you follow me?" Ryn asked her. She should have been terrified to see another Folke this close to her cousin, but… Kai knew her name.

"I didn't know you'd be here," Heva admitted to Ryn. "I came to speak with the priests." Then to the Priesthood, she said, "I know Geovani and her priestesses haven't always gotten along with you—" a few grunts and scoffs lifted through the room "—

but Geovani wanted to know who Estheryn Electus was. After finding no recorded history of her among the Electus family, she sent me to inquire if this woman's presence at the palace was one of your schemes?"

"Schemes?" Kai released a sound from the back of his throat. "Just because the Adriel priestesses have become lazy and obsolete doesn't mean *we* must. Yes, we do things."

Ryn's lips parted at his harsh tone.

Kai's shoulders relaxed. "But no, we aren't behind Ryn going to the palace. I tried to stop the Folke from taking her."

At that, Heva looked from one priest to the next. And, as if deciding they no longer mattered, she walked straight to Ryn and put out her hand. "Come, Maiden," she said.

Ryn blinked down at the girl's open palm. Back at the carriage, Heva had refused to offer Ryn her hand.

"Where?" Ryn asked.

"Back to the palace. You can't be here." Heva's hand didn't waver. "It's not safe."

"And the palace is?" Ryn drifted toward Kai. Ryn was sure this guardswoman would catch her if she tried to run. Even though they were the same height and appeared the same age, they had vastly different builds.

"No, the palace isn't safe either, but I'll try to protect you," Heva stated.

"What do you mean, *you'll* try?" Kai demanded and folded his arms.

Heva's gaze remained on Ryn when she said, "I'm her personal Folke guard."

Kai closed his mouth, but a few of the priests started to whisper.

Heva spoke only to Ryn again, "I'm not going to lie to you, Maiden—at least seven high political powers want you dead, regardless of whether or not they know who you are. Seven influential political powers with a lot of money," she emphasised. "I'm just one person against them. I might be the first Folke guard to die in the trial period trying to keep my maiden alive."

The Priesthood fell quiet; Kai looked like he might be sick.

Heva lifted her chin a little. "But Geovani wanted me to protect you the moment she saw you. And I might not be the deeply spiritual type, but I believe in that woman. So, I will."

Still, Heva's hand didn't move. Still, her gaze remained solely on Ryn.

From the side, Saturn piped up, "We'll take up an offering. We'll fund you, Adassah. *We* will be your benefactors."

Kai's head snapped toward him. "She said she didn't want to go back!" he protested.

"And we can't possibly be expected to work alongside Geovani and the priestesses," Theo muttered.

"Quiet, you two," Saturn scolded. He reached for Ryn's hand and gently placed it into Heva's. But as Heva's grip tightened around Ryn's fingers, a spark of something lifted in her chest—terror? Hopefulness? The urge to run and vanish into the darkness outside? Ryn ripped her hand back and nearly bumped into Kai.

Saturn sighed and turned to Heva. "Tell Geovani we'll get her whatever she needs. Tell her that, for once, we're on her side with this."

Heva gave him a curt nod, but her attention fired to Kai dragging his hands through his hair and pacing in a small circle. Ryn thought Kai might protest again, but he stopped before her and cradled her cheeks. A tear spilled down his face.

"Ryn, you can do this," he said. All thoughts of running melted away as Ryn looked into her cousin's eyes. "You're brave, and pretty, and smart. You can do this," he repeated.

A slow, sharp pain settled in Ryn's chest. She couldn't imagine surviving the next day, let alone three months. There was no way her secret wouldn't come out. And her death wouldn't be easy, either—it would be public and horrid.

Brave. Pretty. Smart? What did it matter if she was dead?

"What if I can't?" she rasped. "What if the King is heartless like gossip claims? What if he really has no heart to steal?" She imagined what the King looked like; a cruel, dark being stamped with the hideousness of all the bad things he'd done. How could she look someone like that in the eyes and keep her food down while trying to be *brave* and *pretty* and *smart* for him? While trying to convince him to fall in love with her?

Kai swallowed and placed a hand atop Ryn's head, like a father, like an older sibling. A dark look came over his eyes and a snarl curled his lip. "Then kill him," he said. "Before he kills you."

Heva's gaze darted to Kai in surprise, but she didn't object. Neither did Saturn, or Theo, or any of the priests. Ryn forgot how to take a breath as that settled in, as she wondered if that was what everyone in this room really wanted. If that was what they'd been hoping to send her in to do the whole time.

"For the Adriels," Kai added. "For your mother, Ryn. And my parents. And all the parents who were discovered and slain unjustly. Do it for them."

Why did Kai mention her mother? Only he knew what her mother's death meant to her. The pain she'd buried.

The torches around the room turned hotter and brighter than a moment ago; Ryn's flesh burned as she looked at the Priesthood, at Kai, at Heva. It was clear to her now what they all were. Ene-mies of the King. Devoted Adriels. Her people. Her hands felt wet as if they were covered in blood, but she lifted them and saw it was only sweat.

"Let's not get carried away." Saturn's objection sliced through her thoughts. "For *now*, we just need you to be our spy. We have three months to decide what to do in the end."

Ryn closed her mouth. Saturn had failed to remind anyone what a spy's death would be. The last spy caught committing trea-son against the King was dragged through the Mother City behind a steed. Ryn had been so afraid when the rumours reached their village; she'd slept in her mother's bed for three nights afterward.

It was absurd. Only a fool would walk back into the palace to die. But death was just the peace at the end of a long, difficult road—that's what Ryn had told herself after her mother's passing. And though she'd never admitted it to Kai, there were days when Ryn had missed her mother so much, she'd craved the reunion death would bring.

But she couldn't win the despicable King's love against the three fairest maidens in the kingdom. So, would she be able to kill him in the end? And could she really *spy* on the most powerful beings in Per-Siana for the Priesthood? Could she will her feet to walk her back into that palace at all?

A phantom clock ticked in her head, rushing her decision. But perhaps she already knew the answer as she looked around the room and saw the desperate faces—faces of people who'd lost loved ones, people who'd been treated like insects because of their heritage, people who'd suffered.

Yes.

For her people, she could try.

But still. Kai was her cousin, whom she loved. Who loved her.

She wished someone else had asked her to do this instead of him.

5
RYN

It was a sin to be an Adriel.

Ryn learned this the hard way more than once. The first time was the day her father had purchased false identity cards and told them they were changing their names and their religion. Ryn's mother had protested—she'd loved their Adriel names, and she'd loved the Adriel God. She insisted there were still places in Per-Siana where Adriels could go without being persecuted. But Ryn's father didn't want that; he wanted to be like everybody else—like the *Weylin* people. Like those who ruled the kingdom and served the seven primary Celestial Divinities. Like the royal family, and the famous warriors, and the renowned magicians. It was an alluring lifestyle, but it was one Ryn's mother had never wanted.

After all his arguments for why he needed a better life than the beautiful, simple one Ryn's mother had built, Ryn didn't miss her father after he left.

She was, perhaps, the reason he left. She did ask him to find her a type of rose that didn't exist, after all. He was simply too dull to realize it, or maybe he knew and only pretended to take the task seriously the day he vanished. It made no difference to Ryn.

It wasn't long after that her mother was arrested for an act of thievery she didn't commit. Even under the pressure of interrogation with the Folke, Ryn's mother never admitted she had an Adriel daughter. The day she was dragged out the front door of their house, she shoved Ryn into a cupboard and said, "Adassah! Go find your cousin Mordekai in the Mother City! He'll keep you safe!"

Adassah Cahana. Her Adriel name. Her birth name. Her mother had used it by accident in the heat of the moment even though local persecution had driven them to start using the false Weylin names her father had purchased a year and a half before.

Her mother had closed the cupboard door, and Ryn listened as the Folke took her mother away. Her mother never returned.

The journey to hunt for Kai in the Mother City had been dreadful and frightening that week, but Ryn finally found him after eight days of living on the streets. She was nearly starved to death when Kai scooped her up off the roadside and carried her home with his friends from the Priesthood. Kai was the one who'd investigated and discovered that Ryn's mother had died after contracting the *cinder plague* in prison.

She'd died alone. All because she was an Adriel, and their Weylin neighbours discovered it and thought it would be funny to accuse her of thievery.

Weylins had killed Ryn's mother and *laughed* about it.

For years after Kai had taken Ryn into his care, he spent his evenings teaching Ryn the scriptures and the ways of the Priesthood. Ryn wasn't that interested in learning, but she let him talk for hours anyway. She let him teach her Adriel songs from the hymnary. She let him guide her through the basic customary prayers. His voice was a familiar comfort, and even though he was only two years older than Ryn, he was more of a father than her real one had ever been.

Ryn's room in the palace was cooler in the morning. The window had been left open for most of the night, even after she and Heva climbed back inside. It wasn't an easy task to get back over the outer wall, to navigate the gardens, and to climb the side of the palace to Ryn's room without anyone noticing. Both girls had barely made a sound during the journey, giving each other glances and signals about when to move and when to wait. But it was much easier travelling in a pair than when Ryn had tried to do it on her own.

Maids brought hot tea, unleavened bread sprinkled with sugar, and fresh pomegranate seeds on a silver tray at dawn. Ryn nibbled on the bread, but found it had no taste. After a while, her stomach rolled with queasiness and she gave up trying to eat. Even as the warm sun spilled gold over the Mother City, Ryn's fingers were stiff and cold. Whatever promises she'd made to the Priesthood the night before sat heavily now. She'd never be Queen because she couldn't steal a heart from a king who didn't have one. So, how could a frail, antisocial Adriel girl assassinate a powerful, murderous King? Never mind that she had no chance of outsmarting the Intelligentsia who surrounded him at all times.

Ryn nearly dropped her teacup when Marcan barged in; the

large doors swung around and slapped the walls with a *thud*. "I was up all night," he announced. Two assistants trailed in behind him carrying a delicate tapestry studded with thousands of tiny, navy gems.

"That makes three of us," Heva mumbled, too quiet for Marcan to hear. She stole the rest of Ryn's bread and took a bite. Sugar spilled down her chin and she swiped at it with her fingers.

When Marcan lifted the jeweled fabric from the assistants, Ryn realized it wasn't a tapestry at all.

She leapt to her feet. "What is that?" she demanded.

A smile broke across her artist's face. "It's your introduction dress, Lady Estheryn. It's a mosaic, like you suggested."

No. That wasn't a simple mosaic made to sit at the back of a dining room. That dress was a centrepiece, the sort of attention-grabbing display that could be featured as the main attraction at a Divinities Museum. With thin tulle skirts and a bodice of enough gems to make the stars envious, it was the last thing Ryn wanted to be caught dead in.

"Wow. Nice," Heva remarked. She tried to poke the navy skirt with a sugar covered finger, but Marcan slapped her hand away.

"I can't wear that!" Ryn exclaimed.

Marcan raised a brow and frowned. "Why ever not?"

"It's... It's beautiful!" Ryn said in horror. "There's real gold *in the skirt*, and how many gemstones did you use? A thousand?"

"*Several* thousand." Marcan smiled, and Ryn slapped a hand over her eyes. "I had a few assistants help me place them all. This, Maiden, is what I call a diamond painting. Can't you see how it resembles the starry heavens?"

Ryn swallowed the lump in her throat. The King would notice her in that dress. *Everyone* would notice her. People would talk about her, look into her background, and discover who she really was.

"I'm sorry, Marcan, but I can't." Ryn fanned her hot cheeks. She was supposed to be a quiet spy. She was supposed to hide. She was supposed to never be here in the first place.

Marcan's smile faded. The wobbly pout that replaced it put a twisting feeling in Ryn's chest. "Please, Ryn. This will save my reputation," Marcan rasped. His brows pulled together, and Ryn wished she'd never looked him in his eyes.

It wasn't fair. It wasn't fair that Marcan was yanked from his home and ordered to be a part of this Heartstealer period the same way she was. It wasn't fair that she could relate to his fear of the unknown to come. It wasn't fair that he looked like a helpless mouse caught in a trap when his eyes grew large and misty like that.

"Divinities, Marcan. Fine." Ryn's shoulders dropped. "I'll put it on."

It wasn't fair, most of all, that Ryn was the one who had to wear the dress. She glanced at Heva, who was no help.

Marcan's face lit up. "You'll be the talk of the introductions this morning, Estheryn. Trust me—this will turn heads."

Ryn wanted to curse.

It took almost an hour for Marcan to fit Ryn into the dress. A number of other artists—Marcan's "friends"—began smearing colours and chalky things onto Ryn's face after that. She winced, until Marcan told her to relax so his friends could work. "I don't do makeup," he explained, not that she'd asked. "But it's important you look like you belong." He stole a repulsed look at where her gardening dress hung over the back of a chair in the sitting room.

Marcan and his assistants left two hours later, and Ryn raced to the mirror the second they were gone.

She didn't recognize herself when she looked in. A girl stood in a glittering dress with silk hair, a smooth face, and shimmering powders. Even Heva's jaw hung open as she crowded into the mirror space to see better. The dirty gardener girl had vanished at some point in the last hours, and now a noble lady commanded the room.

"You still have scrapes on your arms," Heva pointed out. "You'll have to hide those. They'll be a dead giveaway you're not a Weylin noble if people see them."

"Why? Are Weylin nobles invincible?" Ryn rolled her eyes.

Heva shot her a look. "They don't hide when the Folke show up at their door, for starters. They don't try to fight them, either. And they don't sneak around at night, they don't get their clothes dirty, and they don't look so painfully afraid all the time." The guardswoman swatted Ryn's arm, and Ryn winced. "Snap out of it. Don't you want to save your people?"

"Just because you're an Adriel doesn't mean you represent *all* the Adriel people when you speak to me." Ryn rubbed her arm.

"I'm not an Adriel."

Ryn looked Heva up and down, not that Folke armour or her silver-bead hairstyle gave any clues. "You're not? But the Priest-hood…"

"I'm of Weylin blood. I escaped a terrible home when I was little, and I found my way into a priestess's temple not far from here. High Priestess Geovani took me in and raised me," Heva said. "Speaking of which…" She glanced out the window and eyed the sun. "We're going to be late, Maiden." She headed toward the door, but she paused in the doorway. "Do you want me

59

to call you *Maiden* or *Ryn*? Or *Estheryn*?" she asked. Then, before Ryn could answer, she decided, "I'll call you *Maiden* in front of others, and *Ryn* when it's just us."

Heva led the way out.

Ryn scooted after her, keeping close behind. Her nerves fluttered along her skin as she thought about being 'introduced' to the King—especially in Marcan's artwork. She wondered how many minutes were left before the introductions would start.

Down the hall, the other girls slipped from their rooms in dazzling gowns: pearl white with dark blue threads, black stitching over blue taffeta, wide organza cascading to the floor. Everything had the same feel—the dark blue sky, the silver stars, and occasionally, a golden sun. Emblems and hues to bring blessings to the King via their praise of the Divinities.

Heva changed direction. She slid into a dim adjacent hall and waved for Ryn to follow.

Ryn watched the other girls heading toward the Hall of Stars where Marcan told her they'd be announced. But Heva kept waving, so Ryn scampered the other way after her. They scurried down a dark corridor and around a bend where morning light broke through slit windows, bleaching the walls in long shapes and blinding Ryn.

"We're going the wrong way—"

"Shh. Hurry!"

Ryn's gold-spun sandals slapped over the floor as she tried to keep up. The gems in her dress rattled, and she imagined Marcan's outrage if any broke off. She also imagined missing the Introduction Ceremony and alerting the whole palace that they should be suspicious of her.

"Heva," she tried again, but Heva was jogging now.

Finally, they reached an arch that was too narrow to go in side-by-side, so Heva slid in first.

Ryn released a heavy breath before she followed, ready to demand an explanation from her guardswoman. But her lips parted when she stepped into the wide room that was crumbling yet looked more beautiful than the great palace atrium had been with all its dark blue murals and Celestial statues.

Beige stone walls enclosed a room of pillars, most of which were smashed or had deteriorated. Overgrown ivy spilled from a hole in the ceiling's corner that was open to the sky, and soft tweets came from the heights of the domed space where birds congregated in the stream of morning sunlight.

Four inches of water also covered the floor.

"Heva, I can't come in here," Ryn said.

Heva glanced back at her dress. She doubled around and lifted the train of Ryn's skirt, and they walked in that way—Ryn kicking through the water in her sandals. "Are you going to tell me where we're going now?" she asked, wincing as water splashed up her legs.

"This is the old temple, now called the Abandoned Temple after it was deserted when a groundwater stream burst through. No one's bothered to repair it, so no one comes here," a white-haired woman Ryn hadn't noticed before explained from the centre of the room. The hem of the woman's emerald green robe swished through the water as she turned around. She brushed her palms clean of birdseed, and Ryn watched it sprinkle into the stream.

"We only have three minutes," Heva said over Ryn's shoulder to the woman.

"Who is this?" Ryn whispered back to Heva.

The woman chuckled and waved a hand through the air. "Apologies, Estheryn. I'm Geovani, High Priestess of the Adriel God, representing the Adriels in the one hundred and twenty-seven provinces for the royal court." She came a few steps closer, revealing a soft smile and bright eyes amidst many wrinkles. "You have a red 'R' painted upon your forehead. Did you know that?"

Ryn didn't realize she'd taken a step backward until she bumped into Heva. Sure, Ryn had heard of visions. Visions from the Celestial Divinities were what gave the Intelligentsia their power and wisdom to govern daily affairs. Ryn's mother had believed in visions but had then called the palace sages liars. Geovani didn't have the look of a liar, but she talked like a crazy person.

Also, Ryn had just been looking in a mirror—there was no red *anything* on her forehead.

Geovani raised another hand of apology. "I don't know what it means yet, but I know you must be important. Sometimes an "R" stands for *Revivalist*, but I think we'll have to wait and see with you."

Ryn almost turned and yelled at Heva for bringing her here. This wasn't what Ryn had expected when Heva spoke of Geovani.

Geovani grinned like she could read Ryn's mind. "Trust me, this is the most important moment since the day you were born, Estheryn. Or should I call you, *Adassah*?"

Ryn's lips parted. She tried to move back again, but Heva's hand found her shoulder and held her still. "Just wait," Heva whispered.

Geovani sighed. "There was once a great battle between the gods," she said. "Someday, I'll tell you what really happened, and it'll change your mind. But don't worry—I won't tell you now. I know you have somewhere important to be." A strange twinkle lit the old woman's eyes.

That was it. Ryn shook off Heva's hand and turned to face her guardswoman. "Take me to the Hall of Stars," she said. "Let's go."

But Heva shook her head. "I'm loyal to Geovani," she said. "I'll do what she says."

Ryn stared at her guard in disbelief. Nothing since the moment she'd entered the palace was normal, but this encounter was the strangest of all. Was this really the revered Geovani that even the Priesthood knew about? Ryn once learned from Kai that there was only one Adriel representative left on the King's council—one single soul of the Adriel religion; a priestess. And apart from her, any Adriel who set foot on the palace grounds would be executed on the spot.

Ryn glanced back at the woman. Suddenly, all those things Kai mentioned in their candlelit conversations returned to her mind. He'd said the High Priestess was ignored, that she had no voice on the council, that she was just there for show so the Adriel citizens of Per-Siana would feel represented in the palace, obey the Weylin order, and never revolt. She didn't even have a vote in kingdom affairs anymore; only the Weylin councilmen and the Intelligentsia had ballots. Kai once said the High Priestess shouldn't have bothered staying in the palace when she was invisible and never heard, and all the priests wondered why she was still there. How humiliating it must have been for her to exist and not be treated like she was alive.

"Sorry," Ryn said. She wasn't even sure why she was apologizing to the woman. Maybe because she knew the feeling of always staying quiet in public, never raising her voice, never objecting to anything.

The wrinkled corners of Geovani's mouth turned up. "I'm a tired old woman, Adassah. I know my ways are considered ancient for the current times. But if you won't listen to me, at least listen to *him*. And then decide."

Ryn's face fell. "You should call me *Ryn*," she said, fighting the temptation to look toward the temple entrance to see if anyone was eavesdropping. "And who should I listen to, exactly?"

And decide what?

Geovani stepped toward her, and Ryn ducked a little when the old woman raised her hands and placed them over Ryn's ears. "I pray that you would have eyes to see and ears to hear, Adassah."

A net of warmth tangled into Ryn's stomach, and she tore away from Geovani, blinking. A flash of light burned over her vision, and she winced as heat popped in her ears.

What did this crazy old woman just do?

Ryn placed a hand over her stomach. "Are you a witch?" she asked. "Or a Jinn?"

Geovani burst out laughing, startling Ryn more than the heat in her belly. The old woman took her shoulders and turned her toward the arch. "Not at all. Go now. You can't be late." Then to Heva, she said, "Take her quickly."

Heva tugged Ryn out of the Abandoned Temple and back into the hall.

Ryn's hand remained on her stomach the whole walk to the Hall of Stars.

6
XERXES

Xerxes's room was so dark, he could hardly see himself in the mirror as he pulled on his blue coat of nobility, sliding his arms through the sleeves, and positioning the shoulders where they ought to be. He'd forgone the assistance of servants today, wishing for quiet he'd never find. The servants vanished after some threatening persuasion, leaving the King to get ready for the Introduction Ceremony alone with his voices. He shoved things around on his dresser in the dark, searching for the last piece of his outfit he was expected to wear before the court. By the Divinities, he couldn't remember where he'd put his ring.

He glanced over to the water glass beside his bed, recalling how his signet ring had drowned in the middle of the night. The royal ring was a heavy boulder on his hand, and he couldn't stand how it kept him awake. He'd watched it sink to the bottom of the glass, and there, he'd stared at it for hours.

With a sigh, he headed over, fished the ring out of the water glass, and slid it onto his forefinger where it belonged. It was a shiny, gold thing with star runes of royalty and prosperity. Not his style, but certainly his father's sort of thing. Xerxes hadn't inherited his father's plain features, his ruthless confidence, his control over the kingdom, nor his peaceful, care-free slumbers. The only gifts the former King had given Xerxes before he died were a wife he never wanted and this lump of gold that rested heavily on Xerxes's hand.

He took in a deep breath and exhaled through his nose. It was the time he'd been dreading. The time when the Heartstealer maidens he'd been avoiding all morning would get to see his face. They would like it, too—he didn't have to look in the mirror to know he was handsome. Grovellers on his council informed him of such things all the time even when he wished they wouldn't.

He tugged open a curtain before he left, eyeing a rising bout of smoke far in the distance. The smoke had appeared behind the mountains at daybreak, and it was only increasing. The mountains weren't a part of Xerxes's land, but still. He had men out there, enforcing the kingdom boundary. His chest tightened when he thought of them. If his boundary men were attacked, he wouldn't get word until it was too late.

"Just let them die," one of the voices said.

"Don't trouble yourself with such trivial things," another agreed.

"Quiet," Xerxes snapped through his teeth. He released an exasperated grunt. It seemed he needed to visit his tree before the Ceremony began. The last thing he wanted was another *incident* before all the watching eyes in the Hall of Stars.

As the thought crossed his mind, a deep hunger boiled within him. A hunger that could not be satisfied by any food, apart from one. Xerxes rushed for his door and ignored the questioning looks from his room guards as he flew past.

The Hall of Stars buzzed with so much energy, Xerxes could hardly sit still in his gilded chair upon the dais. He shifted in his seat, licked the taste of pears from his lips, patted imaginary dirt off his shoulder, and tapped his toes against the floor. He wished to stand and pace, but he knew that would make people whisper. His robe was too warm for a day like today too, and the organizers had decided to keep the glass doors to the courtyard closed, suffocating everything in the room with still air. It was all unbearable.

Seven Celestial Divinity statues built into the walls gazed down into the Hall of Stars. The servants must have polished them for this event; the white marble glowed beneath the chandelier lights and the two hundred gold lanterns hanging from the ceiling. Xerxes eyed the statue of Nyx, her slender female form taking up half the East wall. For a Divinity who governed the night, she hadn't helped Xerxes sleep much. Perhaps it was because Nyx was claimed to be the daughter of chaos itself. Maybe it was the goddess's nature to bring only restlessness to one's sleep.

Xerxes rolled his eyes at the thought. He'd prayed to Nyx and Hesperus more times than he could count, and they never gifted him a pleasant slumber. He was sure the Celestial Divinities had all forgotten about the King of Per-Siana by now. Which was an easier truth to believe than the alternative; that they knew of his troubles and didn't care.

Xerxes tapped his knuckles against his armrest, thinking of how the Divinities also hadn't lifted a finger to stop him from being trapped on this throne facing the debacle before him today.

"What a fine day to meet the four Heartstealers," one of the Intelligentsia murmured down the dais. Xerxes huffed a quiet laugh to himself. How shocked the Intelligentsia would be when they learned that one of their precious chosen maidens had already escaped the palace and was probably racing into the wilderness by now. Currently, there were only three maidens left, and despite the dreariness of the situation, Xerxes revelled in the fact that he would get to see the Intelligentsia discover this fun little fact up close.

A sweep of glassy wind chimes filled the Hall with music, and hundreds of nobles of the highest rankings turned to face the silver entrance. Only the dark blue centre carpet was empty—a walkway for the maidens. All the Intelligentsia who stood at Xerxes's sides aimed themselves to watch the show, their shadowy faces peering from below their long hoods.

An organizer said a short welcome, and before Xerxes was ready, the first maiden was announced. Xerxes closed his eyes and sucked in a lungful of air. The announcer said her name was *Ulita Sorabata*. At one point, Belorme had informed Xerxes about these young women, but Xerxes couldn't remember a thing about this Ulita person now. He rubbed his temples, waiting for it to be over as the nobles below reacted with gasps and other obnoxious noises.

He finally opened his eyes when the second maiden was announced—just a crack to see how terrible everything was. *Calliope Ingrid*. Unfortunately, Xerxes remembered that one. Only because the Intelligentsia had discussed her the most. This was the horrid woman Xerxes would likely be expected to marry. He released a huff of disbelief at the sight of the large, frilly pale blue and navy dress she wore. "This is utterly impractical," Xerxes muttered.

At his side, Damon tilted his hood toward Xerxes. In his low, dark voice, he asked, "How so, Your Majesty?"

"What good will fancy dresses do for these women?" Xerxes asked, loud enough to challenge all the Intelligentsia down the line, yet quiet enough to keep the conversation from the rest of the nobles. "How will those dresses save them if B'rei Mira attacks? Shouldn't we be more concerned with finding a queen who can defend herself, rather than one who looks nice in a ridiculously large ball gown?" Xerxes didn't hear the third maiden announced through his talking.

Down the line, Belorme tilted his head toward Xerxes too, but he said nothing.

Xerxes closed his eyes and went back to rubbing his temples. He wanted a hot bath and a drink. What a waste of time this all was.

"Estheryn Electus," the organizer announced, and Xerxes's eyes opened. His gaze darted up. He was not interested in her, but perhaps he wanted to know what she looked like—the girl whose father had traded her life for his own freedom. The girl Xerxes, by a deal bound by the Celestial Divinities, now owned.

Xerxes's heart stopped when he spotted her.

It wasn't because she wore a gown inlaid with a depthless sea of gems, or because her sheer skirts whispered of the night breeze as she walked, or because she left strange, wet footprints behind when she came in. It wasn't because it occurred to him that *four* maidens had been named after all, instead of three.

No.

It was because he recognized her from the garden last night when she tried to escape. When she *succeeded* in escaping—with his help.

She'd returned.

A slow, wicked smile threatened Xerxes's face when she lifted her gaze to him. Their eyes locked, and in her expression, Xerxes saw it all: her startled look as it dawned on her that she knew his face, the rigidness that seized her body, and the flash of horror as she must have remembered all those things she said to him in the garden.

"Goodbye, you ugly, heartless King!"

Those dangerous, exquisite, amusing words.

Forget the moment she mistook him for a palace servant. *This* was now the most entertaining moment of Xerxes's kingship.

CHAPTER

7
RYN

The air was different in the Hall of Stars—colder. Ryn studied the nobles, the Intelligentsia, and the great statues around the room through the angled door from where she stood out of sight. Heva was already somewhere inside.

The lighting design in the Hall was unusual. Even though there were more lanterns than Ryn could count hanging from the ceiling, faint black shadows hovered inside like the light was being masked by a misty cloud above the nobles, an even darker shade around the Intelligentsia, and a few wispy breaths of it up by the heads of the Celestial statues. She wondered if the lighting trick was intentional, meant to set the mood.

Maybe the King preferred darkness.

Ryn shook the thought from her mind as the maiden before her finished her introduction. An organizer with a scroll in his hands nodded for Ryn to head in, and Ryn swallowed her nerves. She smoothed down her skirt. She tried kicking the last of the water off her sandals. She took in one last deep breath.

The second she stepped inside, an eruption of whispers came from the nobles who weren't far enough away for Ryn to tune out. Some of the whispers were in admiration for Marcan's mosaic dress, but the rest weren't pleasant. Ryn's cheeks grew warm as she thought of the benefactors and powerful nobles all seeing her as a threat in Marcan's work of art. She regretted agreeing to wear this dress, even if Marcan had flashed his misty eyes at her when she'd refused.

But that all meant nothing the moment Ryn looked upon the King of Per-Siana, sitting on his gold throne atop a dais of glass stairs. His eyes had been closed, but they'd flashed open at the mention of her name.

Ryn took in his rich, fitted robe and the thin gold crown upon his dark hair. He was much younger than she'd expected, not the old troll she'd pictured—that was her first thought. But when he settled his gaze upon her... and then the corner of his mouth tugged upward...

She froze halfway down the carpet.

Ryn imagined him in a dirt-covered landscaping tunic, his hair a mess, his features dimmed by the night's shadows.

A flush threatened to turn her cheeks to roses as warmth speared up her neck. She tried to tell herself her eyes were deceiving her. That this could not really be the same young man she'd spilled her terrible plan of escape to. Whom she'd persuaded to lift her over the wall in an act of betrayal.

Ryn's sandals were sticky against the floor when she resumed walking, each step a chore as she wondered how far behind her the silver arch was. As she wondered how difficult it would be to run for it, to make it through the halls and out the palace front entrance. She could be dead by midnight if she stayed. But the Folke guarded the doors, and the mosaic dress was so heavy, she'd have trouble walking out, let alone running. She pulled her parted lips closed, and she swallowed past her thick, dry throat.

"Maiden!" someone whispered. She tore her gaze off the King and landed it on an organizer beside the walkway. The organizer gave a small nod toward the other three Heartstealer maidens standing near the end of the navy carpet. Where she was *supposed* to be standing.

Ryn's legs quivered as she rushed to join them. She thought she might crumple to the floor and melt into it. The nobles' heavy gazes were like hands squeezing her insides.

The organizers said several things to the room—things Ryn didn't hear. Everything became a blur of sounds and colour. Her lungs were too tight to breathe properly.

Through the distortion of glassy glimmers from the overhead lanterns, the clapping nobles, and the faint smell of fermented fruit in the air, one single, crystal-clear thought entered Ryn's mind.

The King had looked up when her name was called.

She hadn't imagined it. The King had recognized her name.

Ryn's eyes darted back up the dais, finding him. The King hadn't moved a muscle. He sat with good posture on his throne now, facing the room with interest.

He was still looking at her.

Ryn's gaze dropped back to the floor.

A slow procession of events followed where the maidens each took a turn gliding to a designated space before the King and his Intelligentsia and bowing as a form of formal greeting. Ryn twisted her fingers. Her lashes fluttered against a dizzy spell. She was sure she'd pass out when it was her turn.

The third maiden finished a bow and a fine curtsy. She, like the others, said one or two greetings to the King in a soft, sweet voice, introducing herself and stating her intentions to try and impress him in the trials. He never said anything back. Not to the first maiden, not to the second, not to the third either.

The third maiden turned and left down the navy carpet.

The organizer waved Ryn forward, and she dragged her feet in slow steps, one after the other, until she was in the spot directly before the King. It was then she realized she didn't know how to perform a proper bow. She didn't know how to curtsy, either, or say an appropriate greeting to royalty. And, Divinities, she'd been too distracted to overhear the other girls' greetings to copy them.

People noticed she didn't greet the King, didn't look up at him. So, she cleared her throat quietly, and said, "Your Majesty—"

"*Ugly*, was it?" he cut her off, and her wide eyes flashed up to him after all. "And *heartless*?"

Ryn's lips peeled apart. Intelligentsia members tilted toward the King. She had no idea if they knew what he was referring to— if they'd learned of the names she'd called him to his face.

She took in a slow, shaky breath. "You must have me confused with someone else," she rasped. "I don't know what you speak of."

The King stared at her for a moment. And then he laughed.

The entire room hushed, the Intelligentsia staring at the King with startled faces like they'd never heard him laugh before. Like Ryn had done something terrible by making him react at all. One sage leaned forward and whispered to the sage in front of him.

The King's laugh was raspy and deep in contrast to his youthful appearance, and some of the nobles began giggling along with him. Ryn laced her fingers together tightly in front of her, strangling them. After a moment, the King's laughter ceased, bringing the marvel to an end, and he sighed.

"Divinities," he cursed.

The King suddenly stood from his throne and the nobles at Ryn's back burst into shocked murmurs and gasps as he trotted down the glass stairs until he was in front of her. He eyed her rosy cheeks, her throat when she swallowed, her dress.

"And they say *I'm* crazy," he said. He poked her forehead. "You must have the memory of a brick."

Ryn's mouth parted.

A *brick*?!

The King bit his lips together. Then, he huffed another laugh to himself, and he walked past her.

He left the Hall of Stars.

Whispers rose, some Intelligentsia taking steps after him. Even the organizers looked dumbfounded as the King marched down the navy carpet and out the silver arch. Ryn turned to watch him go, and only when he was out of sight did her heart cease its pounding against her chest.

"Well, that concludes our Introduction Ceremony! I'm sure the King was pleased to meet all the Heartstealer maidens," the organizer host said, though, he didn't look convinced the King was pleased with any of it. "Thank you all for coming!"

Nobles shifted around and the maidens excused themselves, one of the maidens glaring at Ryn on her way out. But Ryn remained standing at the foot of the glass dais, staring at the silver arch. Asking herself what she'd done.

Asking if that young, handsome landscaper was really the King of Per-Siana or if this was some kind of trick.

A Folke guard moved by the silver entrance, and Ryn glanced over to him. Her focus sharpened on his red-cheeked face, and for a moment she forgot where she was. A blond-haired priest stood there—one she'd seen almost every day walking past her house, one she often chased down the street for fun, one who always joined her and Kai for dinner on special occasions.

Matthias wore dark blue Folke armour and had a sword strapped to his hip. He cast Ryn a look of warning, and she thought she was dreaming. She took a step toward him, but he gave her a small shake of his head, and she halted.

No, of course she couldn't approach him. But what was Matthias doing here?

"Kai sent someone in as soon as you were taken." Theo's words rang through Ryn's mind, and she nearly gasped in the middle of the Hall of Stars.

Matthias?!

She could hardly believe it. Of all people, Kai had sent in sweet-hearted, good-natured *Matthias* who never crushed bugs because he believed they deserved to live just as much as humans? Did Matthias even know how to use that Folke sword?

Ryn thought of the priests at the Priesthood temple carrying weapons. How Theo was ready to strike her down outside the temple. How he'd worn a black cloak over his green priest garments.

But the priests were wrong. Ryn needed to tell Matthais everything before it was too late; what she'd done in the garden, how she'd insulted the King, how the Priesthood's plan was no longer going to work—

A hand took Ryn's wrist; Heva pulled her toward the arch.

"Wait," Ryn said from a dry mouth. She tugged her arm free and pushed through the crowd to a table of flowers in glass vases. She ripped a white petal from a large bloom.

"What are you doing?" Heva's low whisper found her. "Everyone's looking at you, Ryn."

Ryn grabbed a lead pen resting beside an abandoned organizer's book. The pen hovered over the petal as Ryn realized she didn't know the Per-Siana alphabet. To save her from Weylin bullying, her mother had homeschooled her, but they hadn't studied letters much before her mother's passing. Ryn had only learned the *Adriel* alphabet years later from exploring the scriptures with Kai.

She scribbled a quick note on the flower petal in Adriel symbols, and she tossed the lead pen back down. The petal was delicate in her fingers, and she thought about crushing it in her palm instead. What if someone saw this note and realized she wrote it? What if someone learned there was an Adriel—no, *two* Adriels now—in the palace? What if her Adriel letters got both her *and* Matthias in trouble?

Heva appeared ready to explode when Ryn turned around. The guardswoman's hand was on her sword like she was worried the nobles would rush Ryn and she'd have to draw it. She took Ryn's arm again, gentler this time, and guided her back to the navy carpet.

Ryn didn't look at Matthias as they passed. But she dropped the petal to the floor by his feet. She chewed on her lip as she hoped and prayed he'd know enough to grab it before anyone else did.

Ryn's hand flashed to her chest once they were in the hall.

"What just happened?" Heva asked, stealing a glance back

over her shoulder. "What, by the Divinities, just *happened*?"

"I don't know," Ryn rasped. "But Heva, I can't be a spy anymore." She didn't mention that she expected guards to flood her room tonight, to drag her out to be executed for escaping the Heartstealer trials.

Heva didn't object. "What did you write on that petal?" she asked as they rushed through the atrium toward Ryn's rooms.

Ryn swallowed. She hoped all over again that what she wrote would find its way to the right person, and not the wrong one:

I'VE MADE A MISTAKE

TELL KAI TO GET ME OUT OF HERE

A brick.

Ryn spent hours pacing the length of her room before she finally sent Heva away in the evening. Heva objected, but Ryn argued she wouldn't sleep if Heva was there. It wasn't exactly a lie, but Ryn hadn't told Heva about her encounter in the garden, about why the King was so interested in her at the Introduction Ceremony. The less Heva knew now, the better. If Ryn was going to be taken by the Folke, Heva didn't deserve to be punished alongside her.

Moonlight blossomed over her bedroom floor, and the stars crept from their hiding places. It was a remarkable show of heavenly lights as the late hours swept in. Ryn wiggled her way out of the mosaic dress and looked around for a place to put it. A wardrobe rested at the far side of the room, but assuming she wouldn't know how to hang such a piece of artwork, she tossed it over the back of the nearest armchair instead. She had no other clothes apart from the gardening gown she arrived in. Nothing but a rich white nightdress delivered by an organizer after the Ceremony as a "gift from the King". But after how the introductions had gone, Ryn doubted the King had anything to do with the gifts.

Still though, the choice was between a dirty work dress or a silk nightdress. So, Ryn pulled it on, the thick, shiny silk softly draping over her in a whisper. She sat before the mirror and slid the silver beads from her hair, pulling off the other jewelry Marcan had insisted she wear as well. Her makeup hadn't worn off yet, even after all these hours. She wondered if she should go find the baths.

But what if the Folke barged into the baths while she was *in* them?

No bath, then.

Ryn broke into another restless pace. Every time a small noise sounded in the hall, her heart took off and she thought to run for the window. After the fourth blood-chilling noise from the hall-way, Ryn gave up and headed for the window to sit on the sill, just in case. She flicked the lever, thinking.

Escaping the first time hadn't been easy, but she'd managed. At least she knew her way around the garden now. She wondered if she could find her way to the outer wall again.

It was a crazy thought. The Folke guards were probably on the lookout for her after what had happened. The King would have told them about what she did. She sighed.

"If you go out there tonight, you'll be caught." Ryn's hands tightened on the lever when a voice filled her head. She looked behind her. She glanced out the window, seeing no one. *"He's waiting for you in*

the garden."

Ryn shrieked and stumbled backward, her back hitting the cold glass. "Who's there?" she asked the empty room. She crawled across the floor toward the bed and grabbed a pillow, whirling with it held above her head.

A warm breeze fluttered through the space, ruffling the curtains and making the gems on her mosaic gown tap lightly together on the chair. Ryn's gaze dragged to the window. It was still shut. She brought a hand over her mouth in horror.

"Don't be afraid," the voice said.

"Too late," Ryn rasped back through her fingers. She hugged the pillow to herself and backed up against the wall. The voice didn't sound like a female. It couldn't have been her mother's spirit arriving to look after her. But she asked anyway, "Are you my mother?" She tried not to sound too hopeful.

"Not your mother. But I do know your mother well." Another breath of wind followed the voice, and Ryn lowered the pillow slowly. Her hair fluttered at her shoulders.

"What do you mean you know her? My mother is dead," Ryn stated. But a thought crossed her mind. "Wait… are you a god?" Her mother had known a god. And Ryn had heard of the gods speaking to their most devoted believers. Could it be…

"I am."

Ryn slammed her mouth shut. A god. A *god*? Speaking to her in clear words. She bit her lower lip, her grip tightening on the pillowcase. She was far from the devoted spiritual sort. She hadn't even heard of Kai speaking to a god this way, and he spent his days studying his religion. "Which of the Celestial Divinities are you? Or are you something different? My mother didn't worship the Divinities."

"No, she didn't."

The room filled with the warm wind gently channelling over the surfaces and brushing along the windows. Even though Ryn's bedroom was dark, it felt like being in the daylight under the sun. "What do you want with me?" she asked.

"I want you to believe, Adassah," he said.

"Believe in what?"

"In me."

Ryn huffed out a strange, coarse laugh. "Are you speaking to me because of what that old woman, Geovani, did? I didn't ask her for ears to hear the voices of the gods. I didn't ask for eyes to see either, she just gave them to me." Ryn cursed the moment she met the High Priestess. Heva never should have brought her to that Abandoned Temple. Ryn didn't want religion, and she certainly didn't want a god. She was an Adriel by birth and had been tormented for it. But when the voice didn't reply, she asked, "Which god are you? Be specific. Give me a name."

"Which name do you want? I have many."

Ryn tossed the pillow to the bed and hugged her arms to herself. "One I'll recognize," she decided. "One that will make it clear who you are."

"Brace yourself for the mention of my names. They bear incredible power."

The wind lifted through the room, and Ryn's hair blew back. The bedsheets flipped over themselves, mimicking Ryn's heart doubling over in her chest. She grabbed the bedpost to steady herself.

"I'm called Alpha. I'm the great warrior God known in legends throughout the ages. I'm the First God. The God once forgotten. The God Original," he said. *"And I'm the Last God. Omega."* Then he added, *"You can call*

81

me El Shaddai, El Tsebaoth, or Paracletus, since those are the names of my three branches. Or you can simply call me, El."

Ryn pressed her palm against her pounding chest. Her hands trembled, her ears ringing with echoes of the voice even after he finished speaking as if the utterings had brushed along her very bones.

Yes, this had to be a god. But she couldn't imagine why a god would choose to speak to *her*. And she had no idea what 'three branches' meant.

"El Tsebaoth," she tried one of the names. It felt strong on her tongue. "Why did you come here and speak to me?" Ryn asked. "I'm no one. I'm the least of my family and the least of the religious people. I'm weak in knowledge of the gods, and I'm not good at practicing religious traditions," she admitted.

"I came to bring you a gift. Open your wardrobe," he answered.

For a split second, Ryn thought to refuse and end this conversation. To hide and never come out. But when she looked around at the wind ruffling the room, she rushed for the wardrobe and swung the doors open. She gasped.

A sword hung there, its detailed gold sheath glistening in the moonlight from the windows. A sun rune she didn't recognize marked the handle. There were no dresses in the wardrobe, no shoes, nothing, apart from this masterful blade hanging on two pegs.

"Wear it tomorrow. And when you've decided you will trust me, we'll speak again."

Ryn stared at the glittering deadly weapon. "How did you get it in here?" she asked.

The voice—El, or El Tsebaoth, or Paracletus—didn't answer. Ryn turned around and found the room perfectly still. The breeze was gone, the room was back to being dark and chilly. Ryn was alone.

Something tickled her face. She reached and smeared a finger across her cheekbone, then held it high to see what it was. The moonlight glistened off a layer of gold coloured dust coating her fingertip. It was as though something gilded had swept by and left traces on her flesh.

She turned and slammed the wardrobe shut.

This was lunacy. A god had spoken to *her* of all people, and at the worst time. Did he give her this sword because he expected her to stay in the palace? Now that a god had entered her room, she knew now more than ever that she could *not* stay.

She rushed for the window and turned the lever. Icy wind spilled into the space, entirely different from the floating breeze that had just touched everything. She was an *Adriel*, for Divinities' sake. She was an *orphan*. She couldn't carry a sword like some warrior in the mountains—especially in the palace.

Ryn's feet hit the soil with a quiet patter as the midnight wind tugged her nightdress and tousled her hair. She moaned at her scraped knees after dragging them down the palace walls for the climb, and she shivered as the breeze picked up, sending loose leaves and flower petals dancing through the garden.

Everything looked larger than it had last time—the trees more crooked and pointed, the branches a little sharper, the soil a little blacker. She hiked through the plants, slipping past shrubs as she hustled down the orchard path until she came to the square fountain she recognized. She looked both ways, and seeing no one, she breathed a sigh of relief.

Ryn slipped into the lilac bushes. Their scent engulfed her as she pushed through, reaching for the other side, stretching her fingertips toward that white wall as it came into view; the barrier between her and freedom.

Her dress tightened, lurching her to a halt, and she glanced back to find her nightdress caught on a branch. Was this that "El" god playing tricks on her? Was this his way of telling her she couldn't leave now that he'd gifted her a sword? Was he a scheming god like some of the others? She took a hold of her skirt and *yanked*.

The skirt tore from the branch and Ryn yelped as she flew back, hitting the outer wall. She lifted the hem of her nightdress and groaned at the tear in the silk. Even though the dress was meant for sleeping, it would have been the richest thing Ryn owned.

Now she might as well slice the dress into squares and sell it off as fabric.

"Did you really think you could escape twice?"

Ryn nearly screamed as she whirled. Her heart doubled over at the sight of someone in the shadows leaning back against the outer wall a few feet away. A long, navy robe hugged his body. Ryn turned to flee, but he swung around her and slapped a hand against the wall, blocking the path and forcing her to go flat against the stone before their bodies might touch. His fingers splayed beside her head, his arm hovering by her ear.

Ryn's pulse returned as she stared up at him, noting he was no longer wearing his gold crown. But in his royal kings' robe, he couldn't be mistaken for anything but what he was. She was a fool for ever thinking he was a landscaper.

The King was taller than her by several inches. Ryn worried about the golden dust left on her cheeks as his gaze hovered there for a moment. His stare flickered back up to hers, and she froze, gaze-locked with his dark eyes that were like the bottom of a deep-sea abyss where the light couldn't reach. She couldn't deny that he was just as handsome as the gossiping maidens claimed, especially up close. He was nothing like the troll she'd imagined; even his eyelashes were long and black enough to make the Divinities jealous.

Ryn's toes curled into the grass. She was too afraid to swallow, too afraid to move at all. "*You* let me escape last time." Her whisper was coarse.

What found his mouth wasn't exactly a smile, more like the beginnings of one. "Perhaps I did. But one free escape is generous enough, don't you think, Maiden?" He leaned over her further. "Which makes me wonder why you came back after I lifted you over the wall myself?"

The question left a strange feeling in the air. It was asked with accusation, as if the only explanation was that she was a crazy person.

As if she was an empty-minded *brick*.

Ryn smirked in disbelief. The King's eyes sailed down to her smile and stayed there. His lip twitched.

"Why do you think I returned, King?" she asked. "For the compliments?" There was a slight edge of sarcasm to her words, small enough that she could deny it if necessary. He raised a brow, and Ryn bit her lips together after she said it.

The uneven wall dug into her shoulders. She finally moved to adjust, but she stiffened when she bumped into him. She slammed herself back against the wall again, heat erupting in all the places her nightgown had accidentally brushed his royal robe. Her breath was a hostage in her lungs.

The King didn't react to the collision; he chewed on the inside of his cheek, blue eyes squinting. Then he said, "I think you're curious about the monsters here."

Ryn had to think for a second before she realized he was answering her question. Her voice shook when she replied with, "Ah. You caught me."

The King frowned. He pulled back, his hand sliding off the wall and falling to his side. He kept his dark, steady gaze on her. A moment later, he said, "Guardswoman—" Ryn's eyes widened. She looked over and spotted Heva standing by a bush with a pale face. Ryn hadn't even noticed Heva arrive. Hadn't noticed Heva following her. "—if this maiden escapes," the King said, "I'll have you killed in her place."

The King didn't glance at Heva once as he spoke. That faint, beginning-of-a-smile found him again when he pulled his eyes off Ryn and turned, heading into the dark trees and leaving Ryn in the garden with her guardswoman's fate tied to hers.

Ryn stayed perfectly still against the wall. She had no idea how many seconds or minutes passed before Heva appeared in front of her, took her arm and guided her through the garden. She glanced back at the white wall one last time as it slipped out of view.

Ryn was a prisoner of glass and stardust, soft-petalled blooms and sweet fruit. Anyone else might have craved the position she was in—wouldn't have seen it as imprisonment at all. But she only saw a white-walled cage around her, sealing her in with enemies who would show no mercy once she was caught.

CHAPTER

8

XERXES

Xerxes flew over the side of his bed and rolled onto the floor. His flesh was tight, his hands balled into fists, his breathing heavy. Bedsheets wrapped his torso like ropes.

After a moment, he unclasped his hands and released a deep breath as he slowly pushed himself up onto his elbows. Sweat tickled his hairline, and he closed his eyes in disbelief as his nightmare replayed in his mind.

He'd been a beast. He'd been hunting. Hunting for *her*—that penniless noble girl he'd won in a deal and brought to the palace to live a lavish lifestyle. He'd thought he was doing her a favour, taking her from the dirt and handing her a lifetime of riches and influence. Any maiden should have been thrilled at the opportunity to dine at the palace, eat great feasts, wear expensive dresses, and be forever known across the kingdom as a coveted

Heartstealer; one of the fairest in the land. Someone who'd walked in the presence of the King.

But, by now, it was abundantly clear to Xerxes that this Estheryn Electus maiden did *not* want to be here. He almost huffed a laugh as he thought about it all over again.

Xerxes picked himself up off the floor, letting the bedsheets fall into a heap on the cold stone.

Another day.

Another terrible day.

He headed for his window and tore the drapes aside, searching the horizon for smoke. He breathed a small sigh of relief when he saw none; just clear skies and gray mountains filled the landscape behind the Mother City. He rubbed his temples as he collected his bathrobe, eyeing his signet ring which had landed on his dresser this time—he'd thrown it across the room in the night. He pulled on his bathrobe and headed out.

Steam filled the men's bath chambers. Xerxes could hardly see the furthest bath pools when he came in, but he spotted a fellow relaxing one pool over. He cared not. Xerxes dropped his robe onto a hook and sunk into the nearest pool. He glanced over curiously when the fellow didn't say anything or announce himself. "You do know that no one is allowed in these baths in the morning before I have used them," Xerxes said into the mist.

The fellow shifted, his head of blond hair bowing in the fog like an apology. He still said nothing though, so Xerxes folded his arms.

"Show yourself," he demanded.

The fellow swam across his pool to the edge closest to Xerxes's. His features became sharp then, and Xerxes wondered if he'd ever seen him before. "Are you a Folke guard?" he guessed. "Are you new?"

"Kill him."

The fellow nodded. "I wasn't aware of the rules, Your Majesty," he said in a voice that told Xerxes he feared for his life. The fellow was young enough that it was probably true about him being new. He was still older than Xerxes though, by a year or two, if he had to guess.

Xerxes sighed and sank deeper into the bath, laying his head back against the stone and closing his eyes. "Just make sure you're gone before an Intelligentsia comes in here. They've executed guards for less offensive crimes than this."

His muscles were sore, though he didn't know why. Xerxes reached across himself and massaged his shoulder.

A splashing sound came from the pool beside him like the fellow was preparing to leave quickly, and after a moment, Xerxes peeked an eye open to see if he was still there. He was.

"Do you want something?" Xerxes asked. "I'm not in the mood to be generous."

The fellow's light brows pulled together; his mouth tipped into a frown. He was looking at Xerxes rather carefully, and Xerxes lifted his head from the rock. "You're not a Folke, are you?"

No guard would dare to look the King right in the eyes.

The fellow's face blanched, and Xerxes rose from the bench, standing waist-deep in the pool now, staring down at the fairhaired fellow who had crept into his baths. "My guards are just outside," he warned, tilting his head in a beastly way, eyeing the exact places where this intruder was the most vulnerable. "Not that I need them."

The fellow drew back, his light eyes wide. "I'm a Folke!" he swore. "I'm new, like you said!"

"You're an assassin," Xerxes decided.

"Assassins should be killed."

"I'm not! I swear it on my life, Your Majesty!" the fellow looked like he might pass out, and Xerxes folded his arms again as he thought about that. If this young man was hiding in the pools to assassinate Xerxes, he'd have already done it—or tried anyway. And he'd have quickly found out how foolish it was to attack a monster. So, this young blond fellow couldn't have come to the palace for Xerxes. That only left one other option.

"If you were hired to assassinate one of the maidens, at least tell me which one." Though, Xerxes shouldn't have asked. He didn't care which one. Any of them could vanish and he wouldn't lose sleep over it, not that he slept much to begin with.

Except that he was sort of curious if it was *his* maiden—the one he chose to be here against the Intelligentsia's wishes. Perhaps the Intelligentsia were the ones who'd hired this fool. Perhaps that was why Belorme was so willing to let Xerxes have his way with the Heartstealer numbers. Because Belorme had planned to have the "extra one" murdered all along.

"Just tell me, out of curiosity," Xerxes waved a hand through the air, "is it Estheryn Electus you're here to kill?"

"Ryn?" the fellow breathed then shut his mouth quickly. He tried to cover his mutterings by shaking his head as if to answer Xerxes's question, but it was too late; Xerxes heard it.

Xerxes twisted his mouth to the side as he ran that new name over and over—and over and over and over again—in his mind.

Ryn.

So, she had a nickname. A cute little name people she knew called her by. Truly, this was the first person Xerxes had crossed that knew anything about Estheryn Electus. Xerxes hadn't looked into the maiden himself, but the Intelligentsia had. How delighted Xerxes had been when he saw the legendary sages grow frustrated by how little information they could find on her. It only made him more pleased to have gone against them in the first place.

But Xerxes knew his instincts were right, even if he'd been wrong about this particular fellow being an assassin. The Intelligentsia might kill Estheryn Electus soon, especially after she'd arrived at the Introduction Ceremony in *that dress*.

Xerxes shook the memory from his mind. "If you really know Lady Electus," he said to the fellow, "then you should keep an eye on her. Otherwise, she's not going to live long here."

Xerxes wasn't the charitable sort, so he wasn't sure why he bothered with the warning.

Deciding his bath was over, he stepped from his pool and wrapped himself in his bathrobe. The fellow in the other pool said nothing else. The stunned look on his face had said enough.

Time for breakfast.

The table was colourful with hot meat skewers and eggs, bread, figs, and fruit. The Intelligentsia ate mostly in silence, occasionally discussing things Xerxes knew full well were just to fill the empty space. They never discussed anything important in front of him. They hardly ever even discussed things in front of the council anymore, though the council members at the breakfast table were too dull to realize it.

Xerxes placed a hand over his stomach, finding he wasn't as hungry as he thought. Or maybe he was, just… He glanced toward the kitchens. He could have sworn he smelled pears.

"You're starving."

The *other* hunger had come earlier than normal today, and during the monthly King's Council Breakfast of all places. Xerxes was used to waiting until the evening to feel the effects of his disease.

A particularly presumptuous napkin rose from the pile and flew at Xerxes, dabbing his mouth clean even though he'd hardly eaten anything. He swatted it away. Then he rose from his seat, not bothering to excuse himself or tell anyone where he was going. A few heads lifted, but no one said anything as Xerxes left the dining room, feeling the Intelligentsia's feast magic slip off him, and headed for the long hallway that would take him to the basement stairs.

Minutes later, he studied his tree in the oval room with a sigh. It was still perfect. Not a single leaf turning brown, not a single fruit beginning to wilt. The pear he'd eaten the evening before had already regrown. He plucked it from the branch and rolled it over in his fingers. Here he was again, at the mercy of this tree. Every day it was the same—*boring*. A stale and repetitive occurrence of events. Nothing at the palace intrigued him anymore. The food had lost its taste, the aromas of the gardens had turned bland, and the people—he could not stand to be around them. For seven years, he had done this dance, relied on the knowledge of the Intelligentsia while simultaneously hating them for having insight when he didn't.

At first, Xerxes had been terrified of himself. He'd raced for the tree each evening with gratitude, had worshipped it for saving him from becoming the one thing he hated most in all of Persiana. But after several years, the ongoing need had become a monster of its own. Xerxes often wondered what would happen if he simply stopped eating the spell-covered pears. He wished, just once, he could race through the palace as a free man, as the worst version of himself, and tear everything apart.

"Do it."

"We will help you have fun!"

Xerxes smirked at the thought. He would be dethroned in hours. Probably hunted through the city and killed by the Folke. It would be a sweet end to a long existence of suffering, and the Intelligentsia would rule the kingdom in his stead.

His smirk twisted into a sour scowl at that. Belorme was like an uncle to him; a cruel, arrogant, overbearing uncle. Even so, Xerxes could not stand the thought of that man winning.

He sunk his teeth into the pear, the savoury juice sweet on his tongue. A spark of greed moved through him, an obsessive pull. He devoured the entire fruit in seconds. Then he glanced up through the skylight tunnel, and he hurled the core as high as he could, seeing if he could beat his record. The core slapped against the stone overhead, leaving a juicy mark just below the stain from yesterday's fruit.

He grunted and brought his gaze back down to the luminous tree before him. The branches whispered an invitation as his restless night of sleep caught up with him, and Xerxes found his eyelids growing heavy, his breathing slowing. The next Heartstealers event wasn't taking place for another few hours, and he didn't exactly feel like being around the nobles, the council, or the servants until then. So, Xerxes took hold of the lowest branch and pulled himself up. He climbed into the tree's rafters, his coat of nobility hanging down like a navy curtain as he laid back along a branch. He fell asleep.

He awoke to the voices screaming in his head.

Xerxes fell from the branch, his robe catching a twig and filling the oval room with a tearing sound as he landed on the tree's protruding roots. He moaned, glancing down at his sleeve where a four-inch rip across his shoulder sliced through the face of the white dragon. Then he rubbed his eyes and tried to remember where he was and what he was doing.

The voices in his head were all laughing now. He blinked the sleep away and looked around, seeing a hundred golden pears within reach. He wanted to eat one, desperately. He reached for the closest fruit when a beam of sunlight spilled over his hand from the skylight as though the sun had discovered his hiding place. His hand froze there as he thought about that. Thought about how he was hiding.

As he realized he had somewhere to be.

Xerxes scrambled from the roots and leapt to the cobbled floor. He swatted twigs and emerald leaves from his robe as he marched for the arch and sprinted up the winding staircase. He had no idea what time it was, if the Heartstealers event had already begun. If the whole palace was in a frenzy looking for him.

He swallowed as he broke from the staircase door into the bright hallway, stopping only to tilt his ear toward the atrium and listen. He didn't hear the organizers announcing anything. He didn't hear a crowd of voices, or any evidence of a gathering. He breathed a sigh of relief, his shoulders relaxing as he resumed walking toward the Hall of Stars. Toward the event. Toward the maidens he hated.

He meant to stop by his room on his way to change from his torn robe, but a man in an organizers' coat swept into his view. Xerxes couldn't recall what the man's name was, even though they'd spoken many times. He thought it might be Cornelius. Or Corninaeus. Or…

Whatever.

"Organizer," Xerxes called. "What time is it?"

The man's face lit up when he realized Xerxes was there. "Your Majesty! Where have you been? The Initiation Ritual of the maidens is beginning in just a few minutes, and everyone is waiting in the Hall of Stars! We assumed you were…" the man swallowed "…*ill*."

Xerxes closed his mouth. He imagined the Folke scouring the gardens with spears, looking to herd a beast inside. He tried not to feel disgraced, though the assumption was likely already a palace-wide series of whispers by now.

He set his jaw, annoyance bubbling deep within him.

"Someone should die today, don't you think?"

"I'm fine. Take me to the Hall immediately," Xerxes said. He reached across himself to smooth down the tear in his shoulder, and he brushed a hand over his hair to ease it down. Then he shook his robe to straighten it out.

The organizer—Cornelius or Corninaeus or whatever—bowed in obedience and rushed down the hall to lead the way. Xerxes followed, thinking he might lose it if he reached the Hall of Stars and there wasn't a drink available for him. A dull thudding beat against the inside of his head, and he rubbed his temples.

Intelligentsia members turned their long hoods toward him

when he entered and crossed the dais toward his gold chair. He imagined them breathing a unanimous sigh of relief.

Music began to play across the Hall the second Xerxes sat down.

"Are you ill?" Belorme had the nerve to ask from Xerxes's side.

"No." Xerxes's grip tightened on the armrests of his chair. He wasn't exactly lying. He didn't *feel* ill, but…

"You should have eaten a fruit!" the voices said, all together.

"We're starving!"

Xerxes ignored them. He was fine. Never once had he needed to eat two fruits so close together.

"Then where is your crown, Your Majesty?" It sounded like Belorme spoke through his teeth when he asked. Perhaps the sage was humiliated by having to wait for the King, in front of everyone. Like a subject.

Xerxes fought the impulse to touch his naked hair. His crown…

Truly, he didn't even remember where it was.

Ah, that's right. He'd tossed it into the chandelier in his room. It was dangling by a candlestick.

He almost smirked.

The music magnified, and the arch doors at the end of the navy carpet swept open.

"I need a drink," Xerxes said to whoever was listening.

Belorme refused to acknowledge the request, but Choi slipped away from the line of sages. He came back a second later with a tall glass of deep red liquid.

"May the Divine Eos bless you," Xerxes said to him as he took the glass. Choi dipped his head before sliding back into line.

The maidens began to enter. Xerxes hardly cast them a glance of interest. He studied his drink instead, lifting the red liquid to watch it swirl around the cup. He brought the glass to his lips and took a sip.

His gaze slid over to the maidens performing an initiation dance as he drank. It was a traditional choreography meant to showcase a woman's features and strength that ended with them drawing a pair of scissors and cutting a blue ribbon to signify the barrier between subject and King broken.

Xerxes spat his wine.

Belorme sprang away, and a noble or two gasped from the viewing area. Two napkins tore up from the refreshments table and soared across the Hall; one patting itself over the floor to soak up the drips, the other aiming for Xerxes's face. He swatted it away, staring down at the maidens with his parted, liquid-covered lips.

Armour.

The maidens were dressed in *armour*. No longer were they in soft, sweeping gowns and feminine silks. Instead, metal plates studded with gems and thick leather belts covered their bodies. And were those… *swords* strapped to their backs?

Xerxes swiped his sleeve over his mouth to clean it. He wasn't sure whether to laugh or throw something. They looked utterly ridiculous in their frilly versions of combat garb, and every soldier with sense knew that fitting a sword to their *back* instead of their *side* was laughable because it was difficult to draw. Xerxes's hands balled into fists on his armrests. The women's swords didn't even look real. It was a mockery. A statement by the Intelligentsia because of what he'd said at the last event.

"How will those dresses save them if B'rei Mira attacks?

Shouldn't we be more concerned with finding a queen who can defend herself, rather than one who looks nice in a ridiculously large ball gown?" His own words haunted him. It took every ounce of his self control not to glare over at Belorme, to demand to know what this spectacle was. To throw the Chancellor off the dais before everyone. A slow, cool, watery sensation moved down his arms, down his legs, into his toes.

He hated many things about the dynamics of this palace. But what he hated more than anything was to be mocked. And Belorme had a special way of going about that. Xerxes tried to settle his rising heartrate, tried to calm the temptation burning through his mind. Tried to ignore the strange suggestions of the voices.

He bit his lips together as he watched the maidens. The dance was one performed at the Festival of Stars each year in the Mother City, one of the most common noble dances. Three of the maidens were good at it. One of them was not.

Xerxes's gaze narrowed on Estheryn Electus who had the look of a slender, graceful dancer, yet couldn't seem to pull off the choreography to save her life. The sword strapped to her back appeared to be weighing her down too, and Xerxes wondered what her artist was thinking, giving her a heavy prop like that. The girl who liked to escape through the garden at night performed all the moves half a second after the other maidens. Xerxes couldn't decide if it was funny or cringeworthy. The watching nobles hadn't noticed her ever-so-slight delay—at least, no one was whispering about it. Perhaps they were busy obsessively watching their *favourite* maidens.

He sat back in his chair as the music picked up tempo.

Xerxes also couldn't decide if he found Estheryn pretty, and that bothered him. The armour fit her well, and she danced on her toes like a feather in the wind. Even her hair agreed with her movements as it swept around. Divinities curse him, maybe he did find her a little attractive.

He tore his eyes away from the maiden. He did not need more of a reason to hate himself today. He settled his gaze on something at the side of the room instead—a Folke guard he spotted, standing by the arch. The fellow had blond hair and a familiar nervous look upon him. Xerxes tilted his head, recognizing him as the new guard who'd invaded the baths that morning. The one who claimed to know Estheryn.

Xerxes didn't mean to glance back at Estheryn, but as soon as he did, he caught her stealing a look over at the blond fellow, mid-twirl. It became painfully obvious that the two knew each other. Were possibly close enough that he had a sweet little nickname for her.

Xerxes's finger tapped slowly against his chin.

"You want to kill him, don't you?"

"Of course not," Xerxes replied, not caring that the sages down the dais could hear him.

But it was a lie. Xerxes wanted to tear that guard apart, and he had no idea why.

He sighed and closed his eyes, waiting for the Initiation display to be over. Fighting the call within him and the stream of icy water pooling through his veins. He rarely got urges so shortly after eating a spellbound fruit—It was far too early for this nonsense. He could handle this. He could hold on for one more hour until it was over. And then he could race back into the basement and rescue himself with a pear before he lost his mind.

He. Would. *Not*. Lose. Control—

"Open your eyes, Your Majesty. Or people might think you're

having a hard time," Belorme's voice slithered into his conscious-ness, and Xerxes's skin went tight. The Chancellor had sounded less like he was giving advice, and more like he was laughing.

Laughing. Because he'd pulled one over on Xerxes today. He had, once again, reminded Xerxes who really had all the control in this palace. He had reached out his hand and influenced the maidens who were supposed to belong to Xerxes, yet, who were really only puppets on strings Belorme tugged along himself. Like every other soul in the palace, in the kingdom. Including Xerxes.

Xerxes would destroy him. And his display.

His eyes flashed open, and he found himself standing. He heard himself shouting. All the music and dancing ceased as Xerxes called over the Hall of Stars, "What good is dancing for the wel-fare of this kingdom? Will dancing keep the Per-Siana people safe?"

Nobles gasped and rushed out of the way as Xerxes marched down the dais stairs, across the navy carpet, and through the maid-ens who shrank back at his nearness. He approached the blond Folke guard at the back of the room by the arch. Xerxes stood over him, a swelling hunger creating such a ruckus in his stomach, he was hardly sure he was really seeing the guard at all.

Xerxes reached for the fellow's sword and tore it from its sheath. A noble or two screamed; the Folke guard's face paled.

"Your Majesty!" Belorme called from the dais with no more laughter in his voice. "I need a word!"

Xerxes whirled to face the room. He lifted the sword, pointing it directly at the maidens who had been used to mock him. "I want to know which maiden can overtake me in a fight," he stated. One of the maidens slapped a hand to her chest, the others backed away. Xerxes did not care. He did not stop. He pointed toward the glass door beneath the Divinity statues of Iris and Boreas. "Into the courtyard. Every. *Single*. One of you." His gaze cut to the nobles to assure them he expected their obedience as well.

A shadow swept over the room as if the clouds in the sky had heard his command and taken the sun hostage.

By the dozens, people filed out of the Hall of Stars and into the courtyard. Rain spat upon the stones as Xerxes marched out. The nobles rushed to stand beneath the nearest balcony held up by four large pillars; the only dry spot left in the yard.

The maidens hadn't even gotten all the way outside before Xerxes grabbed the first one, dragging her with him by her outrageously decorated gauntlet. The metal didn't feel real—Xerxes guessed it to be painted bark, or worse, some sort of craft board. He wanted to laugh. He wanted to scream.

He tossed the first maiden ahead, and she whirled to face him with large eyes. "Draw your sword," he commanded her, eyeing her silly, bow-covered belt that was an insult to any soldier who'd seen real battle.

The maiden's hands shook as she struggled to pull the sword from the sheath on her back. When she got it out, Xerxes slashed it in half before she even lifted it, and she screamed as both pieces of her craft board weapon soared to the ground. She fell backward onto her rear and raised her hands to shield herself.

"You fail," Xerxes stated. "Next!" he shouted to the crowd.

When a maiden didn't volunteer, Xerxes marched over and grabbed another one, determined to make every maiden hate him by the end of this. His mind spun with voices that weren't his, his body was ice cold, his pulse a raging drum imprisoned in his flesh. The girl screamed and begged—it only angered him more. "Is this how you will plead for your life if the ruthless B'rei Mira soldiers come?" he shouted at her.

She shrank to her knees and clasped her hands together to beg. When she didn't immediately draw her sword, Xerxes drew it for her. Then he turned and hurled it across the courtyard, far into the gardens beyond. The sword soared like a bird, weightless.

When he turned back, he found the maiden trembling. For just a second, no more, a touch of sympathy moved through him. But it vanished just as quickly as it appeared. "You fail," he told her. He turned for the last maidens, already shouting for another one to come forward, but one already had.

Xerxes stared down at the sneaky, insult-hurling, wall-climbing maiden before him. She stood between him and the last maiden as though she planned to *stop him*. It was laughable. Xerxes's vision turned hazy, and through the blur, all he saw was the outline of another presumptuous maiden in silly, outrageous armour.

A light buzzing sound reached his ears when she drew her sword, pulling it from the back sheath with less difficulty than the others. It filled Xerxes's mind with noise as she held the sword out and lowered herself into a defensive position. Xerxes eyed how the rainwater dripped down the sword—the heavy prop. He tilted his head in thought. Then he smashed his sword against it.

The loud ringing of metal colliding with metal sang over the courtyard. The maiden spun away with the impact, but she wasn't tossed off her feet. The realization was so startling that for a moment, Xerxes was shaken from his trance.

"Is that real?" he asked her.

Her—Estheryn Electus. That was her name. That's who this maiden was.

Estheryn nodded as she tightened her grip on her weapon,

turned back toward him, and raised it again. Xerxes could not believe his eyes. Her artist had given her a *real* sword. What a fool. Yet…

A slow, wicked smile spread across his face.

Finally, a challenge.

"Hit me, then," Xerxes invited. Obnoxious whispers lifted from the crowd of onlookers tucked beneath the balcony. His gaze snagged on the movement of her throat as she swallowed. Rain drenched her dark hair, ran down her face. Made her fake armour look slick. She didn't look afraid though.

"Hit me, then, Maiden," Xerxes said again. "Strike me down. Kill me if you must." He nodded toward the Intelligentsia standing in a line outside the doors in their damp cloaks. Their faces were lost to the dim shadows of their hoods. "They heard me. You'll not be punished even if you strike me down."

Estheryn's gaze darted over to the Intelligentsia, then back to Xerxes. She still refused to move. So, Xerxes lifted his sword and placed the tip gently at her throat. He used it to tilt her face up to meet his eyes. "Don't you know that I own you?" he whispered. "Don't you want to kill me and set yourself free?"

Her brows angled inward, confusion rippling over her features. So, Xerxes added, "Did no one tell you that your father gave you to me to save himself? That you were the price for his freedom?"

Her lips parted. It was the most remarkable, fascinating reaction. Xerxes could not get enough of it. He shoved her sword aside, and he stepped in, standing over her darkly. In some ways, she was the only interesting thing that had entered his life since before he could remember. And for that, he supposed he'd decided already that he wouldn't let her go.

"You were traded to me in a deal overseen by the Celestial Divinities. If you try to run, the Divinities will find you and you'll be punished." Xerxes paused to think. "Or I will. But for your sake, I think you'd rather deal with the Divinities."

Her sword flashed through the air before he could brace himself. Xerxes leapt back, but her blade caught the collar of his coat of nobility and tore through it. Folke guards drew their own swords, and one of the maidens shrieked from the side. But Xerxes laughed, lifting the shredded piece of fabric at his collar to see.

Estheryn raised her sword again, and Xerxes smashed the weapon out of her hands; the metal sending a sharp clatter over the yard as it hit the stone. He grabbed Estheryn by her belt and drove her four steps backward to a pillar, pinning her there. She gaped, her startled gaze meeting his. Xerxes's sword was pointed against her waist, his fist around her belt, his body her cage. He was about to inform her she had failed like the others, even if she had been bold enough to bring a real sword.

"She must die. You must kill her for us," one of the voices stated.

Estheryn's face changed, even though Xerxes had said nothing. The timing was strange. So was her reaction. It was almost as though she'd heard...

Xerxes's smile vanished. The haze cleared from his mind, the ice fled from his flesh as Estheryn looked back and forth between his eyes, her brows tugging together.

Xerxes nearly dropped her and tore back.

She couldn't hear his voices. No one could.

"Kill her before it's too late!"

"Kill her now!"

"We want her dead!"

"Do it! Do it!"

"Quiet," Estheryn whispered.

Xerxes blinked. "What?" he asked, wondering what he was doing here, wondering why he'd brought the maidens outside in the first place. Wondering why the voices wanted her dead so badly and were all shouting at once. He wanted to go back inside.

Estheryn's mouth tipped down at the corners. She had a strange, hesitant look as she studied him. Then she said, "I wasn't talking to you, King."

A ball of heat dropped through Xerxes's stomach. His grip loosened on her belt. He thought he might be sick as she stared. Just stared. And stared some more, like she'd torn open his flesh and could see all the things inside of him he had hidden away.

No, he must have imagined it. *Never* had anyone witnessed or heard his insanity.

But who was Estheryn speaking to then? Terror wrapped his heart. Xerxes thought to turn and march back inside, to run for his tree, until he realized... His mind had gone quiet.

Quiet.

Just his own thoughts were there.

His mouth parted. He lowered his sword from Estheryn's side, and he pulled his other hand back to himself.

Was she a witch? Was she a divine sorceress or a Peri or a Jinn? How could she hear—

Estheryn kicked him in the stomach.

Xerxes flew back, the sword falling from his grip and smashing to the ground, his body slamming into the adjacent pillar. He gasped in shock as a fast, dull pain flooded into his abdomen.

"How dare you?!" Damon's voice was a mere ghost in the back of Xerxes's consciousness, the ringing of the sage's sword being drawn a distant echo. The stomping of feet over the wet courtyard didn't settle in until the sage was standing before Estheryn.

The sight of Damon slashing his sword at her shook Xerxes from his dream. The sage's blade caught the maiden in her side, burning through her false armour and throwing her to the ground.

A Folke guardswoman appeared out of nowhere, blocking the sage off, her own sword drawn. She would die today, Xerxes was sure, as Damon's cold glare settled upon her. "Know your place, Folke!" he said. He smacked her, but she kept balance even when her face swung to the side.

It was Belorme who cut in, walking to the scene slowly with his hands folded behind his back. "No need to make the situation worse, Damon," he said in his collected tone. "This was supposed to be fun. You took it too far."

Xerxes didn't remember pushing himself off the pillar, or walking to where Estheryn was on the ground, or lifting a hand toward her. But he caught himself there, his arm hanging in the air as he wondered what he was planning to do. Help her up? Check her wound? Make sure she wasn't going to bleed out?

He pulled his hand back, balling it into a fist at his side. He didn't intervene when the guardswoman with her red cheek dropped to a knee and lifted Estheryn from the ground. The guardswoman wasn't much bigger than Estheryn, but she lifted the maiden with trembling arms and carried her off through the rain. The blond Folke guard had rushed in, too. The fellow had stopped himself the same way Xerxes had—Xerxes watched him slide back into formation as Estheryn was carried through the doors. No one noticed he'd moved at all.

Xerxes wasn't certain, but he thought he heard the Intelligent-sia members *growl* as Estheryn Electus left. He'd never heard them growl before. It was strange—like something was happening in the air around him, but he couldn't see it.

He was left staring at the doors where Estheryn had disappeared, wondering what it was about her that had gotten the Intelligentsia so worked up. That had gotten his own chest out of sorts. That made the voices in his head beg him to race after her and kill her immediately.

9
RYN

Ryn had made dozens of apple pies when she was young. She did it with her mother at the end of every month to signal a "fresh start" for the next one. The smell of spiced pie put a smile on everyone's face and filled the house with warmth back when Ryn's family was a family. When they all sat around the same table to eat, when her father told her creepy bedtime legends like *The Manticore* and *Gavaevodata*, and her mother would scold him for it. When laughter wasn't a foreign concept, and there was nothing to fear. No enemies. Nothing lurking in the shadows. No fathers deciding they were unhappy for no good reason.

Ryn burnt her fingers on the oven during her first attempt at baking on her own. Once was enough to teach her forever to be careful around things that could hurt you. Pain was only a consequence of carelessness, after all.

Ryn's flesh burned all around the gash. She clutched her side as Heva laid her on the bed in her chambers. "I'll get the physician!" Heva said, but the door swung open and Marcan came marching in.

"I've already brought him!" he announced.

A white-haired man carried a bag of supplies and a weathered book over to the bed. Marcan and Heva stayed back far enough that the physician could work, but didn't step out of arm's reach. The man peeled away Ryn's costume, layer by layer. Every movement felt like Ryn was being cut by that Intelligentsia's blade all over again.

She closed her eyes and pursed her lips as whimpers threatened the back of her throat. If she broke down now, everything she'd just been brave enough to do would be for nothing.

That black-haired Intelligentsia's face haunted her; the wild scowl, the sharp eyes, the purple lips. Ryn caught a glimpse beneath his hood only briefly while Heva had carried her off. She could have sworn she saw a dark hue rippling over his expression like a mask of smoke.

Even so, his face hadn't been as shocking as the King's.

Ryn swallowed when she thought of King Xerxes. There weren't shadows over his face like some of the others. There wasn't a mask or illusion of any kind, there was just... torment. Ryn couldn't exactly decipher what she'd heard in that moment when he'd held her against the pillar and came in close. It was like a murmuring choir of sounds, no actual words. But she could *see* it on him, feel it even: the anguish. The oppressors. The sounds had twisted a muscle in her chest. It reminded her of her least favourite bedtime story about a boy trapped on an island where all the water around him was filled with poison. He only had two options: stay on the island and starve to death or brave the fatal water.

Why did Ryn feel in that moment the King was trapped on an island?

His cold words rang through her mind, *"Didn't anyone tell you that your father gave you to me to save himself? That you were the price for his freedom?"*

A tear formed at the corner of Ryn's eye. She tilted her head away from the others, letting it sail down her cheek onto the bed. Maybe Heva and Marcan would assume her tears were from her injury. She'd let them think that.

Even after all these years, her father was still finding ways to hurt her from afar. She couldn't believe he was the reason she was here. It hadn't made sense when the Folke had shown up to her house at first, but it did now.

A long time ago, her father would make her breakfast in the mornings, dance around the house on holidays, tell her life-lesson fables to make her think, and teach her how to barter at the market. It made her believe the delusion that he loved her. It was what made her believe for a while after he'd left that he might write her a letter or come back to visit. But he never did. She'd waited forever.

Even after her mother was taken away for false crimes, Ryn had sat by the door of her childhood home for a day and a half before she left to go find Kai. Just waiting. Waiting for her father to come back and save her. Waiting for him to tell her she'd misunderstood everything and that he would take care of her since her mother was gone.

But he never came, not after her mother was taken, not after her mother died. He never left behind a whisper of his presence, until today. She hadn't even known her father was still alive until King Xerxes said that to her in the courtyard.

Ryn was nothing. Nothing but a throwaway whose father had used her as a ticket to survive.

Even the King knew it.

She wished she'd never stood up to the King and had to learn about her father. Her sword had given her misplaced courage in the moment, making her think anything was possible.

El's sword.

It had buzzed like a soft, whispering song when she first drew it. White light burned down the blade as if the whole thing was on fire. When no one had commented on it, not even the King, Ryn realized no one else could see it.

It didn't make her suddenly become a good swordswoman though.

"What's wrong?" Heva asked her.

Ryn pushed aside all thoughts of her father and cleared her throat. "I left my sword in the courtyard."

"I'll go find it once you're alright," Heva returned. After a moment, she raised a hand to her own face and touched her cheek. Her jaw flexed and she folded her arms. "I've never wanted to hurt someone so badly," she added.

Ryn thought she was talking about the King, until Marcan spoke. "Yes, well. I don't know you that well, but I indeed felt the same way when I saw that idiot smack you," Marcan admitted, folding his arms too.

"I almost stabbed him for it," Heva confessed. "That sage is lucky I practice self-control for a living."

The physician opened his book, briefly studied a diagram, then began needling thread into Ryn's flesh. Ryn clenched her teeth and released a guttural sound. "Are you two finished?" she asked her guardswoman and artist. "I *wish* that sage had only slapped me."

Both Heva and Marcan unfolded their arms and raised their hands in apology. A second later, Heva folded her arms again. "It's definitely more of an insult to be slapped though," she said.

Marcan nodded.

"You can't be serious." Ryn cast them a look.

The physician finished stabbing and began smearing salve across Ryn's side instead. Heva leaned in to see better. "It's not like he cut you deep. It's just an inconvenient scratch." After a second, she added, "I've gotten much worse injuries in training."

Ryn huffed and gave up. She folded her arms across her chest while she waited for the physician to finish. A light breeze slipped in through the open window and ruffled the sheer curtains and ivies around her bed. She watched them dance for a while.

"You should heal by tomorrow with this salve. It was a gift to me from the Intelligentsia!" the physician bragged, but Ryn didn't feel like being grateful to the Intelligentsia right now. "Which is a relief. I was told that if I didn't fix you by tomorrow, I'd be cast out of the palace forever." The man's face fell.

Heva plugged her nose like she was trying not to snort a laugh at the physician's predicament. Ryn's body drained of tension, and she found a dull smile as she reached for her pillow, dragged it over, and propped it behind her head. Her eyelids grew heavy.

"I should teach you how to fight." Heva's smile faded. "This isn't good, Ryn. The King has his sights on you, and I reckon the benefactors have noticed now. Assassins will start showing up soon."

Ryn's gaze sailed toward her bedroom door, her stomach tightening beneath the physician's needlework. "You can't teach me to defend myself in time," she said. "Isn't there something else we can do?" She thought about asking the King for more guards, but quickly decided it was the worst idea ever. She'd rather fling herself off the palace roof than cross the King again.

Heva's gaze travelled around the chambers and settled on the windows. "Well, we should lay some traps around, at least. It's too easy to get into this room."

Someone cleared their throat by the door, and Ryn gasped when she saw Matthias standing there uncomfortably, his cheeks rosy and his hair wild. She pushed the physician's hand away and sat up, ignoring the searing pain through her middle. "Matthias?" She climbed from the bed with a wince and hobbled toward the door, holding the living space chairs for support on her way.

Marcan looked from face to face in the room. He waved the physician away, then said, "I'll take my leave too." He fled after the physician, glancing back curiously at Matthias.

As soon as they were out, Ryn grabbed Matthias, pulled him inside, and slammed the door shut. Matthias held her arm to keep her steady when she grimaced in agony. It took all her self control not to hug him, to cry in front of him, to tell him about her father's trade—the real reason she was here. But she bit down on her lips, keeping her secrets locked away. Matthias didn't know much of Ryn's family history. Kai never told a soul for Ryn's benefit.

"I shouldn't be in here, Ryn," Matthias said, letting her go and wringing his fingers together. "If someone sees me—"

"Say I called you here," Ryn said. She took in his blue and silver uniform. She'd only ever seen Matthias in Priesthood robes or casual clothing, often with a smile on his face. He looked like a stranger in a Folke uniform and a frown. "What's wrong?"

Matthias took in a deep breath. "Everything is wrong, Ryn." He shifted his weight and glanced toward the door. "You're in a lot of trouble."

"We know that much," Heva cut in. Then, as if realizing she didn't need to be part of the conversation, she turned and studied a speck on the wall. She peeked over her shoulder though, keeping her ear toward them.

"Where do I begin?" Matthias scratched his head. "The Folke have been suspicious of me from the beginning, and now the King has seen me, so I should escape before I'm caught. But there's a bigger problem. I delivered your note to Kai, and you won't believe what he said," he stammered.

Ryn's spirits lifted. "What did he tell you?" She imagined her cousin sending in the entire Priesthood in a palace-wide heist to get her out. She imagined him plotting an escape route through the Mother City and bartering with the tent folk up in the mountains for a safe place to live.

But Matthias's throat bobbed. "First, he told me that you can't come home. That you need to finish what you started."

Ryn didn't blink for several seconds. "He said that?" No, Kai wouldn't have. Ryn hugged her arms to herself and traced her fingers over the bumps on her flesh. She recalled what Kai had said back at the Priesthood temple:

"I know the risk."

"You could save the Adriel people."

"Then kill him," he'd said. *"Before he kills you."*

Matthias nodded. "It was Kai."

Ryn's gaze fell to the floor, her fingers digging into her arms as a burning sensation crawled back behind her eyes.

Marry the King or kill the King. Those were the options Kai gave her. She'd had a moment of bravery at first, but after the escape attempts in the garden and *especially* after today she knew she couldn't do those things. Would Kai really not listen even with Ryn's life in this much danger?

"That's not all," Matthias went on. "You know Kai speaks many languages," he said.

Ryn dragged her watery gaze back up to the priest. Kai spoke seven languages; it was his chosen study focus at the Priesthood. "What does that have to do with anything?"

"He overheard a plot in the market. The men spoke in *Mira.*" Matthias stepped closer, his hand finding Ryn's shoulder. "B'rei Mira spies have entered Per-Siana. They mean to assassinate the King—from *within* the palace."

The sky outside dropped from the heavens and crashed over the ground. Ryn stared at Matthias, unsure if she'd heard correctly. A strange story was coming out of his mouth.

Matthias reached into his pocket and pulled out a note with a name printed on the outside in Adriel letters. It was Kai's handwriting: **Ryn.**

Ryn should have been relieved. Someone else might do the job for her and she would be free—maybe she could go home to her quiet apple tree oasis and vegetable garden if the King was dead. Maybe she could wash her hands of this palace forever.

But a weight sank through her along with the story of the little boy on the island; the one surrounded by poison. She thought of the torment in the King's eyes. Like he'd already chosen the poison and knew what it felt like.

"Why? Why does B'rei Mira want to kill the King of Per-Siana?" she rasped as she took the note and slid it under her shirt for later.

"I'm not sure." Matthias chewed on his lip. "But Kai made me promise to tell you so you can take precautions. I told him I'd pull you out of here the moment swords were drawn. That's why I'm going to stay with you, Ryn, even if I might get caught."

The moment swords were drawn.

Ryn huffed a dull laugh. Swords had already been drawn. The King had drawn one, the Intelligentsia had drawn one, she'd drawn one. More would come.

She teetered. "I need to think," she said to Matthias and Heva.

"You shouldn't stay here alone," Heva warned as she wandered back over. "Not now."

Ryn waved her away. "Please," she said. Her grip tightened on the chair in the living space. "I want to be by myself for a little while."

Heva and Matthias exchanged a look, but they both nodded, went to the door, and shut her in.

Ryn journeyed to the window. She studied the lever that had already given her two chances to escape. Two times she'd failed to leave for good. She couldn't try again. The King might be waiting in the garden, and besides...

The threat of tears turned her eyes hot.

She was here because of her father. And...

Kai didn't want her back.

Even the burning wound in her side didn't hurt as much as that.

The "little while" turned into hours, which led to nightfall. Ryn didn't eat anything in that time, and her stomach groaned. She ignored it as she walked through the garden, the grass and path stones cooling her bare feet, the garden growing colder as the goddess Nyx licked dusk over the kingdom.

She'd found a strange comfort in scaling down the side of the palace into the garden. Just knowing that she could do it—even with an injury—was almost enough to make her forget she was a prisoner. She'd ripped off most of her tacky armour before coming to observe the orchard. She was out of fresh clothes, and so far, the Priesthood hadn't sent any of the benefactor funds they'd hoped to get from the offering plates. She wasn't sure she wanted it anyway—it would have been better spent on the hungry children in the cracks of the Mother City. Marcan's event costumes were the only clothing she owned, and she couldn't imagine waltzing through the palace gardens in her mosaic dress.

As she walked, she unfolded the letter to read it one more time:

Ryn,

B'rei Mira spies will infiltrate the palace at some point during the three-month trial period. They plan to kill the King while he's blindfolded.

Keep yourself far away from him.

Kai

What did Kai mean, blindfolded? Why would the King be blindfolded?

And what did he want from Ryn? Kai hadn't said in the note why he wanted her to stay, if she should continue on with the original choice he'd given her in regards to the King, or if he wanted her to *help* the B'rei Mira spies, or stop them, or avoid them...

Ryn sealed the note and slid it away, then crossed her arms as the wind tugged against the loose white tunic she was left with after the armour was gone. A simple, blood-stained garment, along with a pair of combat tights.

The cool wind slipped down the back of her shirt, and she shivered. When she glanced up, she nearly choked at the sight of something moving in the heavens alongside the great white dragon. Her eyes narrowed.

Back and forth the dragon slithered, its tail a river of white. Dozens, if not *hundreds* of black shadow creatures filled the sky around it, guiding it along, holding it up. It was as though the dragon couldn't move without them, couldn't stay up in the sky on its own.

"Divinities," she cursed. She slid back a step and yelped as she stumbled over a jut in the path and fell on her rear. But she couldn't tear her eyes away. Had those creatures always been there? Was this another thing she could see that others couldn't? Were those shadows what was holding the dragon in the sky? She wanted to find Geovani and force the old woman to reverse whatever 'gift' she'd passed along to Ryn.

"Divinities is correct, for the dragon is theirs."

Ryn nearly choked when the voice entered her mind. She flipped onto her knees and gazed at the path behind her. No one was there. "E… El?" she guessed. She quickly climbed to her feet, studying the shrubs and the branches overhead. She hadn't been able to see a person in her room last time. She wondered if he was here with her now though.

"Do you see it now? The mirage?" he asked.

Ryn's gaze lifted back to the sky. With the dark creatures involved, the dragon looked like a puppet. Something hollow and unliving.

"Most things are not what they seem."

Ryn squeezed her arms to herself again. As soon as she did, a warm wind rippled along her skin, fluttering her hair and chasing off her shivers. "You must have something to ask me," Ryn said, "otherwise, you wouldn't have spoken to me at all."

"I ask one question of all people, Adassah," the voice said. *"My question is this: Will you follow me?"*

Ryn tapped a finger against her forearm. She wanted to ask what exactly 'following a god' would entail. She was in enough trouble as it was. "Follow you where?" she tried.

"Wherever I lead."

"That seems like a dangerous commitment," Ryn reasoned. She chewed on her bottom lip as she strolled down the path. The warm wind trailed beside her. He said nothing else as they moved along, but the silence was comfortable. Ryn's shoulders relaxed, and she stole a sidelong glance at the air around her where she imagined El hovered.

Ryn didn't really have close friends. It wasn't that she didn't want any, but her neighbours were all Weylins. She wondered if this was what it felt like to walk beside a friend—not that El was a *friend*. Whether he was one of the gods or not, she didn't know him, and she couldn't imagine trusting a god either after the legends she'd read about gods tricking mortals and leading them into traps.

But somehow, she was sure El was moving along at her side.

They walked for several more minutes before the wind left. Ryn paused. She looked around. She nearly called El's names to ask where he went when she spotted a white-haired woman a short distance away, lounging back against a rock and staring up at the starry sky.

"You see it, too, right?" Geovani's unmistakable raspy voice reached Ryn. Ryn shivered as the cold air returned. She headed over to the woman. "The dragon," Geovani clarified. "You see that it's just for show?"

Ryn didn't answer. It was Geovani's fault she was seeing things.

"Didn't I tell you there was more to the story? That the great war didn't happen the way we think?" the old woman went on. She twisted a long, white lock of hair between her fingers. Her emerald robe was sprawled over the grass picking up bugs, but she didn't notice.

"I never studied the great war, or the Celestial Divinities," Ryn clarified. "And if you were trying to creep me out with all this *'eyes to see and ears to hear'* nonsense, you're doing a great job."

Geovani threw her head back and laughed. "You'll be glad you've opened your spirit eyes in the days to come, Adassah."

"Stop calling me that." Ryn glanced over her shoulder. The path was empty, the garden quiet.

Geovani's eyes slid closed. The woman's breathing turned heavy, and for a moment, Ryn worried she'd actually fallen asleep like that.

"Won't you catch a cold?" Ryn tried, but she shook her head. It wasn't her concern if the old woman got a cold. "Why did you give me 'spirit eyes' or whatever?" she asked instead. "I don't want them. I keep seeing things no one else can see, and earlier today I heard..." She thought about the King, the chaos. The tormentors. "I heard..."

Why couldn't she say it?

"You heard the truth for once. You heard things as they are, instead of as they seem," Geovani said. She rolled onto her side and yawned. "You'll need to keep listening to what's *really* happening. Watching what's *really* going on. An unseeing mind is completely incapable of representing El and his power," she added. "And don't you want to walk among mortals with his power at your fingertips?"

Ryn made a face. "That's impossible," she said. "I can't wield the power of a god."

"You can," Geovani corrected. "And you will do great things with it."

"Are you a prophet?" Ryn scoffed.

"Yes." Geovani peeked an eye open just as Ryn's face fell.

"Oh," Ryn said.

"Don't you want to know who El is? Why the Intelligentsia refuse to acknowledge him? Refuse to speak of him? Why his names have been wiped from the history books Weylin children are required to study?" Geovani sat up so fast, Ryn jumped. She pointed at Ryn. "It's because he's the Adriel God. The First God. The Highest God," she said. "And those Celestial clowns didn't win the war. El Tsebaoth did." Geovani stood and shouted it over the garden. "El Tsebaoth!"

Bumps formed over Ryn's flesh at the name Geovani called. It was like the name itself had shattered something in the atmosphere. A warmth fell into Ryn's chest, and she placed a hand over it, sure her broken heart had suddenly cried out in response, reaching back, and taking hold of whatever was in the air and refusing to let go.

She spun back to the garden with wide eyes, scanning every tree and plant. Geovani *must* have been heard this time. Ryn and this crazy High Priestess were going to be dragged away and tossed in the palace prisons if Geovani didn't keep it down.

"I'm not really a practicing Adriel," Ryn called back to the Priestess. She thought of her mother though, who was. Who had always spoken aloud a prayer before bed. Who had said that Ryn didn't have to be afraid of anything because the Adriel God was on their side. Ryn never understood that because she couldn't imagine a life where someone didn't have to be afraid of anything. Her mother had been dragged away, imprisoned, and had died of the *cinder plague* afterward. So, where was her "god" then?

Ryn folded her arms. "I can't possibly believe in the goodness of a god who can't save his own people."

Geovani lifted her head from the rock she used as a pillow. "You don't think he saves them? You don't think every single one of his people are free, whether they're stuck here with us, or living in glory at his side?"

Ryn's mouth parted. This High Priestess truly believed Ryn's mother was living in glory? Ryn's mother was *trapped* in the afterlife; she wasn't off somewhere, happy and well. If she was, she would have found a way to send word to Ryn even from the spirit world to let her know everything was alright. There would have been signs.

Geovani sighed. "You still don't believe me." She nodded like that was expected. Then out of nowhere, she asked, "Do you play any harp?"

Harp?

Ryn gaped. She cleared her throat. "I mean... a little."

"Take a harp to the Celestial Divinities temple inside the palace then. Play an Adriel anthem. See what happens." Geovani stretched, collapsed into the grass, and rolled back over to sleep again.

Ryan shook her head in disbelief. "And where exactly would I find a harp?" If she didn't think Geovani was crazy before, she knew it without a doubt now. How had Heva turned out so normal if she was raised by this woman?

"There's a harp on display in the hall not far from the temple entrance," Geovani said, waving a hand as if to send Ryn off.

Ryn suddenly laughed. She wasn't sure what she was still doing here talking about this. She rubbed her eyes, thinking about her bed. Without another word, she turned and headed back down the path, stealing one last glance up at the white dragon swimming in the heavens. Who would have thought the great judge was a fake? A lie she'd believed until tonight.

Her feet came together, and her arms fell at her sides.

It was madness, this lie. Even if Geovani was a little crazy in her approach, she was less crazy than a fake judge ruling the skies.

"What exactly do you want me to do if I choose to follow the Adriel God?" Ryn called back down the path. "Do you really expect me to try and protect myself with the same god that let my mother die?" She hoped El wasn't still nearby to hear the cruel question. It wasn't that she was accusing him.

Though, maybe she was.

Geovani chuckled and stood again, brushing the grass off her green robe. "Protect yourself? No! The opposite, actually." She folded her arms, mimicking Ryn. "I've stayed quiet for nearly forty years. I'm ready to make some noise."

Ryn stared at the harp.

The hallway was dark—all the torches had been blown out hours ago. The palace was asleep, and Ryn should have been too. Only a whisper of moonlight found its way into the hollow space, glistening off the harp's curve where it rested on a low, decorative pedestal. It wasn't a large instrument; half Ryn's height, just big enough to offer a depth of octaves and small enough that she might be able to carry it.

She'd expected to run into Heva guarding her door when she crept from her room, but Heva had disappeared somewhere. Probably sleeping on a bench outside like the crazy woman who'd raised her.

Ryn scratched her head and glanced both ways. It wasn't like anyone would know if she borrowed the harp. If she carried it through the dark palace.

This was insanity.

She grabbed the harp and almost dropped it when it weighed more than she expected, then she scurried as fast as she could, deciding this was a terrible midnight heist now that she was doing it.

The temple of the Celestial Divinities was open to the sky and city. Ryn inhaled a silent gasp as she entered, taking in the thin gold markings around the domed glass ceiling, and the seven statues evenly spaced apart. There was no back wall; it was a gaping window to the city, sucking in wind that encompassed Ryn and her stolen harp.

Everything in sight was a remarkable tribute to the gods. But as she studied the mosaics in the walls, the star patterns in the floor, and the gilded painting across the ceiling, she began to see other things. Limbs of shadows reached around the statues. When Ryn concentrated, they all appeared at once, turning sharp and clear. They weren't exactly figures or bodies, just shadows in various shapes with arms and hollow faces. She had the strangest thought.

"Do these creatures serve the Celestial Divinities?" she asked aloud. "Or are these creatures the gods themselves?"

They weren't beautiful like the statues and paintings depicted. They were darkness, nothingness. Emptiness. They stared at her, watching her. Some of them perked up in interest, others seemed bored and lazy, lounging around the room.

Ryn spotted shadows in the city beyond too, crawling over rooftops, lurking through the streets, winding around roads. Hunting as if they were hungry.

"They're false gods. The gods spoken about in legends. Their power comes from illusions they create that are meant to make you feel fear."

Ryn watched the shadows coil and swerve as the voice of El filled her mind, as if they'd sensed it. Her skin tightened as some dropped to the floor and weaved their way toward her like serpents. Their whispers lifted through the room, though she couldn't make out what they were saying.

"I'm afraid," she admitted.

"Be strong and courageous. I'm with you."

"But there are many of them, and there's only one of you." She swallowed. "You really want *me* to go to war against these gods?" Ryn couldn't believe she was asking.

The shadows drew closer, some forming swirling eyes within their hollow faces. One lifted and grew nearly the full height of the temple. It eyed her harp, and Ryn's hands shook around the wood, her knuckles turning white.

"I'm not a warrior, and I don't want to be a Heartstealer. I have no skills and no benefactor. I have nothing," she rasped.

"You have me."

Warmth brushed along her shoulders. Ryn loosened her grip on the harp and swallowed the lump in her throat. She couldn't imagine wielding the power of a god. But with all that had happened at the palace, she might not live through the next few days without it. She brushed her hand along the wound in her side as she watched the shadows move in slow, slithering motions. And as Ryn saw what was *really* happening for the first time in her life, she knew that no matter where she was, no matter what she chose to do with herself, she would always stand against these gods. She could never be lured into joining them like her father. She would resist them—like her mother.

Shadows drew forward until the whole floor was coated in darkness, apart from a ring of floorspace around Ryn and her harp. Whispers echoed through the space. They invited her to join them with muffled promises of safety. Hands lifted from the black sea and waved her forward.

Lies. An illusion, like their dragon.

A sea of blackness surrounded her, making her feel like she was on an island.

For the first time, she realized why she hated that story about the boy stuck on an island. The boy with no one to help him make the decision: should he starve to death, or should he leap into the poison? Now, she imagined a god like El reaching down to that boy, extending a hand, and offering to lift him off the island and take him to shore.

Ryn hardly recognized her own voice when she spoke.

"Yes. I'm here. Use me."

"Welcome home, Adassah."

Ryn took hold of the harp strings. She didn't know many tunes, but she'd learned songs handed down from her ancestors and taught to her by her mother. She played an Adriel hymn she hadn't heard since she was a little girl.

As soon as she plucked the strings, strength rushed into her veins, and warmth encompassed her. Arms of light rested over her arms. Strong and gentle hands came over her hands.

The music lifted through the temple.

All the shadows in the room began to scream.

CHAPTER

10
XERXES

He'd made a scene. He couldn't believe himself.

It had been months since he'd done something so irrational in public. For a few minutes, Xerxes had *wanted* the maidens to see him at his worst. The foolish, irresponsible part of him had won.

Immediately following the Initiation Ritual, Xerxes fled to the palace pools and dropped beside a cold one, scooping water and splashing it over his face. He hardly knew what had happened in the courtyard. The whole congregation of visitors saw him lose his mind. The rumours would spiral out of control.

And what was worse—one of the maidens might be a sorceress who could hear his manic thoughts and voices…

He didn't care about his coat of nobility; Xerxes leaned forward and plunged his face into the water, holding himself there, feeling the icy caress until he ran out of air. He came up panting, his robe drenched at the collar, his hair dripping water back into the pool as he watched his warped reflection in the ripples.

Slow footsteps filled the bath house, footsteps Xerxes could have recognized in his sleep. Xerxes thought to greet the Chancellor first, but he'd lost his voice somewhere in the pool. It seemed to have sunk right to the bottom.

"What you did was dangerous." Belorme spoke first, to Xerxes's relief.

"Then you shouldn't have provoked me," Xerxes snapped back, finding his voice after all.

Belorme was quiet for several moments. Xerxes wiped the water from his face with his sleeve.

"Who is that maiden?" the Chancellor finally asked.

Xerxes stayed quiet this time. Not that he knew anything about Estheryn Electus to tell anyway. Except that she could kick with the strength of a disgruntled horse.

"The Intelligentsia hired investigators, but her home has been abandoned, and there wasn't much in it to speak of. Even her neighbours knew little about her," Belorme went on.

Xerxes swatted at his reflection in the pool, sending a shower of droplets across the water. He took fistfuls of his hair and squeezed out the moisture. It all ran down his neck.

"She's dangerous, Xerxes," Belorme said. "I think she might be using magic to persuade you."

It could have been true. Xerxes had considered it. And perhaps he should have been more careful around her, but—

"She could get you dethroned," Belorme reasoned. "She could even get you killed. Divinities, she looked like she wanted to kill you herself."

Xerxes burst out laughing, and Belorme finally shut up.

The look on Estheryn Electus's face in the courtyard had told tales; the anger, her piercing eyes, her pinched mouth, and even her tiny scrunching nose. For a moment after he'd uttered those things about her father, she *had* wanted to kill him—he'd practically been able to taste it in the air. And now he couldn't stop feeling that kick colliding with his stomach. It was as though the maiden had the same curse as Xerxes and inherited supernatural strength at the drop of a dime. But her flesh hadn't turned gray and cold, so how did she do it?

It didn't matter. Even if she was briefly charming in the yard—holding that sword of hers like she'd been ready to use it—Belorme was correct. She should be killed off before she might try anything else. Danger was danger.

Xerxes sighed. Laughing still felt strange. He rubbed his throat.

"She should be executed," Belorme stated, echoing Xerxes's thoughts. But Xerxes found his grip tightening on the edge of the pool. "Before she becomes more dangerous. I can make it look like she fell—"

"If you touch her," Xerxes said, sliding his grip off the ledge and sitting up, aware that his back and neck were fully exposed to the Chancellor, "I will kill you next."

Belorme went deathly quiet. The coiling mist stilled in the room. Far across the chamber, a waterfall tumbled into one of the pools; the only sound remaining.

Xerxes heard Belorme's sandals shift over the floor at his back. His skin pulled tight as he imagined the sage quietly drawing a blade. Xerxes glanced over at the rippling reflection of the Chancellor in the water.

"I warned you not to threaten me, Xerxes," Belorme said

calmly. Articulately.

Xerxes rose. He turned and took the last step toward the Chancellor, closing the gap and towering over the man by several inches. There was a time when Xerxes was just a boy at this man's feet, but those days had passed long ago. It was time the Chancellor realized.

"Have you forgotten who I am?" Xerxes asked. "I'm the King. With just one word, I can have you executed for disobedience before this whole kingdom. I can have your reputation ruined for ten generations—I can have you written in the history books as a shameful traitor."

Belorme's black eyes flickered back and forth between Xerxes's. A slow, terrible smile spread across his face. "Can you?" he wondered, and Xerxes frowned. "I don't think you have it in you after what you did."

Xerxes's hands balled to fists at his sides, his toes curling.

How dare he? How dare this foolish man bring up the one thing Xerxes dreaded talking about the most?

"I have helped you at every turn, Xerxes. You would be a raging beast in the garden without me. What do you think would happen to you if I was gone? What would happen to your tree? To your only source of medicine? Don't you think I would have a plan in place to have it burned, should any harm come my way?"

Xerxes staggered back, his stomach dropping as he imagined his tree up in flames. Suddenly, he wanted nothing more than to race down to the basement and make sure it was still there, to stand guard, to keep it safe.

"Destroy him!"

"Keep our tree safe!"

Belorme had the nerve to raise a hand and shake a finger in

Xerxes's face. "Careful," Belorme warned, like he was scolding a child. "Don't forget how much you need me."

Xerxes clenched his jaw as the Chancellor turned and glided from the pool room in slow, easy steps.

"Belorme," Xerxes called, and Belorme stopped at the arch. "We were friends, once." It pained Xerxes to say it aloud, to have to beg for the Chancellor to remember the time before he became Chancellor. Back when Xerxes's father was still alive and the King. Back when Xerxes got along well with the Intelligentsia. Back when the Intelligentsia taught him many important things—things that had raised the only great parts of him. Belorme used to sneak Xerxes sugar-coated peanuts after council meetings, and he'd bring double if Xerxes memorized a whole chapter of the Divinities record books.

Belorme's face had looked different back then. His eyes had been a little brighter, his smile more genuine—not the dull, forced thing it was now.

The Chancellor cast a look over his shoulder. Xerxes studied the man's unblinking eyes that were looking his way but still didn't appear to see Xerxes standing there. And Xerxes's shoulders dropped. By the expression on Belorme's face, Xerxes knew once and for all that what he feared was true.

The man he once considered an uncle was gone. Belorme saw Xerxes as nothing but a tool to be used now.

After Belorme left, Xerxes stood in that very spot, staring at nothing for a long time.

"We want her dead."

"She is our enemy."

"She is dangerous! Hurry, before it's too late!"

"Kill her!"

"She must be stopped—"

"WHAT IS THAT NOISE?!"

Xerxes's eyes peeled open.

Somewhere in the darkness of his bedroom, a clock was ticking. The sounds were evenly spaced apart: *tick, tick, tick*... He'd lived in this bedroom for almost four years now, and he never knew there was a clock. He lifted his head from his pillow to look around, finally spotting it far across the room—a small oval of gold high upon his wall, blending into the gilded framework of diamond paintings gifted to him over time. Xerxes studied it, realizing it was the middle of the night.

The quiet buzz of a bug lifted by his window. His gaze darted to it. The tiny insect landed on the closed drapes.

Xerxes climbed from his bed and wandered over. He took hold of the drapes, but he didn't draw them. Instead, his hands hung there, fingertips grazing the velvet. He waited for someone to tell him something. Anything. He waited for dark instructions and cruel messages.

A faint, distant humming he hadn't noticed until now tickled his ears. It sounded like...

Xerxes glanced toward his bedroom door instead.

Music.

He didn't bother getting dressed. He grabbed a silk robe and pulled it around himself as he headed from his room, grateful he'd sent his guards away earlier. He felt like a part of himself had fallen out of his head while he was asleep, leaving an empty space in his mind. He rubbed his temples and scratched behind his ear.

What was that noise? It was like the plucking of strings, a sweet melody that spilled into the hallways. And with the sound came… utter quiet.

How could music bring quietness? It didn't make sense. Also—where were his voices, and why didn't they care about what he was doing at this moment?

Xerxes padded over the cold stone, following the music around a bend. His heart picked up speed as he drew closer. He jogged the last few steps to the Celestial Divinities temple to catch the musician before he or she could disappear.

He swung around the temple entrance, grabbing the arch frame to keep himself from barging in and startling whoever was inside. He pressed a hand against his chest where his heart drummed along to the music's rhythm, his gaze settling on a young woman with long, dark hair. She faced the city, strumming a harp beneath the silver moon.

Xerxes nearly ran for her—grabbed her, shook her, demanded to know how she was doing it, how her music could bring silence to his mind. But when she tilted her head ever so slightly to reach the furthest string, Xerxes recoiled into himself, drawing back into the arched frame and slumping against it with his shoulder.

It was Estheryn Electus. The maiden who'd *raised a weapon* at him.

Her hands glided along the instrument as she offered a tribute to the statues of the Celestial Divinities in the temple. Though, she didn't cast the statues a single glance.

She must not have noticed he was there.

Xerxes stood straight, eyeing her back. She wore a common

shirt, ripped at the side and stained with red where Damon's blade had found her. Xerxes wondered why she hadn't changed into her nightdress yet, why she was here instead of sleeping.

His mouth twisted to the side. Why had he chosen to save this woman against Belorme's wishes at the pool? Was it because her presence was Xerxes's choice, not the Intelligentsia's? That was motivation enough. But that hadn't been the only thought in his head when he'd stood against Belorme. Estheryn had heard his voices, hadn't she? She told them to be quiet, and they'd obeyed.

Estheryn paused her playing and lifted her hand, glancing at a chipped nail. The second she did, Xerxes gasped and grabbed the side of his head.

"She must die!"

"Do it now!"

"Kill her! Kill her! Kill her!"

"Don't stop!" Xerxes called into the temple, and Estheryn spun around on her knees. She stared, looking him over with wide eyes, her gaze snagging on his nightclothes. She didn't keep playing.

Xerxes became aware of his robe hanging half open, his white knuckles gripping the arch frame, the pleading in his voice. He shrank back a step. Then he swallowed. "Never mind." He swept back out of the temple, back around the bend, back into the hall-way. He kept a steady hand on the wall as he caught his breath.

"Go back in there."

"Destroy that woman!"

Xerxes pinched his eyes closed. A shameful hunger filled his belly, worse than before. He inhaled, exhaled, stumbling toward his room, the walls tipping left and right as he put one foot in front of the other.

He made it by the grace of the Divinities. He slammed his door behind him as he dragged his feet toward his bed. He should have gone downstairs. He should have found a fruit, but the headache was so terrible he wasn't sure he'd make it that far.

Xerxes grabbed his bedpost for support. Sweat tickled his hairline, the cold rivers of water brushing over his flesh. He wanted to die.

There was a knock on his door. He ignored it.

When the door creaked opened, Xerxes set his jaw. "I'll have you executed for entering my chambers without invitation..." His words fell off when he turned back and saw her there.

Estheryn Electus was in his room. Holding her harp.

The door drifted closed behind her.

Xerxes's lips peeled apart as he faced her fully. "You're brave," he remarked, not sure if it was a threat.

"Kill! Kill! Kill!"

His hands balled into fists. He eyed her most vulnerable places, same as every person's most vulnerable places, only hers seemed far more delicate and easily breakable to him in this moment.

"Lay down, King," she said, and that snapped Xerxes out of his trance.

"What?"

What, by the Divinities, was she suggesting?

"I'll play for you so you can sleep," she clarified, and the eruption of flutters that had taken over Xerxes's chest settled—he shook all improper thoughts from his mind, clearing his throat and dragging his fingers through his messy hair as his rational judgements returned to where they were supposed to be. Such as: How dare she come in here?

His hands flexed, tempting him to do something about it.

But when she set the harp down and knelt before it, Xerxes

found he couldn't speak to stop her from playing. He waited, hoping she would. Wishing she would never stop once she started.

"Slay her right now!"

"This is your last chance—"

The tune lifted through his bedroom, and all went quiet. Just the light, soft sound of harp strings remained.

Xerxes's muscles loosened. But instead of falling onto the bed like she'd suggested, he found himself moving toward the maiden. His walk was strong now, instead of the clumsy staggering it had been in the hall. He saw her clearly for the first time since that day he'd helped her escape the palace in the garden.

She'd called him ugly. She'd called him heartless.

And he was.

Heartless, anyway. Not ugly. He was a pretty King.

And truthfully, she was not ugly either. A flutter returned to his chest at the hazardous thought.

Divinities, she was not ugly at all. She was prettier than he'd perhaps let himself notice. Not in an evident way, not in comparison to the typical fair maidens of the Mother City. She was a disorderly sort of pretty with her ruffled hair and torn, stained garments. But seeing how she'd entered his room without his permission, likely knowing the consequences if he decided to inform on her, and how she'd kicked him into a pillar in the yard before witnesses... It proved she was fearless. And that perhaps was the most attractive thing about her.

"If you're a witch, I'll have you hanged," he warned as she played. It was a lie. He would keep her, no matter what.

But a smile cracked over her mouth. Any rational person would have been afraid at the threat of death. Only a lunatic would smile.

Xerxes smiled too. Just a little.

Then he whirled around before she could see it. "You aren't, are you?" he asked just to be sure. "A witch?" He should go to bed. He should take this rare opportunity to sleep before it passed him by. Before she left and he'd be disrupted all through the night by voices again.

"How insulting. Are *you* a witch, Your Majesty?" she asked. He twisted to glance back at her in surprise. "If you are, I'll have you hanged," she added.

Xerxes blinked. He turned away from her again, and he bit his lips together. He could *not* laugh before this maiden. What if someone in the hallway heard? Divinities, she was trouble.

He climbed into his bed without another word. He thought he might have difficulty falling asleep with her there, but his body relaxed against the mattress and his eyes drifted closed almost as soon as his head found his pillow.

Xerxes had hired magicians, a magus, and the best physicians to try and silence his voices. Not even the Intelligentsia who heard from the Celestial Divinities had been able to find a solution. He'd changed his diet, used medicine for sleep, undergone needle therapy. Xerxes had tried everything.

He didn't care if this maiden was a witch and was lying through her teeth. He didn't care that she might cast a spell over him. That she might feed him a potion and trick him into making her Queen. That she might try to assassinate him with magic, like Belorme warned.

In this moment, Xerxes didn't care that she was dangerous.

He would keep her.

CHAPTER

11
RYN

Tranquillity rested upon the Abandoned Temple of the Adriel God. The birds overhead sang in their softest voices as though they knew the power moving through this space was divine. Ryn sat cross-legged in the shallow water with her eyes closed. To anyone watching, she would have appeared to be meditating. But she was listening.

She'd arrived at the Abandoned Temple at first light, tired and ready to fall asleep right there in the water after creeping from the King's quarters before he woke, bringing the harp with her and returning it to its decorative pedestal in the hallway. She hadn't planned to study the King's face before she left—lying there in absolute serenity; his cheek smooshed against his pillow, his mouth parted, his eyes closed, his black hair splayed. But she'd wanted to see his dark lashes up close. He didn't look crazy as he slept. In fact, he didn't actually look like a king at all. Just a young man who'd found a moment's peace.

She could have sworn that last night in his room, she'd caught him smiling at her.

Ryn's eyes flashed open in the temple when she realized what she was thinking about. Along with it came visions of how desperate the young King had looked when he'd begged her to keep playing music in the other temple, and after that when she went to his chambers, obeying the unspoken orders she wasn't sure he even knew he'd given. In that moment, she didn't know what had come over her when she saw the desperation in his eyes. It reminded her of a starving child in the street looking for a morsel of food and a warm place to sleep. It was strange to see that in a king, of all people.

She wondered if King Xerxes had any idea he was in danger. That B'rei Mira had numbered his days. She pictured him sleeping again, his face relaxed upon his pillow. She imagined an assassin sneaking up on him that way and...

She shivered.

"Sorry," Ryn whispered into the Abandoned Temple. She adjusted her legs and closed her eyes again. Then she said, "Why must I do this each morning though?"

"You're like a Scarlet Star," El whispered. His voice brushed along her mind, settling into her soul.

Ryn pictured the flower; the layered green stem, the deep red shoot at the top that made the blossom. It was only due to Kai's flourishing garden that Ryn even knew what a Scarlet Star was.

"The cup in the flower's bloom must always remain filled, or it will dry out and eventually die. It's the same with you, Adassah."

140

"I'm like a flower." She made a face. "Warriors aren't like flowers. They're like smoke and fire and chaos."

"And when a warrior goes to battle alone, he dies amidst his smoke and fire and chaos."

Ryn's mouth twisted to the side at that.

"I want to hurt people," she admitted. She bit her lips. "I want to take the Weylins down. You said you had great power, so can't I do that with your power in my hands?"

"You're not fighting a battle of flesh and blood. It's not people you're after."

Ryn sighed and folded her arms, struggling to keep her eyes closed. She felt an itch on her back. "It sure seems like it's people I'm after." She thought about the neighbour who brought the false charge against her mother. She thought about all the other Adriels across the city in prisons for unjust reasons. She thought about the rule that Adriels weren't even allowed to set foot in the palace, simply because of their 'tainted' bloodline. Yes, people were exactly who she was after.

"Just be still."

Be. Still.

Easy.

Ryn disobeyed the instruction almost immediately—she reached around and clawed at the terrible itch on her back. "Sorry," she said again. She returned her hands and clasped them together so she wouldn't do it again.

"Your hands aren't to blame. It's your thoughts that must be still."

Ryn peeked one eye open and studied the decaying statue that had once represented a god. She wondered if El really looked like that statue. She wondered if any mortal had actually seen the god face to face.

"El Tsebaoth," she said one of his names. When she spoke it, warm wind flittered through the temple, rippling over the waters and shaking the curtains of ivy spilling from the ceiling. So, she said it again. "El Tsebaoth!" This time, she gasped as wind surged against her, brushing back her hair, spiralling into her stomach.

She huffed in disbelief.

"Do not use that name irresponsibly, Adassah."

"Sorry." Ryn bit down on a smile. All she was doing was apologizing, but she had fairly warned this god that she was not the ideal, devout, religious kind of person he should use, nor was she a warrior, nor was she the best candidate to summon godly power. "When will I get to use that sword again?" she asked.

"That sword represents my spirit. It's for fighting the darkness," he said. *"Not people."*

Ryn's face soured.

"How far will you go for the Adriels?" El asked. *"Will you go to the ends of the earth for your people?"*

The expression fell from Ryn's face. "I'll do whatever it takes."

Death was just a doorway, after all. Pain was just the consequence of carelessness.

"Will you lay down everything you have and follow me?" he asked.

"Yes." She had nothing anyway.

"Will you learn how to love?"

"Y—" Ryn closed her mouth.

Love? What did love have to do with anything? She was going to be fighting against the gods, for goodness' sake. Not throwing a tea party.

"You must learn to love even the most difficult people to love. Even your enemies."

Ryn opened her eyes. She glared at that statue of El. "I knew this was a trap," she said.

She climbed to her feet, sending a spray of droplets as she spun and stomped through the water toward the exit, wincing at the shooting pain in her side from her wound. She thought about offering a rude hand gesture to that statue on her way out.

She could have sworn she heard chuckling behind her as she left.

"Adassah." Ryn was already in the hall when he spoke again. She slowed her steps, her toes squishing in her watery sandals. *"Visit the First Temple in the city. Go see the priestesses."*

"Why?" she asked. Then she slammed her mouth shut and looked around to see if anyone might have heard her talking to herself.

"They need to be awakened. That's where we'll start."

Ryn chewed her lip. She started walking again, around the turns, through the long halls, all the while imagining the trouble she'd be in for trying to sneak out of the palace to visit the 'First Temple'—wherever that was. Didn't this god know she couldn't waltz out of here whenever she wanted? Didn't he realize she had larger needs, that she didn't even have clothes to wear? Did he really not have insight into her situation?

She sighed as she headed around the last bend to her chambers.

An arrow spiralled past her face, and she screamed.

Ten feet ahead, a body flew out her bedroom door. Heva marched out after him and raised her sword to stab. Ryn shrieked and slammed her eyes closed, spinning away, but a shuffling sound filled her ears and she peeled her eyes back open. She almost screamed again at a man in a black cloak before her, holding a curved blade inches from her throat. Ryn staggered back a step until she noticed the *other* blade—the one coming out the man's stomach.

The *other* blade retracted, and the black-cloaked man fell to the floor in a heap.

Xerxes stood behind, holding a silver sword. His navy coat was fastened, his hair was neat. But his eyes... His eyes went in and out of focus, not quite settling on what was before him, and his flesh had a slightly grey hue. He grabbed the side of his head and squeezed his eyes shut.

"Look out, Ryn!" Heva shouted.

Xerxes's eyes flashed open again. He grabbed Ryn's sleeve and yanked her toward him just as half a dozen Folke guards flooded the hall and wrestled the last man in black to the ground who, Ryn realized, had been inches away from sending a serrated blade into her back.

"Interrogate them," Xerxes instructed the men. "Find out who sent them. I don't care if it's an esteemed duke or an Intelligentsia; imprison whoever paid these butchers to come here. Show no mercy."

The Folke spoke all at once. "Yes, Your Majesty!"

Folke lifted the bleeding men and carried them off. Trembling maids rushed in with cleaning soaps and cloths, trailed by a few wet sponges that flew into the hall on their own and began scrubbing at the mess. Ryn pointed at one of the sponges, realizing her hands were shaking. She forgot to speak or ask a question, and her arm dropped right back to her side.

The servants looked ready to vomit as they scrubbed up the blood. Ryn took a step toward them, her mind spinning with thoughts of helping, imagining she was in her house with Kai and there was a mess on the floor and... The vision of her house snapped away, and she glanced up at Heva.

Heva was gaping at the King, not moving a muscle even as the maids washed the floor around her feet. Ryn dragged her attention back to Xerxes, realizing he still gripped a fistful of her sleeve.

Xerxes's gaze fell to it, and he dropped her arm immediately. Then he looked around at the mess for a moment, and he put his sword away.

Ryn didn't know if she should dare to speak to him in front of others. If she should ask him why he was here. Her gaze flickered to two pale-faced servants behind him pushing carts of clothes and shoes.

He'd brought her clothes? Ryn brushed a hand over the tear in her white shirt where the bloodstain had turned brown. Her tights were drenched from sitting in the temple too. How did the King even know she needed clothes? And why, by the Divinities, would he deliver them himself?

She glanced at the man's body at Xerxes's feet. If the King hadn't been standing there, Ryn would be dead.

Xerxes blinked rapidly, his chest expanding, moisture appearing over his flesh. "I need to leave," he said. Without explanation, he turned and marched down the hall, his royal coat fluttering behind him.

Ryn watched him go. For a split second, she imagined running after him and telling him, *"You're in danger. Assassins will come for you next. The B'rei Mira army will enter the palace."*

He just saved her life. Why couldn't she find her voice to save his?

"Maiden?"

Ryn turned and found a man in an organizer's robe approaching. She watched him tiptoe over the mess in the hallway, cradling a scroll beneath his arm. He didn't seem surprised a fight had taken place, though he cast repulsed looks at the blood spots. He flicked the scroll open when he reached her.

"I'm here to help you select your charity. I apologize for the inconvenient timing." He flashed a toothy smile. Ryn glanced at where the servants were finishing their washing. The hall looked new again—there was no trace anything had happened. It was over too fast.

The organizer held the scroll closer to Ryn's face, and her gaze fell upon symbols and Weylin letters she didn't recognize. She realized her hands were still trembling when she took hold of the scroll. She moved her eyes back and forth like she was reading it.

"You must choose a charity to support for the duration of the Heartstealer trials," the organizer went on. "It's part of the ancient custom. Every Heartstealer in our history has done service to the kingdom—"

"What about the First Temple?" Ryn said, lowering the scroll. "Can I do charity with the priestesses?"

Heva looked up in surprise from where she was still glued to the spot outside Ryn's door.

The organizer made an odd face and took the scroll back, turning it toward himself. He dragged a pair of spectacles from his pocket and began scanning the list. "I'm not sure that's an option, but— Oh! Would you look at that! It is." He made another face and scratched his head. "Well, it's only on the list for the purpose of tradition. That building isn't still recognized as a temple even though it's run by High Priestess Geovani—"

"I wish to volunteer my services to the priestesses," Ryn said again. It came out strained past her thick throat. "I'll check in with High Priestess Geovani in a couple of days after I've healed."

146

"Uh… Well, I suppose it would be fitting for a Heartstealer to walk among the graceful and quiet priestesses. But the First Temple is in the Mother City—off the palace grounds…" The man's brows tilted in, and he hesitated for a moment like he hoped Ryn might change her mind. When she didn't, he nodded and added, "Perhaps they could use assistance in their daily meditations, acts of kindness, and soft-spoken teachings."

Before the man could say anything else, Ryn swept around him. She placed a hand over her roiling stomach as she walked. She kept it there until she made it into her room, and her jaw dropped when she looked around.

The drapes were torn. The bedsheets were stabbed. There were gouges in the walls.

"By the Divinities, Heva! What happened in here?"

The King's servants rolled in the carts of clothes: silk dresses, fresh nightgowns, glittering robes, leather sandals, and gold belts. As soon as the carts were inside, the servants bowed and excused themselves.

"I know I said assassins would come, but I didn't expect them to come in packs," Heva admitted bitterly as she closed the door behind them.

"How did you survive against three opponents?" Ryn eyed a torn painting on the floor. It was peeled down the middle in strips like blades had sliced clean through it—as if Heva had used it as a shield.

Heva folded her arms with a scowl. "I told you. I trained my whole life for this." She tilted her head. "But enough about me. Did you really just volunteer to serve with Geovani? Don't you think that's dangerous? Aren't you worried people will start to suspect you're an Adriel?"

147

Ryn's gaze flickered to the racks of clothes. Only minutes ago, she'd accused El of not having insight into her situation.

Even though she'd nearly been stabbed, Ryn laughed.

The First Temple wasn't huge and glorious like Kai's Priesthood Temple. In fact, it looked more like a shelter for the homeless. The whole right side was an open pavilion with beds where rugged-looking people slept and lounged. Ryn's heart sank when she imagined Heva growing up that way—a young girl sleeping out in the open among strangers.

To the left of the temple were sparkling fields of wheat that went on for so long, Ryn couldn't see the end of them. A wheat worker waved at her when he saw her looking.

Ryn waved back and rubbed her eyes. She hadn't slept a wink the last few nights. Her side still ached, but the salve the physician put on every evening helped. She could walk normally and move around now, though she hadn't gone anywhere except to a mandatory 'royalty customs training session' with the other maidens, and there was one breakfast banquet the maidens were forced to attend with the King. Xerxes hadn't eaten a thing. He'd sat at the head of the long table with his chin resting on his fist, staring out the window and ignoring everyone. He'd looked so miserable that Ryn had snorted the tiniest, quietest laugh. She didn't think anyone heard it over the chatter, but Xerxes's gaze dragged back to the table and settled on her. He didn't smile, but his frown evened out for a moment. Then he went back to staring out the window.

One of the maidens—Calliope—glared at Ryn for the rest of breakfast, so Ryn hadn't made another sound as she ate her pilaf, omelet, and meat kebab.

Apart from those two events, she only left her room in the mornings to visit the Abandoned Temple in the palace and sit in silence in the quiet presence of El.

"You stay outside and stand guard," Heva directed the six Folke guards that had accompanied them through the city. The temple wasn't far from the palace gates—it only took them a few minutes to get there on foot, and even though Ryn wore a disguise, the rest of the Folke hadn't which drew stares from all who passed. Organizers had insisted Ryn travel by palanquin, stating it would be "catastrophic" for her image if normal citizens were to get too close or, heaven forbid—*touch* her, but she refused and promised to keep her face covered and her guards close.

Ryn had never breathed air fresher than the air outside the palace walls. She wanted to take the opportunity to visit Kai, but one look at her hovering Folke guards reminded her she was still a prisoner whether she was within the palace walls or not.

And Kai didn't want her back anyway.

"This way," Heva said to Ryn as she pulled open the thick, wooden temple door. Ryn tugged off her hood and followed Heva up a set of stairs.

An emerald carpet invited them inside. It stretched between two rows of pews lining a large room. Old books lay open across tables in a wide space to the left, surrounded by shelves jam-packed with bookstands, scrolls, and artifacts. The temple was dim; the windows looked like they hadn't been washed in years.

Several young priestesses slept in the pews. Their limbs were flung in random directions, their emerald skirts hiked up carelessly to their knees. One snored, and another talked in her sleep.

Ryn bit her lips together. When El made the comment about 'awakening the priestesses' Ryn didn't think he'd meant it literally.

Heva sighed. "So embarrassing," she murmured.

She smacked the back of a pew, and four priestesses startled awake. The nearest one snorted, launched up to a sitting position, and shouted something indecipherable. She blinked the sleep from her eyes then glared at Heva. "You monster. I haven't slept that well in weeks!" she said.

"Then go sleep in your *bed*," Heva articulated. "It's not that difficult to find."

The girl snorted and tried to lay back, but Heva grabbed her shoulder and rolled her off the pew. Ryn slapped a hand over her mouth as the girl tumbled to the floor. The other priestesses hid grins.

The girl leapt to her feet and sprang for Heva with her fingers out like claws. Ryn's jaw dropped as Heva and the priestess went channelling into the pews across the row, punching, kicking, and shouting threats.

The other priestesses stretched and yawned. One rose and twirled down the aisle, her dress fanning out around her. When she spotted a cricket on the floor, she reached down to scoop it up, whispering sweet words to it as she carried it by Ryn and out the door of the temple.

Ryn could not believe her eyes. What was El thinking sending her here? These girls were freaks.

Heva finally rose from between the pews, wiping a bead of blood from her lip. The other girl's foot shot up, catching her in the stomach and sending her staggering into the aisle. Heva's face went taught, but she released an exasperated breath and marched to Ryn without retaliating. "Crazy priestess," she muttered.

"I'm not crazy, you troll!" the girl shouted as she climbed to her feet. "Also, you look like a wild forest nymph with all those silver beads in your hair!"

Heva stopped walking, biting down hard on her lips.

Ryn tried not to grin as she took Heva's arm. "Let's find Geovani," she said.

Heva nodded and headed around the pews toward a door with a nameplate that said in Adriel letters: OFFICE OF THE HIGH PRIESTESS. She knocked and opened it.

"Seeda is still exactly the same as I left her," Heva remarked without missing a beat as she led Ryn inside.

A large news scroll was open, covering the top half of someone at a desk. The corner of the scroll flipped down, and Geovani's white hair appeared, along with one peeking eye.

"Yes, well. Seeda is a lunatic most days," Geovani agreed. She flicked the paper to fold it in half, then she placed it on her desk. "Why do you think I hide in here and pretend to read the news scrolls?" She flashed a smile at Ryn. "Welcome, Adassah."

A loud crash lifted from the main room, and Geovani's smile faltered. She released a sound in the back of her throat. "It's like living in a menagerie. They're all animals," she muttered as she stood from her desk.

"So, lock Seeda in a cage." Heva shrugged a shoulder.

Geovani snorted through a smirk and walked around to the door. "I imagine you're here because you've chosen the First Temple as your charity, Adassah. Well done. Let's get to work."

Ryn raised a brow in surprise. Maybe the organizers had sent word ahead of time.

"We'll start with a lesson," Geovani preached as she led the way out of the office. She cleared her throat and launched into it before Ryn was ready. "Adriels were a devout people who once had a rich history of miracles, you know. But the miracles went dead for over a hundred years, and the Adriels were conquered by their enemies—the Weylins. After, we were held captive beneath the thumb of the Weylin royals and were no longer recognized as 'people' at all. Many of the original Adriels who survived the conquering did not conform to the Celestial Divinities religion of the Weylins, causing much persecution for our people." Geovani pointed at a large mural on the wall of the wide room. A battle took place in one corner, and groups of people were tied up in the other. An old King with a white beard, dark eyes, and a frown stood above them all, holding a gold scepter.

"The Adriel history was forgotten after that, and the Adriel God was *supposedly* silent for nearly a hundred more years, making most scholars wonder if he'd ever really existed or if he was just a mythological character in old literature. Because of this, naturally, the Adriel people either went into hiding, changed their religion, or forgot who they were. Many Per-Siana dwelling Adriels eventually were swayed to rely on the Celestial Divinities, who spoke in wisdom through the Intelligentsia and guided the kingdom into prosperity."

Heva made a face and shook her head.

"Celestial Divinities are the reason Per-Siana has not yet been dragged into the great war beyond its borders." Geovani smiled. "At least, that's how it's taught in seminaries nowadays." She flung a hand through the air. "Even the Priesthood are forced to read only Intelligentsia-approved books and historical accounts that have been warped and played with. It's all a battle for control. If you keep pushing the same information down people's throats long enough, they'll start to believe it even if it's a bunch of lies woven together."

Geovani dragged a large book off a shelf and carried it to a table. Dust spat out when she dropped it, and Ryn coughed. "But here—" Geovani flipped the book open "—we have the real records. If the Intelligentsia ever found out, they'd burn this whole place to the ground." She cackled a laugh. "But they think we're a lazy, obsolete bunch, and not much of a threat." Her smile faded. She cut a glance over to the pew area where some of the priestesses had dozed off again. "Unfortunately, they're not wrong." She spun to face Ryn and her smile returned. "But I'd like to become one. A threat."

Ryn tapped her finger against her thigh. The first time she'd met Geovani, she thought the old woman was bizarre. But the white dragon had been an illusion. Geovani had been right about the harp too.

"How do we become a threat to the Intelligentsia? How do we fight gods?" Ryn asked.

"False gods," Geovani corrected, then tapped the open book with her knuckle. "And to fight them, we must spend time in the presence of El to grow our light. Then we study." After a second, she added, "Or, sometimes we sing."

Ryn cast Heva a doubtful look to see if Geovani was being serious. "I don't study," she said. "Even when my cousin brought home his Priesthood work, I didn't study. He read it aloud to me to pass the time." She didn't have to mention that singing was also an outrageous idea to fight gods. She could only imagine how horrifying it would be to come face-to-face with the shadows again and expect to survive by *singing* at them.

In fact, this whole approach was different than anything Kai had taught her. None of the priests at his temple had suggested these methods to go to war. Instead...

Kai had only suggested murder.

"Ladies!" Geovani snapped toward the pews. Two priestesses' heads poked up. "Get the others. We're going to read through as many chapters of this book as we can before dusk. And we're going to ask *our* god—God of the Adriels—to give us great insights while we do."

Heva dragged over two chairs and slumped into one. Ryn sat in the other.

"In the beginning..." As soon as Geovani began reciting the passage, colour filled Ryn's vision, and she gasped. In her mind's eye, she watched a great war in the heavens. She saw the Divinities be cast down from the sky. She saw them rise above humans as gods and give themselves positions over Per-Siana and the surrounding kingdoms.

She saw how bitter they were. How much they resented the God Original for defeating them, and how much they hated the Adriel people—how much they hated *all* people. She saw these dark gods chasing after Adriels, influencing minds to hurt them, to hunt them even. Not seven—thousands, if not *millions* of Celestial Divinities, hiding behind pictures of beauty, persecuting El's people and serving words of knowledge to the Intelligentsia who interpreted their false 'goodness' and provided guidance. It was a constant battle.

Only when the blue daylight began sinking to purple over the city did Ryn and Heva come outside to find all six Folke guards sleeping. Heva thought they should leave the men behind, but Ryn shook them each awake. Her mind spun with stories and a secret forgotten history as they set off for the palace.

The sun threatened to disappear behind the mountains, leaving the distant sky layered with bright orange and silky violet. The palace shone in the evening light, casting rainbows along the ground and making the city glow.

The Navy Road bustled with women in sweeping gowns and men in silk coats drawn in glass carriages. Magic speckled the air in glowing buds, and songs seeped from nearby revelries. It was strange to be around so many people. It was strange to be outside at all. From beneath her hood, Ryn studied faces, wondering why she'd avoided this area all her life when the road didn't seem that frightening anymore.

Her stomach growled. She longed for the trays of food and sweets that were delivered to her chambers on a silver cart.

A silver cart…

Ryn shook her head at herself, wondering how she could think such a thing. She hadn't been in the palace that long. Was she really getting used to things there? She stole a glance down the Navy Road at the Priesthood Temple and its domed gold roof. She wondered if Kai was in there right now. She wondered if he was sleeping well, if he was eating.

"Help!" a coarse voice called over the street.

Ryn slowed her walk, spotting a young man in a blindfold sitting at the roadside. His thin arms shook when he lifted them, his hands grasping at air. "Is he blind?" she asked no one in particular.

"Ignore him. He sits there all the time yelling at people," Heva said. "I think he's a beggar."

"Ah…" Ryn nodded. The streets were busy at this hour; steed-drawn carriages passing each other and Per-Siana citizens pushing by. She watched the blind man try to stop each person he heard pass. She watched him reach out his hand, never finding anyone to take it.

She took it.

Ryn wasn't sure why she did, but when her warm hand clasped around his cold one, the man went quiet. His mouth moved like he'd practiced what to say, but now that someone was there, he couldn't find the words.

"Do you want to see what a real warrior looks like?"

Ryn dropped to a knee, holding tight to the man's hand. "What's your name?" she asked him.

"Ryn!" Heva called when she realized.

"What, by the Divinities, is she *doing*?" one of the Folke guards asked. "She's a Heartstealer. This is shameful!"

Someone else behind Ryn gasped. "A Heartstealer?"

Ryn glanced up and instantly realized the mistake in revealing her face when people began slapping their hands over their mouths and whispering as they stared at her. A woman pointed toward the palace, and Ryn's gaze flickered that way.

A new banner hung before the white wall that hadn't been there when Ryn had first crossed through the gate. The rest of the Heartstealers were depicted on expensive, rippling fabric alongside the Intelligentsia, but now—*now* there was one more.

Ryn's eyes widened when she took in the image of herself at the same time as everyone in the street: the tall, cascading picture of her in Marcan's mosaic dress with her dark hair gliding down her back, her lips stained red, and her shoulders back like she owned the world.

"It's her! She's the new Heartstealer!" someone shouted.

Ryn almost dropped the beggar's hand and fled, but the man answered her question, "My name is Candello."

"What if you stay?" El suggested gently. *"What if you abandon your fear so this man can see again?"*

"Why should I?" Ryn whispered. And how exactly did El think this man would be able to see again?

"Didn't I tell you that you must learn how to love?"

Ryn's gaze drifted back to the man in the blindfold. El wanted her to love this beggar? She'd already felt compassion toward him after he'd reached out for help and didn't find it.

"Is he an Adriel?" Ryn asked quietly.

"He's not."

She huffed. "Then why?"

"What if he can become one?"

Ryn's face changed. She'd never heard of a Weylin choosing to become an Adriel. Only the other way around.

She took in a deep breath and squinted, trying to see the man differently. She wasn't sure how to turn her 'spirit eyes' on and off. But the longer she stared, the more she made out the edges of chains. Lots and *lots* of chains. Some around the man's legs, and one large one around the man's eyes. The chains were of the same shadowy substance as the creatures in the Celestial Divinities temple, and Ryn swallowed.

"I don't have my harp to chase these shadows away," she reasoned.

"What are you doing, Ryn?" Heva called again. The Folke began nudging people back who got too close. A crowd was forming. "We have to go!"

"She's a Heartstealer!" citizens shouted to each other, waving more people over.

"You don't need your harp. Just tell these false gods to leave this man alone. Tell them you speak on my behalf."

Ryn squeezed the man's hand. A warm wind tickled her neck. "Celestial Divinities," she called to them, "pay attention." She eyed the chains over the man's eyes and spoke to them next. "Leave this man at once. In the name of El Tsebaoth."

Fire burned through Ryn's stomach, and she inhaled, tearing her hand away from the man in surprise. A snapping sound filled her ears. She didn't know what had happened, but something had changed—the air had shifted, something had *moved* between the two of them.

No… something had *broken*.

A gasp escaped the man. His hands trembled as he reached for his blindfold.

"Ryn!" Heva shouted. But Ryn kept her gaze on the man as he pulled down the cloth and blinked at the sunset in the distance.

The loud ring of Heva drawing her sword brought Ryn to stand. She whirled to find the Folke guards holding back a crowd who shouted at her, reached for her, tried to hand her things.

"Don't you know how foolish it is to linger in the streets, Maiden?!" the same Folke as before snapped, and Ryn's cheeks warmed.

"I'm sorry…" She watched people toss their dignity aside.

They acted like she was one of the Divinities themselves and they wanted to grab her and feel her magic.

Wailing lifted at her back. Ryn found the beggar pointing up at the setting sun in disbelief.

"Well done, Adassah."

The warm wind fluttered away.

The beggar stared at the buildings, at the people, at the streets left and right. Ryn was sure he could see. A slow, awe-filled smile found her face.

"You are wildly irresponsible, Maiden!" the Folke grabbed Ryn's arm and her hood fell back. She reached to yank it up again, but realized the crowd wasn't looking at her anymore; the crowd gasped and pointed toward the palace, their shouts lowering to whispers.

"Is that…?"

"That can't be…"

Ryn tugged herself free of the guard.

"You think you can cause a ruckus for the Folke because you're famous now? Ha!" The guard turned and grabbed the beggar instead, yanking him to his feet. "All this so you can give attention to a worthless street rat?!"

Ryn screamed when the guard grabbed the beggar's hair, tilting his head back so his throat was exposed. The beggar didn't cry or protest; he gazed up at the sky in amazement as if seeing the clouds for the first time. When the Folke guard tightened his grip, the beggar finally shrieked, the sound echoing down the street.

"Are you crazy?! Let him go!" Heva shouted at the guard.

"And look at him making another ruckus!" the Folke growled. Ryn tried to pry the guard's hands from the beggar's hair, but the guard shoved her backward so hard she stumbled over her own

JENNIFER KROPF

feet. Heva reached to catch Ryn but missed, and blurs of colours sped by as she spun into a fall.

Two hands caught her forearms, steadying her.

Ryn blinked at a navy coat inlaid with gold. Stitching of a white dragon coiled up the sleeve. A drop of fear sank through her as it dawned on her whose coat that was. Whose hands held her.

She lifted her eyes slowly to find a king looking back at her.

King Xerxes's blue eyes were sharp. He lifted his gaze to the Folke guard harassing the beggar, then he dropped Ryn's arms. At least thirty Folke followed him as he walked past.

"Is that the King?" the crowd whispered. "*Outside* the palace? Can that really be him? Is this really what he looks like?"

"Your Majesty!" The guard dropped the beggar's hair when he noticed. He forced a strange laugh. "I'm just dealing with a disruptive beggar."

Xerxes smiled. Ryn studied it, trying to decide if it was real. Xerxes was striking when he smiled, even when it didn't appear genuine, and a few young women in the crowd started giggling. But Ryn couldn't be happy the King was pleased at the sight of a beggar being tormented. She wouldn't have helped the blind man see if she knew the whole kingdom would turn against him.

All the Folke guards—including Heva—stood at attention now, silent.

"I wonder if it hurts when someone's hair is grabbed like that?" Xerxes thought aloud, and the guard chuckled.

"I imagine so, Your Majesty! This man was making a terrible ruckus, so I—"

Xerxes grabbed the Folke guard's hair. Citizens in the crowd gasped and drew back as Xerxes held the guard exactly how the beggar had been held. The guard wailed in alarm, his eyes open

160

wide as Xerxes forced him to look up at the sky.

The King leaned in, and Ryn heard him whisper, "Anyone would make a ruckus if their hair was grabbed like this." Xerxes's face darkened. "How dare you wear my colours, represent me, and harass my people in the streets? And how *dare* you grab my maiden like that?" He tossed the guard away.

Ryn's mouth hung open as the guard scrambled backward and clasped his hands in pleading.

"Folke," Xerxes called, and the Folke down the line lifted their heads. "Strip this guard of his uniform. He's not worthy of it."

Xerxes turned like he meant to leave, but he paused, glancing over at the beggar. Then at Ryn. Back to the beggar. "Give this beggar a year's salary and food for this inconvenience," he added. His throat bobbed as he left the crowd behind.

He caught Ryn's hand on his way. A rhythm lifted in Ryn's chest as Xerxes pulled her with him through the palace gate. She wasn't sure if it was an accident when his thumb brushed over her knuckles, or when his fingers tightened around hers. Xerxes didn't react to the crowd lifting hollers and cheers and shouting questions at his back while he took a shortcut through the garden.

Ryn's knees trembled as they reached the wide palace entrance, and she nearly stumbled up the stairs.

Twice. Twice now, King Xerxes had shown up and saved her.

Xerxes didn't let go of Ryn's hand until they were in the atrium, and there, he turned so they were face to face. He was frowning.

Ryn folded her hands in front of her and glanced toward the entrance to see if Heva had kept up.

"Are you mad?" Xerxes asked, and her attention darted back to him.

161

Mad? No one had ever called her that. "I was trying to be kind—"

"What were you doing outside the palace in the first place after being *attacked by assassins* only days ago? You really must have the memory of a brick," he said. "And getting that close to a beggar?!" His chest expanded, and he exhaled as he dragged a hand through his hair, scuffing it out of its neat state. "What if he'd drawn a dagger and held you hostage for ransom? Don't you know how often that happens to rich nobles?"

"I'm not a rich noble," Ryn murmured. The King should have figured that out by now since she didn't even have her own clothes to wear. She bit her tongue after she said it though, hoping he understood that she was admitting to not being *rich*, and she wasn't at all admitting to not being *noble*.

Xerxes pinched his lips and blinked slowly. "Don't make me angry," he warned. "It won't be good for anyone." When she didn't reply, he took her arms and turned her wrists up. He began inspecting her thumbs, her knuckles, the undersides of her hands.

"What are you looking for?" Ryn asked. He tugged her sleeve up an inch.

"Bruises," he said.

Ryn yanked her arms back. "I'm fine," she said.

"That's not why I'm searching." He rolled his eyes.

"Then why look for bruises?" It came out like a scold, and she closed her mouth when maids around the atrium scowled at her for raising her voice at *the King*.

"I'm trying to decide if he should die today," Xerxes said, and Ryn's stomach dropped.

"W… What?"

"The guard," Xerxes clarified. His brows tugged in when he

studied the look on her face. "You don't want him dead?"

"No!" Ryn said in horror. "Of course not!"

Xerxes squinted his eyes a little like he didn't believe her. After a moment, he said, "Fine." He took in a deep breath and released it, glancing to the Folke trailing into the palace. "Don't go outside the palace walls, Maiden. I thought I warned you that your guards-woman would pay the price if you did."

Ryn raised both hands. "I wasn't escaping! It was for my charity work."

His mouth went thin at the corners again. "You chose charity work *outside* the palace? I'll have you switched to something else."

"No!" Ryn released a breath and reached for him. "Please. I want to stay with the First Temple."

Xerxes stared at her. He glanced down at where she clutched the sleeves of his royal coat. Ryn dropped her hands and clasped them in front of her again, wondering if the nearby servants were scowling at her all over.

Heva appeared at the entrance panting and with flushed cheeks, so Ryn dipped into a strange curtsy.

"Farewell, Your Majesty," she said. She turned and fled toward Heva.

But the King's deep voice followed her. "Don't you know it's a crime to depart from the King's presence before you've been dismissed?" he said, and Ryn's feet came together. Even though the King's tone was calm, maids in the atrium inhaled. A few pointed, and Ryn wished she'd thought to pull her hood back up before she came inside.

She released a breath through her nose. How much more ab-surd could the rules in this palace get? No leaving, no Adriels, no self-dismissing from the King.

"So then chase me down and put me in prison, Your Majesty," she invited, keeping her back to him. It came out with a sweet touch of sarcasm. "I'm sure it wouldn't be much different than this." She twirled a finger through the air at the palace where he knew full well she was being forced to endure as a Heartstealer. She carried on and fell into step beside Heva.

A second later, the King's laughter lifted through the atrium behind her.

12
BELORME

Citizens of Per-Siana milled about in the city below, pulling out their coin purses to make trades, stepping into the vast collection of temples lining the roads to pray and offer tribute, and gossiping with their neighbours as they strolled in pairs. Belorme watched them from the balcony off the Intelligentsia's Room of Knowledge. He watched how they chased their desires, went about their little hobbies, and made every choice of their day based on their fears. The fear of going hungry. The fear of growing ill. The fear of being harmed. The fear of losing their family.

Belorme had once thought that way. He'd spent most of his life serving a king who swung fear around like a sword—right up until the day he died. Day in and day out, those dwelling in the palace had served the late King with every ounce of their devotion. King

Draco had been a king chosen and blessed by the Celestial Divinities, a king who all believed would be a ruthless conqueror in his years and expand the borders of Per-Siana. A king the people believed would take back the sacred desert lands stolen by B'rei Mira a hundred years ago. There were prophecies about it. Even the Intelligentsia had been convinced.

But the late King was rash. The King made one terrible mistake in the last years of his reign that had cost him the legendary life the kingdom had anticipated.

Belorme could still taste the tension in the air from that day. He could still feel the sweat on his flesh from nerves even now, as if he was back standing before the whole council, placed there by King Draco. He could still hear the King's condescending words, *"What have you done, Belorme? How could you be so foolish?"*

Foolish?

Belorme had served the King faithfully at his side, had even raised his son. He'd been family, and still, the King dragged him out in public and made a scene, blaming Belorme for mixing the wrong remedy for Xerxes's morning medicine. Many of the magic brews and medicines had been switched around during the annual cleaning, and Xerxes's medicine had been merged with a dreadful potion. And when magic is mixed with medicine, only terrible things happen. Terrible things like… an innocent young prince transforming into something beastly.

But *Belorme* hadn't mixed the young Prince's medicine. *Belorme* hadn't even been in the medicine cabinet that day. It was Damon—Belorme's new apprentice at the time—who had made the medicine that morning.

Despite Belorme's claims of innocence, the King had never believed him. And what a terrible thing—to speak the truth and not be believed.

That was the former King's single greatest mistake.

It was also the reason Damon owed Belorme his life.

Belorme wasn't responsible for the King's untimely death afterward, but he hadn't done anything to stop it either. Even the medicines Belorme had made for the King's sickness were fake—water and blossom paste. A concoction good for nothing more than watering the gardens outside.

The King's funeral had been a grand spectacle. Xerxes had cried for days. And Belorme, who had once spoken softly to the boy and taught him how to read, did not say a word to him. Even when Xerxes tugged his sleeve and begged Belorme for a bedtime story to ease his pain, Belorme had ignored the boy and told him to go read a book by himself.

Xerxes had, after all, been far more loved by the King than Belorme. Something Belorme had learned the hard way. It was difficult to feel sympathy for the weeping boy after that.

Belorme flicked a crumb off the balcony ledge as he thought about these things. He watched the crumb sail down the side of the palace and disappear into the courtyards below. From where he stood, he could see into the glass rooms of the palace, he could watch the staff going about their chores. He could spy. He could collect all sorts of knowledge from up here. And knowledge, after all, was power. And power equalled control.

And only control could keep Belorme from ever having to suffer at Xerxes's hands the way he'd suffered at his father's.

"We hate the late King," the voices chimed together.

"We hate Xerxes."

"Chancellor."

When Damon's low tone filled the balcony, Belorme realized

he was gripping the rail with bleached knuckles. He loosened his grip and peeled his fingers off.

"The Intelligentsia are meeting soon to discuss the Heartstealers issue. As you can imagine, everyone's a little on edge."

A little on edge. Belorme grunted. Everyone was more than 'a little' on edge. Ever since Xerxes's additional maiden had made the King laugh.

He'd *laughed*.

How horrifying. Belorme had not seen Xerxes laugh since he was a tiny boy giggling through pranks he'd pull on unsuspecting noblemen in the palace. And now, Xerxes had threatened to come after Belorme if the Intelligentsia had the maiden killed.

What a mess this was.

"I want you to go apologize to that maiden," Belorme said to Damon.

"What?"

"The one you raised your sword against," he clarified. "The one starting all the rumours among the nobles."

Damon was quiet, but Belorme imagined he was seething. "Why?" the sage asked in a dark voice.

"Because you're young, attractive, and the perfect candidate to make the King jealous. And there are more refined methods than killing to get what we want," Belorme stated. "I want you to get on Estheryn Electus's good side. I want you to talk to her sweetly. And if you can, I want you to put her in a compromising position," Belorme said. He turned around to face the sage. Only one of Damon's near-black eyes showed through the slit of his hood. "I want to catch her in the act of betraying the King."

Damon's shoulders relaxed, the anger fizzling from his gaze. "Being sweet will take too long," he said. "I can move things along faster if I'm pushy." There wasn't a spark of doubt in Damon's appearance. The unreserved confidence almost put a shiver in Belorme's spine as he nodded.

"Yes, befriending her does seem like a waste of time," he said.

"Kill her immediately! We want her dead!"

"She's dangerous!"

Belorme folded his arms and paced around the balcony. "I'll arrange something scandalous," he decided. "Be ready. And Damon…" The young sage raised a brow in question. "I've been watching the Adriel priests in the city—They're getting bold. Grab one of them when you have time and bring him here in secret. I'd like to interrogate a priest."

Damon nodded. "Of course." After a shallow bow, he returned to the Room of Knowledge, his cloak sweeping around with him.

Belorme turned back toward the Mother City. And to his voices, he said, "Consider it done. What shall I do for the gods next?"

.

CHAPTER

13

XERXES

The door to the Folke assembly room made a clatter when Xerxes swung it open, striking the adjacent wall. A dozen nearby Folke jumped in surprise, and everyone in the room leapt to their feet to stand at attention.

Xerxes scanned their faces.

The problem was that Xerxes wasn't sure he could trust any of these fools. He was aware the Intelligentsia were lining the pockets of Folke guards, he just wasn't sure which ones. All Folke looked the same—blue and silver with slightly fearful faces whenever he got too close. Only the Divinities knew how to tell a trustworthy guard apart from a crooked one.

Xerxes stepped into the room, and even the sounds of breathing vanished.

He searched the guards nearest the door first, then those in the middle, those furthest away...

A blond fellow with rosy cheeks stood at the very back of the room, half in shadow where the window's light didn't reach. He cowered amidst his fellow Folke, keeping his gaze down on his feet.

Xerxes pointed. "You," he said.

The Folke parted all the way down the assembly room, looking backward to see who had caught the King's attention.

The blond fellow's face paled as he realized an open path now lay between him and the King of Per-Siana. That the King was pointing right at him.

"Come with me," Xerxes said, dropping his hand. He turned and headed back out of the assembly. Faint sounds of the fellow scrambling filled the dead-quiet room behind him.

Xerxes headed down the twisted palace hallways and up a tetrad of stairs until he reached the library, and there, he glanced between the shelves to ensure no one else was present. He turned to the fellow. The only Folke who might be immune to bribes in this particular situation.

Xerxes meant to inform the guard of his new assignment, but "Did I not warn you she was in danger?!" was what came out instead.

The fellow's mouth hung open. Xerxes released a heavy sigh and reached over to shove the fellow's jaw back up so his mouth wouldn't dry out.

"She was attacked several days ago, like I warned you she would be," he added. "Didn't you hear about it?"

"Wh...who?" the guard stuttered.

"Your friend. *Ryn.*" Xerxes bit his lips together after he said it, liking saying her nickname far too much. "Since you're the only guard I can trust with this, I'm charging you with her safety. Stand outside her door at night and always keep her in your view. Do you understand, Folke?"

The fellow nodded with red cheeks and startled eyes. Xerxes scanned the fellow's uniform, finding it all fitting strangely.

"I can *not* lose her," Xerxes articulated.

"Yes, you can."

"If she gets a single scratch, you'll take responsibility and be punished," he added.

Again, the Folke nodded, and Xerxes was beginning to wonder if the fellow had gone mute in the last few seconds.

"Go to your new post." Xerxes waved in the general direction of the maidens' rooms. "And go see a tailor too," he added with a mutter as he turned for the library door. The scent of undusted books washed over him, and his nose wrinkled. Maybe he ought to remind the cleaners to pay more attention to the library.

The fellow finally found his voice again when Xerxes was half a step out the door: "I would give my life for hers."

Xerxes hesitated. He turned back around, studying the Folke to see if he was serious.

It seemed he was. A crease hovered between the fellow's brows, his head was held high, his eyes were even glossed with a strange message that made Xerxes draw back into the room.

"What sort of relationship do you have with that maiden to make you say such a thing?" he asked. Xerxes wasn't the jealous sort, but his jaw slid to the side as he waited for the answer. He looked the fellow over afresh, finding him handsome enough— blond, strong, possibly sweet in an odd way once one got to know him.

Xerxes interlocked his fingers behind his back and squeezed them. Even though he was King, Xerxes knew his flaws massively outweighed his attributes. Not that he cared what Estheryn thought of him. He simply wanted her to stay alive because she and her harp might be his only cure.

The fellow's cheeks flushed again, and Xerxes suddenly did not want to know. "Never mind," he said, turning to leave. If Estheryn had romantic feelings for a Folke, that was not his business. Though, if she was discovered, he as King would be forced to cast her out of the palace, put her in prison, or worse.

Xerxes realized his hands were in fists. He also realized he hadn't taken a single step out the library door.

"Ryn is as good as my sister." The Folke spoke again—wrongfully assuming Xerxes wanted him to.

Xerxes glanced back. He was making an annoying habit of trying to read this fellow's face.

"A sister?" he asked, just to be sure.

The fellow glanced down and ran the toe of his boot along the ridge of the library rug. "It's a long story. But yes."

Xerxes nodded. He found himself fighting an almost-smile that didn't belong on his face. He washed it from his mouth and turned back to the fellow one last time with all the authority of a king.

"Assassins already reached her once," he said. "Do not let them twice."

A loud commotion erupted outside the library. Shouts flittered down the hall and Xerxes forgot about the red-cheeked fellow as he rushed out and marched down the hall to the atrium.

Servants and Intelligentsia surrounded four men in navy war uniforms by the entrance. Dried blood coated the men's hands, and Xerxes's stomach turned. He had not seen one of those uniforms in almost ten years. The Intelligentsia asked all sorts of questions, but Xerxes could only stare at their torn clothing, the scratches on their armour, the cuts on their faces and arms.

Signs they'd seen battle.

Were they from the border? Xerxes couldn't find his voice to ask as he thought of the smoke he'd spotted lifting past the mountains from his window.

When a uniformed man saw Xerxes there, he pushed through the servants and Intelligentsia. "Your Majesty!" the soldier performed the army salute and dropped to a knee at Xerxes's feet. "There's been trouble at the border."

Xerxes's heel drifted back an inch. His stomach squeezed. He wanted to ask for information, to *do* something, but his mind spun.

"Revenge."

"Seek revenge."

"How dare the enemy cross you?"

"Say no more!" Belorme's words overtook the noise in the lobby. "Not here." The Chancellor glanced around at the eavesdropping servants and local dukes arrived for the weekly affairs meeting.

Xerxes's throat was thick when he swallowed, but he stood tall. "What happened?" he asked, ignoring Belorme's instruction. "Tell me."

The soldier bowed again. "Spies got past us," he whispered.

"Not another word more!" Belorme snapped, losing his composure for once. He pulled the soldier back up to his feet. "To the Strategy Hall," he directed. Belorme led the soldier away, and Xerxes watched the three other soldiers follow. The Intelligentsia trailed after them all. And then...

And then Xerxes followed.

The halls felt longer than normal, the path more winding and dizzying.

He marched ahead and slipped into the Strategy Hall seconds after Belorme. The remaining Intelligentsia and council members trailed in, telling Xerxes they'd somehow already been notified.

"How many spies?" Xerxes asked to take control of the meeting. Men spread around the centre table in the room. They eyed the maps always left there—maps that showed the one hundred and twenty-seven provinces of Per-Siana and all their borders.

"I'm not sure," the same soldier admitted. "B'rei Mira sent a diversion. We were fighting for our lives while the spies slipped past."

Xerxes exhaled. It was worse not knowing if there was one or one hundred than knowing for sure there were thousands hiding among the people. "Can you identify them?" Xerxes asked.

The soldier shook his head, and a unanimous exhale sounded through the room.

"They might already be here. They might be hiding among your servants, or your noble guests, waiting to attack you," the soldier said.

"Let them try."

"We will kill them."

Xerxes flexed his jaw. His fingers curled slowly into fists as the touch of cool water rippled over his flesh. He inhaled, and for once, he invited the dangerous sensation of icy power, that darkness inside of him that made him feel like a monster.

"Your Majesty... you're looking a little pale," a councilman commented.

"King Xerxes, what should we do about the B'rei Mira spies

here in Per-Siana?" another asked.

Dozens of blinking eyes looked his way, men dressed in nobleman finery and Intelligentsia hoods alike, their features muted by the dimness of the windowless room.

Xerxes's tongue flexed and he fought the urge to shout.

Instead, he said in a low, calm voice,

"Let them try."

"Go hunt down Alecsander first. Go destroy him."

"First kill the maiden."

"Kill everyone."

Xerxes carried his sword to the training field. "Quiet," he muttered at the voices. It was impossible to focus this morning with their ruckus.

He'd lain awake all night thinking about the soldiers' news. Imagining Alecsander of B'rei Mira making Xerxes his next target. During breakfast he hadn't been able to speak a word as the councilmen talked and talked and *talked*, coming up with lame speculations and pathetic strategies that would never work to hunt down the B'rei Mira spies. Xerxes didn't eat; even the sight of jam had turned his stomach. Instead, he'd watched the councilmen, separating the newest members and wondering how difficult it might be for a B'rei Mira spy to pose as a Per-Siana councilman. He did the same thing with every servant who carried out hot breakfast items. And then again, as he headed out of the palace to the training field. Every single subject he passed looked to have the makings of a spy. He'd go mad at this rate.

Folke stood at attention across the field. The training grounds were just inside the outer palace wall and surrounded by lush flower gardens, pomegranate shrubs, and almond trees—the most beautiful place for any soldier to sharpen his skill. It was where Xerxes had learned to fight.

"We'll be doing extra training in the days ahead. I want every single one of you able to defend yourself against our enemies," Xerxes said. "We'll train from dawn to dusk if we must."

"But, Your Majesty, what about the dance tomorrow night?" a bystanding organizer piped up, and Xerxes closed his eyes.

These wretched Heartstealer trials. They would be the end of him.

"Cancel it," he stated.

He hadn't noticed other organizers were even there, hovering by the footbath of the Turquoise Peri Pond of Blessing, until they all started gasping.

"We can't! The kingdom would be in an uproar! They live for news about the Heartstealer trials!" he said. "Please, Your Majesty, these events are all your people have to look forward to!"

Xerxes opened his mouth to protest and scold the organizer for objecting. But he realized how difficult it was going to be to contain the gossip about the four soldiers from the border. The Intelligentsia would already be overworked trying to conceal the truth and rewrite the story so the citizens didn't panic. Truly, as much as he hated it—*dancing*—it was an event that would be a promise to the people that everything was normal in the palace. Even if it wasn't.

Xerxes rolled his eyes and walked to the edge of the field. He shook off his coat of nobility and tossed it to a servant, then he locked eyes with a Folke and pulled his sword from its sheath. He felt like pummelling a few guards this afternoon. "If anyone goes easy on me," he warned, "I'll get angry. And none of you want to see what happens when I get angry."

Xerxes was slick with sweat three hours later, his silk shirt ruined. His sleep-deprived body begged him to stop, but he refused.

It had been a while since he swung a sword. His extensive combat training had ended when he turned fifteen. He was surprised to discover how much of it was still second nature to him.

Folke guards rolled into the grass in exhaustion when they thought he wasn't looking. Xerxes should have punished them, but instead he sighed and turned away to take a long drink of water, giving them a moment's rest. As he drank, his gaze fell upon a slender silhouette scaling down the palace wall into the garden. He wiped a drip of water from his lip, his eyes narrowing on the dark-haired maiden.

"I'll be back," he said as he handed his water glass to the nearest servant.

Xerxes marched past the pond and into the orchard, ducking around shrubs until he was close enough to hear her heavy breathing over the wind. He waited at the foot of the palace, watching her make every careful move, watching her leap the last few feet, watching her boots find the ground. Watching her turn around.

She nearly screamed. Her hand flew over her mouth and all that came out was a high-pitched shriek.

"Estheryn," Xerxes said. "How many times have I warned you not to try to escape? Hmm?" He raised a brow at her, too tired and sore to show much expression.

Instead of panicking, dropping to her knees, and begging for mercy with repentance—which was what any normal person would do—Estheryn's face broke into a sheepish *smile*. Something flipped in Xerxes's chest when he saw it. "Don't do that," he instructed.

"What?" Estheryn asked. Still smiling.

Xerxes glared at her mouth. He tore his gaze off a second later and glanced toward the nearest tree. The sky. Anything.

He cleared his throat. "I heard you're causing trouble. There's a rumour in the Mother City that you…" Xerxes bit his tongue. He wasn't sure he could spit out such an absurd claim. "…*healed* that beggar."

"Ah. Yes, that man was healed." She nodded and Xerxes's gaze fired back to her. "But not by me, King. I'm not that powerful on my own."

"She's alone out here, did you notice?"

"Now would be an excellent time to kill her."

"Then who was it?" Xerxes asked. He didn't mean to take a step closer, to reveal desperation in his voice, but that's what happened. He also became aware of how soaked with sweat his shirt was, how his face might have glistened. How he must have smelled.

"It was a god," she said, seeming not to notice.

A god.

Xerxes tilted his head. Estheryn Electus had the favour of a god? A god who could *cure* illnesses?

"Which one? Iris?" he guessed. "Helios? Boreas?"

The funny smile on her face vanished. "I can't tell you that," she said.

"Why not?" Xerxes took another step in by accident. They were nearly against each other now, and a light flutter moved through his stomach when she shifted her footing and almost brushed against him. He took the opportunity to search her face for clues. This maiden heard his voices, she made them go quiet. Whatever power was at her fingertips... He needed it.

She didn't explain anything. "Do you trust me, King?" she asked, and Xerxes made a face.

"No, of course not."

She cast him a look. "Fine. I don't trust you either."

His mouth curled into an absurd smile. He bit down on his lips and shooed it away. "I could have you interrogated," he pointed out. "I could learn all your secrets that way."

Estheryn's cheeks paled. Even though he meant it as a joke, she didn't laugh. In fact, her reaction was so strong that Xerxes realized something he hadn't picked up on before in any of his encounters with her. He eyed her blanched cheeks, a twitch of her lashes. The Heartstealer he chose to be here. The young woman almost exactly his age who had a terrible father, yet who apparently had the favour of one of the seven Celestial Divinities.

He took a slow step back. To leave, maybe. Or to give her space?

"Don't wander the gardens for too long," he advised. "I'll come hunting for you if you do."

Neither of them laughed, but she gave him a tight smile that looked forced. Xerxes glanced up toward her chamber window, searching for her guards. He saw her guardswoman climbing over the sill, high above.

At least Estheryn wouldn't be alone.

"Let's dance tomorrow," Xerxes said, bringing his attention back down. "We'll talk then."

Estheryn didn't object with her mouth, but a crease of worry formed between her brows.

Worry that he was showing her favouritism, maybe. That he'd shown her favouritism since the Introduction Ceremony where he spoke to her and none of the other maidens. Worry that his favour would only make her more of a target, when she was already an obstacle in many people's way.

Xerxes wondered if she thought he hadn't noticed what his attention did to her. How absurd; he always saw everything that happened in the palace. In the beginning, he hadn't cared if she was a target of the Intelligentsia—he'd hoped she would be. He'd *wanted* them to become irritated by her presence. But now, Xerxes supposed he wanted other things more.

"I'll be sharing a dance with *each* of the maidens," he clarified. He didn't mention he'd just decided that in this moment. Or that the thought of actually participating in a Heartstealer event repulsed him more than she'd ever be able to imagine.

But she breathed a small sigh of relief, and that was worth it. At least, it was worth it at present. It wouldn't be worth it at the dance tomorrow.

"Of course," she nodded and smiled a little.

Xerxes stole one last glance up the wall where the guardswoman was halfway to the bottom. Another second or two and she'd be by Estheryn's side.

"I'll see you tomorrow, then," Xerxes said. He turned and headed back through the garden, a thousand questions on the tip of his tongue he dared not ask. He pushed through the bushes, catching his damp shirt on a twig.

When he reached the training field, he saw the Folke were back at it. Many of them fashioned swelling bruises or fresh, dripping cuts. But they fought, regardless. Xerxes watched them without really seeing them.

Instead, he saw Estheryn's face when he made that joke about interrogating her for her secrets. He'd found the maiden interesting since the beginning, but he'd never looked at her long enough to realize the most interesting thing of all.

Estheryn Electus was hiding something. Something big enough to make her fear him, even though she had the power to still his voices and give sight to a beggar in the street. What did someone like that have to be afraid of?

He planned to find out what it was.

Cool evening wind rippled over his warm flesh. Dusk was sweeping in. He'd grow hungry soon and would need to visit the basement. But even his precious pears wouldn't be enough of a remedy for the things he was facing today.

Xerxes felt a war coming. It was in the air, like a prophecy woven within the magic. And though there were many things to worry about, what he feared the most was what might happen if his voices were still in control of him when the war came.

CHAPTER

14

RYN

Rumours rose in the palace that the Folke had gone into an intense period of training. No one offered an explanation why. Heva was excluded since she was a Heartstealer guardswoman, but even with her asking around, none of the Folke knew or admitted exactly what it was that had sent the leaders into such a frenzy.

Ryn spent her morning in the Abandoned Temple, resting in El's quiet presence. After that, she went with Heva and six Folke to visit the First Temple. Geovani's teaching had been of old Adriel miracles that left Ryn with a buzz in her stomach. The woman spoke of seas being parted, of fire falling from the heavens, and of manna coming from the sky to feed the Adriel people when they were hungry—all by the power of the God Original.

Ryn wasn't aware how many hours had passed until Heva interrupted and said they needed to get back.

"Bye, Ryn!" Nebulin, the youngest priestess, blew a kiss and accidentally let go of a butterfly she'd been nurturing all day. She chased it through the temple until Seeda flung the front door open and let it be free.

Ryn's Folke guards wore disguises now, posing as a band of travellers. It worked—few people noticed them on the journey back. They pulled off their cloaks and travel bags as they came into the palace, and organizers were there to receive them.

Ryn smoothed down her ruffled hair on her way to her room. She slowed her steps when she recognized Calliope's voice drifting from the largest set of maidens' rooms above the crackling fireplace inside.

"He turned me away last night." It was said in a hushed state, barely a whisper.

Heva glanced back at Ryn in question when she didn't follow, and Ryn waved her forward. The guardswoman shrugged and went into Ryn's chambers alone, likely to find a snack after she'd complained the whole walk back that they'd missed lunch.

Ryn silently leaned against the wall outside Calliope's door.

"What do you mean, he turned you away last night?" Calliope's artist asked with an edge. The artist's voice was scratchy—the opposite of Calliope's. Calliope's voice was pretty, like smooth music.

"I mean, after you got me all dressed up for my scheduled evening with the King, he wouldn't see me," Calliope said. "We only get *one* evening with the King. So naturally, I'm enraged."

Ryn's eyes widened.

An *evening* with the King? What did that mean? She almost

covered her ears and fled from her hiding place, but the artist spoke again and Ryn couldn't help herself. She leaned toward the doorway, keeping a flat hand on the wall for balance.

"So, you're saying first the King refused to spend an evening with Ulita, and then he refused to spend an evening with you? What's gotten into him? Is he really crazy like the rumours say?"

Calliope made a tsking sound. "Obviously he's lost his mind. Didn't you see him in the courtyard that day? I was lucky to be the only maiden he didn't face off with in that state."

In the courtyard. When Xerxes had driven the maidens outside with a sword and demanded they fight him. Ryn remembered every second.

She relaxed against the wall. She wasn't even aware there were scheduled times for evening visits, or what exactly an 'evening visit' entailed, but what did it matter if Xerxes wasn't interested in meeting the maidens at all?

She pulled off the wall and turned toward her quarters.

"It's not that unusual for him. My uncle is Intelligentsia, re-member? He told me King Xerxes never once went within three feet of his last wife." For someone with a pretty voice, Calliope's laugh was ugly and cruel when she let it out. "Not even on their wedding day."

Ryn stopped walking.

The artist made a scoffing sound. "He must have really disliked her if he went straight from avoiding her all the time to *killing*—"

"Hush!" Calliope's voice was loud this time.

Ryn clasped her hands together. She wasn't sure what bothered her more—Calliope's gossip, the idea of an evening visit with the King, or the reminder that Xerxes had... had...

Ryn's chest tightened. Somehow, she'd forgotten Xerxes had

killed his first wife. In the moments between him catching her red-handed in the gardens and showing up to rescue her, she'd started to see him as a boy stranded on an island in this palace. Not as the heartless young man who once did something so unthinkable.

For days now, she'd wrestled with whether she should tell Xerxes his life was in danger. The truth was, she wanted to tell him. She didn't want to watch a stranded person die. She wasn't even sure when her mind had changed about that.

But that meant she'd be the one to assassinate the King in the end—if Kai got what he wanted.

"What do I do?" Ryn whispered into the hallway. She looked up at the ceiling when there was no answer. "I'm asking you, El. What do I do?"

"Go to bed."

She released a heavy sigh.

"Ryn?"

It took Ryn a second to figure out where the soft voice came from. She turned all the way around before she saw Matthias at the end of the hall. She rushed over, turning pink as she wondered if Matthias's greeting had alerted Calliope and her artist to her creeping outside.

She pulled Matthias through the hall, keeping her head down as she passed Calliope's room, flung the door to her chambers open, and shoved Matthias in ahead of her.

Heva was lounging on Ryn's bed with her dirty boots still on, and Ryn scowled. "You know, there might be a reason Seeda despises you so much," she said.

Heva only grinned.

"What news have you brought, Matthias?" Ryn asked as she fell into a chair. "Has Kai changed his mind about me being here?"

Matthias kicked his toe against the floor. "Uh… No. I haven't spoken with the Priesthood."

Ryn's face fell. "Then what are you doing at my room?"

"Well…" Matthias glanced back toward the closed door. "The King sent me to guard you."

"What?" Heva lifted her head from the bed. "Does he think I'm incapable?"

Matthias scratched his head. "Maybe… If I let something bad happen to Ryn, the King promised to punish me. But it's a good thing—I don't have to sneak around to get here anymore." He released an uneven laugh and dropped his hand to his sword awkwardly. Then he turned to Ryn and changed the subject. "Do you remember that time we stole sumac from the park trees and the neighbours chased us all the way down the street for it?"

"How do you still remember that? That was shortly after I moved in with Kai," Ryn said, even though she wasn't finished discussing the King's threat to Matthias.

The sumac heist was one of her favourite memories—she and Matthias had mud all the way up the backs of their legs from running through the rain by the time they returned to the house. "The kabobs we made with the sumac were delicious," she added.

"Of course I remember it. I remember every moment with you, Ryn, since the day you showed up," Matthias said. His cheeks flushed, and Ryn's smile faded away.

She remembered too.

In fact, Ryn hardly had any memories of the last six years without Matthias in them. Matthias was the one who spent the most time around her and Kai, who checked in at the house to make sure she was warm when it rained, who gave her a reason to laugh every year on the anniversary of her mother's death. And with Kai and Theo lost to their plans to make Ryn a Queen or an assassin, maybe Matthias was her only friend now.

Ryn ran a hand down her hair as that settled in, along with Xerxes's threat. "Matthias, maybe you should escape the palace before it's too—"

Marcan barged through the door, and Ryn jumped. The artist was followed by six makeup artists and two more assistants carrying a sparkling navy dress with gold sleeves.

"Do you ever knock?" Heva mumbled from the bed.

"Not really." Marcan waved his assistants over. "Estheryn, come try this on. If I got the sizing correct, you'll be a dazzling goddess on the ballroom floor for the dance tonight." He held up the gown, and Ryn sighed as she took in the remarkable gold threads and glassy blue beads over deep ocean-blue satin.

Another dress that would ruin everything.

The ballroom was grander than the Hall of Stars; more glitter, more lights, louder music. Ryn waited for the host to announce her before stepping into the glowing space—not that anyone was paying attention. The chatter in the room was nearly deafening.

Chandeliers hung from a glass ceiling below a dazzling night sky, and cool wind rippled in from four sets of open balcony doors. The walls were covered in mosaic murals of heroes and villains from Per-Siana myths; The Huma Bird, the Azhi Dahaka, the Peri, the Jinn.

Ryn searched the room for the other Heartstealer maidens first.

Each of them was surrounded by a small crowd, and *five* Intelligentsia hovered by Calliope. She beamed, her smile a velvety crescent of pink. Truly, Calliope was the most beautiful person Ryn had ever known. With dark hair like satin and glassy porcelain skin, she practically glowed in the chandelier lights. Ryn had barely used a hairbrush before coming to the palace; she couldn't imagine ever having hair that shiny.

The other two maidens, Ulita and Lis, stood at opposite corners of the room with their noble friends, and Ryn realized this was the first event where there had been no training, choreography, or order of events; it was strictly social. Her stomach tightened. She had no idea how to be social. If she hadn't promised Xerxes a dance, she might have tried to sneak back out of the ballroom without anyone noticing.

She wandered to a table of refreshments and pretended to study the sugar-coated almonds, dried pomegranates, and chutes of bubbling liquid. She took a glass, lifting it as slowly as possible as she brought it to her lips and sipped. Then, she sipped again. When nothing happened in the room around her, she sipped a third time.

Divinities, this was going to be a long evening.

"Can you spare me a dance, Lady Electus?"

Ryn turned. Warmness bled across the injury in her side when she locked gazes with a pair of dark eyes she only knew from an encounter that left her slashed by a sword. *Damon*. The young Intelligentsia's hood was off now, but he still wore his sage cloak.

"I... Isn't it a rule that no one is supposed to dance until the King has started dancing?" she asked from a dry throat.

Damon smiled, if what he did could be called a smile. His purple mouth curled, but no warmth reached his eyes. There wasn't a single freckle on his glitter-dusted face, and his black hair was as neat and shiny as Calliope's.

"The King has already started dancing," he said.

Ryn glanced past the Intelligentsia and sure enough, there was Xerxes in a special navy jacket with gold details and a dark cape. He even wore a gilded crown inlaid with onyx and diamonds. He held Calliope close, guiding her around the dancefloor while she smiled beautifully with her bright, glistening lips. At the sight of them, Ryn doubted Xerxes had really sent Calliope away the other night like Calliope claimed.

Ryn's glass slipped from her hand—*Damon* caught it. He flashed a smile and lifted it to his own mouth, taking a long drink. Ryn blinked in surprise at herself. "Sorry," she murmured.

Damon chuckled and placed it back on the table. "The King is surprising, isn't he? I didn't think he'd want to come tonight, but it looks like he's enjoying himself," he said, then he extended a hand. "Allow me?"

Ryn looked around, wondering who in the whole ballroom she would talk to if she didn't follow Damon. But of course, there was no one.

She took Damon's hand.

"Hmm." Damon tugged her to the dance floor. "It's strange. At first, I thought the King would only smile at *you*. But it seems he's gotten past that."

Ryn's gaze swept back over to Xerxes. He flashed Calliope a dazzling closed-mouth smile, and Calliope released a soft, feminine laugh in return. Onlookers clapped and nodded, and Ryn was sure she was witnessing the blossoming romance children read about in fairytales. Two glittering young nobles who couldn't take their eyes off each other.

If she wasn't seeing it in person, Ryn might not have believed it. Up until this moment Ryn didn't think Xerxes even *wanted* to get married at the end of all this. He must have changed his mind.

Ryn bumped into Damon's chest. She lifted a hand to her forehead and tried coughing out an apology. "Sorry, I'm just…" Nothing else came after that. She had no explanation for her strange behavior. She closed her mouth.

What, by the Divinities, was she so worried about? Why did she care if Xerxes danced with Calliope first? Or if Xerxes danced with anyone at all? Why did it matter if he smiled at other maidens? It was better this way. Ryn had briefly become the centre of his attention, so if Xerxes liked Calliope, things would only get easier for Ryn. Especially Xerxes being assassinated—

Ryn nearly choked at the thought. She forgot how to keep moving forward, and the lights played tricks on her eyes as the dancefloor went in and out of focus.

She shrieked when Damon pulled her snugly against him, all assassination thoughts vanishing. "What are you doing?" she demanded. She nudged Damon, but he held tight to her waist and studied her with a crooked smile.

"Haven't you been to a dance before, Lady Electus?" he asked. "Don't you know how these things work?"

Ryn took in the room, making a fast study of how the noble women danced. There weren't many other couples dancing though, and she wondered how long it would be before everyone in sight questioned whether she'd ever attended a nobles' dance.

"I wanted a moment with you so I could apologize." Damon guided her a step backward and twirled her beneath his hand. He pulled her close again when she was around. "For attacking you that day. I was only doing my duty to protect the King. You understand."

191

Ryn met his dark eyes against her better judgement. His irises swam with rich, deep brown. It was difficult to tell if his apology was sincere. His handsome features told an unusual story; one that made her sure that even though she could access the power of the Adriel God, she was dancing with a devil.

"I accept your apology," she said. She stole a look at the refreshment tables, wondering if this conversation was over.

A dimple appeared in Damon's cheek when he smiled. "I hope we can be friends then."

Ryn made a face.

Friends?

His laugh rang across the dancefloor, and a few heads turned. "You don't need to be so repulsed by the idea, Maiden," Damon said, and Ryn closed her mouth. He added, "Oh look. The King is dancing with another maiden. I wonder if he's forgotten about you?"

Xerxes was with Ulita. Ryn watched him give Ulita the same smile he'd granted Calliope as he twirled her, Ulita's curls bouncing.

When Damon placed a finger beneath Ryn's chin and tilted her face up, she thought her stomach had fallen out. Damon gazed at her, his face serious. Too serious, and too intense. Their mouths weren't that far apart anymore, but Ryn didn't think he'd dare try something so forbidden. She became aware of people watching, of what they might conclude of a maiden being this close to another man. She impulsively smacked Damon's hand away and tore back.

"Don't touch me," she whispered.

Damon smiled wider, his lips slicing across his pale face. Laughing at her.

Ryn pushed a strand of hair behind her ear as the stares of everyone in the ballroom burned across her neck, her back, and Marcan's beautiful, eye-grabbing gown. She glanced toward the open ballroom doors that led to an empty hall.

Damon sauntered back, his hands in the pockets of his sage coat. She ripped her gaze from the doors when he leaned in and whispered in her ear, "You should get used to running into me."

"Estheryn."

Ryn spun around.

Xerxes stood there. His crown was in his hand instead of on his head, his cape fluttering in the ballroom breeze. He glanced between her and Damon.

Ryn interlocked her fingers so she wouldn't hold her hands against her hot cheeks to cool down. Her mouth was too dry to form a greeting. She kept her gaze on the floor.

Damon gave the King a smile and bowed though. "Your Majesty," he greeted for both of them. "I hope you have an excellent evening." Without being dismissed, he waved at someone nearby and headed in that direction. Xerxes watched him go.

A second later, Xerxes closed his eyes and took in a deep breath. When he opened them again, he tossed his crown at a passing organizer. The organizer fumbled to catch it, barely managing to keep it from smashing over the tiled floor.

Ryn couldn't breathe when Xerxes stepped to her. She placed a hand over her chest. "I feel ill," she said, brushing toward the ballroom door. "I think I should leave—"

"Don't leave," Xerxes said. "Stay with me."

He didn't ask about Damon, or what she was doing so close to him, or why she was flushed. Xerxes just held out his hand, and he waited. He didn't offer her a smile like he'd gifted the other maidens.

His jaw flexed a little when she didn't take his hand. "It's rude to keep a king waiting," he pointed out.

Ryn swallowed. She tried to hide her shaking when she put her hand in his. She didn't know if Xerxes noticed as he guided her over the floor. His fingers tightened around hers. "Be careful around Damon," he warned.

Once in the middle of the room, Xerxes stopped and turned her to face him. He took her waist, keeping a hold on her opposite fingers. Ryn's feet were heavy in her sandals. She waited for him to lead.

"Ryn."

The name snapped her from her daze, and she looked up at him in surprise.

"Can I call you *Ryn*?" Xerxes asked. His mouth quirked at the corner. It wasn't a wide smile—not like the loud, obvious smiles he'd given the other girls. He might have been trying not to laugh. "You can call me Xerxes," he offered. "It's only fair."

"I... Alright." She wondered where he'd heard that nick-name—if Heva had accidentally said it in front of him. But Heva was so careful... How then? Marcan? No, he only called her *Es-theryn*. Ryn chewed on her lip.

When Xerxes smirked like he could read her mind, an unlikely smile threatened her own face. Her feet eased into motion; she followed as he drifted back, pulling her along. The King's dark hair was a stark contrast to the lights above, and the threads in his jacket sparkled as he moved.

"Damon is a troublemaker, and he can be quite convincing when he wants something," Xerxes said. He chewed on the inside of his cheek as he studied her, and Ryn blinked. Did Xerxes really think Ryn had been swayed by Damon just now?

"I don't like Damon—"

"Who do you like then?" he asked, leaning in. The fragrance of sweet fruit and soap swept over her. "Do you like someone else?" And then he added, "*Ryn?*" He paused. "Ryn," he said again.

A grin broke across her face. "Do you like saying my name?"

Xerxes tsked. "Of course not. It's boring. It's only three letters and it's not exciting at all, and it's boring." He bit his tongue, and Ryn laughed.

"How childish of you," she said.

Her gaze fell to his square jaw, the width of his shoulders, his arms. Her smile faded. The first time she saw him in the garden, she thought he was a Folke because of his build. He looked older than her but looks could be deceiving. She wondered if he really was still a child. She wondered if Xerxes had even been old enough to be married when he'd met his first wife.

"How old are you?" she asked, chasing away thoughts of his first wife.

Xerxes tilted his head. "That's rude to ask."

Ryn chewed on the inside of her cheek. "That's the second time you've called me rude tonight. If you think I'm so impolite, Your Majesty, why don't you just send me home?" She flashed him a fresh smile. "Spare me this torture." She nodded down to their 'dance'.

His lips peeled apart. "What...?"

Ryn raised an eyebrow.

He burst out laughing.

His laughter was deep and coarse, the sound pebbling Ryn's skin. Like last time, people whirled, slapped their hands over their mouths, whispered to their neighbours. Those nearby leaned in like they wanted to hear what his laughter sounded like.

"Not a chance," Xerxes said through chuckles. "You're mine, Maiden. Fair and square." He shook his head and nudged her into a twirl. He caught her when she came around.

"It's not fair for me," Ryn pointed out.

Xerxes's smile fizzled away. "Do you still want to leave?" he asked. His hand tightened slightly on her side.

Days ago, Ryn would have had an easy answer to that question. But Kai had abandoned her to this place, and Geovani wanted to use her to fight the gods. Ryn would miss Heva anyway. It was a strange mix of emotions.

"If you want to leave, I'll let you go." His voice was steady.

Ryn's gaze shot up. Xerxes's expression was serious.

She realized they'd stopped dancing. Cool air sailed into the ballroom and brushed across her back as Xerxes adjusted his hand, slipping his fingers between hers and holding her palm tight against his. He leaned in, staring at her with all the seriousness and authority of a ruler.

But the ever-so-slight twitch at the corner of his eyes left her wondering...

He was lying.

Ryn huffed a laugh of disbelief and relaxed her shoulders. "You're a monster," she said. For a moment, she really thought he was going to let her go.

His grin returned. "The sooner you realize it, the better."

Xerxes pulled her in until her cheek fell along his collarbone. His arm wrapped her shoulders like it was the most natural thing in the world. But nothing about the way Ryn's heartbeat picked up speed was natural.

She couldn't remember the last time someone really hugged her. It was unlike being held by Kai, not that Kai had hugged her much. She could hear Xerxes's heart beating through his jacket. She could smell the fragrant soaps his clothes had been washed with. Her throat grew thick, and she held her breath.

The last person who had held her like this must have been her mother.

"Maiden." Xerxes's voice was raspy. He started dancing again, slower than before. When she stole a look up, she caught him glaring at an approaching organizer. The organizer quickly turned around and scurried off.

"I thought you liked calling me *Ryn*," she said.

He paused. Then, "Ryn. I know you heard my voices the day of the Initiation Ritual. Out in the courtyard."

Ryn moved to pull away, but his hand found her back, keeping her pressed against him. Keeping her from looking up at him. Like he wouldn't be able to speak if she did.

"You told them to be quiet," he added in a lower voice. "And they obeyed."

It occurred to Ryn that she hadn't tried to hear his tormentors since. She hadn't had a reason to.

She cleared her throat. "Well, since you think I'm a witch—"

"I don't care what you are." His tone cut through her light-hearted joke. "I don't care if you're a sorceress, if you're here to cast me under a spell, if you truly do have the power of the gods themselves. I don't care if you *are* a god. If you're a goddess of wrath here to trick me and other mortals."

Ryn tugged herself away. She cast him a wild look, but the expression on his face made it clear he hadn't ruled any of those things out.

He said it again, "I don't care what you are."

I don't care.

What you are.

The claim turned itself over in Ryn's mind. He didn't understand what he was saying to someone like her. And what was he thinking, inviting in a goddess of wrath? Legends of men doing that never ended well.

"Are you out of your mind?" she blurted.

He blinked. "Yes. That should be obvious by now."

A moment of silence swept by. This time, it was Ryn who blinked. Over and over.

Of all the things, that particular statement should *not* have been funny. But the corner of Ryn's mouth twitched. What a horrid time to feel laughter bubbling up—

Xerxes pressed his thumb over the corner of her mouth, right where it tugged. "Don't you dare," he warned, but a smile broke across his lips instead as he watched her struggle to keep it in, and despite his efforts, a giggle slipped from Ryn's mouth.

"Divinities," Xerxes cursed. "This was supposed to be a serious conversation." He bit his lip over a grin.

"I'm sorry," she said. "Please, go on with your *serious* conversation."

"Ryn," he tried again, smothering his smile. "Stop it."

She put a hand over her mouth, sealing away her responses, her mouth, and anything else that might get in his way.

Xerxes cleared his throat. His face was straight again when he looked her in the eyes. "I want to make you a deal."

"To leave?" she guessed through her fingers.

"No." The shadow of a smile threatened his mouth again, but it disappeared just as quickly. "To save me."

The humour inside Ryn melted away. Her fingers slid off her lips, her hand falling to her side.

Her mind sailed back to when she stood before a Priesthood, swearing to do their bidding. When she'd agreed to kill a king. For her people—because he was her *enemy*. And despite how many times Xerxes claimed she belonged to him, the truth was she never would. The King would never want an Adriel.

They'd stopped dancing again.

Xerxes's gaze darted back and forth between her eyes. He was holding her hands. She didn't remember him taking her hands.

He spoke again when she didn't reply. "Cure me, Ryn. And in exchange, I'll give you anything. Even up to half of my kingdom if you want it."

Ryn's lips peeled apart.

Half of Per-Siana? Xerxes *was* out of his mind.

The colours in the room bled together. All Ryn could see clearly was Xerxes standing before her; a young King she'd come to destroy, asking her to be the one to save him.

Offering her half the kingdom to do it.

Yes, it was the uttering of a crazy, haunted King. But he was still the King.

Ryn could save the Adriels. She could rescue her people from persecution, give them a safe place to go. And she could do it without killing anyone, or marrying anyone, or any other thing the Priesthood wanted from her.

"What should I say?" she whispered, not sure who she was speaking to.

"Why don't you say yes?"

Ryn's mother had always claimed there was a purpose for why Ryn had been created. What if this was it?

"I'll do it," she said from a dry throat.

They stood in the centre of the great ballroom before hundreds of witnesses, but Xerxes must have forgotten about them. His gaze remained on her as he let his hand slide off her waist, as he set her free.

"I'll give you until the end of the trial period," he said. "Three months."

Three months. The Heartstealer trials would be over in three months. Xerxes would have to choose a queen in under three months. Three months was nothing.

CHAPTER

15

RYN

"El."

...

"How do I make his voices go away?" Ryn squeezed her eyes shut so hard, they hurt.

Water trickled around her knees, soaking up the back of her cream-pink dress and drenching the ends of her hair where she sat in silence, listening to the birds and breathing in the sweet fragrance of the Abandoned Temple.

Per-Siana was a kingdom of temples. Ryn hadn't been inside many before coming to the palace, but she'd passed by them enough. The Mother City temples were made of white stone, sea-blue glass, and gold, and they smelled of Damask roses. Ryn's neighbours grew the same deep pink roses in their gardens and brought them into their homes on the first day of the second month every year for a midnight celebration. Nyx's Day.

Ryn wondered if there was ever an "El's Day." Geovani hadn't said anything like that in her history lessons.

For three days since the dance, Ryn had been visiting the High Priestess whenever she could, but there never seemed to be enough time. Her morning visits to the Abandoned Temple had been briefer too, since the maidens had been required to spend three days studying meal etiquette. The whole thing was a disaster. Three times a day, Ryn found ways to embarrass herself at the table next to the maidens who grew up with wealth.

"Did you hear me?" Ryn asked, opening her eyes and shooting the statue a look. "I *said*, how do I make his voices go away—"

"Adassah."

Ryn's mouth drifted closed.

There was something remarkable that happened when the God Original spoke her name. It reminded her that even though he was a god, the *real* God, he knew her name. He chose to speak to her, despite all his power, the wars he'd won, and his timeless age.

"Well done, Adassah."

A smile spread across her face. She wasn't even sure why. It was silly to sit in the middle of the temple in a soaking dress, grinning like a fool.

When she was little, back before her father had changed, she would climb tall trees and her father would shout, *"Wow!"* at the bottom and clap.

This felt something like that, only better.

"You're going to tell me how to do it, right? Can you give me the formula, or medicine, or whatever it is to make the King's voices go away?" she asked. "I'd like get it over with."

"He will show you how."

Ryn raised an eyebrow. "He? You mean, the King will? Xerxes doesn't know how to get rid of his voices, or he wouldn't have asked me for help. Also—did you hear that part about how I'd like to get it over with? The King promised me half the kingdom."

"Focus on me, Adassah. Not on the deal."

Ryn stood and her soggy dress stuck to her legs. She folded her arms, tapping her toe and splashing water everywhere. "What exactly are you trying to do here? You told me to go to war against the gods. And now I'm going to war against those exact gods tormenting the King, am I not? I'm doing this to save your people. Who are you doing this for?"

"Him."

Him.

Ryn took in a breath to reply but came up with nothing to say. The statue at the head of the temple didn't look like a statue all of a sudden. It looked more like a broken young man needing to be put back together. She'd never noticed before that the statue rested upon a dome of stone slightly above the trickling water.

An island.

Ryn let out a sound of disbelief. "I'm tired," she said as she turned and headed out of the temple. "We can talk tomorrow."

It wasn't until she was halfway to her chambers she realized that the tightness in her back and shoulders had ceased. It was like something heavy had been lifted off them, like a breath exhaling that had been held for too long, and she realized she was relieved.

Relieved that after all those around her had wanted her to kill Xerxes, someone finally wanted her to save him.

The field behind the First Temple was covered in golden wheat, blowing in the wind like a lush carpet over rolling hills. The priestesses said the wheat was used to make bread for the poor, but that hadn't stopped Heva from trampling over it.

"Block!" Heva shouted. Ryn barely had time to stop Heva's sword before it would have chopped her in half. Heva cut clean through a cluster of wheat beside Ryn, sending the seedy heads scattering over the field.

"Easy, Heva!" Ryn scolded. "I'm not as strong as you." She rolled her stiff shoulder. "Can't we take a break? Also, you should think about what the King will do to Matthias if I get hurt."

Heva got a wicked grin. "We should do this in the palace gardens sometime," she said.

"People would see us." Ryn dropped El's sword and fell back to sit. Stalks tickled her cheeks as she uncorked her canteen and guzzled.

"Exactly. Maybe people would think twice before messing with you," Heva said. She raised her weapon in the sunlight, the glow soaring down the blade.

Ryn grunted and wiped a bead of water from her lip. "I'd have to be good at this for them to think twice."

"You're not bad, Ryn," Heva admitted. "I thought you'd be worse."

They'd gone over tackles first. For hours Heva taught Ryn how to outmaneuver a soldier using his strength against him. Ryn wasn't strong enough for most moves, but she had flipped Heva onto her back twice. It made her think about when she'd discovered that Kai and the priests were training in secret. She wondered what Kai would think if he saw her doing this.

"Let's do another round," Heva said when Ryn tossed her canteen aside. "You're going to pick this stuff up fast, I can tell."

Ryn shook her head and pointed to the field's edge where Geovani was wading into the wheat toward them. "The priestesses are here. I think that means we should call it a day."

Heva sighed and slid her sword away. "You and your excuses."

Geovani brushed her fingers over the golden stalks. "Swords were never my thing," she said when she was close enough, "but I do know how to battle." She leaned to see Ryn hiding in the wheat. "Let us show you how we go to battle, Adassah."

"You fight? What weapons do you use?" Ryn asked, tossing her sword to Heva. Heva caught it and sheathed it in the same motion.

Geovani grinned.

Five minutes later, Ryn looked skeptically from priestess to priestess. Heva didn't look happy about it either, but they—along with six priestesses—sat around in a circle in the grass.

Heva scowled when Nebulin started picking her nose beside her.

"This is called intercession," Geovani said to Ryn. "Have you tried it before?"

Ryn crossed her legs. She didn't have to think hard to know she'd never sat in a circle with a bunch of priestesses before. This was weird.

"Let's choose something to intercede for. Any ideas?" Geovani glanced around the circle.

Nebulin raised her hand. "Let's intercede for the kingdom!"

Geovani nodded and tapped her chin. "Excellent, Nebulin. Our kingdom needs us." Then to everyone else, she said, "Does everyone agree?"

The priestesses nodded, and so did Heva—her cheek leaning against her fist in boredom.

"Let's hold hands as we go to war," Geovani said, and Heva shot up, sitting straight again. She cast Nebulin a glare as if to assure her she should *not* try to hold her hand after where it had just been.

Everyone else did though. Ryn reluctantly took Heva's and Kristin's hands at her right and left. "What do we do now?" Ryn asked. She was tempted to ask El what was wrong with all his people that they sat around and held hands for no reason and then called it war.

"We pray," Geovani said. "All together, and all at once. We pray to the First God. The *only* God, some would say."

"I'm ready." Seeda stated as she closed her eyes.

Geovani smiled. "Then begin," she said.

Suddenly six voices lifted: pleading, whispering, and speaking things over Per-Siana. They called for the freedom of the people, for truth to be revealed. Ryn's grip tightened on the hands beside her as her stomach warmed.

"No more pain! No more suffering!" Tears ran down Kristin's cheeks as she spoke it out. Ryn stared at Kristin. The love in Kristin's heart spilled out like a physical force Ryn had never felt. How could a priestess have such love for people who were complete strangers?

"Spirit of fear, be broken off of every household!" Geovani commanded.

Moisture tickled Ryn's face. She didn't let go of Heva's or

Kristin's hands to wipe the tears away. Instead, she glanced over at Heva in question.

Heva's cheek leaned against her fist again, but she was smiling to herself, looking off at the fields. It was like she was back home in exactly the atmosphere she belonged in.

"Heva," Ryn whispered beneath the priestess's prayers. She was ashamed of how her voice cracked, but Heva didn't seem to mind as she dragged her gaze over to Ryn.

"You said you wanted to go to war," Heva whispered back. "Doesn't this feel like war to you?"

Ryn would have never guessed. The warmth spread from her stomach into her veins.

"You're not fighting a battle of flesh and blood. It's not people you're after."

She hadn't understood El's words in the temple that first day. But as the priestesses spoke out their prayers, Ryn looked around with her spirit eyes, and in the distance, she saw shadows shaking, flying off rooftops like they were being torn away. Some dug their claws in and managed to hold on, but it grew harder for them as the priestesses called upon the power of El. In a few places, glimmers of white appeared and overtook the darkness.

It had taken Ryn too long to understand, but it dawned on her as she watched, as she heard, as she *felt*. As she realized the darkness and the light were at war, and the scene before her looked the same as the one Geovani taught from the *In The Beginning* chapter of the old history books.

El never wanted Ryn to fight her way through the palace with fists or a sword. He never wanted Ryn to fight against the King at all or even the Weylins. No, El had said from the beginning that he wanted her to go to war against the *gods*.

Ryn looked up at the sky where the shadows moved the white dragon along. Invisible beings that had wound themselves around unsuspecting people all over the kingdom—including the King.

Nyx. Boreas. Iris.

The gods.

False gods.

It was war.

Ryn was still buzzing with energy when she got back into the palace, back into her room. She paced for nearly twenty minutes until Heva piped up from where she leaned against the wall, "You're going to sprain both your ankles if you keep that up."

"Heva," Ryn said loudly as she tapped a finger against her chin, "if it's a matter of breaking off the King's shadows, then can't I just bring the priestesses here, they can intercede, and his shadows will flee? That's how it works, right?"

Heva sighed. "You're too enthusiastic for me right now." She stepped away from the wall and caught Ryn's shoulder mid-pace. "Your eyes are very wide and you're shouting. Let's go get a snack to calm you down," she suggested.

Ryn shook her head. "But listen—It would work, right? If I brought the priestesses here?"

Heva had been skeptical about the deal Ryn made with Xerxes ever since Ryn told her about it. Maybe this would change her mind.

"I mean, I've seen crazier things happen while hanging around those priestesses," she admitted. "But you know Adriels aren't allowed in the palace. Only Geovani is," she said, and Ryn's face fell. "And if the God Original wants you to help the King, then don't dump it on somebody else. You do it, Ryn. The priestesses can support you from afar."

Ryn sighed and folded her arms. She paced again. "I barely have two months left."

"Geovani always says El's timing is perfect. And Geovani has been doing the High Priestess thing for a lot of years. I trust her when she says stuff like that," Heva said. "Just wait it out."

A loud knock filled the room, and both girls hushed.

Heva placed her hand on the hilt of her sword as she crossed the living space and cracked the door open. She flung it all the way, revealing an organizer—the same one who'd helped Ryn pick her charity.

"Maiden," the organizer greeted. "I'm happy to inform you that tonight you'll be visiting the King for an evening alone with him in his chambers." And then he added, "Overnight."

Heva glanced back at Ryn with wide eyes that said, *"What, by the Divinities, does that mean?"* which only told Ryn, she knew exactly what it meant. Ryn cast her a small shake of her head for assurance. She already knew from eavesdropping that Xerxes wasn't interested in evening visits with the maidens.

"He'll turn me away once I get there," Ryn told Heva as she went to her racks of clothing. "I suppose it doesn't matter what I wear for the walk over if I'll just be back—"

"Actually, he specifically requested that you come." The organizer's statement left a ringing sound in Ryn's ears. She turned back to him.

"I'm sorry, I don't think I understand."

The organizer cast her a knowing smile. "Your artist should be here shortly to dress you up. Your guardswoman and I will escort you to the King's chambers when you're ready." He gave her a small bow, and lo and behold, Marcan came in.

No... Ryn slid back a step—sure she wanted to stay far away from her artist.

The organizer shut them in, and Ryn called after him, "Don't close that door! We don't need you to close the door! I won't be getting dressed—"

Marcan smooshed his hand over Ryn's mouth. "Are you trying to get me in trouble?" he scolded. "I don't want to be here any more than you do."

"Oh, trust me, I think my situation is worse!" Ryn said back.

Marcan smirked. "Yeah, I suppose it is."

"What..." Ryn chewed on her lip. "What do I do when I get there?" she asked, and Marcan looked at her like she was crazy.

"How should I know? Why are you asking *me*?"

Heva bellowed a laugh by the door.

"This isn't funny!" Ryn said. She put the backs of her hands against her hot cheeks. She didn't have enough information to go on, only what she'd gathered outside of Calliope's door. What did a late evening visit entail? She'd thought about it enough to come to her own conclusions, and—oh, for Divinities' sake—she wasn't ready.

"Maybe he'll just want to play mancala." Heva shrugged. "Don't jump to conclusions, Ryn."

It took all of ten minutes for Marcan and Heva to wrangle Ryn into silk nightclothes. It should have taken longer—most events required hours of work, but Ryn didn't feel like playing dress up and she refused every bright piece of jewelry Marcan suggested.

She inhaled deeply during the walk through the palace. Her exhales were loud, and she should have been embarrassed, but she wasn't. In fact, she blew out a heavy breath down the back of Heva's Folke coat when they reached the King's door. Heva squirmed in surprise and sprang to the side. She was voicing silent threats at Ryn with hand gestures, and Ryn was voicing the same silent threats back when the King's door swung open.

Xerxes stood there. He looked between the two arguing women, ignoring the organizer and the guards stationed outside his door. Then, he reached into the hallway, grabbed Ryn, and he pulled her inside with him. He shut the door behind her.

"Wait!" Ryn almost screamed it. She slapped a hand over her face. "I can't do this." Her voice was pitifully strained. "I'm sorry, but I can't. I know you're the King, and I'm getting myself into trouble by objecting, but…"

Raspy, quiet sounds reached Ryn's ears. She lifted her hand slowly and peeled her eyes open.

There Xerxes stood, *laughing*, leaning against his bedroom door like he was trying not to fall over. "Shhh!" he warned with a finger over grinning lips. "The guards outside can hear you! Do you want the whole palace talking about how you refused me?!"

Ryn blinked as she realized he wasn't wearing nightclothes like she was. A fitted Folke guard uniform covered him, complete with a navy cape. She suddenly wanted nothing more than to run away and hurl her nightdress at Heva and Marcan.

Xerxes found his footing and came to stand with her. "I would apologize," he said, shaking the humour from his face, "but I had no other way to get you here without stirring up unwanted attention. And also—" he pointed at her "—that was quite funny."

Ryn's fingers tingled with the urge to poke him or smack him.

"I'd really like to go hide somewhere you can never find me," she admitted through thin lips.

"Was that an official request? Because my answer is no." Xerxes reached for a spare folded Folke uniform on his living space table. He handed it to her. "Put this on."

Ryn took the garment and held it up, wondering why, by the Divinities, he would want her to wear such a thing. He folded his arms while he waited, and so, Ryn looked around his chambers. There wasn't really anywhere to change. There was, however, a collection of ten glorious paintings high on the wall she hadn't noticed when she'd been here last time with her harp. Every one of the paintings was torn or damaged from water, or some other deformation. It looked like he may have even flung water at them on purpose.

Xerxes pulled on the hood of his cape, shadowing his face. "I'll wait outside," he said. "Be quick. And try not to ogle at my painting collection. It's rude." With that, he opened the door and slipped out in the blink of an eye.

Ryn looked down at the uniform. "Divinities," she cursed. She did one full spin around, making sure the room truly was empty. Then she dropped her nightdress and slipped into the Folke uniform, wondering all the while what she was doing this for.

The cape was falling off her shoulders when she came out of the King's chambers. "How lucky I am," she whispered at Xerxes as he turned to see her in the oversized uniform, "to have been specially chosen to spend alone time with the King."

Xerxes adjusted her cape. Then he pulled the hood up and fitted it around her face. Even though two guards stood outside Xerxes's door, they kept their attention ahead and didn't react to the two Folke frauds in their midst.

"Your sarcasm is charming," Xerxes told her, "but I won't be turned down twice in one night." He flashed her a cynical smile. "So come with me." He took Ryn's hand and led her down the hallway, but he dropped it when footsteps sounded around the bend.

Two Folke guards emerged, discussing something in hushed voices. They paid Xerxes and Ryn no attention, apart from a small nod in their direction. After they passed, Xerxes tugged Ryn's sleeve toward an adjacent hall. Moonlight spilled in through tall slat windows in even intervals, washing over them every other step. Xerxes led her to a door barely noticeable within the décor of the walls. She might have not known it was there if he didn't reach for a lever.

He hesitated, his fingers hovering in the air, barely brushing the metal.

Ryn waited, but instead of opening the door, Xerxes turned back to her.

"People don't go down here," he explained. "No one enters through this door except for me. If you're ever caught here…" He didn't finish that sentence, but Ryn filled in the blanks with the look in his eyes. The message was clear: Never, *ever* come here after today.

Xerxes grabbed the lever and pushed the door open. He stepped onto a dark winding staircase, and a cold breeze lifted through the stairwell that sent chills up Ryn's arms as she followed, descending into darkness.

At the bottom of the staircase was a modest arch, and through the arch…

Ryn gasped at the sight of an enormous tree, laden with pears of gold and rich green leaves. She wandered into the room ahead of Xerxes, marvelling at the prettiest fruit tree she'd ever laid eyes upon. Above the tree, a tunnel channelled far up into the palace toward a crystal window that let the moonlight in, making the tree glow.

She reached for the nearest pear, wondering what a fruit of such colour might taste like.

Xerxes grabbed her hand, his fingers wrapping tight around hers. "Don't touch it," he warned. He pulled off his hood, letting the moon light his face.

Ryn dropped her hand and studied the pears. "Are they poisoned?" she guessed.

"No. They're medicine." He glanced at them too, but not in a grateful, admiring way like Ryn. "Medicine for *me*." His throat bobbed when he swallowed. "Even being near them makes me want to…"

"To what?" Ryn realized his hands were balled into fists, his flesh tight.

"To…" He looked at her strangely now. Fearfully. Ravenously.

Ryn took a slow step away from the tree, away from him, and Xerxes slammed his eyes shut.

"Can't you hear them?" he asked. "Can't you hear how the voices go wild when I'm here?"

Ryn looked between him and the pear tree. "I told you I'm not a witch," she said. "I can't just…" But as she looked between the crooked branches, she wondered why she couldn't? She stared at the glistening bark, the shapely leaves, the plump pears…

She saw shadows.

Ryn nearly stumbled backward into the wall at how many there were, at how encompassing the blackness around the tree was;

limbs woven through the branches, strangling the trunk, misting from every fruit. And, Divinities, the voices...

"Kill her!" they shouted.

"Kill the maiden!"

"Kill her before it's too late!"

Ryn dragged her gaze over to Xerxes standing in the same place with his eyes pinched shut. Before, when she'd heard his torment, she hadn't been able to make out clear words. She hadn't realized the anger, and hatred, the fear channelling through his mind. She hadn't realized just how convincing the voices could be.

"Are your voices telling you to kill me?" she rasped, her hand finding the wall at her back.

"Yes," Xerxes admitted. "Always."

When his eyes peeled open, they were bloodshot.

"Are you thinking about doing it?" Ryn's mouth was dry. She wished she'd left the palace. Forget what Kai wanted, forget what Geovani wanted, forget what El was hoping for from her. The King was being tempted to do something terrible to her. *Always*.

"I don't want to," Xerxes promised. "I want the voices to leave. I want to be a king with a sound mind. And I want to save my kingdom from being destroyed by my enemies." He paused, and he glanced at the pears with resentment. "I want back the years I lost while relying on this wretched tree." His gaze cut to Ryn. "You can cure me, right?"

Ryn wasn't sure anymore. A sharp, metallic sound came off the tree, twirling in her ears and growing louder by the second. "Where did this tree come from?" she asked. If Xerxes was consuming fruit that looked like this, wrapped in spirits and false gods, no wonder he was losing his mind.

"The Intelligentsia. The Celestial Divinities had mercy on me for my illness and gifted it to me through them. When I eat its fruit, I'm cured for a little while. Most of the time," he said, looking off.

Ryn released a breath. "So, they gave you the illness, then they gave you the medicine," she remarked, and something in Xerxes's eyes changed.

"What?" he demanded.

Ryn shook her head. "I don't know how to fix you, King," she admitted. "But I made a deal to figure it out. So, I will." Her body buzzed with the desperate urge to leave this basement, to escape these painful noises and the ice-cold air. She frowned at the tree once more. "El," she whispered, calling on the most powerful name she knew. "El Tsebaoth… is coming for you," she warned the gods.

"Ryn!" Xerxes shouted.

A thousand chilling voices screamed. Xerxes grabbed her wrist and tore her toward the staircase. He glared at her as they jogged up. "Why would you do that? Why would you irritate them?" he asked.

"Kill her!"

"Kill her now!"

Ryn shook the dark noises from her head, the chaos from her ears.

They burst from the stairwell into the palace hallway, and Xerxes slammed the door shut. He leaned back against it, pressing a hand over his heart as he caught his breath. "Don't irritate the voices, Ryn," he warned. "Don't do that to me."

Ryn took in his rising and falling chest, his glazed eyes. "You must be exhausted hearing that all the time. I bet you can't even sleep."

Xerxes ground out a despicable laugh. "You have no idea." He pulled himself off the door and turned, gazing down at her with drooping eyelids. "Sleep is one of many things I want."

Ryn raised a brow. "What else do you want? Aren't you the King? Can't you have anything?"

Xerxes took in a deep breath. He studied her for a moment, then he let it out slowly.

He turned and started walking down the hall. "Well, for many years, I wanted to laugh," he admitted. "And then a maiden appeared who started making me laugh all the time."

"Wait." Ryn tilted her head as she scurried to follow. "Are you talking about me?"

He spun, and she almost walked into him. "Of course I'm talking about you," he stated. "And while I'm talking about what I want, I want these Heartstealer trials to be over, and I want to never have to think about spending an entire evening dancing with maidens I can't stand to be around again."

The statement sounded like Ryn was at fault for something, though she couldn't imagine why.

"And I want everyone to stop trying to force me to take another wife," he added, his voice rising. "And I want my kingdom back! And I want somewhere *quiet* I can go in this cursed palace where I won't run into people *all the time*. And I want…" Xerxes realized he was shouting. His chest fell as his wild blue stare settled back on Ryn. Her knees weakened when his gaze dropped to her mouth. But he tore his eyes back up to hers just as quickly. "Divinities, I don't know what I want anymore," he rasped.

He stared at her. She stared back.

Finally, Ryn looked at the floor and folded her arms. "I know of a quiet place where no one in the palace goes," she said.

When Xerxes didn't reply, she took his hand. He remained silent as she led him down the halls, creeping along on her tiptoes and avoiding nearby guards. After a few turns, she ducked into a side passage.

Minutes later, they stood in the narrow arch of the Abandoned Temple.

"It's wet," Xerxes remarked, dropping her hand. "That's why I don't come here."

Ryn stepped inside, letting the water trickle over her Folke boots. "Yes. It's also why *no one else* comes here," she said.

Xerxes's mouth twisted as he eyed the river on the floor, and Ryn chuckled.

"Are you scared of a little water, King?" she asked.

His jaw slid to the side. "You do know I can get you in trouble for referring to me as '*King*', right? The proper address is 'Your Majest—'"

Ryn kicked water at him. It splattered up his Folke jacket, over his neck, and across his mouth, cutting off his words. His eyes widened. "Did you just…"

Ryn flung a hand through the air. "You complain too much."

His blue gaze narrowed, and he was still frowning. So, Ryn kicked water at him again.

Xerxes ducked this time, springing backward through the arch with his arm raised like a shield. He lowered it slowly, dark lashes blinking, a bead of water trailing down his neck.

Ryn wound up to do it a third time, but she waited, giving him a chance to try and talk her out of it.

His jaw clenched. "If you *dare*—"

Water sprayed over his body, soaking his hair, and sprinkling his shoulders. Ryn's laughter soared into the temple heights with the birds, and she slapped a hand over her eyes. She didn't even know she had a habit of taking things too far until this moment.

She dropped her hand. "Fine, stay over there and be grumpy—"

Xerxes grabbed her waist, sloshing through ankle-deep water as he hooked his boot behind hers and kicked out her foot. Her legs buckled, and she dropped. Xerxes must have meant to throw her into the water, but he changed his mind at the last second and held on. His eyes rounded as he sailed down with her, using one hand to brace against the floor and the other to catch her, breaking her fall.

Ryn found herself flat on her back, water leaking into her clothes. A king was over top of her, holding onto her. She lifted her head just high enough that her ears were out of the stream in case Xerxes spoke. His jaw was dropped; his body frozen in place.

A slow smile broke over Ryn's lips as she took in that expression.

When he saw it, the edges of his mouth curled up, too. "Stop that," he warned.

"Not to be *rude* again, but how long has it been since you had fun? Do you even know how, or are you completely incapable?" Ryn asked, and his smile wavered. She made a scoffing sound. "What do you think, King? Is *fun* one of your many wants?"

He dropped her the rest of the way into the stream and flicked a dollop of water into her face. "Not all of us are allowed to have fun, *Maiden*."

"Ah. Is that why no one here has ever seen you laugh?"

His smile vanished at that. "Careful."

Ryn thought about Heva's training in the wheat fields. Sure, the King was built like a Folke, but she quietly raised a leg and hooked it around his anyway. Then she yanked his supporting arm free and rolled.

Ryn came over him, her hair flipping to the side, her hands braced against the floor by his head. Xerxes lay flat in the water, his dark hair floating in the stream that covered his ears. Ryn cast him a shallow smile. He wouldn't be able to hear what she said now.

And so, she whispered, "I like you."

Divinities.

She *liked* him.

Ryn chewed on her lip as it dawned on her. Maybe she hated herself for it.

She'd thought they were opposites in the beginning, but she was wrong. Xerxes was the same as her. He was a boy who'd lost everyone and had grown up with no one to tell him what to do. He was the boy on the island in the story. She was the girl on the island. The only difference was that Ryn had a cousin who'd stepped up to raise her. Who had been there for Xerxes?

Why? Why did she feel all that about the King, of all people? Why had she even said that to him, even if he couldn't hear it?

She realized her smile had left moments ago. She didn't know how long she'd been staring at him, or how long he'd been staring back.

"King..." she began, suddenly worried he'd read her lips or that he could somehow hear below the water. She adjusted to climb off him—to stand. But she stilled when Xerxes rose onto his elbows, his face drawing close.

He pressed his lips against hers.

Ryn's heart leapt in her chest. Drips ran down her cheeks, her mouth wet with stream water. Xerxes raised a damp hand and slid it into her hair. He kissed her lightly, and he sat up, bringing her with him and kissing her deeper, sending trails of water running down into their collars. Ryn's pulse thundered as the air in the room warmed, as the walls teetered, as everything around her spiralled away.

Xerxes slowed his movements. He pulled back an inch, and he hovered there, just a breath away, his chest rising and falling. His fingers were still tangled into her hair.

"Ryn," he whispered, and she could hardly fathom him speaking her name after what had just happened. "Don't ever say that again."

Don't ever say... *That*.

Ryn couldn't move.

Xerxes stood, pulling her up with him. She remained in a trance as he took her hand and led her out of the Abandoned Temple and down the halls, leaving a trail of water across the floors.

He brought her right to the door of her room, and he left.

She didn't remember anything that took place after that. Going inside. Getting ready for bed. Falling asleep. It was all a blur.

CHAPTER

16

XERXES

There was something wrong with that woman.

Xerxes could hardly focus at the council meeting the next morning. He twirled his lead pen over and over, staring at the candlesticks in the centre of the table, hardly remembering they were lit with magic and that the sages who wielded that magic sat around the table with him.

Xerxes had made a practice of reading lips when he was eight—the day he began to suspect the Intelligentsia of working against his father. He never uncovered exactly what instinct it was that made him think such a thing. That had put his nerves on edge and made him suspicious of them ever since. But one could learn a lot when they could read lips from a distance.

"It's Lady Estheryn Electus's charity work," someone said,

snapping Xerxes's attention from the candlesticks. He fumbled his pen—it flew from his fingers, rolling all the way down the table past every single Intelligentsia and councilman, the lead crumbling from the impact and leaving an ashy trail behind. Everyone leaned to look at Xerxes, to see what was wrong with him that he'd toss a pen in the middle of a meeting.

Xerxes cleared his throat and sat straighter in his seat. He didn't apologize. He didn't really want to be here anyway. "Carry on," he said instead, waving a finger through the air.

The Intelligentsia who was talking—Soya—turned back to the councilmen. "Do you know what she asked the organizers this morning?" Soya went on. "She asked if we might provide a special pass to bring those obsolete First Temple priestesses here. *Inside* the palace." For a sage, the man was quite rattled. "Adriels! She's asking us to commit a crime! What is a noble maiden doing hanging around Adriel priestesses to begin with?!"

Xerxes found a slow, terribly inconsiderate smirk spreading across his face.

"It's her charity work, Soya," Belorme said in a calm, articulate voice. "The organizers helped her choose it. I imagine she's just trying to do a good job." But Belorme clasped his hands tightly on the tabletop. The sight of it was glorious, and Xerxes sank in his seat a little, biting back another teensy smile that threatened him before all these people.

Xerxes couldn't have asked for a better outcome for Ryn's efforts than to bear witness to this meeting of frustrated old men.

The Intelligentsia switched to another topic, and Xerxes let out a long, loud, bored sigh. A few heads turned as he rose from his chair. "I have to get to Folke training," he said. And with that, he headed away from the perturbed councilmen and Intelligentsia alike.

"Xerxes," Belorme stopped him.

Xerxes.

Not 'Your Majesty' in front of the whole council. But 'Xerxes'.

As though the King was still just a child. And now the council would see him that way too, due to Belorme's apparent mistake.

"Perhaps you'd be better off if he was dead."

"Will you turn away Lady Lis tonight? I hear you're taking the maidens in now for overnight visits. At least, rumour has it you did last night," the Chancellor said, and Xerxes's skin tightened over his body.

Of course the Intelligentsia would have had informants reporting on his every move. He wondered if anyone had followed him and Ryn when he'd taken her to the tree. He wondered if the Intelligentsia knew he'd shown her that sacred place. He wondered how much he might give away to the council if he appeared rattled now.

Xerxes lifted his head. He turned, and he looked Belorme and the Intelligentsia dead in the eyes one by one as he said, "I did."

"Ah. So, you'll see Lady Lis then tonight?" Belorme asked. "I wonder if I should send Lady Calliope instead? She was quite devastated you weren't feeling well the other night."

Xerxes couldn't stop his glare from cutting through the room toward the Chancellor. His tongue moved to shout at the man to stop meddling, to keep his thick, prying fingers to himself. But Xerxes had gotten used to biting his tongue, even if what he really wanted was to declare to this council that he wouldn't entertain these maidens anymore—that they should all be sent away forever and leave him in peace.

Except for one. One maiden he needed.

Xerxes released a breath, knowing that Ryn was already in Belorme's sights and would be hunted through the palace like an animal if Xerxes wasn't careful. He'd resolved to try and treat all the maidens the same for the next weeks in hopes of keeping the Intelligentsia's curiosity off her. But it pained him to think about giving his attention, his painfully forced smiles, and even his evening hours to the *other* three maidens the Intelligentsia had hand selected for him.

Divinities, he felt sick just thinking about it.

"Send her," Xerxes decided, and a flicker of surprise crossed Belorme's face. Xerxes turned his back to the sages and councilmen, letting them think whatever they liked about his decision. He cared not. This would not be his first time driving a maiden away. What should he do this time around? Would he let himself turn beastly? Would he tear the curtains and scare the maiden half to death? Would he tell her about his voices so she'd run from his room screaming? Would he pretend to be sleeping when she came in and hope she kept her greedy hands to herself?

What was her name again? Calliope?

Xerxes made a sound in the back of his throat. Even her name was hideously elegant, like a lollipop too sweet he wanted to spit from his mouth.

He marched to the Folke assembly room, and when he got there, he announced through his teeth, "Get to the yard, all of you. We're going to train until we're rolling in pain today."

He'd torn his shirt off hours ago, too enraged by the heat to put up with it. Xerxes's skin glistened in the early afternoon sun as he eyed the one Folke he had not faced off with yet; a pink-cheeked blond fellow. Xerxes hadn't noticed him until now; he'd been acutely focused on tossing Folke to the ground—sometimes two at a time. They'd trained right through lunch, and it was clear some of the men were hungry.

Still, Xerxes marched across the yard and stopped before the blond fellow. "What are you doing here?" he demanded. "I thought I gave you a job."

The blond fellow stood a little straighter. "Well, yes, Your Majesty. But then you appeared in the assembly room and said, 'Get to the yard, *all* of you,' and I thought—"

"By the Divinities, I wasn't talking about *you*," Xerxes said. "Has Estheryn Electus been alone all morning?"

The fellow appeared frazzled as he scratched the back of his head. "I imagine her guardswoman is with her."

"You imagine?" Xerxes folded his arms. "What an imagination you have."

"Well, she prays in the mornings anyways in a place no one can find her," the fellow said, and Xerxes's abdomen warmed. He thought about that place—the temple she'd shown him last night. Where he'd…

Xerxes swallowed when he remembered how she'd looked with her damp hair and water running down her cheeks. How she'd whispered to him, her lips shifting with such slow, gentle movements—how he'd kissed her in a fit because of it.

"I like you."

Xerxes slapped a hand against the side of his head. "Ah!" he scowled, and a few Folke looked at him like he was crazy—which he was. "Why," he whispered. "Why, why, why." He dropped to lean his palms against his knees. He closed his eyes and thought about anything and everything else. The wind was nice. There were sounds in the trees. Somewhere in the distance a bird squawked.

"Are you all right, Your Majesty?" the blond fellow asked.

No. He hadn't been all right in ten years.

"I'm fine." Xerxes stood to his full height again. He wanted to find Ryn and make this right so there weren't any misunderstandings. He wasn't a fool easily swayed by pretty maidens, even if they made him laugh, tempted him with fun, and silenced his voices.

He wanted her.

Xerxes smacked the side of his head again.

Divinities curse him for it. He wanted her and he couldn't think of anything else.

Why?

He spun to face the Folke. "Let's end this. I have important things to do," he called over the yard.

The library looked small from the ceiling heights. When there was an irritating stir by the entrance, Xerxes leaned carefully to look over the side of the shelf he hid high upon. He'd only been there for an hour reading a book of short stories he'd read a thousand times before. He sipped water as he scanned the pictures which had been his favourite part as a boy, the sketch of the large, black dragon especially.

There was something about the mighty creature that Xerxes liked. The villagers in the story were afraid of its size when it first appeared over their village. And so, they fetched their clubs and ropes, and they hunted it day and night. But despite their best efforts, the dragon couldn't be tamed or locked away. Every time the villagers tried, it escaped.

Eventually, the villagers grew weary from all the hunting and lack of sleep, and their bones grew brittle in their skin. They gave up trying to trap the dragon, stopping all desperate attempts to put the great beast in a cage.

When the dragon turned and saw no one following him anymore, for the first time in many years, he looked to the sunset instead of constantly watching over his shoulder. And to the villagers' surprise, the mighty creature left, flapping away until it was merely a speck on the horizon.

In the end, after suffering greatly, the village learned that if they'd let the dragon go free from the beginning and had stopped trying to imprison it, it wouldn't have had a reason to continue tormenting them. It would have gotten bored and left long ago.

Xerxes took another long drink of water as he eyed the sketch. He was sure he could draw the dragon by heart now if he wanted.

There was another shuffle at the library entrance, and Xerxes lazily glanced over to see who was responsible for disrupting his reading. He sat up straighter when he saw Calliope sweeping into the library in a dress the Intelligentsia had probably paid for. Not that she needed it. The maiden was likely as rich as Xerxes.

Behind her came the other two—whatever their names were.

Xerxes set his water glass down when he spotted the last

maiden, the one who was convinced he didn't know how to have fun. She wore one of the garments he'd supplied her; a silk red dress customary of the nobles who visited the palace. She didn't look bad in it.

She would soon.

Fun, she'd said? She'd even accused him of being incapable of it.

It was a wonder she even knew how to laugh, considering she grew up poor—or so Xerxes guessed—and had an evil father—which Xerxes had witnessed himself—and was trapped in the palace—which was Xerxes's fault, really.

Xerxes rolled onto his knees in silence and gently closed his book. He picked up his water glass and watched as the maidens travelled around the shelves toward the learning centre. Calliope passed beneath Xerxes. The two nameless ones followed. And then…

Xerxes held out his water glass. He tipped it just as Ryn swept by below.

She stopped walking when the first sprinkle hit her head. She scrunched her nose as she looked around. The other maidens made it through the shelves and disappeared out of sight.

A wide, terrible smile spread across Xerxes's face. He dumped the entire glass.

Ryn shrieked as water splattered into her hair, tumbled down her arms, and soaked her sleeves. She whirled, her gaze climbing up the shelves.

Xerxes slapped a hand over his grin just as she locked eyes with him. And, hand over his mouth, he winked.

Her jaw dropped, deadly accusation crossing her face. With her eyes and a few undecipherable movements of her mouth, she pointed to her wet sleeves and said something along the lines of, *"You're dead, King!"* and *"How am I supposed to explain this?"*

He cast her a feigned pout as if to assure her it wasn't his problem.

There it was—Ryn smiled, just a little. Not a happy smile, but a wicked one that promised he'd suffer revenge beyond his wildest imagination.

And for that, Xerxes leapt from his hiding place and landed in front of her on light toes, grabbing the shelf by her face to catch his balance. He decided to keep his hand there. He leaned toward her and when he spotted a bead of water on her lower lip, he dragged his thumb over her mouth to wipe it off, smearing her lipstick. She gasped, fresh fire lighting her pretty eyes.

"Look what you've done to me," she whispered.

Xerxes smiled.

"Maiden?" an organizer called through the library, and Ryn froze against the shelf. "Maiden? Lady Estheryn Electus?" he called again.

"You'll pay for this, King. Sleep with one eye open," Ryn warned him quietly.

"I don't sleep. Good luck trying to get your revenge." He placed a hand against her back and shoved her toward the learning centre. "And I hope you learn lots of interesting things today about how to become a queen!" he whispered after her.

Ryn pointed back at him. It was a threat. A promise. It was everything.

She turned and marched from the cover of the shelves into the open space of the learning centre. As soon as she did, Xerxes heard the organizer ask, "What, by the Divinities, happened to your dress?!"

"Some ugly, heartless fool splashed water on me," Ryn replied without missing a beat, and Xerxes grunted. He smirked and made a tsking sound as he turned to go.

He took one step around the shelf toward the library door when someone brushed into his path.

Xerxes took in Calliope in her dress fit for royalty. She smiled sweetly at him, and he hated it. He raised a brow at her, waiting.

"Your Majesty. I've been told you summoned me to visit you overnight tonight," she said, loud enough that those in the learning centre area would hear.

Something turned in Xerxes's stomach. He fought the urge to glance toward the learning centre, to see if anyone was watching, to see if anyone had heard—which they all must have. Not that he cared what she—*they* thought…

"I'm looking forward to it," Calliope added. "Aren't you?"

Xerxes worried he'd swallow his tongue if he spoke. He peeked at the scholars by their desks around the library with their ears turned toward him. He thought about how difficult it was to treat all these maidens the same. He thought about why he had to, no matter what, at least make it look a certain way so that *no maiden in particular* would become a target.

And so, he said, "Yes." He pulled a smile across his mouth. "I'm very much looking forward to it, Maiden. I'll see you later."

He tilted his head as he left the library. Being King had made him immune to feeling the gazes of onlookers wherever he went, but for some reason, in this moment, he was aware of every crawling stare upon his back.

CHAPTER

17

RYN

Ryn brushed her hair in slow, even strokes. Every few minutes, she remembered where she was—that she'd been brushing her hair for ages in front of her vanity mirror and she ought to stop. But she'd think about that, and then a second later, she'd start brushing again.

Ryn didn't classify herself as pretty. Kai always told her she was, of course, but he must have felt obligated to. Ryn eyed her tiny nose in the mirror. Her normal-ish cheekbones, her few freckles, and her dark brown hair. Even her eyes were common; most of Per-Siana had deep brown eyes like hers.

Except Calliope. Calliope's eyes were a wild blend of blue and green. They sparkled effortlessly like gems extracted from the rarest caves in the kingdom.

Calliope never returned to her chambers last night. The whole palace was in a buzz about it all morning. Ryn hadn't been able to focus during her morning prayers, and so she'd left the Abandoned Temple and wandered back to her rooms instead.

"It's odd," Heva said as she sprinkled extra sugar over the leftover bread on the breakfast tray. Her feet were up on the table in the living area, legs crossed. "I actually thought the King was starting to have feelings for *you*." She bit into the bread, then with her mouth full, she added, "I know the King is dangerous, but the two of you... Ah. I don't know how to explain it."

Ryn didn't really want Heva to explain what she meant, but the guardswoman rattled on anyway.

"You two are like magnets. You always get pulled toward each other." Another large bite of bread. "For a moment, I actually thought to myself, *'Divinities, he might really choose her. Maybe the Priesthood was right!'*" Heva shrugged. "I guess I was wrong though. My gut was right in the beginning. Calliope was always the clear choice."

Ryn dropped her brush to her lap and leaned her elbows on her vanity, placing her face in her hands. Her huff came out in a shudder, and she worried Heva heard, until Heva said, "It's for the best anyway. He hates Adriels like his father did. It's better if he marries someone else, and then we can stay quiet and not interfere when the B'rei Mira assassins come for him."

Ryn's stomach turned. She slid around in her chair. She needed to tell Heva that she wanted to warn Xerxes, but she hadn't been able to speak much all morning and now was no exception.

Last night, Ryn saw Calliope all dressed up and headed off to visit the King. Ryn wouldn't have believed it was possible before she saw Xerxes and Calliope cross paths in the library. Until she saw Xerxes smile at her—again. Calliope talked about how the King had *personally* summoned her throughout the entire lecture in the library afterward.

Ryn had never felt more humiliated. She cursed the moment she'd uttered such forbidden words to Xerxes in the Abandoned Temple. How could she assume he wouldn't know what she was saying just because his ears were under water?

She lifted a finger to trace her lips. The way he'd kissed her though…

Flutters moved across her stomach.

Maybe his kiss was impulsive. Maybe he regretted it, and inviting Calliope to his chambers in front of her was his way of telling Ryn he didn't like her back.

What was she thinking allowing feelings to appear for him anyway? For a moment, she'd forgotten he was a king, powerful enough to have every one of her people hunted down and killed with the snap of his fingers. Ryn was ashamed she'd let her guard down simply because he was young and said he needed her. That one, single person had the power to have everyone she knew and loved slaughtered on a whim. There was a reason Kai thought Xerxes should be killed.

Ryn turned back toward her mirror, feeling uglier than ever. Inside. Outside. When she looked at her reflection, all she saw was a naïve girl who'd been too desperate for a friend and too presumptuous around a king. She'd agreed to return to this palace for the Adriel people, and for the Priesthood. She'd agreed to shake up the false gods with Geovani, and in turn, had agreed to follow El.

But then she'd agreed to help Xerxes be free of his voices.

Ryn dragged her fingers into her hair. She wanted to race back to the Priesthood where it all began and tell them they were wrong about her. Yet, until she found a cure for the King, she knew she had to stay.

"Let's go to the First Temple," Heva said, standing and brushing the crumbs off her Folke uniform. "Apparently there's another Heartstealer event in a few days, and all charity work will be put on hold soon for preparation. Let's stay with the priestesses until dusk tonight since it'll be our last chance for a while."

Ryn could not have agreed more. She didn't want to still be around when Calliope finally returned to her chambers in all her glory.

Geovani shared her favourite stories of ancient Adriels all afternoon. The air in the First Temple came alive with her tales. It was exactly the sort of distraction Ryn wanted. She found herself laughing at the old woman's animations.

The priestesses dined together afterward. Geovani prayed to the God Original, and everyone ate fresh grapes from the local vineyard and hot bread straight from the ovens dipped in oil and herbs. Minutes in, Kristin accidentally spilled oil on Seeda's priestess gown, which triggered a food fight that lasted for nearly an hour and had every priestess in the temple—along with Ryn and Heva—scrubbing walls and floors until the sun went down. They thought it was over until Seeda lobbed a handful of squashed grapes into Heva's hair.

Ryn grinned through the whole thing. She was grateful for it all, even the labour. Even the mess she became, with a grape-stained dress and her hair dripping oil.

Everyone was exhausted by the time the First Temple was clean. Ryn hadn't worked so hard to clean anything in a while. She rubbed the tightness out of her lower back as she and Heva came outside to the startled blinking of their six accompanying Folke guards.

"Are those… grapes?" one of them asked as he pointed to Heva's hair.

"Mind your own business," Heva warned, then she moaned. "I forgot my sword! Wait here," she said to Ryn as she jogged back into the First Temple. Voices arose from inside a second later and it was clear she got into another argument with Seeda.

Ryn sighed and shook her head.

Cool wind ruffled the wheat in the field as she glided into the stalks to wait. She wanted a minute alone anyway. Apart from her short time in the Abandoned Temple, Ryn hadn't been alone all day.

She looked up to the stars where the white dragon did its serpentine dance and the crystal night had grown black and hollow. "El," she whispered to the sky, "can't you get me out of the palace? Can't you summon a great miracle like you did in the ancient days of the Adriels?" A cold breeze brushed along her face. "Must I stay?"

Ryn imagined her mother standing in this field. Unlike Ryn, her mother's eyes had been a light toffee, warm and inviting. If her mother were here, she would have said something like, *"You were created for a purpose, Ryn."*

Tears threatened Ryn's eyes. She wished her mother really was here, and it wasn't just all in her imagination. Still, she asked, "Why would you say such a thing?"

Her mother might have smiled at the question like the answer was obvious. *"Because what if this is it?"*

Ryn thought about Geovani's words the second time they met. Geovani had claimed every single one of El's people were free, whether they were stuck here or living in glory at his side.

"Where are you, Mother?" Ryn asked the phantom woman before her.

"Ryn." Ryn imagined her mother taking her hand. She wished she could feel real flesh against her own, instead of the empty embrace of the cold wind. *"Be courageous. What if this great task is what you were created for?"*

Things hadn't died down at the palace. Music lifted from the courtyard where nobles were having a nighttime Celestial revelry with hired dancers, but Ryn was so tired from scrubbing down the First Temple that she fell onto her bed without changing into her nightdress. She was asleep in minutes.

CHAPTER

18
RYN

Ryn awoke to Matthias gently shaking her shoulder. "Ryn," he said. "I was calling for you outside, but you didn't answer."

Ryn lifted her head from her pillow. She scanned the room with tired eyes until she spotted Heva snoring on the couch in the living space.

Matthias held up a card of thick, glossy paper. "The organizers were here. I wouldn't let them in without your permission though, so they left this." He passed it to her.

Ryn rubbed her eyes and took the card. When she unfolded it, gold letters glimmered across the page in the Weylin alphabet. She flipped it over. There was nothing on the back. "What is this?"

Matthias scratched his head. "Well, the organizers wanted to explain the rules to you themselves, so I kept calling, but… Anyway, I think I got the basics out of them on my own. It's for your first match."

"Match? Like a duel?"

"A *theoretical* duel. It's a contest," he explained.

Ryn climbed to her knees. "You mean there are actually *trials* in the Heartstealer trials? I thought that was just a flashy name."

"Let me read it for you." Mattias took the card and cleared his throat. "Trial Card: A Battle of the Senses. Sound, Touch, Smell, or Taste." He tossed the card aside. "You need to pick one of the five senses, except for sight. So, no paintings or anything. And you need to present a skill to the King to try and capture his interest. I suggest you play the harp. Sound is a lovely choice." Matthias smiled. "It's the day after tomorrow, so you'd have plenty of time to practice."

Ryn huffed in disbelief. Xerxes wanted all the maidens to try and impress him? That didn't sound like him at all.

Although… she wasn't sure she knew what he wanted anymore.

"He's going to be blindfolded," Matthias went on. "That's why you can't choose sight. You have to appeal to one of the other senses."

Ryn dropped the note to her lap. "Blindfolded?"

Blindfolded…

The room tilted as that settled in. Kai's letter said the King would be blindfolded on the night B'rei Mira spies would assassinate him.

"Why do you look so pale?" Matthias asked. "Are you all right, Ryn? Do you want me to get you a cup of water?"

Ryn glanced up at her friend. Her oldest friend in these palace walls. He hadn't put the pieces together yet, she realized. It hadn't crossed his mind that whatever trial this was, it was happening on the same night the B'rei Mira soldiers were coming. And as Ryn saw the soft flush of Matthias's cheeks, and the kind look in his eyes that made her wonder if he'd ever had to raise a sword against someone, she decided it was better that way.

"Matthias," Ryn said, folding the card and setting it aside. "I think you should stay back from this contest. I have something for you to deliver to the Priesthood anyway, so you can go that night since I'll be... *safe*... around hundreds of people."

Matthias shrugged. "Sure. What is it?"

Ryn's face changed; she hadn't thought that far. "I'll... let you know."

Her lie was too obvious. Matthias studied her for a moment, then he grinned. "Why don't you want me to be there, Ryn? Are you going to flirt shamelessly with the King? Are you worried I'll be repulsed?"

A hot blush hit her face. "Absolutely not!" She grabbed her pillow and threw it at him.

Matthias snorted a laugh and waved her off. "You should bathe, Ryn," he advised as he headed to the door. "You smell like rotting food."

Ryn glanced down at her dress from yesterday, stained with grape juice and shiny splotches of oil. She lifted her skirt and sniffed it.

Divinities, she did need a bath.

She slid off the bed, snuck past snoring Heva, and followed Matthias outside, gently closing the door behind her.

"You're going to the baths alone?" Matthias asked. "What about Heva?"

"She's exhausted. You should have seen what we did yesterday. And it was twice as bad for Heva because she spent the whole day yelling on top of everything." Ryn smirked as she remembered. "I'll slip to the baths and return before she wakes."

"I'll accompany you," Matthias decided.

"No! Matthias, you can't accompany me to the *baths*." She rolled her eyes. "Just stay here. I'll be right back."

Matthias looked unsure, but he stepped back to his post outside her door.

Ryn headed down the hall toward the women's bath chambers, listening to the chatter seeping down the hallways from the atrium. She ignored it as she rounded the bend. Her arms and legs were itchy from the dried fruit juice, and she wondered what sort of condition her bed was in after she'd slept in it like this.

"Maiden." Ryn looked up as she entered the atrium. She was at the edge of the great glass room, not in everyone's view, but where enough people could see her. She crossed her arms to hide her spoiled dress and kept her head low.

Damon stood there, eyeing her attire. "Did you roll around on a table of food?" he guessed.

Ryn took inventory of those nearby. She stepped left so the fountain would obstruct the view between her and a group of nobles. "It's none of your business," she said. "I'm on my way to the baths. Excuse me." She moved to pass him, but Damon took hold of her sleeve. She lurched to a halt when he didn't let go and her sleeve nearly slipped off her shoulder and revealed her bare skin to the room.

A choice word burned on her tongue as she turned back, but the words locked in her mouth when she found Damon hovering close, his purple lips right by her ear.

"Are you trying to run away from me, Lady Estheryn?" he asked quietly. He tugged her sleeve again, forcing her to brush up against him so it wouldn't slide off.

The servants throughout the atrium parted, standing at attention. Ryn's gaze snapped to them, and her gut recoiled when she spotted Xerxes coming their way, his brows furrowed, his jaw set. It was the first she was seeing him since...

Since...

Ryn took hold of her sleeve and yanked, but Damon held tight. She glanced to the hallway, toward her chambers. The sage bit back a smile and leaned in ever so slightly like they were sharing a secret. He did nothing else; he just stayed that way.

Xerxes passed by them. He looked indifferent, focused on something else. It was just the brief dart of his gaze over to Damon's back that made Ryn flinch.

Xerxes's stare was ahead again when he marched out the front doors of the palace and into the gardens with several dozen Folke trailing him. Ryn's shoulders dropped in relief. He hadn't seen her while she was such a mess, hadn't spotted her this close to Damon and formed the wrong idea—not that it mattered, she realized. Xerxes had gotten serious about choosing a queen, and Ryn was just the maiden he needed for a cure.

Ryn leaned forward to peer out the lobby's front entrance where he left. No, she hadn't wanted him to see her. But still, her chest grew hollow when she thought of how he hadn't even noticed she was standing right there.

She tore Damon's fingers off her sleeve; he let it go this time. A slow, crawling smile found his mouth. "Enjoy your bath, Maiden," he said. It left a dirty feeling over Ryn's skin as he turned and left.

She shuddered and headed for the baths, not stopping again even when servants noticed her dress and asked her questions.

She spent two hours scrubbing herself clean, and still never felt clean enough.

The air grew chilly. Rising winds dried Ryn's hair as dark storm clouds rolled over the garden. Rain covered the Mother City in the distance, and it would reach the palace soon—the distant echo of pattering drops swept in.

"El," she whispered. "Tell me how to silence his voices so I can leave."

The wind was too loud for anyone to hear her prayers, even if others had been in the garden.

A warm, breezy embrace surrounded her amidst the cold. She closed her eyes, letting it soothe her aches and worries.

"It's not about his voices, Adassah. It's about all the other things you'll do first."

She opened her eyes and chewed on her lower lip. Then she tugged at her damp hair.

"Ryn!" Heva called from her chambers window high above. "Come up for a fighting lesson!"

"Here?" Ryn asked in dismay.

"In your rooms! It's not like we can go to the First Temple anyway! And it's going to rain soon so the garden will be full of mud—"

"All right, all right! Just stop shouting!" Ryn waved at her. She looked around the garden for witnesses, then she climbed back up to her rooms.

"Which skill are you choosing for the senses trial?" Heva asked as Ryn pulled herself over the windowsill. Heva fetched El's sword from the wardrobe and went to a large woven sack on the floor. She opened it and began pulling out armour plates.

"I don't know," Ryn admitted. "What's all that?"

"It's my spare armour. I'm not going easy on you this time," Heva stated, "so you should wear this. Otherwise, everyone at the senses trial will wonder why you're covered in bruises."

Heva threw a pauldron at Ryn before she was ready. It flew past and smacked off the bedpost, sending a loud ringing sound through the room.

The door tore open, and Matthias rushed in. "What happened?" he asked, and Heva grinned.

"Nothing, Priest. Just stay outside and make sure *no one* comes in for the next hour," she said.

Ryn stifled a moan and rolled her shoulder as she headed through the winding halls toward the Abandoned Temple. The whole palace smelled of baking ginger cookies. Whispering servants claimed they were for a traditional celebration relating to the royal family, but Ryn knew nothing about it.

She passed a domed window feature, and the late afternoon sun burned against the glass, momentarily blinding her as she moved into the next hall, squinting and rubbing her eyes. Not even a torch was lit to warn her what was waiting on the other side.

She walked into someone leaning against the wall. "Sorry—"

Hands took her waist, lifting her and placing her on her feet with her back against the stone in exactly the spot where the person had been standing. A dark silhouette blotted out the orange sun in the dome, and Ryn froze, blinking rapidly when her eyes didn't adjust.

"You should watch where you're going."

Xerxes's voice.

Ryn realized she'd grabbed his sleeves like she'd been ready to toss him aside and run for her life. She wondered what she was so afraid of, but she shook her head when it occurred to her she'd imagined an Intelligentsia hood, thin purple lips, and dark eyes.

She glanced up, able to make out Xerxes's features now. She was still squeezing the life out of his sleeves. He looked irritated about it.

Ryn dropped her hands. "Sorry," she rasped again. She inhaled quickly and let it out just as fast. His face didn't change from its frown, his pulled-together brows, his hard jaw. A strange coldness drifted from him, encompassing her like she'd stumbled into a dark cellar.

He didn't speak for several more seconds, and she couldn't take it. "Is this about Damon?" she asked.

He blinked. A few times. "What about Damon?" His expression morphed into an odd mix of things she couldn't interpret anymore.

"Well, he and I..." It occurred to Ryn that Xerxes really might not have seen anything in the atrium. "Nothing," she said, waving a hand between them.

Xerxes was quiet for a moment, but after several more seconds of hard staring, he drew away and let out a huff. He put his hands on his hips and began to pace. "I'm angry, Ryn," he said. When he turned around to wander back, his eyes were closed, a crease on his forehead. "You shouldn't be here."

She noticed his collar was scuffed, his royal coat was undone, his boots were only half laced. She hadn't been able to tell before in the darkness, but now that she could see him, he looked a little bit... monstrous.

"Why are you angry?" she dared to ask.

"Because everyone lies to me," he said. "I can't trust the people here. I can't stand liars."

Ryn closed her mouth. When would Xerxes figure out that a liar stood right in front of him?

"Do you want me to leave?" she asked in a small voice.

Xerxes took in a deep breath and let it out slowly. "Honestly? No," he said. He folded his arms and settled his miserable, pointed gaze on her again.

Ryn swallowed. "What do you want to do, then?" she asked.

He didn't avert his stare. "I just want to look at you, Maiden. To prove to myself that you're real and not a figment of my delusions. Because if you're real, there might be an end to this torment soon, and all I have to do is hang on a little longer." Ryn's heart squeezed. She'd been so distracted by everything; she'd momentarily forgotten that he'd begged her for help. "But most of all," he went on, "I want to go steal those cursed cookies." He unfolded his arms and resumed his pacing.

Ryn thought he was joking, but his frown didn't waver. He glared in the direction of the kitchens where the smell of baking came from. And Ryn couldn't stop herself—she laughed.

He tore his gaze back to her again, a look of shock etched over his features. He watched as she slid down the wall a few inches, losing her balance. As she slapped a hand over her mouth to quiet herself.

"How many?" she finally asked when she could speak. "How many cookies do you want to steal, I mean?"

Xerxes bit his lips together. The shadow of a smirk found his mouth. The ominous glaze had left his face—In fact, there was a twinkle in his eye when he leaned toward her and whispered, "All of them."

It wasn't easy to sneak into the kitchen without anyone noticing, but the hardest part was rolling out two carts piled with baskets of cookies before the guards did their rounds or the kitchen staff emerged from the break room. Only three baskets remained inside the kitchen, and Xerxes and Ryn risked the journey back in to get them.

They bumped into each other on the way out, and Xerxes dropped a basket to the floor. Two dozen cookies shattered and bounced away, and he looked up at Ryn with wide eyes. "Run," he whispered. He grabbed her hand and tugged her out the swinging doors just as the staff door screeched open across the kitchen.

They each took a cart and fled down the halls, the metal wheels squeaking and rattling from the weight. "This way!" Xerxes veered into an unlit passage.

Ryn's heart raced; it would be one thing if the King was caught stealing from the kitchens, but it would mean something else entirely if she was caught. She grinned as they veered around a bend and came to the foot of a spiral staircase.

Xerxes grabbed the baskets from his cart and two from Ryn's, and he darted up the stairs with them. Ryn took her remaining baskets and chased him up, their tapping footsteps echoing through the narrow space.

They emerged at the top of an outlook tower. Heavy winds stole Ryn's breath, tossing her hair from her shoulders. The storm hadn't let up yet, and rain pattered over the glass palace below.

Xerxes dropped his baskets, letting them spill over the ground, and he grabbed a cookie. He hurled it into the storm. "This is for you from your King, Per-Siana!" he shouted. "Enjoy it!" He grabbed a basket and flung the whole thing from the tower next, sending a sprinkle of soggy chunks onto a glass roof below.

Ryn sighed and took a cookie from her own basket. She bit it while she watched him release his wrath upon the baking.

Xerxes unleashed a roar over the city, a spiteful laugh mixed with a victorious sound that rivalled the thunder crackling in the heavens. His navy coat fluttered in the wind as he staggered back, his chest pumping while he caught his breath.

His face changed when he noticed Ryn. "Don't eat them." He walked over and tried to flick the cookie from her hand, but she maneuvered out of the way, and he huffed. "They're cursed. I told you that," he said.

Ryn raised a brow and licked the crumbs from her lips. "But they're delicious."

Xerxes's mouth twisted in contemplation. "Fine." He took a cookie, stared at it, then he ate it in two bites. "But the rest of them must die," he said from a full mouth. He lifted two more baskets and dumped them down the side of the tower where they smacked the same roof below and melted in the rain.

Ryn leaned against the rail on her palms. She could see the whole Mother City from this high up. She could almost spot the hills surrounding the village she grew up in with her mother and father too. Her gaze dropped to the spoiled cookies littering the palace roof when she thought about that. Her home village was a harsh reminder of what she was, and that the King beside her hated Adriels.

A slow, ferocious urge lifted through Ryn's chest. She eyed the baskets of cookies. She found herself grabbing one and throwing it with all her might into the rain like Xerxes had. She imagined it splattering against the faces of those who would see her dead, all those who continued to persecute her people in the kingdom, and all those she had to hide from in the palace. She didn't mean to imagine Kai among them, but the moment she pictured her cousin out there, she grabbed a handful of cookies and threw them at him, one by one. He'd sent her here. He was the reason she was in this position. He hadn't stopped her from coming back to the palace even though it could mean her death. He chose the Priesthood over her. Divinities, he *abandoned* her. Ryn threw a cookie with every ounce of strength as a tear broke loose and warmed her face.

A silent sob escaped, dissolving into the noise of the storm. Because she didn't hate Kai. She loved him.

That was why it hurt more.

As she watched her last cookie descend over the side of the palace, she traced the trajectory and gasped. "Oh no…" She looked around the tower for a place to hide and dropped to her knees behind the rail as the cookie splattered onto the head of a passing Folke guard.

The guard spun around far below, drawing his sword, and Xerxes's coarse laughter erupted through the tower. Ryn giggled, smacking a hand over her mouth as she peeked over the rail from her hiding place. The guard started running through the garden like he was chasing someone and disappeared into the orchard.

Xerxes tossed the last basket away. He breathed a long sigh of relief and leaned out the opening, sticking his head from the cover of the tower just enough for rain to drizzle into his hair.

"What were those cookies for anyway?" Ryn asked.

"You don't know?" Xerxes panted, drawing himself back. He dragged a hand through his messy, damp locks. "Every Weylin knows why we make ginger cookies in the seventh month. Didn't you ever have to sing that terrible 'ginger song' for the King's prosperity when you were a child?"

The blood drained from Ryn's face. She turned toward the city, away from Xerxes. "Ah. Right," she said, her fingers gripping tight to the rail.

She heard him chuckle behind her, his foot scraping over the stone floor as if he was nudging cookie crumbs around with his toes.

"Ah. That relieved more stress than even the drills I've been doing with the Folke," he admitted.

"What are you training so hard for?" Ryn asked.

When he didn't answer, she dragged her gaze back to find his smile vanished. The lightness that came with destroying the cookies had left, replaced by the dark look he had before in the hall. "I did a bad thing," he said. His throat constricted. "And I think very soon, I'll pay for it."

Ryn's toes curled in her sandals. She never dreamed she'd be standing this close to the King of Per-Siana in her lifetime back when she first heard the rumours about his wife. She was too afraid to ask now—too afraid to learn the truth and have this image of the boy before her be destroyed. But she knew she couldn't go on anymore without the truth. Divinities, he'd asked her to *save* him. Whether it was what El wanted or not, how could Ryn do that if she didn't know who she was saving?

"What happened, Xerxes?" Her voice came out dry even with the humid air. "What did you do?"

Xerxes closed his mouth. For a split second, Ryn regretted asking, worried he was angry. He pulled his gaze off her and settled it on the city. She thought he wasn't going to answer, but after several moments where the only sound was the rain slapping over the glass roofs below, he said, "I never went near my wife. Not once. Not even at the wedding. I didn't care what the people thought of me."

Bumps formed over Ryn's arms, and she hugged them to herself.

"I hated her," Xerxes whispered. "I hated everyone. She was working against me, forcing my hand at every turn. She thought I didn't know she was manipulating the council, pretending to be my voice to get what she wanted, having anyone who stood in her way executed in my name." His throat bobbed. "There are times when I think she deserved what happened to her. I just wish it hadn't been me who did it."

A gust of wind slithered through the tower. Ryn shivered and tightened her grip on her arms, trying to keep still. Trying not to draw attention to herself as the weight of this moment pressed upon her like a boulder inching its way down from the heavens.

Ryn wasn't sure what to ask next, if she should even speak. Xerxes turned, angling himself away from her. His hand found the balcony rail, and Ryn realized he was trembling.

"I swear, I never went near her. She wasn't even allowed to enter my room. That's why it didn't make sense when I awoke that morning and found her beside me…" His eyes glazed over, like he was seeing something Ryn couldn't. "I don't remember doing it."

Ryn exhaled softly. "Maybe you didn't," she said—the first words she was able to utter in response.

Xerxes cut her a look. "I did. I know I did. It's not the only time I've lost control of myself," he said. "And I knew full well she was sent here by the War King of B'rei Mira to spy on me, and that she was cruel, and that she only wanted to see Per-Siana citizens die. I had reasons to *want* her dead." He moved from the rail and took a step toward Ryn. She fought the impulse to move and stay out of his reach. "You should be more careful around me, Ryn," he said.

The wind blew the storm against them, and Ryn tasted rain.

Xerxes's story wasn't what she expected. Based on the rumours, she thought she'd meet a king who went on killing rampages, who was a poison to the kingdom, and who lacked a heart. But Xerxes wasn't any of those things. Even if his heart had been burned a few times, it was there. It was beating.

"I trust you," she said, surprising herself. "I think I trust you with my life, King."

His lips peeled apart, a bewildered and horrified expression finding him. He shook his head slowly. "You foolish maiden," he whispered.

Somewhere in the distance a temple bell rang over the streets. Ryn stared at Xerxes. Xerxes stared back.

Finally, he swallowed and dropped his gaze. "If you ever see me and my flesh is deathly pale or gray and my skin glimmers with moisture... Run. It doesn't matter what I say to you in that moment, even if I try to convince you to stay, just run."

"Why?" Ryn rasped.

"Because I need you alive. You're the only one who can silence my voices."

The words rattled in Ryn's mind, eating their way through her, slowing her heart to a dull beat.

He needed her alive.

He needed her... for his voices.

She realized she'd crossed a line in asking about his wife. She'd already been foolish enough to tell him she liked him in the Abandoned Temple, only to have him invite Calliope to spend the night with him shortly after. Only to watch him give smiles to all the maidens—which was his right as King. As a young man searching for a wife.

Ryn linked her hands together, feeling more foolish than ever. She looked at the stone floor as it dawned on her all over again that he was a powerful King, and she was just a maiden he needed. The shattered cookies on the ground reminded her how easily things were broken. How fast something sweet could be ruined by reckless thinking. That pain was just a consequence of carelessness.

Suddenly his warning for her to be more careful around him felt reasonable.

The three months he'd given her for their deal were dissolving quickly. After only a few more weeks, Ryn would have either cured him or failed. Either way, she'd probably never see him again—unless he decided she needed to stay at the palace for some other reason, which would be horrifying if she was forced to watch him parade through the atrium each morning with his new wife.

"Will you still need me once the voices are gone?" she asked.

Xerxes's brows pulled together. He opened his mouth, then closed it again. "No," he seemed to realize.

"So, you'll let me go? Once you're cured?"

He had no response ready for that. Seconds passed before he said, "I suppose I will. If that's what you want." His jaw slid to the side.

Ryn nodded.

She had to focus on saving her people. The only reason she came to the palace in the first place was for them. "I want to add something to our deal," she said. "I want you to promise me no harm will ever come to Matthias."

Xerxes looked at her blankly. Then he asked, "Who's Matthias?"

Ryn folded her arms and huffed. "The extra Folke guard you stationed outside my door," she told him, baffled Xerxes hadn't even learned Matthias's name when he'd been threatening him. "Matthias is an old friend. And if I'm going to help you, I need to know my friend is safe, no matter what. He's the only friend I have here." The corners of Xerxes's mouth tightened when she said that. "And I want you to send him on an errand—somewhere far away from the palace—during the Heartstealer senses trial."

Xerxes raised a brow. It didn't look like jealousy. Curiosity, maybe. Even so, all he said was, "Fine. I'll keep your guard safe."

"With your life?" Ryn pressed.

Xerxes made a face and folded his arms too. Ryn knew she was making a preposterous request. But to her surprise, Xerxes said, "Yes, with my life, I shall keep that fellow safe for you."

Ryn relaxed and nodded. "And about the senses trial where

you'll be blindfolded…" She inhaled a light breath as she thought about the assassins. If Xerxes died—she could hardly think about that—her deal would fall through, and she wouldn't inherit half the kingdom and save the Adriel people. But…

Would he be angry she'd known all this time and was only telling him now? Would it break the delicate trust they'd built? And worse, would the King demand to know where she got her information from? What if Ryn was dragged away as a suspect? Would she utter the names of the Priesthood under interrogation? What if she gave up Kai?

A headache formed behind her eyes. She rubbed her temples, and a strand of her hair broke loose.

"What about the blindfold trial?" Xerxes asked when she didn't finish. He unfolded his arms and took a step toward her, eyeing the strand of hair over her face. He raised a hand slightly, but he pulled his fingers in and dropped it back down again.

Ryn met his gaze. Despite all the things she felt since entering the tower, she couldn't imagine those dark blue eyes lifeless and cold. Yes, she would save Xerxes from those assassins. She would ensure he wasn't killed that day, she would complete their deal, and she would inherit half the kingdom for her people.

But she could not tell him. She would find another way.

"Ryn," Xerxes said when she didn't answer. He bit his lips and squinted his eyes. "That blindfold trial will be the death of me," he remarked, and Ryn nearly choked. "I'm going to have to sit there with my eyes covered like a fool. I have to endure whatever nonsense the maidens come up with, and I'm only supposed to take the blindfold off if I'm truly entertained to give my approval. I hate the thought of it," he admitted. Then he guessed, "Will you play your harp?"

Ryn shook her head. "I'm not sure what will happen to the gods in the room if I do." She didn't explain.

A devilish smile tugged on Xerxes mouth. "Give me a hint then, so I'll know when it's you."

"Never." Ryn fought an untimely smile. "You'll have to guess."

"*Ryn*," he urged, dragging in another step.

There they were, smiling at each other. Again.

By the Divinities, Ryn was sure she'd be responsible for her own demise if she kept letting him smile at her like that. She thought about what Heva said, *"You two are like magnets. You always get pulled toward each other."*

There was a reason for that. Xerxes was a boy on an island, after all. He was a boy who saw a ship passing by with Ryn on it. He'd found a way to escape the poisonous sea.

She had no idea if her ship was about to sink with both of them on it.

19
KAI

The storm swallowed the Mother City whole. Rain pattered over the Navy Road, turning it slick and forcing the silver carriages to slide off course. Per-Siana citizens rushed indoors to escape the downpour, leaving most of the streets empty of souls.

Apart from two.

Kai followed the B'rei Mira spy, rain drenching his black cloak that shadowed his face and concealed his green robe of the Priest-hood. He hadn't taken his sights off the man for days. He'd hardly eaten as he crept into revelry taverns to listen, as he hid behind temple pillars, as he dangled from rafters—all to eavesdrop on these intruders who had come to cause mischief in Per-Siana. He'd written down as much as he could interpret of their objectives, but some things he couldn't understand. The B'rei Mira language was a complex linguistic challenge, even for him.

The intruder entered a bed house up ahead. Kai climbed the

side of the building to spy into the room. When he was sure the man had fallen asleep for the night, Kai leapt from the windowsill, back onto the muddy road, and ran for the Priesthood Temple.

The grass was heavily watered when Kai reached the temple and swept around to the back door. He knocked, and Jonathan opened it immediately to let him in.

"Saturn has been waiting for you for hours," Jonathan informed him.

Kai sighed and marched through the temple to the great room. Only a few torches were lit—most of the priests had gone to bed, but Saturn stood by the fireplace, watching the flames.

"It's nearly time. B'rei Mira will strike at the palace soon. I don't think they have the numbers inside the kingdom to send an army; I think they plan to infiltrate quietly. Possibly with only one person," Kai reported as he approached.

Saturn didn't answer right away. When he did, it came out quiet. "Do you think perhaps we're in the wrong?" he asked. The young priest had been strange lately, lost in self reflection for days while the battle waged on around him. "Sometimes I wonder if raising weapons against the Weylin people in secret is only causing more harm."

Kai set his jaw. "I had the same thought once. But then I came upon an Adriel family being harassed and beaten in the street. It's not fair what they're doing to us."

Saturn nodded slowly. "There have been strange things happening around here, Kai," he said. He lifted a finger to the temple. "I can't explain it. The air feels colder, and the priests are restless. It used to be peaceful here."

The logs on the fire made a popping sound.

Kai sighed and folded his arms. "Maybe you're right," he said.

"Maybe we've gotten a little off course. But I can't very well abandon these B'rei Mira intruders if I know they plan to go where my cousin is."

"You warned Adassah. She will take precautions," Saturn assured. "Maybe we should let these intruders go, and we should focus on feeding the poor again. Just today I saw a boy sitting at the side of the road who looked like he hadn't eaten in days."

Guilt prickled Kai's stomach. "Was he an Adriel?"

"I don't know," Saturn admitted. "But when I looked at him, I didn't care what he was. I just wished I had bread to feed him."

Kai tapped his forefinger against his arm. "It's better the people be a little hungry and we keep them safe."

"Is it?" Saturn turned to face him. His cheeks were flushed from the fire's warmth. "I wonder if that's what the starving boy would have said."

"Saturn—" Kai shook his head "—let's leave the acts of kindness and the grieving prayers to the priestesses. They can't carry swords like we can. They don't understand battle."

Saturn's mouth tipped down at the corners. He didn't exactly object, but his face made Kai wonder if he disagreed.

"I'm going to keep following the spies for now. As I do, I'll continue rescuing Adriel people with my sword," Kai said. "For our people, we must be persistent."

"You're going to get caught," Saturn warned. "It's only a matter of time before the Folke discover it's the Adriel priests out in the streets being vigilantes and causing a ruckus. You boys will only be able to raise your swords against the King's guards for so long."

Kai chewed on his bottom lip. "Don't lose hope, Saturn," he finally said.

"I'll never lose hope. I just wonder if we're putting our hope in the wrong things." Saturn turned to face the fire again. The light of the flames danced along his cheeks. "What if our anger is opening doors that should not be opened?"

Kai huffed. "If the Adriel God spoke to me and clearly told me to drop my sword, I would. But you know he doesn't speak anymore. Some old Adriel scholars claim he never actually *spoke* to anyone, and that such things were just a figure of speech in the old stories."

"Maybe we just can't hear him." Saturn looked like a green-robed statue with his long white hair. Kai was sure the priest was wasting time with all his thoughts.

"Get some sleep," Kai suggested. "You'll feel better in the morning."

With that, Kai headed back to the hall and didn't stop until he reached the room of cots where dozens of others in emerald green lay sprawled in sleep. He unfastened his sword, took off his boots, and sat on his cot.

For several minutes, he didn't lay down. His mind raced with thoughts of purging the kingdom of Weylin people, the way Weylins were so desperate to rid the land of Adriels. Kai considered himself a religious and devout man. He'd done enough kindness in his lifetime, including raising his younger cousin. He'd fed many hungry mouths, he'd taught the Adriel scriptures in seminaries, and he'd been a listening ear to countless Adriels in distress. But there was a proper time for everything.

When he finally laid down and drifted off to sleep, his last thoughts were of Ryn.

He wondered if Ryn was all right. He wondered how she was feeling. He wondered if she was safe.

CHAPTER
20
XERXES

"So, you'll let me go? Once you're cured?"

Xerxes heard Ryn say it to him in his sleep, over and over. A never-ending nightmare.

Xerxes spent most days surviving. From dawn to dusk was a slow passing of time, hour to hour, leaving Xerxes searching for the next escape or a place to hide. But this day was not like most days.

Xerxes found brief pockets of enjoyment sprinkled amidst the dark moments. He wasn't exactly happy per se, but he didn't spend the whole morning and afternoon frowning, either. The cooks were in an uproar, the council was restless, and even the Intelligentsia had opened an investigation—complaining and questioning what had happened to all the King's Prosperity Day cookies.

One Folke guard swore a cookie had fallen from the sky and struck him over the head as though the Divinities were angered. He showed leftover crumbs in his hair as evidence. That had sent many of the highly religious to their knees, begging the Celestial Divinities for mercy. The temple had been full of wailing and weeping all morning.

It was astoundingly hilarious.

But the fuss had become too much to bear after a while, so Xerxes spent the afternoon training with the Folke. His men were getting better, but they weren't ready for war. In fact, he could hardly imagine them being able to handle the *sight* of war, should it come their way. Though these men and women guarded his palace, they'd never seen the secret reports that made their way into Xerxes's hands from his Per-Siana spies hiding in B'rei Mira. They had no idea of the slaughter and horrors taking place just outside the kingdom borders. The Intelligentsia refused to let the Per-Siana people find out that even the neighbouring kingdom of Messa had been overtaken by Alecsander of B'rei Mira in the last six months. Per-Siana had closed its borders—no news or people in or out. It was the Intelligentsia's way of preventing panic. Xerxes had rolled his eyes at the command, wondering how the legendary sages could be stupid enough to think that if they closed their eyes and plugged their ears, Alecsander's armies would suddenly no longer exist and Per-Siana would be safe.

Xerxes had once visited Messa alongside his father when he was young. He'd marvelled at the kingdom's glasswork which his father claimed 'almost matched the skill level of Per-Siana's'. It was impressive for such a small nation. Xerxes had made a friend there during the weeklong visit; a seven-year-old Prince named Norkin. Norkin was the second Prince of the small kingdom and had the lightest hair Xerxes had ever seen. The Messa Prince had reached out to Xerxes with letters a couple of times over the years, but due to Xerxes's illness, Xerxes could never bring himself to offer a response.

Xerxes assumed Norkin was dead now. That the impressive castle filled with crystal artwork was a heap of rubble and shattered glass.

The air strained in Xerxes's lungs when he thought about it. His grip tightened on the sword in his hand, and he waved forward his next partner to spar with. He would force the Folke to practice twice as long today. They would hate it because they didn't understand why they needed it. Like all of Per-Siana, they were clueless.

"Ten more rounds," he called over the field. "Then we'll break and do ten more."

Not a peep rose from the Folke, but Xerxes knew they probably grumbled under their breath when they looked at him who, even though he was King, was younger than most of them by at least several years.

A feminine squeal lifted from the garden across the field, and Xerxes spotted maidens there.

Only three of them—the fourth was missing.

It was clear they came to watch the Folke practice, or had come to watch *him* practice, by how the two nameless ones clapped. Xerxes's gaze landed on Calliope a foot away from the others, wearing a gown twice as rich in colour as the other two's. She was scowling in his direction, standing with her arms folded and her hip jutted out. Xerxes grunted and went back to his spar partner. He cared not for the maiden's mood, though, he understood why she resented him. But any woman with an ounce of grace would have let things go by now.

"We're hungry."

In three swift moves, Xerxes batted the sword and shield from his partner's hands. The blade rolled across the grass and the Folke jogged after it. Xerxes sighed and shook his head. He'd been intensely trained in the art of swordplay since he was strong enough to lift a sword—but he still should not have been able to overtake every Folke so easily. Who had trained these idiots? Blind, mute cave goblins?

The next Folke stepped up, and Xerxes glared at him. "I thought I told you to stay outside Ryn's door," he said and then added, "*Matthias*, was it?"

The Folke, Matthias, scratched behind his ear. "Ryn is busy all day preparing for the trial tomorrow night. She told me to leave for a while."

Xerxes's next question should have been, *"And why would you disobey my orders regardless of what she wants?"* But what came out was, "What is she doing for the trial? Do you know?" and "Did she happen to mention which sense she chose?"

Matthias raised a shy laugh and shifted his footing. "She wouldn't tell me."

Xerxes huffed and glanced off, thinking about that. "Well, be off, Guard. You're excused from Folke training today."

"W... Why?" Matthias's sword drooped at his side.

"Because I made a promise not to hurt you, and I don't see you being able to defend yourself against me right now. Go read a book or something." Xerxes flicked his hand back and forth, telling Matthias to get out of the way for the next Folke.

Matthias's mouth opened and closed, but he dipped into a shallow bow. After he left, the next Folke came to face Xerxes. The Folke swung before Xerxes was ready, and Xerxes almost didn't have time to leap out of the way. He blinked up at the guard in surprise, and he almost smiled in his cold, strange way.

"Finally," he muttered. He stood tall and said to the guard, "I'll give you a thousand pieces of gold if you can make me bleed."

The sun began to set in the late afternoon hours, glowing through the infirmary in sizzling yellow. Xerxes propped his leg up on the medicine bed while the physician wrapped his arm in slow, delicate movements. The grey-haired man had three pharmacopoeia tomes open as he followed several sets of instructions. Even with all the knowledge at his fingertips, the physician's hands still trembled as he worked. He wouldn't meet Xerxes's eyes either.

"Just do it," Xerxes urged, wishing everyone wouldn't be so careful and waste his time.

Coming to the palace infirmary was a mistake. Xerxes originally wanted to train, bleed, and heal alongside the Folke to show they were all soldiers with the same flesh, blood, and ability to learn. Now, he knew it wasn't worth it to refuse special treatment. Even being lonely in his bedroom with his personal doctor would have been better than having the physicians here too frightened to tie a knot or sew a stitch. The medical students at their desks on the far side of the infirmary couldn't keep their attention on the pharmacopoeia books open before them either, and Xerxes scowled at them.

Xerxes had driven the Folke to their knees in the yard. A guard had even passed out from exhaustion by the time training was finished. Xerxes suffered three minor cuts; one to his arm, one to his leg, and one along his side. The pain was dull and unimpressive, and Xerxes welcomed it. He was pleased the Folke were no longer going easy on him like they had in the beginning.

"We're hungry."

"WE'RE HUNGRY."

Xerxes cursed and knocked his knuckles off the side of his head. If the physician noticed, he didn't dare comment on it.

A few Folke were scattered around the infirmary, including the one who'd passed out. Maids brought them water and refreshments and offered them little words of encouragement upon seeing their cuts. Xerxes could not believe all the fuss taking place before him.

"You're finished," the physician said, sweeping away with his spare bandages and gently closing his books.

Xerxes rolled his sleeve down as he stood from the medicine bed and marched from the infirmary. He stopped paying attention to everyone he passed in the halls, forgetting faces as soon as he saw them. He slipped into the hall with slat windows and came to the door no one dared to enter but him.

Xerxes descended the spiral staircase into the basement. His voices magnified as he drew closer to the tree—to his *real* medicine those physicians in the infirmary hadn't the slightest insight into. He breathed in the smell of fresh, crisp pears, muddied by the damp scent of the palace's deepest room.

He stopped short when he saw a dark figure standing there, covered in a long hood. He would have recognized Belorme's frame anywhere, even though the sage was growing thinner these days.

"What…" Xerxes drew a step in. Icy moisture tickled his flesh. "…are *you* doing here?" he demanded.

Belorme turned his head, but his face was cloaked in shadow.

"He's trespassing. Kill him."

"We would like to see him die."

"Kill him and then kill the maiden upstairs."

Belorme didn't move, but his voice lifted from inside his hood, detached and ugly sounding. "I suppose I was just… hungry." His hood tilted toward the tree.

A crawling sensation moved over Xerxes's flesh. "Hungry?" he articulated.

"Or just curious, I suppose. I haven't seen this tree since the day we planted the seed. How long ago was that?" Belorme asked, looking up the tree's height.

Xerxes drew in another step closer while the sage's back was turned. A deep, overwhelming appetite burned through his abdomen, his head clouding with a horrid desire to do something terrible. "Ten years," he said.

"No one is allowed down here. He should die."

"You made the rules."

"He didn't follow the rules."

"He doesn't respect you. It would be better if he was dead."

Belorme turned, and Xerxes stopped walking.

"I came to inform you what the Intelligentsia has decided," the sage stated in a clear voice.

"Why did you come *down here*?" Xerxes asked again, carefully.

"I figured this was where you'd be hiding." Belorme didn't address that he broke Xerxes's one strict rule. That he'd tossed Xerxes's authority out the window. "I know you despise that we invoked the Heartstealer trials and disrupted the palace's routine. So, the Intelligentsia has decided to shorten the trial period. For *your* sake."

Xerxes glared.

For his sake.

He could have thrown Belorme across the room by his lips for uttering such a lie. This man was the reason Xerxes hated liars. He was the reason Xerxes hated waking up in the morning.

"Tomorrow night, Lady Calliope will be performing a bandari dance at the senses trial," Belorme said. "She's chosen the sense of *touch*."

Anger rippled over Xerxes's body. "Don't you dare let her touch me," he warned.

"It's too late, Xerxes. She's been practicing how to keep a hand on you at all times during her routine. I've ensured none of the other maidens have chosen *touch*. I've even warned them not to lay a single finger on you, no matter what, or there will be consequences. It will be easy and obvious for you to know when it's Calliope's turn."

"You want me to take off my blindfold?!" Xerxes growled. "You might as well tell me not to come. I have no intention of rewarding a maiden at this ridiculous trial."

"This is your punishment!" Belorme shouted, his voice echoing through the room, and Xerxes jumped. The sound rang in his ears.

It had been years since Belorme raised his voice to scold Xerxes for doing something wrong. Belorme always had a way of putting Xerxes in his place, but the last time he'd truly shouted like a disappointed father was long before the death of the late King. Back when Xerxes had a father. And an uncle.

"You didn't meet with Calliope in your chambers like I told you to," Belorme said from his hood. "You weren't even at your room when she got there. She waited all night!"

Xerxes released a heavy breath.

"You're angry."

"You will feel better if you kill him."

"There are no witnesses down here."

Xerxes grabbed a pear from the tree. He squeezed it so hard, the flesh crushed in his fingers. But he took a bite, furious at the shame that washed over him at having to succumb to his illness, to devour his medicine, right in front of Belorme.

Belorme watched him eat it in silence for several moments. "We've chosen her," he stated before Xerxes was finished.

Xerxes's lips paused on the fruit. He took his last bite slowly, sucking in the juice. He turned and hurled the core up into the skylight tunnel. It smacked the wall and bits of pear showered down over the tree.

"It's going to be Calliope," Belorme stated again. "The Queen."

Xerxes did not acknowledge the claim. He refused to reply as he tugged a leaf from the tree, dropped it, and watched it flip through the air until it met the cobbled ground. He crushed it with the toe of his boot, strangling the leaf to death beneath the pressure. A green smear was left on the rock.

"If you reward Calliope at the first trial, and if you offer to meet with her in the evening as her prize, we will cancel the rest of the trials, send the other maidens home with riches, and you will no longer have to suffer through this. Once you're married, Calliope will leave you alone, just like your last wife did."

Xerxes's glare rose. His blood boiled at the mention of the woman who was never to be spoken of. But that wasn't all.

Ryn. He'd promised her three months. He could not let her leave—He could not stay trapped by his voices forever. He would rather die.

Xerxes fought the urge to blurt the truth to this man who had been playing puppet master for too long. The truth that Xerxes would never marry Calliope and that if the Celestial Divinities threatened to strike him down if he did not choose a wife…

It would be Ryn. He would pick her.

His heart tugged him toward the spiral staircase at his back as he realized. He felt the overwhelming need to find her immediately. He didn't know why.

Or maybe he did. Ryn had been the sole recipient of Xerxes's sincere laughter since the day he caught her escaping through the garden. She'd been the sole recipient of his heart flutters, the one to prove that beneath all his monstrosity, he did have a heart after all. She'd been the focus of his interest, the obsession of his thoughts every time she was within view, and all the more when she wasn't. Ryn even made him believe, briefly, that he wasn't a monster.

Divinities, he wanted her more than he'd ever wanted anything. With or without his voices, he could not let her leave the palace or be sent away. Because if she was gone, he was sure he would never smile again.

"Answer me, Xerxes. Do we have a deal? I can make these

trials go away." Belorme tilted his head, waiting.

Xerxes stood taller, the beastly parts of him on edge. "I will not get married," he articulated. "Not to Calliope, not to anyone. Fake my death and choose a new King if you must. I will not be a husband again." He grabbed Belorme's collar, and the sage's hood fell back. The man's eyes weren't big and startled like Xerxes had expected; they were dark. Menacing. At the sight of them, Xerxes had no doubt Belorme could devise a plan to have Xerxes murdered in his sleep and choose a new, more obedient King.

"If Calliope touches me on that stage," Xerxes went on, "I will kill her before everyone."

It was a bluff, but it worked. Belorme's face changed, his cheeks falling white. Xerxes kept his gaze on the sage as he reached to the tree beside him and plucked a pear from its branch. He grabbed Belorme's hand and placed the pear into it.

"For your hunger," Xerxes said.

He turned his back to the sage, and he marched up the stairs, thinking only of the girl he could not let go.

The moon found its place above the palace. Ryn wasn't in her chambers, and the organizers were being obnoxious about not letting him see her anyway, stating how important it was that he not get a hint of what sense she chose for the trial. As if he cared a dime about the trials anymore.

"Tell her I'm looking for her when she comes back," he told

the organizers hovering outside her door, but he knew they probably wouldn't. Belorme had likely gotten around to everyone already. The whole palace had probably been instructed to cause interference so he'd never run into Ryn again.

Xerxes rubbed his temples as he walked, his skin growing tighter, his headache becoming more irritating by the second. Voices he'd pushed aside for a little while began slipping back in. Tempting him to do ugly things. Making him notice how vulnerable every person he passed was.

How easy it would be to break something large and cause a great ruckus that would turn heads and strike fear into his subjects throughout the palace. Xerxes eyed the statue of Eos in the atrium, imagining hurling the goddess across the room and watching her smash to a thousand pieces. The Intelligentsia would be enraged he'd dared to insult one of their precious goddesses. Xerxes stopped before the statue, thinking about doing it.

"Your Majesty?" A soft voice brought him to glance over his shoulder. The blond fellow stood there. Xerxes had already forgotten his name, but he eyed him until it returned.

Matthias.

Xerxes raised a brow as he waited for the guard to spit out his request.

"I'm wondering if you know what happened to Ryn?" the Folke asked.

Xerxes turned to face him. "Explain what you mean." He didn't intend for it to sound demanding, but it did.

"I can't find her anywhere," Matthias apologized. "I was told she was with a man, and I assumed it was you…"

Xerxes did a sweep of the atrium, taking in every servant and statue and painting and councilman. He'd already visited the

Abandoned Temple, and Ryn wasn't there. He hadn't seen her guardswoman all day either. "Does..." Xerxes pursed his lips as he thought about how to ask. "Does she have *other* friends here who are... men? That are like brothers? Apart from you, I mean?"

Matthias's brows furrowed. "No," he said.

The clouds in Xerxes's mind swallowed him for a moment as he recalled how he'd stood across from Ryn in the tower last evening. How he'd stumbled over his thick throat and had shared things with her he'd never shared with anyone. And how, in the end, she asked for permission to leave as soon as she'd dealt with his voices.

"So, you'll let me go? Once you're cured?"

She was a prisoner here, Xerxes knew that. It had been obvious since the day they met at the palace wall. She'd always been trying to run away.

But he'd been convinced something had changed. It was the way she'd looked down at him in the Abandoned Temple. The way she'd mouthed those words.

"I like you."

He couldn't stop hearing them, putting a voice to them, even though he'd only seen it with his eyes.

No one liked him. Xerxes was incapable of being liked in any of his forms—or so he'd believed until that moment. He'd lost count of how many people despised him, were disappointed in him, wished he'd move out of their way. No one in the kingdom of Per-Siana *liked* him.

Just Ryn.

But the Intelligentsia would execute Ryn on the spot if she was caught alone with another man while she was a Heartstealer. Xerxes swallowed, hoping she wouldn't be that foolish. Trying not to imagine it if she was.

"Your Majesty."

Three Intelligentsia glided across the atrium toward him. "We can't seem to find Damon. I don't suppose you know where he is?" The way Yelenos asked made Xerxes worried the sage knew exactly where Damon was.

Xerxes's fingertips grew ice cold. He wondered if his skin was glistening.

"I do," he lied. "Go back to your mediations. I'll go get him for you."

A moment passed where no one spoke, and there was a lot of staring. Maids and guards exchanged pleasantries at the far end of the atrium. Carts were pushed past by attendants serving tea. Though it was all exactly as it should be, nothing about it felt normal.

Finally, Yelenos smiled and dipped his head. "Your kindness knows no bounds, Your Majesty." The Intelligentsia trio turned and drifted back across the atrium.

The Folke guard at Xerxes's side moved to leave, but Xerxes grabbed his arm. "Folke—I mean—*Matthias*," he said in a hushed voice. The red-cheeked fellow looked at Xerxes in question. "We must find Ryn before anyone else does. Do you understand? Move through the palace as fast as you're able—check *every* room."

"Why, Your Majesty?" Matthias whispered back. "What's the urgency?"

Xerxes watched the Intelligentsia disappear through the arch in the direction of their Room of Knowledge. The sun was setting outside, pushing shadows into the atrium.

"She's in danger right now," Xerxes said.

21
RYN

The sun was so bright in the morning, it woke Ryn from a deep sleep. She squinted at the light crawling into her eyes and rolled over to drift off again. But Heva poked her nose.

That was the start of what should have been a simple day.

The maidens suffered through a long meeting with the organizers during which Ryn stood behind the others and tried not to doze off. They were given a strict list of rules and told to spend the day preparing for the senses trial. A middle-aged Intelligentsia showed up to the meeting minutes before it should have ended and warned the maidens to *stick to their senses*. He couldn't have made it more obvious he wanted none of the maidens to touch the King, apart from Calliope. Calliope had a gloating smile like she knew a secret. The girl had been strangely quiet for the last day or two, so it was an unexpected turn of attitude.

Taste. That was the sense Ryn chose. She didn't have many skills in comparison to noble maidens, but she knew how to bake an apple pie better than most women twice her age.

The kitchens were busy—the staff spent the morning trying to re-bake the cookies they'd lost. Ryn listened to the stories floating through the kitchen as she dragged her hot pie from the oven, filling the air with the fragrance of sweet apples and crisp crust.

She should have baked more than one pie; a few to taste test would have been smart. But she didn't bother wasting her time, knowing that regardless of what skill she came up with for the senses trial, Xerxes probably wouldn't notice since he'd made it clear he didn't want to go. Adding the right amount of sugar wouldn't miraculously make him change his mind.

So, Ryn decided to make better use of her time. She trained in her room with Heva for the afternoon. She watched Heva closely, studying her moves and mimicking them. Ryn got several good hits in, and for the first time since the guardswoman had started showing her how to swing a sword, Heva hadn't succeeded in landing a single strike on Ryn.

When Ryn lifted El's sword, music floated into her ears; a quiet hum lifting off the metal, moving with the weapon. When she looked at it with her spirit eyes, she saw it glow bright enough to light the darkest corners of her room.

"I should take my sword with me," she said to Heva. "To the senses trial. I think I can convince Marcan to weave it into my outfit again."

"I told you I'd find the assassin before he makes a move on the King," Heva said, stretching her wrists and rolling her sword. Their new plan wasn't perfect, but Ryn was relieved Heva had agreed to save Xerxes.

"I'm nervous for you," Ryn said. "Maybe you should stay away from the trial instead. What if it becomes an all-out war in the Hall of Stars?"

Heva smirked. "Then I'll be in my glory." She wiped a bead of sweat from her forehead and slid her sword away. "I'm going to the baths. Do you want to join, or… By the Divinities, Ryn, I don't think you're actually sweating," she remarked.

Ryn looked down at herself. She wasn't even tired yet.

Heva shook her head and made a tsking sound. "Maybe I should start praying every morning. Or carrying a god's sword. Or… whatever it is you're doing. Your strength isn't natural, you know. Look at you, then look at me." She pointed back and forth between their bodies. "I'm built like a soldier. And you're—no offense—totally scrawny. There's nothing natural about it. What you can do is miraculous." She smacked her forehead like she thought of something that should have been obvious from the start. "I've heard of this somewhere—when El himself is your strength, it can be like another arm in alignment with your arm, his hands over your hands, that sorta thing."

Ryn glanced at the clock as Heva rambled on, wondering if anyone had gotten snoopy and discovered her pie hiding in the back of the kitchen beneath a straw mat.

Heva waved a hand through the air to dismiss her thoughts. "Anyway, I'll be back soon."

Ryn placed her sword in the wardrobe after Heva left. She thought about Heva's comments about her god-strength. She lifted her hands and arms, looking them over. She hadn't developed the sort of muscles Heva had—not even close. But sometimes she felt like she could hop into the air and float. She'd been noticing that the more time she spent in El's presence, the lighter she felt.

Heva never returned.

Ryn paced for a while, tossing a book into the air and catching it again. Then she tried reading it. Several hours passed and Heva still didn't come back.

When it grew stuffy, Ryn opened her window and filled the room with breeze. She glanced into the garden where the trees ruffled and flowers swayed below. She decided to climb down.

The fragrance of the garden washed over her as soon as her sandals hit the grass. Ryn folded her arms and breathed it in as she walked, heading along winding paths she hadn't walked before and noticing new kinds of trees and flowers. She ventured beneath bridges and oval glass rooms that reminded her of bubbles in gold clasps.

It took her hours of slow strolling, but she made it all the way around the palace and back to where she started. Her stomach growled with hunger, and it occurred to her she'd long since missed dinner. The sun had slipped behind the mountains on her walk too, and dusk left everything gray.

Ryn headed toward her room. She was steps from the palace when, from the corner of her eye, she noticed a shadow move out from behind a tree. She slowed her walk, bumps forming over her flesh as she realized it was a person. *Someone* stood there, far to her right, by the trees.

Even though she knew she needed to look, Ryn couldn't will her body to turn and see who it was. She remained still as coldness crawled up her legs, down her arms, prickled inside her ears.

"Where are you, El?" she whispered. Her hands felt empty. Her sword was still in her room.

"Help is coming."

Ryn finally dragged her gaze over. Maybe it was because of all the mornings she'd spent in the Abandoned Temple, but the sight of spirits came easily now.

She recognized Damon's face. But covering him was a black shadow creature, clinging to him like another person. It wrapped itself tightly around his shoulders and waist. She'd never noticed it in her previous encounters with the sage.

"Maiden," Damon greeted, approaching with his hands clasped behind his back. His dark eyes looked hollow at night.

"I have somewhere to be," Ryn lied, and Damon released an unusual laugh.

When he reached her, he came close like he had back in the atrium when Ryn wore the spoiled dress. His purple lips curled upward. "Are you afraid of me?" he asked, and something heavy moved through Ryn's chest. She was sure the shadow was asking. Sure she was talking to a false god.

"What's your name?" Ryn asked. She thought of the blind beggar in the streets with the chain of shadow over his eyes. How she'd spoken directly to the shadow and told it to leave.

Damon tilted his head and studied her. "Why do you ask that?"

"I'm not talking to you," Ryn said to Damon. She glanced at the shadow whose back sharpened into spikes like a cat with its hair standing on end. "Are you part of the body of Nyx? Or Helios, maybe? Selene?" She named the gods she could remember. "Which one do you belong to?"

Damon looked startled at first.

The shadow refused to offer its name, so Ryn swallowed and

turned back to Damon, finding his black eyes narrowed. "My God is far more powerful than yours," she said. "If you want, I'll tell your shadow to leave so you can be free—"

Damon grabbed Ryn's jaw, and she gasped. "What makes you think I want to lose my gods?" He drove her back against a tree trunk with a look that turned Ryn's blood cold. "Don't go near my gods!" he threatened. Ryn shrank beneath the wildness in his voice, the harsh tilting of his brows.

She shoved him off, but he caught her shoulders instead. "Heva!" Ryn screamed up toward her room. "Matthi—" Damon grabbed the bottom half of her face, encompassing her whole jaw and holding it shut.

A heavy sigh came from Damon. "I came here with a simple task, Maiden. But you keep doing unexpected things." He paused, his head tilting to the left like he was listening to something in the distance. A grin sliced over his face, and he unpeeled his fingers from Ryn's jaw. "Right on time," he said.

"Heva—" Ryn's cry was cut off when Damon took both sides of her head and pushed his mouth over hers. Ryn shrieked in protest, hot tears forming behind her squeezed eyelids. She pulled at his hands, kicking at his shin, and *finally*, he tore back with a grunt, grabbing her wrist in the same motion as she tried to slap him and slamming it against the tree trunk. His dark lips curled up as she gaped at him in disgust.

"I adore you too, Lady Estheryn," he shouted into the night. "But you cannot keep persuading me to meet you like this in secret..." Damon glanced to the left, and his words trailed off, a strange look coming over him.

Xerxes stood there, capturing the first traces of moonlight. His royal coat was covered in twigs and leaves, his chest rising and falling, his breath steaming in the cool air.

Ryn's lips burned, revulsion sinking through her along with horror at what Xerxes would have just seen. Damon's nails dug into her arms, but she didn't move a muscle.

Xerxes's glare hovered on Damon and Ryn beneath the tree. She wanted to shout at him, to beg him not to believe what he'd just witnessed. But all she knew was the heat of tears rolling down her face. She was done for because of this crime, forget being an Adriel.

Damon leaned and looked past the King, searching for something in the trees.

"X... Xerxes," Ryn finally rasped out, but he ignored her.

"Damon," Xerxes said calmly, and Damon dragged his attention back. "Leave before I tear you to a thousand pieces and scatter them across this garden."

Damon released an exasperated huff. "Your Majesty—this maiden pressured me to—"

Xerxes took a step toward him, and Damon ripped himself back from Ryn, nearly stumbling over himself. The intimidating Intelligentsia Ryn had seen a moment ago vanished.

"Wait!" Damon tried, raising his hands. "You witnessed it! You know how this works now—It'll be my word against hers," he reminded the King. "That's how it is before the council's judgments."

Xerxes took another careful step toward him. His skin was damp and his cheeks were pale, almost gray. Ryn pressed back further against the tree. "No," Xerxes said. "It will be your word against *mine*."

Damon's face fell. He moved away.

"I'll give you three seconds before I start chasing you," Xerxes promised.

It was enough. Damon turned and rushed into the garden, his dark robe flapping at his back. Ryn watched him until he was lost to the vine-covered trees.

Xerxes's gaze snapped toward Ryn, and she grabbed the bark at her back.

"If you ever see me and my flesh is deathly pale and gray, and my skin glimmers with moisture... Run."

"Xerxes," she whispered.

Rustling lifted in the garden a short distance away, along with muted voices. Ryn wondered if they would hear her if she screamed. If they would even come help her.

"I didn't do that with him... with Damon," she stammered. "I know I'm a Heartstealer—I would never—"

"Stop, Ryn. I'll fix this." Xerxes took four steps toward her, the shadow of the tree swallowing him. "Make it look real," he whispered as he brought himself nearly against her. He inhaled, his gaze tracing her face, finding her lips. He exhaled.

He kissed her.

Xerxes's warmth spilled in, erasing the chill on Ryn's skin. He wasn't aggressive; he moved carefully. His hands brushed over her cheeks, swiping off the tears there, then moved into her hair, delicately taking hold of her head to tilt her face to his.

"Who is that? Is that a maiden of the Heartstealer trials?!" a voice boomed over the garden, and Ryn flinched. Xerxes slowly took his mouth off hers. His dark lashes were pointed downward. He stared at her mouth. He swallowed.

"Arrest them!" the voice in the garden shouted. "This is punishable by—"

Xerxes turned and stepped from the tree's shadow, making the voice stagger to a halt. Two members of the Intelligentsia and six Folke filled the garden. The Intelligentsia man at the front gaped at Xerxes, his mouth hanging open like he was seeing a ghost.

"Are you going to arrest me for being with one of my maidens?" Xerxes asked. "Isn't this exactly what you all want me to be doing?"

The Intelligentsia man didn't blink, didn't speak. The Folke guards looked uncomfortable—a few of them glanced off at random shrubs or a passing leaf blowing in the wind. Ryn knew they could recognize her in the dark, but she was grateful to be in the tree's shadow in this moment.

"What's the matter? Did you hear a rumour this maiden was out here with a man?" Xerxes asked. He rolled his eyes. "You've seen me, now leave. And, by the Divinities, don't bother us anymore," Xerxes said.

The Folke bowed in obedience and turned away, rushing back through the flowers. It took the Intelligentsia a few more seconds to move, but they too turned their backs to the King and left. The two of them whispered between themselves until they were out of sight, abandoning the garden to a quiet, still state with only bushes and treetops ruffling in the breeze.

When they were gone, Ryn peeled herself off the tree. She interlocked her shaking hands.

"Xerxes," she said. He turned around to face her. The moonlight was crisper now, emphasizing his drawn brows and his frown. "I wasn't doing anything out here with Damon—"

"Just say thank you," he advised. A small touch of humour lit his face. "For saving you, and for that excellent kiss."

Ryn's gaze expanded. She closed her mouth, grateful for the night hiding her blush. The tightness in her body unspooled, and she dropped her hands to her sides. She said nothing as several seconds slipped by. She'd stopped shaking, the pressure of forming tears was gone.

Xerxes waited, lifting a brow.

"Oh…" Ryn shook her head to clear it. "Thank you," she said. "For saving me. And…" She paused, and his smirk widened. She bit down on her lips, wondering if he really wanted her to say the next part. But he didn't stop her, so she took in a deep breath and blurted, "…for that excellent kiss."

"You're welcome. I'll wait here until you've climbed back into your room," Xerxes said, but his smirk fell and his lashes fluttered like his vision was misting over. He tapped against the side of his head with his fist and jammed his eyelids shut. "But hurry," he said. "I need to go, urgently."

Ryn watched moisture crawl back over his skin, glimmering in the moonlight.

She quickly turned and took hold of the palace wall. She imagined he'd run off the second she was out of reach, but she was only six blocks high when he called up in a loud whisper, "Ryn!"

She glanced down over her shoulder. He stood directly below her now.

"What are you doing for the senses trial tomorrow?" he asked.

Ryn released a sound of astonishment, wondering how he could be thinking about that at a time like this. And why he assumed it was easy for her to hang off the side of a wall. "I've chosen the sense of touch. I'm dancing!" she whispered back. Why did he want to know so bad? It only made her want to hide it more.

A moment passed. Then a slow smile spread across his face. "No, you're not," he said. But he swept back from the wall, shaking his head as he blended into the orchard's shadows.

She didn't know what to feel as she resumed her climb. There was a great wave of things starting with Damon and ending with Xerxes. Heva was going to lose her mind when she found out what Damon did. And what Xerxes did...

Ryn rolled over the windowsill and tumbled onto her chambers' floor minutes later. When she climbed to her feet and looked around, she realized none of the torches were lit. A dinner tray rested on her dining table in the dark with a large plate of untouched food.

"Heva?" Ryn called into the room.

When there was no answer, she tiptoed to the door and cracked it open to peer into the hall. No one was there, not even Matthias. So, she closed herself in.

Heva still hadn't returned by morning. Ryn picked at her bread and sugar. Her first bite of breakfast felt like a stone sliding into her stomach. She was sure she'd vomit if she took another, so she shoved the bread aside.

She'd thought all night about telling her guardswoman of Damon's act in the garden. Ryn's abdomen still warmed thinking about what happened after Xerxes had shown up too. With all the extra Folke training taking place, she figured her two guards had been dragged into it all. She tapped on the armrest of the chair to keep busy.

Someone knocked gently against the door, and Matthias let himself in. Ryn breathed a sigh of relief.

"Thank goodness!" she shouted, jumping to her feet and jogging to him. "I worried about you two all night. You're with Heva, right?" She leaned around him to glance into the hall.

Matthias made a face. "No. I haven't seen Heva since… Well, early yesterday morning when you two sent me away."

Ryn's smile fell. "Heva was never with you…?"

Another knock sounded on the open door, loud this time. Marcan flashed Ryn a grin as he walked in. "You're going to be blown away by the gown I made you for the trial tonight, Estheryn," he said.

Tonight. Ryn had already forgotten the Heartstealer trial was tonight.

Tonight?!

It nearly knocked her off her feet: the assassination attempt on Xerxes's life would happen *tonight*. She'd been so flustered by the garden incident, and with her Folke guards absent, she forgot how important this day was.

Ryn had a plan with Heva. Heva was going to release whispers through the Folke from "anonymous sources" that there would be an attempt tonight at the contest, so the Folke would be on high alert. At least if the Folke knew an attack was coming, they'd take measures to prevent it. Then Heva was going to take up a position by Xerxes and watch the crowd like a hawk.

But where was Heva and why would she not at least send word to Ryn if she was going to leave for a while?

"I need to go," Ryn apologized to Marcan. She moved for the door.

"Why? We need to do sizing immediately so I can make alterations to your gown before this evening," Marcan said.

"I just... I need to talk to someone." Ryn slipped into the hallway, rushing on bare feet over the cold floors. She didn't realize she was still in her nightdress until she was halfway to the pools.

She came into the women's bath chambers to find mist coiling off the two-dozen naturally formed rock pools. "Heva!" she called into the mist. She slipped into the haze, balancing on the narrow rock barriers between pools. "Heva!" she called again.

She searched every pool, but there wasn't a single body in sight.

Ryn ended up in the Abandoned Temple. She stared at the crumbling statue at the end of the room. She pointed at it.

"You'd better not let something bad happen to Heva," she threatened. In legends, it never ended well when a mortal threatened a god. But after what had occurred in the garden with Damon, Ryn's gut twisted when she thought through every possibility.

She didn't stay to hear the voice of El. She turned and marched back to her chambers, her bare feet leaving watery footprints down the halls the whole way.

It took Marcan nearly the entire day to fit Ryn into her dress after she demanded he find a way to work her sword into her outfit. He'd huffed at first, but after a while he got to work on a silk braid down the back of Ryn's dress for her sheath to rest in.

When hours went by and Heva still didn't return, Ryn started scratching at the flesh on her knuckles, pacing in circles, yanking her hair—only to have Marcan slap her hands away so she didn't destroy everything he'd worked so hard on. Ryn glanced at her door every few minutes, wondering if Xerxes was getting ready. Wondering if he had any idea what was coming. Wondering if she should have warned him when she had the chance.

The makeup artists were placing tiny navy gems around Ryn's eyes when she decided she couldn't take it anymore.

"Am I all ready?" she asked Marcan, glancing at the clock in the corner of her room. It was less than an hour until the trial. If she was going to warn Xerxes, this was her last chance.

"Yes. You're perfect." Marcan stood and looked her over, admiring his work.

"Good." Ryn headed for the door again, and Marcan's face changed.

"Where are you going?! You can't let anyone see you until the trial!" He chased after her and caught her arm.

"I need to see the King," Ryn said.

"What?! You especially can't see *him*!" the artist objected, pointing down to all her skirts and tulle and gems.

Ryn tugged her arm loose. "I'll be right back. If Heva shows up… don't let her leave until I return."

The hallway was warm when Ryn swept out, her skirts whispering as they fluttered behind her. Her sword pressed into her back, and she tilted her head back and forth to try and loosen it. Music lifted from somewhere in the palace as the rehearsals began for the event taking place very, *very* soon.

Ryn broke into a run. Her footsteps echoed as she came around the bend to Xerxes's chambers. The guards outside his door looked at her oddly, but they didn't stop her from knocking.

"King!" Ryn called.

"He's not here," one of the guards said. "The organizers took him away a few moments ago. You're not allowed to see him until the trial." His eyes narrowed a little. "And you would do well to address him as *'Your Majesty'*," the guard added.

Ryn ducked into a shallow bow. "Yes, of course," she apologized.

Marcan flew into view at the end of the hall, staggering to a stop. "Estheryn!" he scolded. He marched to where she was and turned her around. "You cannot be here! You're expected at the Hall soon to prepare for your trial!"

Ryn swallowed as Marcan escorted her back. When they reached her room, she dug a hand into her hair, and Marcan smacked it away again.

Where was Heva?

Ryn lost track of the seconds passing by as she was led to a room off the Hall of Stars with the other maidens. She hardly noticed the other three women standing around. She wrung her fingers and poked her head back out the door into the hallway. There were no female Folke guards in sight.

Music lifted inside the Hall, signalling the beginning of the trial.

"Relax. Just relax," Ryn whispered to herself as Calliope passed by.

Calliope cast her an odd look. "Madwoman," she muttered.

Someone appeared at the door, and Ryn spun around too fast to see who it was. A blast of dizziness swept over her, and she grabbed a table for support as she took in the organizer entering the room with a large book in his hands. Ryn's shoulders dropped.

She stood in silence after that as Calliope took up nearly the whole space to practice her dance. Ulita cleared her throat and quietly sang through a few lines of her song, and Lis arranged her cart of perfumes and practiced fanning the scents in specific directions.

Ryn took in a deep breath and let it out slowly. "It's going to be all right," she whispered to herself as she leaned back against the wall and closed her eyes. Her sword pressed against her spine with too little assurance.

All she had to do was get through tonight. She didn't even know for sure the B'rei Mira assassins would be at this event—she'd only assumed it based on a guess. And maybe Heva was somewhere out there, doing her job. Maybe she'd discovered something and was working to end the threat, if there was one.

"Are you nervous, Estheryn?" Lis asked, drawing Ryn's eyes open.

"A little," Ryn admitted, though Lis wouldn't understand why.

"Me too," Lis said.

Ryn cast her a small smile of assurance.

An organizer appeared and escorted the maidens to a backstage area. Ryn had a clear view of the stage, and the large crowd of nobles filling the room. There were more people here today than at past events. Ryn eyed them one by one, guessing which one might be a spy hiding in plain sight.

When she saw Xerxes in a gilded chair with a blindfold over his eyes, nausea and relief washed through her at the same time. At least he was still alive.

Xerxes's lip was slightly curled into a scowl, and he held tight to the armrests of his chair. His royal coat wasn't even done up. It looked like the organizers had wrangled him into that blindfold and dragged him to the stage, and contrary to Ryn's nerves, she smirked.

Ulita went into the trial first. Ryn watched the crowd, studying each face, catching each movement. After a few minutes where nothing happened, she relaxed. It didn't make sense for an assassin to wait this long if they had something planned.

Ulita sang a lovely tune, and the guests clapped her praises when she was finished. Unlike the whistling and cheering nobles, Xerxes hadn't moved a muscle. Nor had he found it within himself to offer Ulita a nod or smile of assurance. Ulita bowed to the nobles and returned backstage, fanning her cheeks.

Lis went next.

Xerxes did move this time. He reached up and plugged his nose the moment she began fanning perfumes at him. Ryn bit down on a smile, and a few nobles in the crowd chuckled.

The tension drained from Ryn's body as it became clear she'd gotten herself worked up over nothing. Even Matthias hadn't imagined something might happen tonight. She let out a long, heavy exhale as she went to her cart and lifted the silver tray of apple pie. As soon as this ridiculous show was over, Ryn would go find Geovani so they could search for Heva. Maybe the guardswoman had simply fallen ill and was sleeping it off in one of the spare palace rooms.

Lis returned.

"You're next," an organizer urged Ryn.

Ryn took in a deep breath and carried her tray out. She moved slowly, letting her footsteps tap in spaced out beats across the stage, letting the nobles—and the King—wait. Truly, she had no desire to rush through her turn, then be forced to watch Calliope run her hands all over Xerxes's shoulders and face while he was blindfolded. Naturally, the organizers had decided to save Calliope's skill for last.

However, Ryn revelled in the thought that Xerxes would be shocked to realize there *was* someone who'd chosen 'touch' and was doing a dance. She almost smirked in front of all the nobles when she pictured Xerxes thinking it was Ryn who was dancing because of what she'd told him in the garden. As it was, her boring pie would be the least exciting thing Xerxes would experience during this trial.

Ryn dropped the silver platter on the stage table with a clatter. She grabbed the fork and gouged out a large bite of pie, then carried it over to where Xerxes miserably waited. His frown was priceless.

"I'm going to have to sit there with my eyes covered like a fool. I have to endure whatever nonsense the maidens come up with," he'd said. *"I hate the thought of it."*

Ryn bit her lower lip so she wouldn't laugh and give herself away. She leaned over him, bringing the pie toward his mouth, but realized she didn't know how to make him open it without telling him to—which would reveal her—and she'd been given strict orders not to touch him.

The nobles watched and waited around the room. A man in the front row folded his arms and began tapping his foot against the floor. So, Ryn nudged the pie against the King's lips with the fork, leaving a dollop of whipped cream on him.

Xerxes sucked on his teeth a little. But he opened his mouth, and Ryn stuck the bite of pie in.

There, it was over.

Ryn pulled the fork out.

Xerxes chewed once, then stopped. Ryn moved to stand, to glide toward backstage and never think about this trial again, when

Xerxes's hand flashed out, catching her wrist in midair and holding her still. The fork hung between them. Ryn's mouth parted as whispers flittered through the room. As it dawned on her she was *touching* Xerxes against the strict instructions of the organizers.

A slow smile spread across Xerxes's face. He swallowed the pie, holding tight to Ryn. He licked the whipped cream from his lips.

He yanked his blindfold down.

Gasps and chatter erupted in the Hall of Stars.

Xerxes's blue eyes settled on Ryn standing there. She gaped back at him.

"Your pie tastes salty," he remarked. "I almost spat it back out."

Ryn closed her mouth, biting hard on the inside of her cheek and feeling warm beneath so many pointed stares. "Liar," she finally said. "My pies are delicious."

"Go back there and eat a bite." Xerxes nodded toward her pie on the table. "It's fit for cattle, not kings."

Ryn made a snorting sound and tried to pull her arm free, but Xerxes stood, keeping his hold on her wrist. He turned and shouted at the room, "This trial is over. I've chosen the winner."

Visitors clapped and cheered in an explosion of noise, but the Intelligentsia leapt from their chairs at the back. It was impossible to see their expressions beneath their hoods, but everyone in their section was rigid, their hands balled into fists.

Ryn managed to yank her arm free from Xerxes, thinking only about the cover of backstage. She forced a smile across her face. "What are you thinking?" she asked Xerxes through her teeth.

He flashed the room a smile, too—one a little more gloating that glided right to the back of the room where the Intelligentsia

294

stood.

"I was thinking I'd like to end this before Calliope's turn," he murmured back.

Ryn released a doubtful grunt. "I thought you liked Calliope," she said. She wasn't prepared for the look on Xerxes's face when he turned his head toward her. His wild, accusatory, horrified eyes nearly made her jump.

A hooded man nudged someone out of his way halfway through the crowd. Ryn's gaze darted to the movement, taking in the man's pale face that didn't belong among the tanned Per-Siana skin tones.

Her stare lifted to someone *else* at the back of the gathering, far behind the pale man, positioned in the oval archway where he was mostly darkened by the hall. Someone Ryn knew from the years they spent together growing up in the same house. Someone who'd lit candles so she could see at night and had put bread on the table for her in the mornings. Someone who had left her in the palace all this time.

A small gasp escaped her lips.

Kai.

She thought it was an illusion.

Her cousin's green priest robe was gone. Instead, Kai wore a sleeved cloak that brushed the floor. Ryn wanted to scream, *"What are you doing here?!"* but she realized Kai's gaze wasn't on her. It was trained on the pale-skinned man in the hood pushing through the crowd.

And the pale-skinned man's eyes were set on Xerxes's back.

Ryn's stomach dropped when the man reached for something beneath his cloak. "King!" she screamed, grabbing Xerxes and shoving him behind her as the man lifted a loaded crossbow.

He fired.

B'rei Mira.

Assassin.

They came. After everything. They came.

Ryn's breath stalled as the arrow spiralled for her chest. She braced for it as a streak of blue fabric flashed in the corner of her eye—a Folke leapt into the crosshairs. The Folke took the arrow instead.

Visitors screamed and pushed as they raced for the exits. Folke guards drew their weapons, a unanimous ring of metal around the room. Ryn felt her sword be taken from its sheath at her back. But she only stared down at the blond Folke shuddering at the foot of the stage with an arrow through his body.

She was vaguely aware of the pale-skinned man loading another arrow and aiming his weapon.

An arrow from somewhere else plunged through him first, and Ryn jumped as the pale-skinned man was thrown to the floor. He rolled over once, then went limp.

Kai stood several paces back, bow raised, his arm pulled back from releasing the bowstring.

Guards leapt upon the B'rei Mira assassin, yanking his lifeless arms behind him.

No one rushed to help the blond Folke bleeding out at the foot of the stage.

No one tried to save her friend now that he wasn't moving.

Matthias.

Matthias was dead.

22
XERXES

The screams in the Hall were deafening. A window shattered from people trying to escape through it. The air buzzed with frantic shouts, with terror.

Xerxes had spotted the assassin the moment Ryn leapt in front of him.

He couldn't move fast enough; he'd grabbed Ryn to spin her, to pull her out of sight, to turn his back into her shield even—but someone else got there first—a blond fellow.

The whole Hall of Stars erupted into chaos. Arrows were flying, bodies were falling to the floor. Xerxes unsheathed the sword fastened to Ryn's back. He wanted to shout at her, he wanted to scream and demand to know why she'd recklessly put herself in his place. Instead, he stepped off the stage, and he scanned the crowd for other threats as his blood boiled, as his flesh turned ice-cold, as the whisper of water crawled over his skin.

Someone had tried to shoot him. The King.

"Kill! Kill! Kill!"

Yes, he would. He would kill today.

He moved to charge the crowds and annihilate every enemy when a delicate cry filled his ears. His gaze brushed over the blurs of colours and commotion in the room, finding her.

Ryn had moved off the stage and now hovered over the blond fellow on the floor. She was covered in his blood; her dress stained red, her cheeks wet with tears, her sobs an agonized symphony to the Divinities in the sky as she clutched his collar.

The dampness fled Xerxes's skin. The fire left his veins.

He let the sword slip from his fingers. It clattered to the ground as he marched toward her, but he stopped short when Ryn lifted her watery eyes to him. The look on her face was one he didn't recognize.

She pointed at him with a trembling hand. "You said you'd keep him safe," she rasped, and all the stars in the heavens fell upon Xerxes in that moment. "You promised me. You broke your promise, Xerxes!" Ryn screamed it, and Xerxes found he couldn't move, that his feet had frozen together. "You promised... My friend..." She broke into a well of sobs, a shuddering frame that was once a glass monument of joy, now shattered to a thousand pieces across the floor of the Hall of Stars.

It occurred to Xerxes that he had, in fact, made a promise. And he'd kept it. He'd gone out of his way to request that Matthias do a long scout around the outside of the palace wall tonight—which should have taken him hours. But Xerxes hadn't personally seen to it that Matthias had left; with everything going on in his battle of wills with the Intelligentsia, he'd been distracted. And now...

Now Ryn would hate him forever. He was sure of it.

Someone unfamiliar appeared over Ryn; a young man in a cloak, holding a bow. He dropped to a knee, and he dragged her to him. Ryn leaned into his shoulder and his cloak caught her tears. Xerxes could only watch.

"Your Majesty!" A Folke appeared at Xerxes's side. He pointed to where Xerxes was already looking. "That young man just shot the B'rei Mira assassin, but none of us recognize him."

Xerxes did a quick study of the fellow's street clothes that made it obvious he wasn't a visiting noble for the trial. But he couldn't be dangerous if he'd shot the assassin.

"Bring the Folke commanders to the Strategy Hall. And I don't want the Intelligentsia there for the meeting. Bar them out," Xerxes stated. "No exceptions."

The Folke glanced at Xerxes in question, but he bowed and left obediently.

Broomsticks rushed into the Hall and began sweeping up fragmented glass. Whatever visitors were left were ushered out by the Folke. The Intelligentsia were in a heated discussion at the far end of the room. Belorme had vanished.

It took Xerxes several seconds to find the courage to move. He swallowed and marched to where Ryn and the fellow were. He looked at the young man, unable to make eye contact with Ryn. "How did you get into the palace?" he asked.

The fellow had a hard gaze. He glowered at Xerxes; the coldness coming off him was enough to chill the room. "I followed the spy here. When he snuck in, I snuck in after him," he finally said.

Xerxes nodded, eyeing him. "Who are you?"

The fellow hesitated to answer. But when he did, he said, "Just a concerned Weylin citizen looking out for my King."

Xerxes let his eyes flicker to Ryn for the first time. She looked like a ghost, pale and lost to another place. Her lips had grown dry, her eyes puffy. By the way the fellow clutched her, Xerxes had his doubts about who the fellow had come here to protect.

He opened his mouth to challenge the fellow.

"He's my cousin," Ryn rasped, and Xerxes went silent.

Cousin. Ryn had a cousin?

Xerxes didn't know why it surprised him that Ryn had family in Per-Siana. Perhaps he'd assumed that because her father was evil and her house had been empty, the rest of her family weren't in her life.

"How did you know to stop that assassin? How did you know what he was here to do in the first place?" Xerxes asked the fellow again.

"I overheard their plan." The young man climbed to his feet, gently pulling Ryn up with him. She leaned against his arm as though she'd fall over if she didn't. She finally—*finally* pulled her empty gaze up to Xerxes. It sent a chill down his spine.

"I speak the B'rei Mira tongue," the fellow added.

Xerxes nodded. "You said '*their*' plan," he pointed out. "That means there are more assassins here."

"Yes."

"Can you identify them?" Xerxes asked.

The fellow nodded. So, Xerxes nodded, too.

"Good. Come with me then. And Ryn…" Xerxes swallowed. He was having a hard time not reaching for her. She stood close to him, but she felt very far away. "I'm sorry."

It wasn't enough. It was a fool's response to what had happened. Xerxes had never valued human life enough—it was the worst side effect of his constant torment. But in this moment, he wished he cared for others the way she did.

A young, panic-stricken artist jogged through the Hall of Stars on loud-heeled shoes. He caught Ryn dramatically when he reached her. "Estheryn," he said. "Come to your rooms. I'll take care of you."

The fellow let Ryn go to the artist, but he followed her across the room with his gaze until she disappeared through the arch.

When it was just the two of them, the gaze of Ryn's cousin cut back to Xerxes. There was a strange glow there. Xerxes had the strangest feeling the fellow was thinking of doing something rash right there in the Hall of Stars. Like attacking a monster.

"Let's be honest with each other now," Xerxes said. "You never set foot in this palace out of concern for me."

"No," the young man agreed. "I didn't."

Xerxes nodded slowly. "At least you're honest," he muttered as he turned for the arch that would take him to the Strategy Hall. "Follow me," he said. He heard the fellow's footsteps over the tiled floors a second later. When he got to the Strategy Hall, he made one loud announcement as he came in:

"I give this man full authority over the Folke," he said. The fellow behind him choked through an inhale. "Provide him with whatever he asks for until we find every one of the B'rei Mira spies in the palace and in the city. Anyone who disobeys or undermines his orders will answer to me."

The Folke stood a little straighter. One of the commanders bowed slightly and asked, "Of course, Your Majesty. What is this leader's name?"

Xerxes opened his mouth. It hung open there. He glanced over at the fellow when he realized he hadn't a clue.

Ryn's cousin seemed to have lost his tongue. But he cleared his throat after a moment and said in a strange, quiet voice, "Kai Electus."

"I trust Head Commander Electus with my life," Xerxes stated, and the fellow's head snapped toward Xerxes. Xerxes met his gaze. "We'll begin our hunt at dawn."

No, Xerxes did not expect this Kai Electus fellow to care about him one bit. But as long as Ryn was here, her cousin would fight for her. That was obvious.

And maybe Xerxes was tired of fighting for Ryn alone.

He turned back to the Folke. "One last thing," he said. "If I discover any of you are taking bribes from the Intelligentsia... You'll be cast into prison for the rest of your life. Do you understand?"

The number of faces that went stricken was telling.

The following week was chillier than normal. Xerxes wore a wool sweater and sipped hot tea as he leaned against the archway to the Abandoned Temple. He watched Ryn in silence. Her eyes were closed. She hadn't moved a muscle in nearly an hour from where she sat cross-legged in the water. Xerxes knew he had to leave soon, that he couldn't just stand here and watch her forever.

Seven days had passed since the senses trial. Xerxes hadn't been able to sleep much.

He had, however, been able to leave the spy hunting to Kai Electus—which was more of a surprise to Xerxes than anything.

The bow wielder had proven to be better at tracking down and cornering Xerxes's enemies than Xerxes was himself.

Eight spies from B'rei Mira had been captured so far—one more in the palace, seven out in the streets. According to Commander Electus, there was still one more to be found that he knew of.

Xerxes planned to interrogate the spies now that they were rounded up. He'd been on his way to the dungeons when he found himself standing outside the Abandoned Temple instead, watching a maiden pray.

He downed the last of his tea, and he turned to leave her alone. He would make things right with Ryn when she was ready, but she wasn't ready yet. He had work to do anyway.

Xerxes had foregone his coat of nobility and crown the last few days. Only his signet ring indicated he was the ruler of Per-Siana. But it was difficult to get dressed in his royal robes in the mornings when he didn't feel like much of a king.

After the assassination attempt, Xerxes had issued a decree that the Heatstealer trials be put on hold until every spy was captured. The council had agreed—thank the Celestial Divinities. Though the senses trial had destroyed many things, it had also opened people's eyes. Citizens were starting to wonder about B'rei Mira now. Wondering if something terrible was coming to Per-Siana.

Despite all that had happened, Xerxes expected it to be a fairly normal, non-eventful day.

But that was not what occurred.

The evening came with a headache.

"Hungry."

Xerxes knocked his knuckles off his head as he sank into the hot baths. He tried to relax against the stone, but the voices wouldn't shut up.

"You must kill the maiden."

His eyes opened slowly.

"She must die today."

"She is the enemy."

"Quiet," Xerxes muttered. He smacked the water, sending a wave of sprinkles into the next pool over. He adjusted his head along the pool's edge to take a nap—

"YOU MUST KILL HER."

"KILL FOR US."

"KILL!"

"YOU WILL ONLY FEEL BETTER IF YOU KILL!"

Xerxes leapt from the stone bench, splashing water out of the pool. He gripped the rock, his heart beating faster, his skin growing tight. His vision blurred.

"KILL THE ENEMY!" many voices said.

The headache turned to searing pain, and Xerxes held his temples. "Ah!" he growled. "Why are you *so obsessed* with death?!" he shouted at the voices. "Leave me alone!"

Every voice in his head flooded in at once. Xerxes gasped as the noise became unbearable; he couldn't understand what they were saying anymore. Half his vision turned black. His lungs tightened as he pulled himself out of the pool and stumbled for the bathrobes. He barely got one around himself before he tipped out of the pool room and collided with the opposite wall, blinking against blurry shapes and dragging himself forward in clumsy steps, following a path by memory.

The door to the spiral staircase banged open. Xerxes nearly fell down the stairs on his way down. The further into the basement he got, the louder his voices shouted, and he released a screech as he raced the last steps to his tree.

The golden pears were the only thing crisp in his vision. He took one. He ate it in seconds.

It wasn't enough.

He took another.

Xerxes ate eleven pears before he realized they weren't helping.

"No!" he shouted at the voices. "I will not do what you want! I will not kill for you again!"

The only way to be free of pain is to give us what we want.

"Kill for us, and you will have great power. All your needs shall be satisfied."

"Kill! Kill!" they all chanted.

The pain erupted, and Xerxes screamed. He fell back against the wall, damp with sweat as icy water crawled over him. His mind spun, his flesh turned gray, and his belly ignited with hunger.

He lifted his trembling hands to find them beastly.

CHAPTER

23
RYN

"Why? El, why?" It had been the quiet whisper of Ryn's soul for days. At first, it was through weeping, and then she'd screamed it. Afterward, she sat quietly for a long time, letting the warmth ease her crushed soul.

"I don't want to do this anymore." It was her first claim.

"Matthias's family must be devastated."

"Why am I alone again?"

Even the water in the temple had turned warm. It was part of the reason she didn't want to leave. Because if she tried walking the palace halls again, she wasn't sure she could face the cold.

"You have a purpose."

"Matthias is more alive than he's ever been. You'll see him again after your long journey home."

"You will never be alone."

A quiet splash told her someone was approaching. She peeled her eyes open and found Geovani lowering to sit at her side.

"Still no sign of Heva," the old woman said. Her green skirts absorbed the water quickly, saturating her knees. "The priestesses are praying for you, Adassah. I hope you feel it."

Ryn nodded. It had been a warm embrace and a deep peace during her lowest hours of mourning.

"We're praying for Heva too. I'm hoping and believing she'll turn up." Dark rings of exhaustion rested beneath Geovani's eyes. She shook her head slowly. "Something is shifting in the atmosphere. I sense a great war of body and spirit coming this way fast."

A light pull came over Ryn's flesh. She had to admit, she felt it too. She'd been feeling it all day.

"I hope I've been a sufficient mentor to you, Adassah. I suspect you'll face even greater trials than what you have until now. But so did every Adriel who said *yes* to El in our history. Those *'yeses'* resulted in great change."

The old woman's words stirred within Ryn's bones. Ryn wanted to be brave. She didn't want to be a little girl too scared to leave her island, too broken to move from her place in this temple where she sat alone and cried. She knew now that the waters around the island had never been poisoned. That she'd simply believed a lie she'd been told. That she could have swum to a new shore any time she wanted... and that was perhaps what El had been trying to make her realize all along. That looking at an impossible situation through El's eyes made it possible.

When men with great influence lied, a whole nation could fall under a spell of blindness. And the blind were the most difficult to convince, the most difficult to change when they'd grown comfortable in their dictated values. But Ryn thought of the blind beggar on the Navy Road. El's power had changed him and allowed him to see.

"The false gods have noticed you," Geovani went on. "But we knew they would, didn't we?" The High Priestess stood and brushed water from her skirts. "They'll retaliate. All seven of those devils and their underlings will try to stop you from now on. Things are going to get worse; there will be signs like never before."

"Let the gods try," Ryn said. "I'm ready."

Geovani nodded with a smile. "Go to your room and rest while you can." She extended a hand to Ryn. It was just a gesture, but as Ryn stared at the old woman's wrinkled hand, she realized she'd been stuck in this spot for a long time. She saw how important it was that she move.

She took Geovani's hand, and the woman pulled her to her feet.

Ryn stared out at the night, watching the white dragon rule the sky, a mighty illusion of strength in the heavens above. Her bedroom was unlit, but the moonlight angled in, glowing over her floor. She didn't feel like wearing a nightdress, so she dressed herself in Heva's spare set of clothes and armour. She hugged the clothes to herself when they were on. They smelled like her guardswoman; a blend of powdery soap and the grassy wheat fields outside the First Temple.

She thought about how she'd yelled at Xerxes in the Hall of

Stars. That terrible moment when she realized Matthias was gone from this mortal world, and she'd blamed the King. He was the most powerful person in Per-Siana. He should have been able to save one person.

At least those were the thoughts that had channelled through Ryn after that dreadful end to the senses trial. But over her hours of reflection, she grasped what a foolish assumption that was. Xerxes had his hands tied more than anyone else.

Maybe Adriels were always blaming the King because it was easy. When things went wrong in the city, it was his fault. When they were hungry, it was his fault. When they were being persecuted, it was always the King's fault.

She sighed and rubbed her forehead as she pondered these things.

A commotion sounded in the hall, and she spun around. A crash followed. Glass shattered.

"Ryn!" Someone screamed her name, and bumps formed along her flesh. *"Ryn!"*

The voice sounded like Xerxes but… she'd never heard him scream.

Her bedroom door banged open, and there he stood with a robe tied loosely around him, his hair a dripping mess. Ryn took in his state—his pale, grayish body, how he grabbed his head, how he struggled to stay standing. He looked like a child caught in a nightmare.

"Ryn." It came out a dry growl. "I'm…" He shook his head. His lashes fluttered as he backed away toward her door like he wished he never came. "You should run," he said through his teeth. He reeled backward into the hall.

Ryn followed him out, listening for his voices, catching the words they hissed. Understanding exactly what Xerxes was being told to do. "El," she whispered as a bead of fear moved through her.

"KILL HER NOW!"

"She must die RIGHT NOW!"

"KILL HER."

"I'm here."

Ryn took hold of the sides of Xerxes's head. His eyes flashed open, and he stared, unfocused. A warm wind fluttered along Ryn's hands, and she knew El was with her, standing there in the dark hallway. Right at her side. It was on his behalf she said to the voices, "Be quiet."

A gust of air was sucked out of the space. Xerxes nearly lost his balance, but he caught himself on the wall. Unshed tears filled his bloodshot eyes as he stared at her in disbelief, in horror, in question. The scent of spoiled fruit wafted from him, so potent Ryn nearly choked. She took in the bits of pear on his robe, the stain of fruit juice on his mouth.

She thought of his tree, the one webbed in shadows. That trunk of crooked limbs that produced both his curse and his treatment.

His treatment.

His *curse*.

Ryn wanted to kick herself. She huffed in disbelief as it dawned on her that the answer had been right in front of her the whole time. How long had this been going on right under her nose?

"It's been long enough," she said quietly. She said it to Xerxes, to El, to herself.

Xerxes was frozen to the wall, so she left him there. She marched back into her room, threw open her wardrobe and grabbed her sword. Xerxes was still where she'd left him when she came back. His gaze fell on the sword as she passed, as she went to do what needed to be done.

"Wait..." Xerxes rasped. "You're not going to..." His voice turned panicked. "You can't, Ryn, you *can't*!"

Ryn heard him shuffle after her, so she broke into a sprint, staying well out of his reach as he teetered. She raced through the halls, past startled servants, making her way to the door at the top of the spiral staircase.

"Ryn!" Xerxes shouted. The plea echoed through the stairwell as she descended.

A thousand dark voices screamed in protest when she reached the bottom, when she came into the oval room and looked upon that great, terrible tree. The shadows swivelled, turning their heads in her direction.

"Leave us alone!"

"We will kill you!" they threatened.

Ryn drew her sword. She took in a deep breath as Xerxes stumbled into the room behind her.

"WE ARE GODS."

"WE SHALL DESTROY EVERYTHING YOU HAVE—"

She swung for the tree. Her sword released an anthem of song as it collided with its base, sailing into its wooden throat like it was cutting the head off a snake.

The shadows screamed, growling as she hacked, her sword gliding through the wood. She swung again, and Xerxes reached to grab her, but the volume of voices electrified the room, and he fell, gripping his head.

Chips of wood flew everywhere, releasing a great torrent of wind that ripped around the oval room and pulled at her hair. She hacked until the sweet snap of the last stronghold broke, and the whole tree tipped forward.

Branches shattered against the cobbled stone, pears tore from their perches and splattered to the floor. Ryn watched the shadows unlatch and race into the tunnel above, going around and around. They broke through the window overhead and disappeared, sending a shower of glass raining down. Ryn raised her arm to shield her face as spiralling shards whisked by and pierced the floor. She turned to race out of the palace, to follow the gods but...

Xerxes leaned back against the wall, staring at where the tree had been. Staring at the nothingness that was left. Water dripped down his cheeks from his damp hair. He clutched his robe closed at the collar, his body trembling.

Ryn lowered her arm.

The room rested in complete silence: no more voices, no more threats, no more temptations. The only sounds left were Ryn's and Xerxes's panting.

"They're gone," Xerxes whispered, to himself or Ryn—she wasn't sure.

She looked at the tree's remains, then at her sword. The buzzing music had hushed, and the blade was no longer glowing. She slid it away.

"You're free, King," she said as she wiped a bead of sweat from her forehead.

Xerxes didn't reply.

Ryn headed for the staircase, but she paused at the doorway of the room. She waited—not sure what she was waiting for.

Then she heard Xerxes whisper, "Don't leave me, Ryn."

Something inside Ryn's chest swelled. She didn't know exactly what he was asking, if he was talking about this moment or something else.

It didn't matter.

Ryn doubled back.

He caught her. She hugged her arms around his middle, crushing his body as she listened to the pounding of his heart. They breathed together.

Seconds passed, and neither of them let go. Ryn's fingers curled around the fabric of his robe as his chest rose and fell, as his rapid breathing slowed down.

The quiet, melodic buzzing of her sword returned, filling the space with a serene tune, calling for her.

It felt wrong to pull away—Ryn's muscles flexed in denial as she moved, as she unclasped her fingers from his robe.

"I have to go do something," she said from a dry throat.

Xerxes's hand flattened against her back as if to keep her there. He clung to the base of her armour with the other hand, right by her hip.

"I'll come back," she promised.

Xerxes's brows twitched, his lips starting words he didn't say. But after a second, he closed his mouth and nodded.

Their hands slid off each other as she dragged her heels toward the archway. His watery gaze stayed on hers with every step.

Ryn turned. She didn't look behind her as she jogged for the staircase. As her boots thudded over each stair. As she went to finish what she started.

When she reached the top, her hand paused on the door's lever. Beyond, turmoil tore through the palace in shouts and screams, and a loud, dark, cruel laugh consumed it all. Her flesh tightened, and she pushed through the door.

24

BELORME

"We shall destroy her!"

"Make way for the gods of mortals!"

"Revere the great goddess, Nyx! Revere Boreas, Helios, and Iris!"

"We come with a rage!"

Belorme clutched the wall, his hand pressed over his heart. He lifted his gaze to the chandelier in the atrium where it rattled as a magnificent wind tore through. The guards shrieked as windows smashed and curtains ruffled behind them. Coldness brushed past every soul, causing servants to drop their trays and nobles to fall to their knees as though trying to duck from something swooping overhead.

The lights flickered. Lanterns went dark.

"The Celestial Divinities are angry!" someone shouted over the atrium. "We have committed a great sin!"

Those in earshot crumpled to their knees to beg the stars for mercy. The entire palace filled with the chaotic sounds of pleading and shouts. People pulled mourning satchels from their belts and sprinkled ashes over their heads as they wailed.

Belorme turned and marched from the atrium. Anger coursed through his veins as his mind spun, as he plotted. Who would dare stand against him? Who might have the audacity to send the gods into turmoil under his rule?

He swept into the Celestial Divinities temple, but he stopped short when he found someone already there. Belorme studied the sage uniform. The man's long hood turned, and in the dimness of it, he saw Damon.

"What's happened?" Belorme asked his apprentice.

Damon didn't answer, and it was only then Belorme noticed the sword in his hand. Drawn.

"Kill the failure," the voices urged.

Belorme released a sound from the back of his throat. Were the gods angry because Damon had failed to be caught scandalously with Estheryn Electus? Because the sage failed to get her executed? No, Belorme could not kill Damon over that.

"Kill him now."

Belorme tilted his head, listening carefully. Damon took a slow step toward him, and it was then Belorme realized the voices were not speaking to him.

He slid a step back. "How have I failed?" Belorme demanded of the gods. "I have followed every sacred order of the heavens."

Damon finally opened his mouth to speak, but the words came out strangely. Darkly. "You cannot control the King. And now a follower of the God Original has infiltrated the palace and done an unspeakable thing," he seethed. "An *Adriel* walks among us. A powerful one."

Belorme was sure Damon was delusional. Belorme had carefully watched every soul who'd gone in and out of the palace for

315

years. The only Adriel was that crazy High Priestess he'd managed to silence long ago. And Adriels only became powerful when their eyes were opened to the truth—no one knew the truth.

"The gods must restore order. Starting with you. You have failed the Divinities," Damon said to Belorme.

The blade came swiftly, and Belorme gasped, a thousand thoughts rushing into his mind all at once. His blood ran hot from the puncture in his stomach, soaking the temple floor. Damon retracted his blade, and Belorme fell there, lying beneath the statues of his gods as they watched.

"Save me," he begged the Celestial Divinities. "Save your servant!" But his pleas became too difficult to utter as his mortal life slipped away.

His eyes closed, his face pressed against the ice-cold floor, and his mind went to a little boy he'd raised. A boy who had tugged on his pant leg and asked him all sorts of questions which Belorme had answered with true love and laughter. A boy who had been curious about everything, who had pointed to clouds in the sky and seen shapes among them. A little boy who'd had a big smile once—before it was taken away.

A boy who had been asking Belorme for help for a long time. And Belorme had told him to go read by himself. Figure it out by himself. Belorme had told him to go be alone.

A tear broke loose from Belorme's closed eyes. As he died, Belorme prayed one last time to the Celestial Divinities he had served. "Please…" His voice shuddered. "Please spare that boy…"

And the Divinities answered.

"No."

CHAPTER

25
RYN

With the palace in turmoil, no one tried to stop Ryn when she left the palace grounds, following the shadows across the dark sky as they beat their wings and screamed. The front gate was abandoned; the Folke were dispersed throughout the gardens hunting for the cause of the commotion.

The gods split off in several directions at the Navy Road, but Ryn followed the ones racing to the Priesthood Temple, to *Kai's* temple.

Ryn's sword buzzed as she burst through the wooden door behind the temple, sprinted down the hall and into the main space with an outstretched hand, ready to grab priests and warn them. But she entered a silent, dusky room. Tables were tossed over and books lay scattered in pieces on the floor. The chandelier had been ripped from the ceiling, leaving a hole above and all the gold pieces scattered over a tabletop.

A cloud of darkness swirled in the heights of the rafters like a black lake.

"She's here!" the gods whispered to each other.

Ryn raised her sword, holding it with both hands like Heva taught her. "I'm not alone," she warned them.

Black limbs and tails began to drop, swooping in from all sides and coming together to form a body of rippling gloom in the shape of a woman with long, shadowy hair. Something like stars subtly twinkled within her, but otherwise, she was hollow and featureless.

"What are you? And where's my cousin?" Ryn asked as her heel drifted back a step. Other shadows crept along the walls, surrounding her and painting the walls in darkness. A curtain rod snapped nearby, and Ryn jumped as the velvet fabric toppled into a heap on the floor.

"We're Nyx," the shadows said in an ugly voice. *"Goddess of night."*

Ryn stifled a shudder as the temple filled with a cool breeze that slid along the back of her neck and legs.

Nyx, the 'daughter of chaos' in her true form; horrid and hollow. So, this was the creature all Ryn's neighbours had been growing their pink Damask roses for, had been revering as a great and beautiful deity, had been worshipping and offering tributes to all their lives. If only they could see what their god really looked like—not a god at all. Just a shadow of one. An imitation.

"And who are you?" the shadows asked. *"Are you not just a little girl with weak flesh and breakable bones? Did your god really say he would protect you from us? Did he really tell you you'd be safe?"*

Ryn kept quiet, waiting for El to contradict them.

After a moment, she looked around. The wind grew freezing; not a breath of warmth appeared in the empty, dark temple. Her teeth chattered as the cold slipped down the back of her clothes, leaving prickles along her spine.

The shadows of Nyx tilted their head, darkness curling off in smoky tendrils from her hair.

"Why is your god quiet?" the shadows asked. *"Are you sure he's with you right now?"*

"Of course!" Ryn finally replied. "Tell them, El," she whispered.

Silence.

Ryn looked behind her, not sure what she expected to see, but sure she'd see *something*. Bits of torn pages floated through the room, picked up by the wind and carried into the far hall. A wax candle rolled over the floor.

Her mind wandered back to her conversations with El. All her morning meditations, all the time spent in his presence. El promised to be with her if she followed him, but he hadn't actually promised her she would always be safe, had he?

"We see a girl who's all alone here. A girl who trusted the wrong god. A girl destined to fail, destined to hurt, destined to lose everyone. Do you really think this is the end? This is just the beginning." The shadows' words crawled over Ryn, hiding inside her ears, tucking themselves into the corners of her thoughts.

"I didn't trust the wrong god. You're not even a real god," Ryn said back, her voice weak.

Dark laughter erupted through the temple.

"Are you certain? We shall ascend to the heavens and raise our throne above the stars. We shall sit in the utmost heights and make ourselves like the God Original. If you bow to us now, you shall gain our power, and you can have everything you've ever wanted,

even the Weylins if you wish. Did your god ever offer you that? And are you sure he said Nyx is not a real god?"

Ryn's gaze fired up to the hollow form of Nyx. Her mind went blank, and for the first time, she couldn't recall anything El had said. Her chilly hand shivered around her sword, and the handle slid down an inch, almost falling from her grip.

"I don't trust your power," Ryn whispered. "You're a god of the Weylins—my enemies. You've worked hard to crush people like me."

Nyx lowered from her hovering state, coming face-to-face with Ryn. Shadows spread out from her back like wings, creeping through the air in slow movements.

"Did your god really say you could not use our power? El knows that if you use our power, if you eat of our fruit, your eyes will be opened to even greater possibilities."

Suddenly, Nyx's wings latched onto Ryn's wrists like fingers, wrapping her ankles and her midsection, and Ryn was pulled out a smashed window, up the side of the temple, and all the way to the gold-domed roof. She yelped when she was dropped on a narrow ledge—she grabbed a spire and held it for dear life, her sword sailing down the side of the dome and falling to where she couldn't see. The people on the Navy Road were like ants below.

"All this we will give you," Nyx said, *"if you will bow down and worship us."* A limb of shadow swept out from the gloomy figure, presenting everything like a hand sweeping across the horizon as evening sunlight glimmered off the buildings, towers, and villages across Per-Siana.

Ryn lifted her eyes to the Mother City. From this height, she could see most of the kingdom, stretching from the deserts all the way across the provinces and to the mighty shelf of mountains in the distance. She imagined tens of thousands of homes all filled with people, streets and markets and temples and gardens and valleys and everything else that had belonged to the Weylin royal family for the last century.

"Don't you want to save your people from the Weylins? With our power, we can make you Queen over all this land."

Queen?

Ryn once had the thought that if she were Queen, she could save her people. Kai told her that if she could take the Queen's throne, it would change everything. In that moment, Ryn had considered doing whatever it took to get it. She would have been a hero to the Adriels pinned beneath the mighty Weylin thumb—the one who finally rescued them from decades of oppression. She could have avenged her mother from the throne, she could have made the childhood neighbours who brought the charge against her mother pay, and she could have arrested the guards who hadn't given her mother a fair trial and had thrown her in a dark cave to die. She could have been someone the Weylins looked upon with awe and fear and trembling. Ryn could have turned this entire kingdom upside down. With the snap of her fingers, she could have set everything right.

But she wasn't Queen. And she hadn't come here to fight for that title.

"I'm loyal to El Tsebaoth," Ryn decided. She adjusted her grip on the spire. "I'll stay loyal to him no matter what you offer me."

"Skin for skin!" the shadows snapped back. *"You think yourself sincere, but once your flesh and bones are struck, you will surely turn from your god and curse his face."*

"I won't!" Ryn shouted back.

Nyx tore Ryn off the spire and smothered her with shadows, dragging her over the side of the dome, off the edge and into a freefall. Ryn screamed as she descended, the shadows' voices all raging against her ears:

"Kill her!"

"Kill!"

"Kill the maiden!"

"El!" she cried.

Warmth wrapped Ryn's hands, burning down her arms as her sword tore upward from the ground and sailed into her hand like a blazing torch of light, casting gold against the shadows that flung her back through the window and onto the temple floor.

Ryn rolled over twice before she caught herself, dizzy and out of breath. "Where were you?!" she shouted.

"Right beside you."

"Then why didn't you speak up? And how come Nyx couldn't see you?!" Ryn gritted her teeth and pulled herself to her feet as Nyx's shadows separated from each other and turned into a storm of racing black insects. They rained down, sailing toward Ryn with shrieks.

"She could."

There was no time to marvel—Ryn sliced through screaming creatures, sending gods rolling away. They dissolved into nothing once they met the blade.

The gods tried to fight back. They threw books; Ryn caught a corner against her cheek, and a papercut along her knuckles. Light flashed through the temple like a thunderstorm as two wills collided.

The battle lasted until midnight. And when it was over, the air was clear, and the Priesthood Temple was clean. Hundreds of false gods were no more.

26

GEOVANI

What came were the forces of hell themselves.

A strange voice lifted in the sanctuary. Geovani heard it from where she sat in her office penning letters. She'd been there most of the night, unable to sleep like some of the other priestesses. Something foul was in the Per-Siana air tonight; it left an irritating itch on her elbows.

"We can offer you power. You don't have to be quiet anymore."

The High Priestess lifted her eyes, wide and sharp as her flesh tightened. Surely the priestess in the sanctuary knew better. Still—she dropped her lead pen and raced around her desk, flinging her office door open wide.

"Don't answer!" she shouted as Quinn gasped in the sanctuary, a water glass slipping from her fingers and smashing over the floor.

"I didn't!" she promised as she dropped to her knees and held the sides of her head. The girl wept and cried out, "Leave me alone!" It was then Geovani lifted her spirit eyes and beheld the horrors—the dark beings crawling along the ceiling of her temple.

"Priestesses!" Geovani's shout echoed through the sanctuary to stir every soul from their sleep.

The High Priestess swept toward the pews as young women opened their doors and emerged from their rooms, yawning and rubbing their eyes.

A dark wind channelled through the temple, smacking open books on tables, making the pages roll. Candles tipped over while sacred objects fell from shelves and smashed on the floor. Priestesses screamed in alarm.

"Make a fence! This is war!" Geovani called, positioning herself in front of Quinn. The priestesses swept around the girl, facing outward in a circle. They all began to shout.

The darkness shuddered as intercession wove light in radiant branches that spread over the floor and up the walls. Geovani pointed at her enemies, calling them out one by one. Some shadows fled, but the braver ones grew, giving the appearance of height and strength and demanding undeserved fear. Nebulin shrieked, and Geovani grabbed her hand.

"It's an illusion! *Don't* fear them!" she reminded her priestesses. "The enemy is full of air while El is full of power!"

The door to the temple swung open, startling the priestesses into silence, and turning the shadows' heads. A quiet breeze swept through the sanctuary from the entrance, cooling the sweat on Geovani's brow.

Someone stepped inside. A great blade of light was in her hand, its glow rippling off the walls and illuminating the path at her feet. Geovani released a shaky breath, clutching her chest, holding fast to Nebulin's hand.

Every dark thing in the sanctuary turned to face the maiden at the door, and a smile spread over Geovani's dry, cracked lips. "El," she murmured, "what's happened?"

"Adassah faced her first test."

Geovani huffed a laugh. It seemed Adassah had passed.

She wondered if Adassah knew she was glowing.

CHAPTER

27

XERXES

A breeze rolled into the lookout tower, fresh and clear. Xerxes shook as it brushed along his skin. He stared, not really seeing the sprinkles of dawn lighting the Mother City.

Silent tears streamed down his cheeks, dripping off his jaw, hitting the ground at his feet. He couldn't stop them. He simply stood there as they came.

The quiet was overwhelming. Birds sang softly in the distance, whispers of the wind brushed over his ears. He heard it all, and yet, he heard nothing he didn't want to.

So, this was what freedom felt like.

He'd spent the whole night in the basement, sure a hole was growing inside of him. Waiting for the voices to come back and fill it. But they never came. Nor did the hunger. Xerxes felt nothing when he thought about the pears, even now. It was an empty feeling, and yet…

Xerxes almost smiled.

After he'd finally picked himself up off the basement floor and came upstairs, people had tried to speak to him. But Xerxes hardly heard them. They'd said things like, "The palace is haunted!" and "Everyone is going mad!" and "Belorme has been found dead!"

Belorme.

Xerxes finally found his voice. "You kept me in bondage for over a decade," he rasped, though he knew no one, especially Belorme, could hear him. "You lied to me. You must have known that tree was keeping me ill." Xerxes dragged his gaze up to the morning sky where pale blue was beginning to form. "How could you do that to me?!" he shouted.

Weakness took his knees. He nearly lost his balance, but he grabbed the rail for support and leaned against it.

"I hate liars," he whispered.

Belorme was gone now. Xerxes couldn't even yell at the man in person. It didn't feel fair.

"Xerxes."

Xerxes's hands tightened on the rail. He looked behind him at the stairs. When he saw they were empty, he leaned out the balcony and looked down at the palace, wondering if someone had miraculously scaled the wall. No one was in sight.

No. That could not be…

A *voice*.

Warm wind brushed along his white knuckles. He couldn't remember the last time he felt warmth; he'd been ice cold for so long.

Perhaps he'd imagined it. Perhaps it was a side effect of being set free from his torment.

"Xerxes," it called again, and Xerxes inhaled a sharp breath.

"Who are you?" he asked.

"I have many names," the voice said. *"Do not be afraid. I'm your friend."*

Xerxes released a raspy huff and swiped the tears from his cheeks. "I've been told that before." Though, only *one* person spoke this time, not many voices. Even so. "I want no part of you," he said. "I'll never trust a god again."

"I'll be here when you're ready."

Xerxes swallowed. He closed his eyes, willing himself to create a shield around his mind to block the voice out. Waiting for the voice to spew more nonsense. For a flood of voices to join it and take over…

Xerxes peeked an eye open after a moment. He looked around.

"Where did you go?" he asked warily.

Only the quiet breeze and the warm sunlight responded. He grunted. "Am I still crazy?" he muttered, dragging a hand through his hair and rubbing his eyes. He glanced down at his clothes, noticing he wore a mangled shirt with holes and old dirt stains on it. He hadn't been paying attention when he got dressed. Someone might mistake him for a gardener if he wasn't careful.

He smirked at the thought. Then he bit his lips, his smile fading.

"I don't want you," he said to the new voice, just to be sure it was really gone. "Don't waste your time with me—I won't listen."

Exactly ten years ago Xerxes had responded to the call of a voice in his head. He'd been lured by promises during his most broken moments. He would not make that mistake twice.

No, he wanted nothing to do with voices. There was only one thing Xerxes wanted now, and it happened to be the one thing he'd been sure he never wanted again.

Ryn did what she'd promised, and whether it was by her power or her god's, Xerxes was cured.

She might leave him now. The thought sent a different sort of fear into his body.

For all his utterings of not wanting a wife, of refusing to marry ever again, he was ready to announce himself a fool. Even when he'd made the deal with Ryn at the dance, he knew full well he couldn't *actually* give her half his kingdom—not without her becoming Queen. At the time, he told himself he would just go back on his promise if it came down to it. But now he wondered if he'd always hoped to choose her since that day.

Ryn didn't know yet that Xerxes would choose her.

That was... if he could convince her to stay.

Xerxes left the tower, descending the stairs and coming into a dim hallway lined with useless unlit lanterns. Thankfully, pockets of early sunlight crept in through the glass at the end of every hall.

Only now did Xerxes hear the wailing through the palace. Only now did he notice the miscellaneous items scattered over the floor like people had dropped things and fled. Even some of the windows were shattered and glass was strewn everywhere. It crunched beneath his boots as he marched around the bend into the atrium, trying to guess what had happened.

The atrium was in shambles. Xerxes raised a brow at the destroyed chandelier, its crystal pieces scattered from one end of the floor to the other. He wondered what fool had been swinging from it to have made it fall. But his attention tore to the entrance when a series of men raced in from outside. Soldiers.

Soldiers who were battered, bleeding, and breathing heavily as though they'd sprinted a great distance. They shouted for all to hear, "The B'rei Mira armies have attacked!"

The news dropped through Xerxes's stomach like a hot coal.

"They've crossed the border! Our men can't hold them off!" one bellowed. "They've already destroyed three villages! They're coming for the Mother City next!"

Xerxes found himself waiting. Waiting for voices to tell him what to do. To tell him to rush into the battle, to hunt for King Alecsander and brutally kill him for daring to set foot in Per-Siana.

But the voices were gone now, and Xerxes realized he had to make the decision himself.

"Your Majesty?!" Folke guards appeared around him. One Folke drew his sword and fumbled it, dropping it to the ground. The commotion alerted the battered soldiers, and the moment the soldiers saw the King, they rushed over and dropped to a knee at Xerxes's feet.

"Please," a soldier begged. "Tell us what we must do, Your Majesty."

Xerxes took in the crowd of men surrounding him, wearing his colours in two different uniforms; Folke and Army. He glanced around the atrium where nobles clutched each other and servants' faces were pale. None of these people would survive if the B'rei Mira armies made it to the palace. Xerxes would be a deceased King, his home would be shattered like the palace in Messa, and his people would become subjects beneath the vicious rule of Alecsander of B'rei, the war legend.

For once, every person in the palace saw the danger they were in.

"Arm the men, and gather our armies," Xerxes instructed. No members of the Intelligentsia were around to object, not that he would have stood for it if they did. "Per-Siana will prepare for war."

Gasps and whispers surged through the room; a councilman released a loud wail of agony. Xerxes turned and headed toward the Strategy Hall to prepare. He was sure he was the only one in the palace who'd seen this day coming.

"Your Majesty!" someone called after him. He didn't stop, and whoever it was chased him to catch up. "The great white dragon has fallen from the sky!" the man shrieked. "It's lying dead in the streets! The people are in an uproar—they believe the Celestial Divinities have abandoned us!"

And that was it.

Xerxes whirled on the man. He drilled him with his cold gaze, and he shouted, "The Celestial Divinities were never fighting *for* us. Can't you see that?!" The man drew back in alarm, and the Folke in the hall held their breath. "The gods do not care about *any* humans. They don't care for Per-Siana, or Messa, or even B'rei Mira. Don't you think the B'rei Mira armies serve gods too?!" he growled. "The gods just want to see humans die. They want to see *turmoil*."

Silence was thick in the hallway. No one dared to even adjust their weight.

Until someone else spoke. Xerxes hadn't heard anyone approach, but he turned around when Damon said, "I have insight, Your Majesty."

Xerxes's fingers curled into fists. "Out of my way, Sage. I have work to do." Xerxes pushed past the presumptuous Intelligent-sia—and the other two sages standing there with him. His thoughts were back on the soldiers' report.

"It's about Estheryn Electus," Damon said, and Xerxes stopped walking. He silently cursed himself for it—he had no plans to ask

331

or show interest. But then…

"She's an Adriel."

Xerxes didn't hear it. His ears were faulty. They must have been.

He glared down at his treacherous feet. Why weren't they moving?

"She lied to you about her name and her heritage. She's been hiding in plain sight all this time, Your Majesty." Xerxes heard Damon take a step closer to his back. "I have evidence that she was sent here by a rebel group of Adriel priests responsible for a secret uprising. That maiden came here with a mission."

Xerxes could not breathe in the air required to speak up and stop Damon from continuing. He fought the impulse to slap his hands over his ears and run.

But his ears betrayed him. His feet betrayed him. He stayed. He listened.

"Estheryn Electus came here to kill you," Damon said. "On behalf of her people."

The nerves in Xerxes's body went numb. He wasn't sure how he was still standing.

Ryn had come to the palace because Xerxes had made a deal with her father. Xerxes was the one who brought her here.

"You're lying," he whispered. But as much as Xerxes would have given his own kingship to ensure this moment wasn't real, he'd always found it strange that Ryn appeared poor. And her father had tried too hard to claim she was a noble. Her cousin had been dressed for the streets. She hadn't known how to properly address him as the King, she'd tried to run away shortly after she arrived, she didn't even know why ginger cookies needed to be made for a Weylin holiday.

Xerxes had helped Ryn escape.

But then she came back. She never gave him a reason why.

"I have a priest under interrogation in the palace prisons. He's confirmed everything. I do hope this doesn't bring you too much distress, Your Majesty." The sage's words were bland and detached. Deep within them, Xerxes was sure he heard the ever-so-slight tone of gloating.

Xerxes dragged himself around to face Damon. Trying to decide if he should kill him on the spot. There were no voices begging him to. After ten years of wanting desperately to be free, right now Xerxes wanted to slip back into that monstrous flesh he'd just escaped from.

Ryn.

Was.

An.

Adriel.

CHAPTER

28

RYN

Every once in a while, someone stopped on the Navy Road and looked a little closer at Ryn sitting on the stairs of a trade building amidst dirt and dragon scales. Sometimes they pointed, sometimes they whispered, and sometimes they took a step toward her only to realize Ryn was holding a sword, before carefully stepping back again. But even her sword didn't stop the loud gossip passing down the streets from mouth to mouth.

"…Heartstealer maiden…?"

"Did she do this? The Heartstealer?"

"…Are you sure that's the same Hearstealer from the banner?"

"Is the Heartstealer cursed? Is that why our dragon fell?"

If Ryn heard the word "*Heartstealer*" one more time, she'd lose it.

Even hours after she'd shouted at the gods in the night sky to release their dragon, to come down and face her, she still hadn't found the strength to stand. Her calves ached, her back was sore, her eyes stung from lack of sleep.

The dragon had fallen as soon as the gods let go of it. The battle was short, and they'd flung pebbles. Ryn's lip was busted, and her cheeks were scratched up. But by El's power, she won.

She smirked as she remembered.

Thankfully, a man passing by had been kind enough to offer her water. Ryn had accepted gratefully. The man asked her if she was a Heartstealer maiden a moment after, and she'd scowled. Then she'd said, "No. Not at all."

The great white dragon's body took up half the Navy Road, almost reaching the palace. The creature's mouth gaped open, its tongue hanging out the side. Overall, it was an embarrassment to anyone who'd ever revered it. People screamed when they saw it. They turned pale—one noblewoman even fainted. It had been like that all morning; a slow current of people discovering the great judge of the sky was dead. Unfortunately, Ryn was far too tired to explain to them that it had never actually been alive.

Ryn chugged the last of her water and eyed the sky where the sun indicated it was almost noon. She set the canteen aside and released a moan as she climbed to her feet. She leaned her hands on her knees, swaying a little. Her legs shook. She took in a deep breath, then she stood tall, grabbing her sword and dragging it along behind her.

She thought of her soft sheets in the palace. Her plush bed. She craved bread with sugar.

"I don't want to do that again for a while," she told El as she walked the length of the dragon's serpentine body. Its tail nearly brushed the palace gates. "Also… I'm starving," she added.

The gates were wide open when she arrived. The guards still weren't back at their posts and Ryn looked around as she walked through. She took the shortcut through the gardens, flicking the blooms of unopened flowers, and she headed to the entrance stairs.

She took in a deep breath as she went over what she would say to Xerxes after what happened in the basement. She chewed on her lip. There wasn't an easy way to explain that she could see shadows and that she'd battled them late into the night—and that's why she'd left him there.

"Ugh." She dug her fingers into her hair.

She stopped on the stairs, imagining telling him the truth. Telling him that even though his voices were gone, she didn't *want* to leave the palace. She didn't *want* to leave his side. But reason reminded her that she was just the maiden he needed, not the maiden he'd choose. And now that the gods had left him, he didn't need her anymore.

The Heartstealer trials had been delayed anyway, and Ryn doubted Xerxes would be in a rush to start them up again.

Her sigh filled the entrance as she climbed the last stairs and went inside. Her feet came together when she saw the atrium.

Statues had been tipped over. The fountain was smashed, and an enormous puddle covered the floor, almost reaching her toes. It was empty—not even a servant was to be found.

Ryn drifted in, eyeing the puddle.

She was grabbed.

Her hand fumbled for her sword as someone pulled her into a hall and shoved her into the nearest bedroom. Ryn nearly raised her sword at him, until she saw Marcan's face.

His eyes glistened. His bottom lip quivered.

"What are you doing?" Ryn asked. His normally polished hair stuck out in all directions.

"They know, Estheryn," he said. He slapped a hand over his mouth as soon as he said it, like he couldn't bear to hear his own words spoken aloud.

Ryn would have asked what he was talking about, but with the way his eyes hung on the verge of tears, something rolled in the pit of her abdomen.

They *know*…

His fingers slid off his face. "They know everything: what you are, the laws you broke, what you came here to do." Marcan squeezed his arms to himself and chewed on his thumbnail.

Ryn's lips peeled apart, a thousand explanations rushing to the surface. "I…" What was there to say though? She couldn't deny anything. Marcan must have put the pieces together already—it was probably obvious to him now based on things he'd seen and overheard her say.

"I need to see Xerxes," she said.

Marcan released a gawking sound. "You should never call him that again!" he warned. "And no, Estheryn, you should *not* go see him." He took a deep breath and let it out. "I am and always have been a Weylin—your enemy. And I know it's treason, but if you want, my makeup artists and I can get you out of here right now."

Ryn's jaw dropped. "Marcan, you can't be serious—"

"We can disguise you as one of us and leave. But you must decide in the next thirty seconds. I'll be long gone from here in five minutes," he went on. "The palace has been evacuated of all non-essential personnel. It's a safety measure now that Per-Siana and B'rei Mira…" He waved a hand through the air like that was off topic. "Now would be your best time to escape. Everyone might forget about you soon with what's coming."

Ryn watched a crease form between his brows. His shoe tapped against the floor. He glanced toward the hallway, then back at her.

Run? Leave the palace?

Forever?

The sword slipped from Ryn's hands and clattered over the floor. Marcan's hand flashed out as if to silence it, his eyes turning wild.

"I didn't know there was goodness to be found in the Weylin people," Ryn admitted. "Weylins killed my mother and swayed my father to leave."

Marcan sighed and folded his arms again. "Estheryn," he said impatiently. "Decide."

Ryn ran her fingers through her long, knotted hair, thinking. "I just want you to know that since I've come here, I've discovered several Weylins who have changed my mind. Including you."

Marcan's face fell. "That sounded like a goodbye," he said. "You're not coming, then?"

Ryn shook her head. "I need to see the King."

Marcan looked like he might argue, but he pursed his lips, and then said, "He's in the Throne Room. But if you go in there, you'd better be prepared to never come out again."

Her throat thickened as she put a hand on her artist's shoulder. "Thank you."

Marcan tsked. "May the Celestial Divinities watch over you," he whispered. With that, he gave her a teary-eyed nod. He opened the door and held it for her, his lip quivering again as he did.

"I hope they don't," Ryn murmured as she walked through.

She turned for the atrium. When she reached it, she heard Marcan scamper the opposite way and flee out the entrance. She

stepped over chunks of broken statues, kicking aside fountain water as she headed toward the Throne Room. The halls felt empty
without nobles and palace attendants fluttering around. There
were no dancing napkins or dusters either; the sweet taste of magic
was missing from the air.

Ryn had never been in the Throne Room—rumours in the palace claimed it was hardly ever used. She wasn't certain where it
was, but she followed the map in her head until she heard murmuring voices; *lots* of them. She imagined the Throne Room was
full of all the people missing from the rest of the palace.

"Ah…" Ryn paused just outside the vaulted entrance and
glanced back the way she'd come. Her sword was still back in the
bedroom.

"There she is." A voice lifted from the hall, and Ryn spotted a
dozen Folke approaching. One grabbed her arm before she could
form her next thought.

"I need to see the K…" Ryn went silent as she was pulled into
the room. The ceiling reached several stories high and gold-
framed windows stretched the full stature. It was bright and
packed with nobles.

Folke guards lined a gold carpet down the middle of the room
that led to a glass dais, and on the dais was a gold throne, and on
the throne…

Xerxes.

He wore his crown. His royal coat. His frown.

His eyes were closed. He held tight to the armrests of his
throne, still as a statue.

Ryn took in a deep breath as the small army of Folke inched in
around her. She studied the Intelligentsia lining the dais behind
the King, and the enormous council of richly dressed people she

realized she didn't belong to. They stared down their noses at her. They scowled.

The Folke released her and stepped back, leaving Ryn to stand on her own before everyone. She rubbed her arms where they'd grabbed her.

"Estheryn Electus—or whatever your real name is—you have been caught committing the crimes of impersonating a noble, spying on the King, plotting treason, and entering the palace, which are crimes punishable by death." Ryn didn't look at Damon as he read from a scroll in his dark voice. She waited for Xerxes to open his eyes. She waited for him to look at her and say something.

Damon lowered the scroll. "The King, the Intelligentsia, and the King's council hereby sentence you to be executed immediately."

The words rang in her ears.

Guards grabbed Ryn from all sides. They yanked her wrists forward and slammed heavy metal cuffs over them. "King..." It came out a near-silent rasp. Ryn's throat was too thick to shout for Xerxes. She waited for him to intervene as the Folke took a strong hold of her shoulders.

Xerxes didn't move.

"Additionally, all those who aided you in your crimes will also be punished. The Adriel Priesthood shall be hunted across the kingdom, destined to live out the rest of their days in prison. And Kai Electus, the traitor who fooled us all, shall similarly die by execution once he's caught."

A tear rolled down Ryn's cheek, leaving a hot trail on her skin. She wasn't sure what she'd expected. She *had* betrayed Xerxes. She *had* fooled all these people. She *had* committed crimes. She knew she would be in trouble, but she thought she'd at least be able to explain herself to Xerxes.

The Folke pulled her backward, and Ryn shook her head. Was he really going to let her die like this? What about Kai—where was her cousin? A well sprang up within her. "I thought we were allies!" she shouted at the young man sitting on the throne. "*Xerxes!*"

A hundred horrified gasps filled the Throne Room.

"How dare you?!" Damon growled. "You should have your tongue removed before you die!"

Xerxes's eyes opened slowly.

Dozens of people held their breath as Xerxes lifted his gaze to Ryn. She closed her mouth. She hadn't meant to use his first name, especially not in front of all these people.

Xerxes stood. The silence remained while he descended the dais, every step echoing through the room. He kept his cold blue gaze on Ryn as he walked over the golden carpet. Her knees weakened, but the Folke held her up until he stood before her.

He stared. Ryn searched his face for hidden smiles, for a spark of assurance. For anything.

Xerxes's brows tilted in. The corners of his mouth tipped down. Every movement was so slight, almost too small to see.

Then he said, "Liar."

. . .

Time stopped.

Ryn no longer felt the rough hands of the Folke as they dragged her back from him.

Liar.

Xerxes was left standing in the middle of the Throne Room as they pulled Ryn through the vaulted entrance and into the hall. She didn't fight them, even when their fingers dug into her flesh. Her gaze drifted down to the metal cuffs binding her wrists, weighing down her arms. It was nothing.

Nothing compared to the weight of Ryn's heart sinking to a place she'd never find it.

All sound was muffled and distant as she walked, like she was standing at the bottom of an ocean. Like none of this was real, and soon she'd wake from a terrible dream and colours would return and she'd be able to hear again.

She was hardly aware of her feet moving. Of the halls changing. Of the stairs she descended.

Cold enveloped her in the dungeon below the palace. Only thin windows allowed any light inside. The cells were empty apart from one at the back where Ryn spotted a man passed out in a green robe. She didn't recognize the priest.

She was shoved into a cell. The loud ringing of the door slamming shut behind her filled the whole prison. When she turned around, the Folke were already walking away.

She tried to inhale a deep breath, but pins and needles scratched her lungs. She placed her bound hands against her chest.

Liar.

Yes. Ryn was the biggest liar of all. And now, everyone knew it.

For several moments, she didn't move from where she stood, staring at the cell bars. Her knees began to shake, her breathing thinned. She thought she would die standing up.

Execution.

Immediately.

A commotion sounded at the prison doors. Heavy footsteps echoed down the hall.

"Your Majesty!" someone shouted.

Ryn lifted her eyes. She came to the bars just as Xerxes marched into view, his navy coat quivering behind. Three guards chased after him with their hands on their sword hilts.

"Everyone, leave us!" he shouted at them. The Folke bowed and fled; noises of pattering boots carried them back to the stairs. The prison door squeaked when it slid shut.

Xerxes waited for several more seconds before he moved. He came to the bars where Ryn was, but he stayed just out of reach, staring at her with a gaze empty of life or warmth. The same heartless being he'd been when she'd first arrived at the palace.

"I trusted you," he said. "You became the reason I smiled here."

Ryn shrank behind the bars. She cleared her throat. "King, did it really seem like I was pretending to you?"

"No!" Xerxes growled. "Which is why I'm so impressed, Ryn!" He bit his tongue like he was mad at himself for using her name. "Your acting was impeccable. You really fooled me."

Her breathing hitched. "A... *acting*?" But she realized she couldn't deny it—that to say she hadn't tried to fool him would be another lie. Her lips grew numb, her tongue heavy. "I really did want you to be free—"

"You're an Adriel!" he said through his teeth, and she slammed her mouth shut. Xerxes grabbed the bars on either side of her. His mouth thinned as he drew in just an inch, no more. "You deserve to die for deceiving me." Ryn could hardly meet his eyes, even when a flicker of remorse crossed them. "But you cured me, like you said you would. And for that, I've reduced your sentence to lifelong imprisonment in the Mother City jails instead. This is the *only* mercy I'll show you. We're even now, and I owe you nothing." He flexed his jaw. "I don't ever want to see you again. I hope we never cross paths."

Ryn backed away from the bars, thankful, for the first time, that a prison wall separated her from him.

Xerxes swallowed. "I will lose my mind if I see you again," he rasped.

Without another word, Xerxes turned his back to Ryn. She watched him march out of the prison. She watched until he disappeared up the stairs. The loud *thud* of the door slamming followed.

The jail grew quiet. Ryn slumped back against the far wall and slid to sit. She didn't move for hours. The sky grew bluer, the sun got brighter, then the heavens fell to ashy shades of gray.

It was nighttime before Ryn made a sound. She stood to her feet.

Her gaze crept up, taking in the chipped ceiling.

"El," she croaked. "What is this?"

Silence.

She screamed. At the ceiling, at the nearby guards, at El. "Is this what I signed up for?!"

She grabbed a loose rock off the floor and hurled it against the far wall. It smashed into the stones and rolled away. She kicked off her boots next, then she picked them up and hurled them out of the prison cell. She slammed herself against the bars. "Let me out!" she screamed at whoever was listening. "Let me speak to the King!"

How could Xerxes have said all those things and not given Ryn a chance to reply? How could he not have at least let her process all he'd said before leaving? She'd never see Xerxes again, and her last memory of him would be of him calling her a liar, all because she'd done what everyone else had asked her to do.

"You'd better not let them find Kai!" she threatened El next. She pointed at the heavens. "If this is the end for me, at least don't let it be the end for him!"

"This is not the end, Adassah. It's only the beginning."

Ryn laughed. It was a cruel, cynical sound that burned her throat on the way out.

"You tricked me! I believed you! I... *fought* for you!" She clenched her teeth, her moisture-filled eyes drilling the ceiling as her legs lost all strength. "We're done! I'm done with you!"

She fell against the wall and sank back to the floor where she belonged. Tears dripped off the end of her cheeks, hitting her bound hands. She looked at the cuts still there from her fight at the Priesthood Temple, and in the First Temple, and in the street. A sliver hid in her pinky from cutting down the pear tree too.

"I'm here."

Dust floated around Ryn's cell. She coughed.

She imagined what Geovani would say about this. Probably something outlandish like, *"There's more than one path to the end, Adassah,"* or *"The God Original works in mysterious ways."*

Ryn had always known deep down the woman was crazy. Thinking about Geovani's 'wisdom' now only made her hands ball into fists. She'd trusted Geovani just as much as she'd trusted El, and now she was headed to the place where her mother had died of the *cinder plague*, likely to meet the same fate.

"I quit," she whispered into the silence. "I quit, El. El Tsebaoth. Whatever your name is." She laid on the ground and curled into a ball. "Leave me alone."

She stayed that way for several more hours until she fell asleep.

CHAPTER

29

RYN

The Mother City prisons smelled like garbage. Ryn moved in slow steps as she was escorted inside and down a set of stairs into an underground network of caves. Not a speck of sunlight made it inside. She blinked to adjust her eyes as she reached the bottom of the stairs and went through a tunnel. She wasn't given any sort of explanation or warning before she was shoved through a gate. It was closed and locked behind her.

Ryn rubbed the bruises on her wrists. After twenty days of waiting below the palace and eating small morsels of food, guards had finally come to escort Ryn to her new home. She hadn't said a word to them. She'd forgotten how to use her tongue. She'd forgotten what it felt like to be alive.

She looked around the new prison, wondering if she might find any priests here from the Priesthood Temple. She didn't know most of them personally, and she wasn't sure they'd acknowledge her in a place like this anyway, even if she did cross one. But maybe they would know something about Kai.

Flickering torches were high out of reach every few feet, and large craters speckled the walls in bubble-like pockets where people stored things or made beds to sleep in. Tunnels branched off the main area, their curves blocking Ryn from seeing what was at the end of them. Men and women—mostly men—sprawled around the edges of the cave, some napping while others sat on overturned buckets and played mancala at rickety tables. They all eyed her as she came in.

For a moment, Ryn wondered if this was what her mother felt when she'd walked into this place for the first time. If she'd looked around at all the faces. If she'd been scared.

If she knew she was going to die.

A man built like a bull dropped his mancala stones onto the table and stood. He wandered Ryn's way. When he kept coming, Ryn dragged herself back, her feet scraping over the floor. "Seems like you got lost and found your way down here with us." He looked her up and down in a way that made her insides turn. "Why don't you come—"

"If you lay a finger on her…" A voice lifted from a crater. Ryn and the man both looked over to where someone lounged inside, hidden by the rock. Only a single dangling leg was showing. "…I'll break off every one of your fingers. And not all at once either; I'll snap them one at a time." A pause. "I might even make you eat them."

The large man released a grunting sound as he drifted a step away from Ryn, his gaze trained on the crater now. He wiped his palms down the front of his shirt, sweat appearing on his forehead.

That voice.

Ryn stared at the crater, her mouth peeling apart as dozens of memories from the last months flooded in. She almost rushed for the hole in the rock, but the figure sat up and hopped out first.

A dark-haired guardswoman.

Ryn gasped, the weak, dead thing her heart had become finding a small beat for the first time in over twenty days. "Heva?" she breathed.

A loose white tunic and black pants were all Heva wore, and neither were clean, but Ryn could have cried at the sight of her. Heva chewed on a piece of straw; it hung from her mouth as she wandered over.

The man took an even larger step away, holding up his sweaty palms in apology. He scratched his belly, then behind his ears.

"Don't forget what I did the last time you bothered me, Reedy," Heva snapped at him.

The man drifted away until he was back at his table, and there he bristled. "You should be careful, Folke," he called once out of arm's reach. "Not everyone around here fears you."

Heva grunted a laugh. "Yet."

Ryn wanted to throw her arms around her guardswoman. "Divinities, you're here! You're okay!" She almost added, *"I'm not alone here,"* but she let her mouth fall closed, offering a smile instead.

When Heva smiled back, it lit up the entire prison. Her gaze dropped to Ryn's outfit; the training outfit typically worn beneath armour. She tilted her head. "Is that my shirt—"

"What happened to you?" Ryn asked.

"I think you need to tell me what happened to *you*." Heva folded her arms. "My story's boring. I was snatched up on my way to the baths and dragged here. That's it. I've been beating the snot out of handsy criminals ever since." She stepped in and took Ryn's shoulder. "I'm guessing you were discovered after I left. Come on." Heva turned her toward the biggest tunnel. "Let's eat while we talk. I don't know how much you've heard, but we just got some big news down here, and everyone's freaking out about it."

"News? Down here?" Ryn looked around at the inmates. There were so many things she wanted to ask. She knew nothing about Kai, had no idea if he was caught and waiting to die. Or...

Or if he was dead already.

Everything had been so quiet below the palace.

"You won't be excited when I tell you what it is." Heva nodded at a burly woman who passed them. The woman gave a Folke salute back to Heva. "Listen—Now that the King has gone to war, a census might be made for *every* eligible prisoner—"

"The King went to war?" Ryn stopped walking. Heva noticed a few steps later and turned to look at her like she was crazy. "How did you not hear about this if you were on the outside?"

"What do you mean *the King has gone to war*?" Ryn asked again.

Heva sighed. "King Xerxes went to the border, Ryn. He's leading the army. He's probably in the middle of a bloody battle as we speak." She shook her head and waved a hand through the air. "That's what this is all about. Now that Per-Siana is at war, they might empty the prisons and make burn divisions. Everyone here is restless about it."

Xerxes... was at war? Fighting for his life every day? Raising a sword against B'rei Mira soldiers in the desert mountains? Ryn clutched her chest when it grew tight.

It wasn't her concern. Xerxes had cast her out of his life forever.

"I don't know what a burn division is," she admitted to Heva.

"It's a military term," Heva explained as she started walking again. "A kingdom at war will sometimes make divisions of throwaway soldiers and send them to the frontlines where it's the most dangerous. They use common criminals they're comfortable 'burning through.' It means no one cares if the division dies. The burn divisions will pave the way through an enemy line or be a distraction, or bait, or whatever else the commanders need in the moment."

"That's heartless," Ryn murmured as they entered a large cave with three dozen tables. A group of women at the back eyed them, shovelling rice into their mouths with flat spoons.

Heva took Ryn's shoulders again and looked her in the eyes. "It means we might go to war, Ryn. It means the Intelligentsia will decide any day now if they want to use us lowlifes for the *war*."

Ryn stared at Heva as that settled in. As she imagined the Intelligentsia in their gaping hoods, sitting around a table in the Room of Knowledge, penning their 'infinite wisdom.' She rolled the word over in her mind. That ugly word grew heavy, sinking into Ryn's stomach.

War.

War was something from a dream. It was a word only used in history books and told as entertaining legends before bed to remember great heroes of old. War was something priests did in the shadows with forbidden swords and priestesses fought on their knees.

War was the hands of wrathful gods at work.

It was smoke, fire, and chaos.

It was harps, prayers, and songs.

War was such an ugly, beautiful, complex word.

END OF BOOK 1